CUTTING THE SWEETNESS

CUTTING
THE SWEETNESS

Peta Tayler

HEADLINE

First published in 1996
by HEADLINE BOOK PUBLISHING

10 9 8 7 6 5 4 3 2

British Library Cataloguing in Publication Data

Tayler, Peta
Cutting the Sweetness
1. English fiction – 20th century
I. Title
823.914 [F]

ISBN 0-7472-1705-X

Typeset by Keyboard Services, Luton, Beds

Printed and bound in Great Britain by
Mackays of Chatham PLC, Chatham, Kent

HEADLINE BOOK PUBLISHING
A division of Hodder Headline PLC
338 Euston Road
London NW1 3BH

DEDICATION

For Jean, whose inspired phrase was the first title,
and for Christopher, who claimed it.

Chapter 1

'Just *look* at the weather!' Mary lowered the potato she was peeling and swished it half-heartedly in the sink. With her hands in the tepid water – she could not bring herself to use just cold at this time of year – she peered through the window. A vicious wind flung handfuls of raindrops that clattered like gravel against the glass, and threw the shrubs and young trees in the garden into wild gyrations, like dervishes or how Mary imagined teenagers at a rave, high on Ecstasy and techno music. The bare twigs glittered as they moved, their wet bark picking up bilious sequins from the dingy orange of the street lamp beyond the garden. Mary sighed, remembering with nostalgia the white lighting of her early childhood.

'Pull the blind down, then you won't have to see it,' said her lover. Mary knew he was talking about the sodium light, not the weather. He always knew what she was thinking. She re-focused her eyes on the window rather than through it. Lightly misted with steam, the reflection was hazy, each ceiling light rimmed with a milky halo. Mary gazed dreamily at it, her eyes lingering on the things she loved best: the old dresser, its pine aged to the soft gold of oak leaves in autumn, its shelves displaying the motley collection of dishes, jugs, plates and mugs that she had garnered over the years; the rocking chair in the corner with the tortoiseshell cat curled on its faded patchwork cushion; the bunches of herbs and dried flowers hanging above the Aga; the old copper pans that gleamed with an almost velvety softness; the big scrubbed pine table . . .

'Hey!' Her lover's voice broke in on her reverie. 'What about me?'

Her eyes moved to consider him.

'I was just getting to you,' she said. The big scrubbed pine table, with its bowl of just-opened blue hyacinths scenting the air and its scattering of cookery books, magazines and novels. And her lover, perched on the

1

corner of it, where he often sat, his long legs stretched out over the quarry-tiled floor, his eyes as blue as the hyacinths looking at her with a quizzical expression.

'You love the kitchen more than you love me.'

'Of course I don't!'

'As much as, then.'

She smiled at him, not denying it and knowing that he needed no reassurance from her. Her eyes caressed him with their look and he smiled lazily back, his eyes crinkling at the corners – something which for some reason always made her think of the feel of hands stroking her back. A small shiver of pleasure spread from her spine down to her fingers and toes, netting her skin with a sparkle of electricity.

He was, she thought, quite devastatingly good-looking in an understated way that she preferred. Though tall, he was far from the 'tall, dark and handsome' of romances, neither saturnine nor with the glossy, plasticised look of a film star. His face was a happy blend of ruggedness and intelligence: she sometimes thought he looked a bit like Charles Dance – what was it they called him, the thinking woman's beefcake? – and indeed his hair was the same auburn, receding slightly at the temples. He was about the same age as Mary. At forty-eight she was rather thankful that her fancy showed no sign of turning to younger men. With his well muscled, lightly tanned body her lover might look a bit like Action Man, but a toy boy he definitely was not.

He was laughing at her, his teeth white against the darkness of the garden.

'You're making your potato more and more dirty,' he pointed out. 'That bowl of water is practically liquid mud.'

'Oh dear.' Mary looked down to the forgotten potato. Its flesh, that had been white when she had peeled it, was now a patchy brown and it was true that the water where the peelings sat was silted and thick. She turned on the tap and scraped the potato briskly.

'There's nothing much left, once you've got the mud and the peel off,' she said ruefully. 'I was stupid to buy them in all that heavy mud.'

'I thought they were always sold ready washed, nowadays?'

'Only in supermarkets. I got these in the market. It's very good value, as long as you're careful what you buy – like I wasn't this time! Only I thought that they might have a bit more flavour. Because of the mud. It made them look more *real*, you know. Sort of organic.'

'And do they? Have more flavour, I mean?'

'No. And they disintegrate on the outside while the inside is still hard, so you end up with soup. As potatoes go,' she said cheerfully, 'they're a complete dead loss.'

'Gratin Dauphinois?' He was interested in cooking. 'Janssen's Temptation? The anchovies would give them some flavour.'

'Shepherd's pie,' she answered primly. 'With *no* garlic—'

'And not too much onion either. I know.' They exchanged a glance, which was the nearest she ever allowed herself to go, even with him, towards criticising her husband.

'A few slices of tomato on the top?' he begged plaintively. 'Tomatoes aren't foreign.'

'Love apples,' she said thoughtfully. 'That's what they used to be called. Before they got domesticated, and lost all their flavour. Still,' she brightened, 'at least they're a good colour.'

'Remember the market in Spain?' He leaned back, stretching his legs out further. Mary thought it was lucky she never tripped over his feet. 'Those mounds of tomatoes, all knobbly and mis-shapen, but so sweet!'

'Oh, yes.' She glowed at the reminder. Her husband had disliked the market, thinking it crowded and insanitary, but she had adored it and her lover, of course, shared all her memories. 'And the peppers, and those heavenly aubergines ... that colour ...'

'And the melons. Remember the smell of the melons?'

'And those little artichokes ...'

'Fartichokes.'

'Yes, *weren't* they! Agony, but so delicious. And so young they didn't have any choke in them, and you could eat the stalk. They stuffed them ... And the peaches, and the grapes, and ... oh, dear.'

'Some day, darling.'

'Yes, some day ...'

They both knew it wouldn't happen. Briskly, Mary salted the pan of potatoes, and carried it to the cooker.

'Hang on a minute! Cook them in the microwave, why don't you?'

'Well, I could, but why?'

'Potato soup,' he said succinctly. 'You only need to put a little water

3

with them, in the microwave. That way you won't lose half of them when you drain them off.'

'Brilliant! Why didn't I think of that? In fact, I could just put in a bit of milk and butter, and cook them with that. Thanks, love.'

'Raymond Blanc, eat your heart out. Anything on the box tonight?'

'Nothing much. Quite a good nature programme at eight. We'll be having supper then, so I'll record it for after the News. Oh, and a Pasolini film in the middle of the night. I'll tape that too; we could watch it tomorrow while I do the ironing.'

'You'll be in the office tomorrow, fluff-brain.'

'Goodness, is tomorrow Friday already? How time flies.'

'When you're having fun. I know. Next Tuesday, then?'

'Or Saturday. John's playing golf, as usual. And I'll still have plenty of ironing left to do.'

'You're so romantic. Let's make it Saturday, then. What about David? Isn't he coming this weekend?'

'Yes. At least, it is one of his weekends, but if he isn't out with Alison he'll probably go with John. He's decided that golf is a good thing.' She listened to what she had said, and heard the sourness in her voice. Surely mothers weren't supposed to use that tone when speaking about a son, a much loved only child?

'It's an enjoyable game,' her lover said reasonably. 'Fresh air, a good walk, all that sort of thing. Better than being a couch potato.'

'Doing the ironing and watching Pasolini is hardly being a couch potato! But he doesn't *do* it for that! And what sort of exercise is it for a young man of twenty-two, anyway, sauntering round a golf course?'

'Carrying his clubs? And his father's?'

'Wheeling them on a trolley,' she snapped. 'It's all very well for John, not allowed to play tennis or squash because of his back, but David used to play rugby! I used to go and watch his matches and it was terrifying, really, worrying about the scrum collapsing on him, or seeing him being neck tackled. But at least it was a proper *sport*.'

'Ballesteros.'

'Ballesteros to you too.' She wasn't going to be cajoled too easily out of her little spurt of temper. 'At least he plays golf seriously.'

'Doesn't John? And David?'

'John does, I suppose,' she admitted reluctantly. 'But David only plays because it's useful. Contacts, networking, that sort of thing. Deals at the nineteenth hole.'

4

'Very sensible. You should be glad he's so sensible. Level-headed. Ambitious.'

'I am.' She sighed, her rage evaporating. 'It's just so terribly *dull*. All those hours playing a game you don't much like, just to get in with some overweight businessman or impress the bank manager.'

'Are bank managers impressed by the smallness of your handicap? I thought it was the smallness of your overdraft that mattered.'

'Not funny. How did I manage to produce such a sensible son? If I hadn't been there at the time, I'd have said he was somebody else's.'

'John's sensible. And so are you, really.'

'Do you think anyone who could see me now, talking to you, would think I was sensible? And I'm not, not really. Not inside.'

'You appear sensible, then. On the outside.'

'Do I?' Mary turned back to the window and looked at what she could see of her reflection in it. Misty and slightly distorted, her face looked back at her and she lifted her hands to touch it, testing its reality. Her hands, large, well shaped and capable, the skin slightly roughened and stained by gardening and housework, the nails filed neat and short, stroked at the skin of her face and neck. She lifted her chin, ran her fingers over the soft triangle within her jaw bone, and down her neck. Not too much sag or wobble, thank goodness. Her cheeks were firm and smooth, the fine lines at the corners of her grey eyes were from smiling, as were the crescents on either side of her mouth. Her eyes, slightly short-sighted but needing glasses only for close work, were still clear and bright, the whites untinged with yellow or the marbling of red blood vessels.

Not bad. Her hair, too, showed no more than the odd grey hair – one advantage of that particular shade of dispiriting light brown – and was still twisted into the plaited knot that she had adopted when, at thirty, John had suggested she was a bit old to have it hanging loose down her back.

'You used to like it like that,' she had said sadly.

'I did. I do,' he reassured her earnestly. 'It's just more *suitable* . . .' He had looked anxious, almost like a child worried that his mother would embarrass him by coming to Speech Day in a wildly unsuitable hat. So she had plaited it and pinned it up, and been rewarded by his admiring 'very elegant, dear'. Was he really calling her 'dear' even then?

Maybe, she thought without sadness, it had never been suitable, that curtain of hair. Long flowing hair was for young girls: more specifically,

5

for pretty young girls. For Laura Ashley dresses and Liberty prints and 'Rapunzel, Rapunzel, let down your hair', not for large, solidly built girls with sturdy ankles and broad shoulders.

For Mary had been a large girl, and now she was a large woman. Not fat. Her waist, even now, was clearly, even well defined between a generous bosom and the smooth rounding of hips and thighs. The flesh was firm, undimpled, and Mary knew that the pinch test advocated by beauty experts would fail to raise any sign of a loose layer of fat over it. In the time of Victoria she might have been called statuesque: in Rubens's day, she sometimes thought, she might have been considered beautiful. Now, in her well cut, camel-coloured Jaeger skirt and beige V-neck pullover over a plain cream blouse, she looked ... well ...

'Blast it, I look *sensible*!'

'You look adorable.'

'Steady on.'

'Well, to me you do.'

'To *you* ...'

'Yes, to me. Doesn't that count?'

Mary frowned. This was one of the anomalies inherent in her situation that she found popped into her head with disconcerting frequency, no matter how hard she tried to ignore them. Of course she wanted her lover to think her adorable – what woman of any age wouldn't – but when he told her so she was unable to find it anything but embarrassing. Unused to compliments, her lack of self-confidence was eroded rather than boosted by her lover's admiration. He, not unnaturally, thought as she did about almost everything, and she was unable to believe his praise, however much she wanted to. As an exercise in ego-boosting, it was definitely a lead balloon.

'Not really. Well, yes, but ... no. You don't really see *me*, do you?'

'I think I do. I think I see the real you, the you that nobody else sees. All right, then, to the rest of the world, how do you look? Comfortable. Capable. Cuddly.'

'How alliterative.'

'But true. Not *fat*, but nicely covered.'

'Well upholstered. Like a sofa.'

He laughed. 'If you like! And what could be nicer or more welcoming than a really comfortable, well-made, expensive sofa?'

'Expensive?'

'Beyond price.'

'Beyond rubies.' She knew he meant it, but she also knew that he was saying what she wanted to hear, and therefore, although pleased, she still found it impossible to believe him.

Glancing at her watch she saw it was getting late, and hurried to the cupboard for a dish for the shepherd's pie, briskly putting in the mince she had already cooked. She tasted it. Had she overdone the Worcestershire Sauce? John hated anything too strongly flavoured. There had been a time, a few years earlier, when he would have complained bitterly if any dish she gave him assaulted his taste buds in an unseemly fashion.

'Since I am working hard all day to keep a roof over our heads, and put food on our table, is it too much to ask that when I come home in the evenings I be given a meal I can eat without needing a gallon of water to wash it down? With my stomach as delicate as it is, and with all the stresses and strains of my work, you must know that this kind of thing will keep me awake half the night with indigestion, and with going you-know-where.' And Mary would have stifled the urge to say 'No, where? If you mean to the loo, the bog, the lavatory, why not say so?' and apologised. Now he no longer made such forceful complaints but would sigh, and eat slowly, and spend the evening bearing the results with so pointed a patience that it was far worse. Mary made what she privately called 'nursery food', and appeased her own longing for culinary excitement with bottles of exotic sauces.

The microwave pinged. Mary took out the dish of potatoes and began to mash them. Her lover turned to watch her. He did not offer to help: he never did, and Mary would not have wanted him to. It was easier to talk to him while her hands were busy.

'That book I'm reading,' she began now.

'Which one? *Miss Smilla* or the one in Egypt?'

'The one in Egypt, about Lucy Duff Gordon. It's so extraordinary, having to abandon your husband and children and decamp to Egypt like that. Romantic, really, though I expect in some ways it was all a bit sordid – she was always short of money, and it must have been rather terrifying. Still . . .'

'Maybe you'd better develop consumption, and be sent abroad for your health. I'll come with you.'

'On the National Health? Dream on, they're more likely to put me on a waiting list and lose me in the system. You only get to go on trips abroad if you're a juvenile offender. Perhaps if I were to hot-wire a car

7

and go on a ram-raiding spree, *and* have consumption ... it were my condition what made me do it, yer honour...'

'Darling, they'd say you were menopausal and put you on a nice course of HRT and some counselling.'

'I suppose so. Maybe that's the answer. Perhaps I'd better go and see the doctor.'

'Oh dear, you *are* low. It's the weather, you know. You always get depressed on these dark, gloomy days. You need something to look forward to. What about a holiday? It needn't be anything too expensive, but it's fun going through the brochures, daydreaming over those lovely photographs...'

'Daydreaming. I think I do too much of that already, don't you?'

He gave a wry shrug of his shoulders. 'Where's the harm?'

Where indeed? thought Mary. All her life she had fled from the unpleasant side of reality, taking refuge in reading and in the seductive pleasures of her vivid and inventive imagination. It enabled her to bear the necessary tedium of day-to-day existence, as well as the deeper rooted anxieties and insecurities she preferred not to confront. It might be weakness, but it worked. Or did it? Of late she had found it increasingly difficult to retreat into her alternative universe. If not quite Eve cast out of Paradise, she had felt sometimes like a child on the borders of adulthood, looking back into the sunlit innocence of childhood and seeing, with precocious clarity, that not only was that world closed to her, but that it was in some ways already a self-created myth.

'Come back.' Her lover's voice was gentle, recalling her. 'The book, remember? In Egypt? What were you going to say about it?'

Mary blinked, and gave her head a little shake as if it were a misbehaving child.

'Oh, only that she treated her maid so badly, sent her home in disgrace when she had a baby but let the father – and the baby – stay with her. And I thought, would I have been like that? Is it *just* upbringing? I can't believe I could have done it.' Mary invariably put herself into the role and situation of characters she read about.

'It's hard to imagine. But then, look at the way you used to browbeat that poor, downtrodden cleaning lady.'

'Oh, *don't*!' Mary turned from putting the pie in the oven, her face flushed with the heat. 'If you only *knew* how that woman terrified me!'

'If I only knew! The way you rushed around tidying for her, and getting the special biscuits for her coffee, and doing all the nasty bits to save her from them! I always thought you only took that part-time job to have an excuse to be out of the house on the days she came.'

Mary glanced over her shoulder, guiltily haunted.

'Look at you now! Just talking about her, and you're behaving as if all the Furies and Jack the Ripper were after you! You gave her the sack, remember?'

'As if I could have done!' Mary shuddered at the memory.

'Well, you let her go, then.'

'Thank goodness she wanted to change her days and have more money! It was such a relief to be able to tell her it wouldn't be convenient. And her face! She was stunned, do you remember?'

'I'll never forget it. She'd got so used to treating you like a cockroach it had never occurred to her you might not just grovel and thank her so much for messing you about.'

'I really wonder what she used to do for all those hours she was here. John didn't notice for months that she'd gone, and really the house doesn't look any worse than before, and it doesn't take me long, except for the ironing and I don't mind that. It's a very easy house to run, big as it is, and of course John's very tidy ... typical accountant.'

'Yes, you're lucky there.' He spoke briskly to counteract the gloom in her voice.

'Mm.'

'What *you* need,' he said, 'is a drink.'

Automatically she glanced at her watch.

'It's a bit early...'

'After six,' he encouraged her. 'Perfectly respectable, after six. A nice glass of sweet sherry.'

'Ugh!' She laughed. 'You are ridiculous! You'll be offering me port and lemon next!' She went to the fridge, poured herself a glass of wine, swallowed a large mouthful and closed her eyes for a moment. The taste of the wine in her mouth, thin and sharp though it was – it wasn't very good wine, and the bottle had been opened two days earlier – brought an illusion of comforting haziness. She opened her eyes to have another sip. 'I don't really like to drink alone,' she said.

'You're not alone!'

'You know what I mean. And anyway, you're not drinking.'

'Yes, I am.' He raised the glass in his hand to her. 'Down the hatch,' he said primly.

'Bottoms up,' she responded sadly.

A glare of light from the uncurtained window, like the travelling beam of a lighthouse, moved across the room, accompanied by the crunch of tyres on gravel. There was a small pause as the garage door, operated by a remote control in the car, lifted smoothly, then the sound of the car moving into the garage.

'John's home,' said her lover unnecessarily. 'Better get the broccoli washed.'

'Yes. And I think I'll do a salad for me, too. Blast it, I haven't laid the table. I'd better hurry, you know how he likes everything to be ready when he gets home, so we can sit and have a drink before supper.'

'Dinner.'

'Oh, all right, dinner then. Though I can't really see shepherd's pie as dinner, can you?'

'Dinner,' he said, gently mimicking John, 'is what you eat in the dining room. Supper is eaten in the kitchen, or off trays in front of the television.'

'Oh yes, don't I *wish* . . . I did suggest a television in the dining room, but it didn't go down very well.'

'I'll bet!' The garage door hummed shut, and there was the sound of a key in the front door. There was a side door from the garage to the lobby outside the kitchen, but even when it was raining like tonight, John always came round to the front door. Mary remembered guiltily that she had forgotten, yet again, to put on the carriage lamps in the porch. Thank goodness for the infra-red triggered spotlight, anyway. 'I'd better be going,' said her lover.

'Yes. Bye.'

'Bye. Love you.' His lips shaped a kiss, but already he was fading. She could see the sterile white melamine of the kitchen cupboards through him, and through the vanishing table, rocking chair, Aga and pine dresser. By the time John came through the kitchen door her lover was gone, though she could still see the faint outlines of the dresser with its multi-coloured china and pottery glowing over the stark featureless cupboards that hid even the refrigerator behind their clinical masks. Her last thought, as she leaned her cheek for John's ritual tickly kiss, was of rueful, amused dismay. Oh dear, she thought, he was right. I *do* love the kitchen more than I love him.

Chapter 2

'How was your day, dear?'

'Oh, fine, thank you. Quiet. How about you?' Once, she would have said, 'Did you have a good day at the office, darling?' and laughed in her mind at the triteness of it, but such questions were no longer possible. She waited, as always, to see how he would answer her.

'Quite busy,' he said in a thoughtful tone, as one casting his mind back over a day of meetings and office work. 'Quite busy, considering.' Considering what? she wondered, knowing it was no more than a manner of speaking. John had always preferred to speak in cliché's, finding safety in the familiar pattern of words and disliking any use of language he regarded as 'fanciful'. In his appearance, too, he might have been created by a television series as an extra, so precise was his chameleon-like ability to portray 'an accountant'.

He was tall, over six foot, but inclined to mitigate any tendency to stand out from the throng by stooping slightly. Over the years the body that had once been elegantly slim had become thin and sinewy, almost stringy, and the bland good looks of his unremarkable face were pared down to reveal the bones of the skull, a process made still more apparent by the baldness that now extended over the top half of his head. The habit of combing his dark hair to cover the early signs of thinning had become, by degrees, a desperate rearguard action that involved keeping strands of long hair on one side of his head, and smoothing them carefully over the shiny dome. Mary, saddened and embarrassed by this, found herself unable to tell him how ridiculous it looked – it was yet another thing they never spoke of. Nor did she tell him how much she disliked the small bristly moustache that he had recently sprouted, as if to prove he could still grow hair somewhere, which, being a lighter brown than his hair, made him look (without her glasses) as though his nose was running with dark mucus.

'What did you have for lunch?' A safer question, this one. He brightened.

'Well now, I went to that new sandwich place that's just opened. I wasn't sure about it at first – some of the sandwiches have rather strange fillings, and they do foreign stuff as well – but I'm glad I gave it a try. Egg and cress, on brown bread of course, and really not unacceptable. The egg nicely mashed, not too lumpy, and not too much salad cream in it. And tomato soup, as it was such a cold day. They sell it in polystyrene cups, with lids, so it stays hot. It's really quite handy, and not at all dear.' He looked mildly triumphant, and Mary looked at him with exasperated pity. Where, she wanted to ask him, did you eat this sumptuous repast? On a park bench, in the rain? In a bus shelter? The library did not, of course, allow the consumption of food within its doors, and where was there for an unemployed man to consume his egg and cress and his polystyrene mug of gluey tomato soup?

Unemployed, that was the word. The unspoken, unspeakable, no-no word. Not that John thought of himself as unemployed, though, she was sure. Unemployed was for manual labourers, for miners or dockyard workers, not for accountants. If pressed, he might have admitted to having taken early retirement – very early, at forty-nine – but to confront the bald reality that he had been given the sack was beyond him.

And who am I to criticise? thought Mary. With my fantasy kitchen and my fantasy lover, how can I condemn his continuing pretence? Doesn't the fact that, for the past eighteen months, he has got up at the same time and shaved and showered and dressed in his clean shirt and careful tie and conservative suit, and gone off with his briefcase, without once managing to tell me that he no longer has an office to go to, say more about my failings as a wife than his as an accountant? There's no shame in redundancy, nowadays; it's happening to everyone – civil servants, bank managers, solicitors even. But do they all still keep up a charade to their wives that they are working?

She had only made the discovery by accident. John, fussy and conscientious, had always made it clear that she should telephone him at work only in cases of dire emergency, and even then she should think twice and count to ten first. In all the twenty-four years of their marriage she had probably done so only five or six times, and those occasions had been in the early days, and in David's childhood. He had been quite safe from discovery by that route. No, his downfall had been to rely on routine. Not his own routine – that could never let him down – but Mary's.

For some years, since David had reached sixteen and taken his GCSEs, Mary had been working part-time in the office of a local business. She had begun on a whim, feeling that although David was still living at home he had no need of her constant presence, and might in fact be better off having to fend for himself a bit more. Or so she told herself, knowing all the time that what she really wanted to do was to avoid her cleaning lady. She had slightly feared that she might be unemployable except in a fairly menial capacity: after eighteen years as a housewife and mother her rudimentary secretarial skills had seemed as out of date as the ability to illuminate parchment. She had wondered, in her wilder moments, whether she might not end up cleaning someone else's house while Mrs Woodend cleaned hers. She would not have minded, only she suspected that she would almost certainly be offered a lower hourly rate than Mrs W., who was very superior and demanded (and got) both generous pay and plenty of perks.

In the event, rather to her surprise, she was offered part-time secretarial work in a small business that had expanded from repairing household appliances into a repair and second-hand centre that in this time of recession was doing brisk trade. People who would have scorned to bother with repairing a three-year-old iron, or toaster, or washing machine, now made a virtue of necessity and said they owed it to the environment to make do and mend, rather than to buy new. Since the ability to repair electrical goods was one that had largely atrophied in the throwaway boom years, Mr Naseby's little corner shop rapidly outgrew itself and expanded down the street, taking on the premises of a defunct sports shop and a bankrupt clothes shop.

Mr Naseby took on two young trainees, and while they were struggling to overcome the benefits of a modern educational system which had left them unable to perform any mathematical calculation that was beyond working out on their fingers, and painfully lacking in self-confidence owing to their almost complete illiteracy, he had recalled his father and uncle from retirement. These two worthies, delighted to find themselves more of use than ever in their lives before, and even more pleased to be released from the confines of home, sat 'out the back' like two gnomes, carrying on endless reminiscent conversations that were largely incomprehensible to outsiders owing to their habit of removing their teeth and putting them, with careful reverence, on a shelf with the other spare parts. From there they grinned cheerfully at all comers, and were the subject of endless practical jokes by the trainees, who took their revenge on the fierce discipline imposed by the pair by clamping a plastic rose into one set, or rubbing another with garlic. Mary adored the old men, and happily called them Dad and Uncle, like everyone else, the complications of having three Mr Nasebys in one small building being too hideous to contemplate. John thought the whole situation undignified and unsuitable, his worst term of abuse, but for once Mary had disregarded him.

'I enjoy it, and they're nice people. Besides, what sort of job do you really think I can get, with my lack of experience and at my age?'

'But you don't *need* to go out to work. People will think I'm not looking after you properly. Not being a good provider.'

Mary looked at him helplessly in the face of this antediluvian attitude.

'Women like me don't get part-time jobs just for the money.'

'Then why can't you just do charity work? That would fill up your time. Get on some committees, that sort of thing.'

'I'm not very good at committees. Hours of talk and nothing achieved that couldn't have been done in ten minutes. And I go to sleep, or say the wrong thing. No, I'm sorry, darling, but it's Naseby's or nothing, at the moment. You needn't tell anyone at work if you don't want to. But I think you'll find,' she added shrewdly, 'that most people think it more odd for someone in my position *not* to do something other than keep house. It's rather the in thing, really. You wouldn't want people to think you're keeping me tied to the house, would you?' Over the years she had become adept at such small stratagems, despising herself and knowing that she was creating her own small home-bred monster, but unable to contemplate the struggle with her own feelings of inadequacy and guilt that would be involved in trying to change him.

Since the shop was in the nearest small town, while John had to travel into Reading each day, Mary was able to leave the house later, and return earlier, than he. Because of this, and because she never mentioned her work in his hearing, John was able conveniently to forget that she did it, though of course the money she earned was increasingly handy now. As the business grew Mary found herself more and more useful, particularly after she enrolled in an afternoon adult education class in book-keeping, which enabled her to see to the accounts and the

VAT returns. The irony of someone married to an accountant going to such a class did not immediately strike her, but a delighted Mr Naseby promptly doubled her salary.

'As your book-keeper, I'm really not sure if the business can afford me now, Mr Naseby,' she told him severely.

'Nonsense, Mrs Marsh. You should see what you're saving me in accountants' fees. Terrible bloodsuckers, accountants. Charge you to say good morning, they will.'

Mary felt she ought to be disagreeing, but did not. Mr Naseby, of course, had no idea what John did.

Or, now, did not do. And it was, indirectly, as a result of her work that Mary had found him out. It would be true to say that for some time she had been wondering. John had seemed so vague, so much quieter at home and disinclined to talk about the office. She thought there must be some problem at work; she had even suspected that he might be having an affair with someone there. It was not so much the change in his attitude that made her think this, as the change in the way he *smelled*.

A non-smoker, Mary had a strongly developed sense of smell. John, always fussy about his appearance, put on clean underwear and shirt every day as a matter of course, and was meticulous in bathing. His suits went to the cleaners regularly, and were hung up to air overnight after wearing. Even so, on his return in the evening he invariably carried round him, unnoticeable to his accustomed nose, what Mary thought of as the Office Smell. It was compounded of cigarette smoke (the office had not yet adopted a no-smoking policy), beery pub effluvium from lunches with colleagues or clients, faint nose-tickling scents of female staff perfume, and an overall pervasive tang that she thought of as ink, though she knew he never handled such a thing.

The difference was gradual. At first the cigarette and pub smell, and even the powdery scents of other women's perfume, were still there, with only the ink aroma missing. Then, after a few weeks, the pub and cigarettes vanished also. Mary did not consciously notice at first. She continued to hang his suits by an open window to air, and it was not until one very cold wet day when he came home and filled the hall with the greasy, heavy, bacon-and-chip smell of a café, that she realised the loss of the others.

Knowing him, she said nothing, and continued to hang out his suits and take them to the cleaners as usual. She was alerted to changes, however, and soon became aware that John was being more than usually careful with money. Whether she would ever have noticed this if it had not been for the Smell was a moot point – John had always been fussy about such things, budgeting carefully for holidays and living expenses. Not that he was ungenerous: her personal and housekeeping allowances (paid, naturally, into separate bank accounts to keep everything straightforward) were more than adequate to her needs. Simply he did not, as before, change his car after two years, or follow up the week of golf in Scotland he had talked of earlier. Mary, in turn, quietly economised, and suggested in a casual way that, with David away so much, she no longer needed so much housekeeping, and that her own earnings were more than enough to keep her in clothes and extras. He had protested, but Mary saw the relief in his eyes and saw, when the next statements arrived from the bank, that both standing orders had been reduced.

'Do you think he's set up a second home, with some busty bimbo from the office?' she had wondered to her lover.

'If he has, he's not spending much time there,' her lover pointed out. 'He's never late home these days. If anything, he's earlier than ever. It must be the recession.'

'What, the recession the government keeps saying doesn't exist?'

'Yes, that recession, that's putting people out of business at a rate of knots.'

'Ah, that recession. But doesn't that make accountants even busier? Surely the one thing you need if things are wobbly is a good accountant?'

'While things are wobbly, perhaps. But not if they fall over completely. Dead businesses don't produce annual accounts.'

'So what's he up to then?'

'Search me.'

A few weeks later, they found out.

It was a Wednesday, one of Mary's three working days. John had gone off as usual, taking his umbrella as well as his briefcase, his navy mackintosh buttoned and belted neatly round him against the drizzle. Half an hour later, having raced to make the bed and dust the house, Mary went to work. On arrival she found the shop deserted, everyone hovering round the doorway to the workroom where a full-blown row was in progress. That it was serious was clear to her – as clear as Dad and Uncle's speech, for in order to argue properly they both had their teeth in. The point of disagreement – Brunel's reason for creating a tunnel under the Thames – seemed entirely pointless to Mary, but had stoked them up to a fine heat of contention.

'This is ridiculous,' said Mr Naseby firmly. 'What on earth does it matter?'

'What does it matter?' spluttered his father. 'Have you no pride in your work, boy? Don't you care that this old idiot' – his brother was, in fact, two years younger than he – 'who doesn't know his arse from his elbow, has just proved himself totally' – his hearers fell back a pace, as he sprayed them vigorously with saliva, and he repeated the word with relish – 'totally unfitted to put a new fuse into a plug, let alone repair a delicate item like a microwave? Ignorant, that's what he is. Pig ignorant. Do untold damage, he could. Untold,' he said again portentously and wetly.

'An old idiot I may be,' said Uncle furiously, 'but not so much of an old idiot that I don't know I'm right, and you're just about as wrong as you can be. Specially seeing as you're older than me, and going senile into the bargain.' He cackled with triumph at this undoubted hit. The trainees stirred, and growled with delight; there was nothing they liked better than a good fight. It seemed to Mary that at any moment they too would be taking sides and a feud would develop that would take weeks, if not months, to heal.

Mr Naseby opened his mouth, glared from one angry old relative to the other, thought, and closed it again. With some relief Mary heard the bell on the shop door ring.

'A customer in the shop,' she said briskly. 'Better go and see, Mr Naseby. And haven't you two boys got some work to do?' she asked severely, quelling any rebellion with the firm glare she seemed able to summon only at work. Sheepishly, they slunk off. Mary turned to the elderly warriors, who sat side by side on the high stools they liked to work on, glowering and refusing to look at one another.

'Shame on you,' she scolded. 'What sort of example is that for the boys?'

Dad scowled. 'It's him,' he jutted his head towards Uncle. 'Old fool.'

'You know you're both being very silly,' she said austerely. 'It's lucky the shop wasn't full of customers listening to you squabbling like babies. Now there's only one way to settle this once and for all – we'll just have to find out which of you is right. So I'm going straight off to the library, which is *not* at all convenient for Mr Naseby, because the VAT returns have to be in by the end of the month; but I don't see how I can possibly concentrate on doing them correctly with this fighting going on. And,' she added impressively, 'if I do them wrong, I could be put in prison! Or Mr Naseby could, because he's the one who has to sign the form as correct, and that would be even worse!'

'Put him in,' muttered Uncle rebelliously, shooting a glance at Dad. 'Do him good, a few months in stir. Smarten his ideas up. Give him a bit of discipline.'

'Discipline! I'll give you discipline!'

'What, like you did when we was small? A belt round the lug 'ole, or else? Proper bully, you were.'

'And you deserved it—'

'Quiet!' bellowed Mary. 'I am going to the library, as I said, and I am going to *look up* the answer, and *photocopy* the result, and *bring it* back here, at which point whichever of you is wrong will apologise to the other, and give him five pounds.'

'Ten,' put in Dad, who was convinced he was right.

'Ten, if you like. And the person who is *right*,' continued Mary inexorably, 'will accept the apology *gracefully*, without crowing, and will put the ten pounds in the charity box, along with another five pounds because you have both been so nasty, and that will be the *end* of it. Right?'

'Right,' they grinned reluctantly, their teeth gleaming white and even in their wrinkled faces.

'Good.' Mary relaxed and smiled at them, loving them both. 'Now, what about a nice cup of tea before I go? And for goodness' sake take your teeth out while I'm gone. Then if you must argue at least nobody will be able to understand you.'

'*Thank* you, Mrs Marsh,' whispered Mr Naseby as she went out through the shop. 'It's very good of you to take all this trouble, and I'm only sorry you've been put to it. Wicked old chaps, they are. I swear I don't know what gets into them at times.'

'Oh, they're darlings,' said Mary cheerfully. 'Don't you worry, Mr Naseby. It's just youthful high spirits. They'll grow out of it.'

She pondered, as she drove through the traffic into Reading, on the fact that after several years of working together she and Mr Naseby were still so formal with one another. Was it a sign that she was too distant, too unfriendly? Certainly they conversed easily and without strain, but it had never occurred to her to ask him to call her Mary, while the thought of addressing him as Bill was beyond her imagining.

And yet she thought of him as her friend and knew that in need she could, and would, turn to him without embarrassment for help. That there was, in the mournful brown spaniel eyes that were set in his plump face, a particular kind of warmth when he looked at her, and that those eyes were inclined to linger perhaps fractionally too long on her well-defined bust and neat waist, was something she did not admit even to her lover.

At the library, having parked with some difficulty, she went to the enquiry desk. It was not a place she visited often, though she sometimes took out the kind of novels she enjoyed but did not feel were worthy of being bought – light romances and historical dramas – when she had a cold, or was feeling particularly tired or dismal. She had no idea where to look up Brunel. The librarian, a middle-aged woman Mary vaguely recognised, took her to the engineering section and found her an appropriate book, and Mary regaled her on the way with a report on the row between Dad and Uncle, which had them both giggling.

'I'd better photocopy the pages, like I said, or they'll never believe me.'

The librarian took her to the photocopier. As they approached it, Mary caught a glimpse out of the corner of her eye of a familiar head. She stopped, like a horse balking at a jump. Looked again. There could be no doubt – the dark hair, cut short but for the long strand that was flattened so carefully over the polished dome of his skull; the thin neck and tall, thin body; the suit she had, the week before, collected from the cleaners, and the shirt she had ironed two days ago. She even thought she could make out the line of thinned, fraying fabric on the fold of the collar. He was stiffly upright but leaning slightly forward over a newspaper, and as she watched he turned to murmur to the man beside him and she caught a glimpse of cheek and of his dark moustache. In sudden panic she turned her back, knowing that this would scarcely deceive him should he turn any further.

'I won't copy it, I don't think,' she whispered, fast and desperate. 'I'll just check out the book, and take that.'

'Of course, if you really want to.' The librarian was puzzled. 'Are you all right? You've gone quite pale. Would you like to sit down? Have a glass of water?' She spoke with all the sympathy of one who has just experienced the sudden bouleversements of menopause.

'No!' Mary hurried away, fighting not to break into a run. 'No, I'm fine, thank you,' she said, more moderately, as they reached the further end of the building. 'Just a bit of a turn ... er, that man. The tall thin one, rather bald, sitting back there ... I thought I recognised him ... does he come here often?'

Do you come here often, mimicked her mind, summoning an image of teenage couples in old-fashioned evening dress circling, sweaty and flushed with excitement and terror, at the kind of dances she had never in fact attended. She blinked, and shook her head.

'Oh yes, nearly every day,' responded the librarian cheerfully. 'He's quite one of our regulars. Monday, Wednesday and Friday, on the dot when we open, and stays most of the day. He's very helpful, too. Only the other day he came up with a suggestion to reorganise the reference books that was most useful! For an untrained person, that is,' she added with the conscious superiority of one trained in the inner mysteries of her calling. 'So you know him, do you? Would you like to go back and say hello? You can check the book out later.'

'Oh, no, no,' gasped Mary. 'He wouldn't like that at all. In fact ... in fact I'd be grateful if you didn't mention the fact that I'd seen him ... there are problems, you see ...' she trailed vaguely off. The librarian, scenting an intrigue, looked as if she were longing to know more, but was too polite to ask.

'Of course. We don't want to cause any unpleasantness, do we?'

'No,' said Mary numbly. 'No unpleasantness. Definitely no unpleasantness. No.' She checked out the book and tottered back to her car, where she sat for half an hour in the gloomy obscurity of the car park. So upset was she that she did something she never normally did except when she was home on her own, and conjured her lover to sit in the passenger seat. Generally she rationed his appearances to such solitary, secret moments, feeling obscurely that it was unfair, even unfaithful to John to bring her lover into the outside world, but at this moment she needed all the comfort she could summon.

'In the library!' she gasped silently. 'Every day! Every day that I'm working, that is. And who knows where on the other days!'

'He's lost his job,' said her lover gently. 'It's happening everywhere.'

'Yes, but ... after all those years! And they said they might make him a partner, a while ago ...'

'They never did, though, did they? Poor John.'

'Poor John. But not to tell me ...'

'He's protecting you. He doesn't want you to be worried.'

'What's to worry about? We're not poor. We paid off the mortgage several years ago, and he's got the capital from the sale of his parents' house, and all the money they left him. We could live off the income from that. We are living off it, I suppose. He should have told me!'

'He couldn't. It's how he is. You know that.'

'It's my fault. I've failed him.'

Her lover was silent. Her own creation, he could not convincingly deny her deeply held doubts and insecurities.

'What do I do?' Mary cried the rhetorical question aloud. She already knew the answer. Any sensible person – an agony aunt, say, or a counsellor – would tell her to talk to John about it. She herself, if one of her friends were to come to her with a similar problem, would recommend doing just that. That, after all, was the current wisdom. Openness, discussion, sharing. It sounded so right in theory, but Mary could imagine only too clearly how disastrous it would be with John.

In John's book, discussion meant an exchange of facts. One discussed with one's clients, with one's bank manager, even with one's solicitor. One gave, or received, advice. At home, one might discuss the weather, or the political situation, or one's game of golf. To attempt to talk about anything more personal would be regarded by him as a kind of mental rape, an intrusion into his privacy that would be worse, to him, than a physical attack, however violent. If John had decided that he did not want to talk to her about having lost his job, then only he could reverse that decision.

How strange, thought Mary. I thought I was the one who lived in a fantasy world, with my kitchen and my lover and my cat. I regard that as normal – well – fairly normal and yet I see what John is doing as unhealthy. Of all people, I should be able to help him come to terms with this, but of all people, I know I am the person he would most mind knowing. I, and perhaps my father. I wish I hadn't found out.

The discovery depressed her, and made her feel more inadequate than ever. Not for the first time she thought that she was not the right wife for John, though she knew he would be appalled by any such suggestion. That, too, would seem to him like a criticism. Had he not chosen her as his wife?

After that day, six months earlier, Mary gave up going to the library; she managed to tell John that she had found it too inconvenient, and switched to a smaller local branch. At least, she thought, he won't be roaming the streets on Tuesdays and Thursdays in case I turn up there. She also became careful not to ask him too many questions about work, though she felt she should still show some interest in his supposed activities.

Questions about lunch were fairly safe. The fortuitous closing down of the Italian restaurant which, along with the pub, had been the most popular lunching place for the people of John's firm, and the partners' recent policy of scrapping client lunches except for the largest accounts, made it easy for John to switch to the round of sandwich and snack bars he now went to. Mary had tentatively offered to make him a packed lunch, but he had looked unhappy at the prospect and she guessed that the daily search for a bargain was a useful way of passing time, and provided more social contact than the hushed atmosphere the library could provide.

'Shepherd's pie for dinner,' she offered now. 'It's in the oven, and there's apples with mincemeat and a baked custard. I've just got to lay the table, won't be a minute. Pour yourself a drink, I'll be with you in no time. The fire's lit.'

John nodded approval of the menu and the fire, while casting an anxious glance at her empty wine glass.

'Do you want some more wine?' he asked, the emphasis on the word 'more'.

'Not just yet,' she soothed him. 'I had a glass from the bottle that needs finishing while I was cooking the supper. I'll have the rest when we eat, but I'll come through and watch the local news with you in just a moment.'

He relaxed, the skin round his eyes easing. Those hazel eyes that had once seemed so warm and soulful, but which now looked so blank to her. The windows of the soul? she wondered. Oh, I hope not.

Chapter 3

While John was changing from his suit to the corduroy trousers, the checked viyella shirt (worn, daringly, with a cravat instead of a tie), and the V-necked pullover that had been one of the last his mother had knitted him, Mary hurried to lay the dining table.

The dining room was not large; not that it mattered a great deal because they seldom entertained. Two of their neighbours in the close had built conservatories, so that the wide sliding doors that opened to the terraces could be pulled back to double the room size. John had rather pointedly not commented on this, and Mary had been careful to let him know that she was not eager to increase the size of a house that was already, she thought, much too large for the two of them.

The house had been John's choice, not hers. When they had married, John's parents and her own father had each given them a lump sum which, added to the savings John had prudently made, had enabled them to skip the first rung of the housing ladder, the newly weds' flat, and move immediately into a small house. Since this had always been intended as a staging post, a stepping-stone on the way to the family home Mary envisaged, she had not minded that the little house was on a brand new housing estate, one of a street of identical semi-detached two-bedroomed modern homes that looked to her eyes, accustomed to the soaring stone of Oxford college buildings and the self-confident Victorian solidity of the Woodstock Road, mean, flimsy and cramped.

'It's not for very long,' John had reassured her when she voiced her doubts. 'We'll soon be moving to something better, and the great thing about these is that they're very saleable. And of course, being new, there won't be any maintenance worries.'

In fact the house proved to have the endless small problems common

23

to newly built estates, and by the time they had sorted out doors which jammed or would not stay shut, cracks in plasterwork where inadequately seasoned timber had warped, creaking floors and the mysterious knocking in the pipes every time anyone used the cold tap in the bathroom, they were indeed moving on – to a three-bedroomed house on the same estate.

'It's just the next stage,' John soothed her. 'We won't have any of the problems we had with the other house – the previous owners will have ironed all that out already. With a utility room *and* a downstairs cloakroom it will be ideal for you when the baby's born, and we don't need much of a garden while it's little. Nice and easy for you to run, and just think how well all our furniture will fit in!'

Mary, queasy and inclined to be tearful in the early stages of pregnancy, had found herself unable to point out that with the exception of one or two pieces from her old home she heartily disliked all the furniture they had. The small rooms and aggressive modernity of their first home had made it impossible for her to furnish it the way she would have liked, with large, comfortable second-hand sofas and chairs, and the stripped pine that was just coming into fashion. Instead they had gone for what she privately called 'dead new' – with the emphasis on the 'dead' – and although she had kept to simple shapes and, where possible, natural finishes, the end result was in her eyes soulless and bleak.

Nor could she tell him how much she disliked living on the estate. Shy and unsure of herself, she had been nervous of joining in on the coffee mornings, the afternoon teas, and all the many activities that her neighbours enjoyed. The few she had attended had been agonising: somehow she always seemed to be wrongly dressed, either too informally or too smartly; they all seemed to know one another, and made incomprehensible references and jokes at which she smiled politely, her face settling into a rictus grin that left her cheeks aching. They all seemed so sure of themselves, their houses immaculate, their biscuits and cakes home-made, that Mary felt she was taking part in the filming of an advertisement – washing powder, or breakfast cereal – and that she was the one using the wrong brand.

She withdrew into her shell and was relieved when the invitations became fewer, and then stopped. It was, she felt, her own fault, something missing in her that stopped her fitting in, but the estate was so large, with so many streets and crescents and closes of houses that were almost, but not quite, the same. She felt hemmed in, encroached on, as she had never done in the town, but at the same time lonelier than she had ever been – she, who loved her solitude.

It was at this time that the first seeds of her fantasy kitchen had been sown. In the slow, dreamy stages of later pregnancy, when she had given up the secretarial job she had been doing for some years, she had found the days long and empty. The new house was, she had to admit, easy to run, and the varnished or laminated surfaces of the furniture needed little care beyond dusting or wiping down. Stifling in its characterless confines she spent her afternoons exploring the nearby villages, peering into estate agents' windows and pottering happily in antique and junk shops.

She never bought anything – the things she fell in love with would have looked out of place and ridiculous at home – but she stored them in her mind. They became mental comfort objects, things against which she would rest her mind and spirit, buffers against the disappointments of the present. She still believed that one day, in a few years' time, they would move to the kind of house she wanted, and when that happened she would be ready. The actual objects would not still be there to be bought, of course, but there would be things like them, and mentally she wandered the rooms of her future life, arranging and re-arranging them to her satisfaction.

David's birth and babyhood had distracted her only slightly. An easy baby, he seemed to have inherited in his very genetic make-up John's orderly habits and love of routine. Mary, prepared for on-demand feeding and sleepless nights, found herself with an infant who fell, immediately, into a four-hour pattern and who slept through the night within a few months. She knew she was lucky, and indeed when she went to clinics and saw the white-faced tearful young mothers of colicky babies she felt almost humble, but she never deluded herself that it was skilled mothering on her part that had created this enviable situation. David, like John, imposed his pattern on life with quiet, implacable firmness.

Nevertheless, she carefully read all the books on bringing up children that she could find, filtered them through the editing process of her own common sense, and immersed herself in trying to provide the right balance of stimulation and loving calm that she wanted for her children. With the meticulous care John showed when balancing a set of accounts, she planned outings, played music, found books in the library, and when David developed infant eczema put him on a special diet that excluded all beef and dairy products, examining lists of ingredients on everything she bought in the supermarket and usually ending up cooking and sieving his meals rather than using ready-made jars. She had her reward – David thrived, the eczema was kept well under control, and he showed signs of being, if not a genius, at least reasonably intelligent.

When he was three they decided to have another child, and shelved any ideas of moving until the baby should be born. As John pointed out, two children would make a great deal more work; and more than that she was reluctant to move away from her excellent GP and midwife, and the services of a familiar maternity unit and clinic. In the event it was as well she did not, for each of her next three pregnancies ended in miscarriage. The third, and most difficult, miscarried at twenty weeks when she had begun to think herself safe, and she needed all the support of the medical network to get her through the shock and misery. For nearly a year she fought against periods of depression that were not helped by the fact that she did not conceive again. Because of her mental state she did not at first wonder why she, who had become pregnant each time she tried, should suddenly have become barren.

'I can't understand it,' she wept to her doctor. 'You're quite sure there's nothing wrong with me? My tubes aren't blocked or anything?'

'No, nothing like that.' He preserved a professionally bland face. 'Have you discussed it with your husband?'

'Not really. I mean, it's a medical problem, isn't it? Or is it psychological? I've heard of that happening, when the more you want a baby the more nothing happens. Could it be that?'

'It's possible.' His reply was uncharacteristically cautious, and he was finding it hard to meet her eye. Mary became suspicious.

'There is something wrong, isn't there? Something you're not telling me?'

He sighed.

'There is nothing wrong with you. I can promise you that you don't have any kind of ghastly disease, and if you did have you can be sure I wouldn't keep you in the dark about it. As to the other thing, I can only suggest you discuss it with your husband.'

'We are still—' she blushed. Since losing the last baby her interest in sex had almost completely disappeared, but recently she had been trying to think herself into the right frame of mind, superstitiously

26

feeling that the quality of the act itself might influence her chance of conceiving.

'Yes, I'm sure you are. I really can't suggest anything else, Mary.' She glanced at him sharply. He had never, before, called her anything but Mrs Marsh. Frustrated and uncomprehending she went home, and that evening raised the subject with John.

'Another baby?' He looked at her in startled amazement. 'Surely, after all those problems ... and now that David's so much older ... I mean, even if you were pregnant now, he'd be seven before the baby was born. Hardly a playmate ... and besides, there's a great deal to be said for being an only child. After all, I'm one.' She ran through various responses in her mind, and rejected them all. 'With just David, we'll be able to afford a good education for him, send him to private school, holidays abroad, that kind of thing. Give him every opportunity. It's no more than he deserves.'

Mary was far from wishing to deny her son any good thing, but all the same she could not altogether accept this.

'But you don't have a second baby just to be a playmate for the first. And I don't believe we couldn't afford school fees for one more, particularly if David gets a scholarship. Besides, it isn't always good to be an only child. I was one too, remember, and I always longed for brothers and sisters.'

'You can't re-live your own childhood through your children,' he said sententiously.

'Of course not, but ... oh, I *wanted* another baby!'

He looked uncomfortable.

'I didn't know...' For the first time in their lives together, he sounded apologetic.

'What do you mean, you didn't know? Of course I wanted another baby!'

'After all the upset last time, I thought ... and it's not good for you, those miscarriages ... and bad for David, too, when you're ill and unhappy ... so I thought it best not to risk any more...'

'What do you mean? What have you done?' The sternness in her voice startled her as much as it did him. Goodness, she thought, I sound just like Pa.

'I had ... well ... I had a little op. You know.'

This time she had no patience with the prudery that she had once found appealing, even touching.

'If you mean you had a vasectomy, for heaven's sake come out and say so,' she snapped. His look was resentful, but he was in the unusual position of realising he was in the wrong.

'It seemed like the best thing,' he said defensively.

'Without consulting me? Without even mentioning it to me? How could you? And ... *how* could you? Without my noticing anything, I mean?'

'Well, it's not a very nice thing to talk about, is it? For a man, that is. It's ... personal. And you were away for a week staying with the Professor, so ...'

'So you sneaked off and had it done. And if I hadn't mentioned it, would you ever have told me?'

'Of course. At the appropriate time.'

'And when would that have been? Oh, never mind.'

The following few months were full of strained silences during which Mary swallowed back the bitter remarks she wanted to make and concentrated all her energies on David. When she showed no signs of relenting John amazed her by suggesting they look for a new house.

'An older one, if you like,' he said awkwardly. 'In the country,' he added, with a martyred air.

'But I thought ... can we afford it?'

'Yes, I think so. There's the money Father left me, and we can put the mortgage up a bit. They're talking about a managerial position, at the office.'

'Oh, John!' There was a softness in her voice he had not heard for some while. He gave a restrained smile.

'I'll leave it with you then, shall I? The house hunting? Of course, I shall want to see it, and have it thoroughly checked before we buy.'

'Of course. Of course, I understand that. Thank you, John.'

He nodded, taking her gratitude as his right. Mary, remembering the years of putting up with modern houses she disliked, could not believe that when he got used to the idea he wouldn't come round to liking an older place. She chose carefully – not too large, to make the mortgage unmanageable; not too small, so that he could boast at the office about his home. Not too old, either – she abandoned dreams of Tudor timbering and settled on a small Victorian house in a pretty village that was not too far away from his work.

For the first six months she thought it had worked. Slowly, so that nothing should change too abruptly, she began to replace pieces of furniture with older, more harmonious things. She organised carefully planned little dinner parties for his colleagues at work, so that he could see that they were impressed by the house. She kept quiet about the problems that occurred, managing to pay out of the housekeeping for repairs to guttering, the replacement of a rotten windowsill, and learning to deal with blocked drains and a smoking fireplace. When, in the autumn, she found evidence of mice in the kitchen, she got a kitten. She began, cautiously, to join in village activities, and was happier than she had ever been in her life before.

She should have known it was too good to last. When they had lived there for a year they found that the small cracks in the walls, which Mary had been quietly filling and painting over, suddenly split and spread almost overnight into what looked like canyons. An exceptionally dry summer and the roots of a large willow tree in the garden that had been planted by the previous owners had leached the moisture from the soil and caused the inadequate foundations to subside. The whole house would need underpinning, an expensive exercise which, though it would be paid for by the insurance company, would render the building more or less uninhabitable for months. John's face had a long, I-told-you-so expression. The heavy rain that followed the drought shifted the foundations still more, and made the cesspit in the garden overflow, to John's even greater dismay and disgust; the cat was run over and killed, and David developed asthma and had to be rushed into hospital on a night when wild weather had blocked the road with a fallen tree.

Mary knew they would have to move. The thought distressed her less than it might once have done. The house, which she had moved to with pleasure, had come to seem more of a worry than anything else. The pressure of attempting to hide its flaws from John, and now trying to defend it against his spoken and unspoken criticisms, had tarnished the brightness. Apart from that, she had come to see it as a bribe, a sugar comfit to distract her from her anger at his vasectomy. She despised the weakness in herself that had allowed this to happen.

She saw with sudden and painful clarity that the only way to escape from this was to separate from John. The thought dismayed her. To go home and live once again with her father was a still more dreadful prospect, for at least John's assumption of control over her life was undertaken quietly, albeit with equal implacability. Then again, she had no income or capital of her own. Even with her share of the value of the house it would be a struggle to give David the kind of childhood she wanted for him; for one thing, she would have to get a job. More importantly, her own childhood had given her an almost religious belief in the importance of a child having, wherever possible, two parents.

For her to leave John would not, of course, be anything like as cataclysmic as her own mother's disappearance to another continent. David would live with her, naturally, but would doubtless see his father regularly. It could all be done without acrimony, and yet in the end Mary found that she could not do it. Not, in the final analysis, because of David, but because of John himself. Looking at her feelings for him, Mary discovered that what had started out as gratitude and fondness had developed, not into friendship, but into similar feelings for different reasons.

Before, she had thought she needed John, and had been grateful to him for choosing her. Now it seemed to her that in many ways he was not aware of how much he needed her, and in a strange way she was grateful for that, too. To be needed by someone, that was what it boiled down to. That, perhaps, had been at the root of her longing for another baby now that David was beginning to grow up, and her bitter resentment when the possibility was taken away from her. She made a conscious decision, then, to put John in the baby's place. Believing that his fussiness, his irritating insistence on rigidly adhering to pre-set patterns and forms, and his narrow outlook on life stemmed from an insecurity even greater than her own, she resolved to stay with him and make the best of things.

Afterwards, looking back, she frequently wondered if she had been wrong. With the increased self-knowledge of later years, she realised that she had made the kind of choice more appropriate in a fantasy world than in reality. More quixotic and romantic than practical, it owed too much to the books she read and not enough to real life. In moments of depression she thought her attitude to John had been patronising rather than supportive, and that she had wildly over-estimated his need of her. She seldom allowed herself to think about this. Having made her decision, she would stick by it.

John chose their present house, in a neat cul-de-sac in a newly developed area not far from their old housing estate, though snobbishly turning its back on it. 'Nice to be back,' said John with genuine pleasure. Mary saw that this was the only kind of place where he could feel at home, and grimly set herself to work to adapt the house, and herself, to make them at least slightly compatible. She kept some of the older furniture – the dining chairs with the seats she had carefully and lovingly re-covered; the *chaise longue*; the buttoned Victorian arm-chairs that even John admitted were so comfortable. She felt something within her dying, however, and in desperation retreated once more to the world of her imagination.

Now she put the tablemats neatly onto the polished table, set out cutlery with the deftness of long practice, put clean table napkins by each place. By the time John had changed and they had had a drink, the meal would be just ready.

'Have you spoken to the Professor recently?'

John, eating the bland shepherd's pie with careful enjoyment, spoke so casually that Mary was at once alert for trouble.

'Pa? No, why?'

'Something I heard.' He sliced a Brussels sprout in half with meticulous accuracy, inspected its blameless green whorls carefully, then ate it. No matter how tiny the sprouts, or how carefully Mary had prepared them, he never omitted this precaution, convinced that some invertebrate timebomb lurked within each one.

'Oh?' It was better, she had learned, not to ask too many questions, which might be seen as an interrogation. She reached out and pushed a half-opened daffodil more firmly into the bowl of garden foliage in the middle of the table. Its yellow petals were fresh and cheering against the rather tired green of the evergreens that were all she had been able to find in the garden – still, after fifteen years, distressingly new-looking in her eyes. The soil, churned up by the builders and left with the spoil from the foundations covered by a thin layer of cosmetic topsoil, had not been conducive to luxuriant growth, and the trees and shrubs she had put in still looked stunted and poor.

'So when *did* you last speak to the Professor?'

John's voice recalled her. She gave a little giggle.

'You sound like a painting,' she said, and in answer to his pained look, amplified: 'You know – *When Did You Last See Your Father?*' His brow cleared, and he nodded. It was the kind of art of which he approved: representational, and with an illustrative quality.

'Very amusing, dear.' He had a little fleck of tomato caught in his moustache, Mary noticed. She averted her eyes, unable to bring herself to tell him and wishing for the thousandth time that he would stop calling her 'dear'. One of her clearest memories of her mother had been the saccharine way she had called her husband, Mary's father, by that unloving epithet. Even then Mary had been aware that it was unloving, although it had frequently been accompanied by a caress. It was a patronising word with undertones of exasperation, a word that spoke of the tepid remains of what had once been love. Was that how John felt about her? In all their years of marriage he had never, she was fairly sure, been unfaithful to her. Certainly his behaviour consistently made it clear that he needed her which was why, even now, Mary never dreamed of replacing her fantasy lover with a real one.

'And how long ago did you say it was?'

'What was?'

'When you spoke to the Professor, dear.'

'Oh yes. Sorry. It must have been last Sunday. You know I always ring him on Sunday. Why? Have you heard from him?'

'Not *from* him, no. *Of* him.'

'Who from?'

His eyebrows twitched into a momentary frown at her ungrammatical answer, but not even for him was Mary prepared to say 'From whom?' in everyday conversation.

'From one of his old students, as a matter of fact. You might remember him – Rupert Greenwood?' Mary shook her head. There had been so many, over the years, and very few of them were clear in her memory now. 'Well, he remembers you. He was a graduate student when we were courting.'

Courting, mused Mary. What a sublimely inappropriate word. She saw that he expected some kind of sentimental response, and smiled dutifully.

'You ought not to expect me to remember *him*, then,' she said cheerfully. 'Surely all my attention must have been taken up with *you*.' As it had been, she recalled. That this tall, nice-looking young man actually seemed interested in her, in clumsy, ungainly Mary Hill, had inspired in her so much gratitude and pleasure that it had been easy to believe herself solidly in love.

'And what's he doing these days? Rupert Whatever, I mean. Where did you meet him?' Blast it, she thought, there I go again, asking the wrong kind of question. They probably met in the library. Glancing quickly at his face she saw with relief that it was all right. The rather red, almost babyish lips below the brownish moustache (without, she was relieved to see, the bit of tomato) were not compressed, or shaping themselves distastefully to lie.

'That's what was so extraordinary – he was running the sandwich place where I got my lunch! Imagine, a man with his qualifications! Of course I'd never have recognised him, and I must say if it had been me I'd have kept quiet and not said anything, but he came straight out with it! "Professor Hill's son-in-law!" he said, straight off. Very friendly. Rather too friendly, really. I could hardly get away.'

Mary could not quite make out whether it was the indignity of being hailed as an old friend by the proprietor of a small sandwich bar that was bothering him, or what had actually been said.

'And what did he say? About Pa?'

'He said,' John lowered his voice as though someone might be lurking behind the discreetly curtained windows and listening, 'that he was in Oxford last weekend, and he saw the Professor in the Botanic Gardens, with a Girl!'

'Goodness, how dashing. Or is it? It sounds rather like *Crampton Hodnet*. It's a book,' she added hastily, seeing another frown, 'by Barbara Pym. But never mind that now. It doesn't sound like anything particularly odd to me. Pa loves the Botanic Gardens, he often goes there – though perhaps not so often in February, come to think of it. He's not exactly one for the great outdoors, is he, unless the weather's behaving itself. I've often thought he'd be far happier on the Mediterranean – Italy, say, or even Greece. I hope he didn't catch cold.'

'I don't think there would have been any danger of *that*,' said John acidly. 'Or at least, that isn't the worrying thing.'

'What is, then?'

'That he was with a *girl*!' He made it sound as though being with a girl was tantamount to dancing down the High Street wearing nothing but a jewelled G-string and a few feathers, thought Mary.

'It was probably just another of his old students,' she said soothingly.

'I said a girl, not a woman,' he said petulantly, slicing a sprout into quarters, in his agitation. Mary took a sustaining drink from her wine glass. The chilled white wine tasted acid after the chilli sauce with which she had tried to enliven her shepherd's pie, but it was at least alcoholic. She began to wish the bottle had not been finished, and wondered whether she could open a bottle of red without John noticing. Red wine was so much more sustaining, and she had a feeling she was in need of being sustained. 'I mean a *young* girl. And not a nice young girl, either. From what he said, she sounded most unsuitable.'

Unsuitable for what? Mary wondered. 'I should think that would be all right, then. I'm sure if Pa has started fancying young girls, he'd only be interested in ones that looked nice. He never had much time for the plain ones.' She thought of herself as a girl, and the carelessly hurtful remarks her father had made about her skin, her figure, and in particular her thick ankles.

'Your mother had wonderful legs,' he had said crossly, as if she had wilfully rejected her mother's build. 'And so did my mother. No one in our family ever had heavy legs.'

'Sorry, Pa.'

He had looked at her in astonishment.

'What do you mean? I'm not blaming you, it's not your fault. It's just surprising, that's all. They'll probably slim down when you're a bit older.' He frowned, and it was not until much later that Mary realised his anger was with himself and his tactlessness, and not her.

'Really, Mary dear!' John was shocked. 'You surely don't want the Professor to be entangled with a young girl! Think of the scandal, if it were to get out! And besides, there's the house and everything. You know he always said that would come to you. Supposing some little tart' – his use of the word was revealing of tremendous mental perturbation, Mary knew – 'some little gold-digger were to get her hooks into him? It happens, you know, and it's the very clever ones that are the most vulnerable, I've heard. They're not practical, you see. Not worldly. And a man in your father's position, living alone in that great big house, well, it's asking for trouble, isn't it?'

'Oh, surely not!' Professor Hill, his daughter thought, could scarcely have been further removed from the ivory tower, unworldly academic image that John was conjuring up. Cynical, acerbic, as quick-witted as ever even if his stroke made him muddle his words sometimes, she could think of no one less likely to fall for a con trick, or be taken in by the wiles of a woman of any age, charm she never so wisely. There had been more than a few female students, in the past, who had thought to buy better marks or academic favours by leading him into a flirtation or an affair. Too wise, and too careful of his reputation, to be caught in a position where he might find himself accused of sexual harassment, or worse, he had generally punished them by leading them on, encouraging them to think he was on the hook, and then appearing to forget who they were the next time he saw them.

He might present himself as the mad professor stereotype, but his madness was thoroughly and completely self-centred. He merely used it as a subterfuge to disguise his more outrageously selfish demands, and to get away with the kind of rudeness and outspoken bad manners that might otherwise land him in court for slander. However careless he might be of appearances, his recent poor health had taught him that his daughter, while she might be useless to him in most respects, was necessary when it came to looking after him. He took it very much for granted that when he needed her she would drop anything and come, and so of course she had done. She lived in quiet dread of what would happen if he had another stroke and needed constant day and night nursing.

'It was probably some neighbour's daughter, or even the daughter of an old student,' she suggested.

'Hardly,' said John austerely. 'When I tell you that her hair was orange and green, sticking up like a cockatoo's crest, he said, and she had a ring in her nostril, and one in her eyebrow too! And her clothes, he said, he couldn't even begin to describe them – black plastic, and bright striped stockings, and goodness knows what else! And...' his voice dropped again and he even glanced round the room with much the same expression as when he examined the inside of a Brussels sprout, '...she was *pregnant*!'

'Oh!' said Mary, rather faintly. She found the image he presented so extraordinary that she was hard put to it not to laugh. 'And did she have a good figure? Apart from being pregnant, I mean. Good legs, in the stripy stockings? He always liked girls to have good legs.'

John stared at her as if she too had sprouted multi-coloured hair and a nose ring.

'Is that all you can find to say?' he asked. 'Your own father... your son's grandfather, his only living grandparent, is *consorting* with some appalling young drop-out who's probably hooked on heroin and quite likely has Aids, too, and all you say is to wonder whether she's got good legs! I sometimes think you must be as mad as he is!'

'So do I,' she said sadly, 'but I'm afraid I'm not.'

'Afraid? What do you mean, afraid? Really, Mary, you are behaving very oddly. I realise,' he said more gently, 'that this must be a shock to you. Perhaps I should have broken the news more carefully. Are you . . .' he paused delicately, '. . . are you quite well, dear?'

Mary knew what he meant. Men like John, she thought sourly, were always so quick to label any lapse from what they regarded as normal behaviour in women as some kind of hormonal problem. That she was at what he would doubtless call 'a certain age' could not be denied: nor could she pretend that her once regular periods were not now far more haphazard. Other than that, however, she was experiencing none of the menopausal symptoms she had read about. No hot flushes, no panic attacks or sudden mood changes or fluctuating weight.

'Perfectly well, thank you,' she said briskly. 'I'm afraid the wine has rather gone to my head, that's all. I shouldn't have had that glass on an empty stomach. You're quite right to be concerned, John. I can't go and see him tomorrow.' John nodded, his own instincts perturbed by the idea of her being thought unreliable at work. 'But I'll go on Saturday while you're playing golf. Then if there seems to be anything going on we could both go to Oxford on Sunday and sort it out.'

John relaxed. 'Splendid, dear. I knew you'd do the sensible thing. Do you know, I think I could fancy a little more shepherd's pie! It's very nice, dear. Very tasty.'

Chapter 4

It was, predictably, raining again on Saturday. Friday, of course, when Mary had been in the little windowless cubby hole that was grandly called 'The Office' at Naseby's for the entire day, tracking down stray invoices and trying to get the books into some kind of order for the end-of-year tax accounts, had been sunny and warm. As The Office was tucked into a corner at the back of the shop, in space grudgingly inched out of the workroom and store, Mary heard each customer enthusing about the beauty of the weather. After the fifteenth disembodied voice had remarked that he or she had daffodils out in the garden already, she had begun to wonder rather grumpily whether this working woman stuff was all it was cracked up to be.

She had comforted herself with the prospect of a trip to Oxford the following day. There was little pleasure in visiting her father, other than the dreary rewards of a duty done. Depending on the state of his health and mind he would either treat her to a virtuoso performance of the neglected, sick old father whose selfish daughter never bothered with him, or barely tolerate her presence, with ill-concealed impatience and the clear implication that she was thoughtlessly taking up too much of his valuable time. To John's anxieties she had paid almost no heed, believing him to have been misinformed or the victim of a practical joke, but she was determined to enjoy what she could of her day. She would visit the covered market, as she always did, and pick up a little treat for lunch. Professor Hill might disapprove of her ankles, but he had never been able to fault her cooking, and at least he enjoyed the exotic dishes she concocted for him – though without any display of gratitude.

The rain, however, put paid to her other plan of a quiet walk through Oxford. Having lived there her whole life up until her marriage, she knew every street and turning; even now when the tourist population outnumbered the students she still loved every stone of it. Hating umbrellas, and knowing that the crowded pavements made their use all but impossible, the kind of aimless ramble she had envisaged was now out of the question. Her spirits, as she peered through the windscreen that even fast-speed wipers could not clear adequately, were low.

Her father's greeting did little to raise them.

'Did you tell me you were coming?' He glared down at her suspiciously. After his stroke he had started to walk with a slight stoop, favouring the damaged side of his body, but recently he had made efforts to hold himself with his old quasi-military bearing.

'No, Pa. It was such a lovely day yesterday and I was stuck in the office, so I promised myself a day in Oxford today.'

'So that's why it's raining.' He was already turning away from her, but she saw that he was not displeased by her visit. They did not kiss one another – he was so far from demonstrative that he regarded even the routine English handshake as an invasion of his personal space – but she was adept at reading his body language. The tendons in his neck were relaxed, and his large, bony hand was raised to run long fingers through the wild shock of white hair that looked unkempt, like an elderly Struwwelpeter, but was in fact carefully trimmed every other week. 'You may as well s-stoke up the freezer, as you're here,' he said. 'It seems to be running a bit low.'

'Stock it up?' She corrected him, remembering at once that this was something he hated, and continued rapidly: 'Is it? It shouldn't be. You didn't leave the doors open again and let everything thaw, did you?'

'Certainly not. I'm not a complete food. Fool.' Loftily he ignored the fact that he had failed to shut the freezer properly on at least three previous occasions. Professor Hill never saw the things he did not want to see, particularly if they involved his own failings – like the failure in transmission between brain and tongue that resulted in the occasional use of wrong words. 'I've been getting through the meals faster, that's all.'

'Oh.' The hall was cold. The ancient heating system, designed in the days of cheap coal and even cheaper servants to carry it, had never been intended as more than a background to the open fires that were now seldom lit anywhere but in the study. With its high ceiling, its dark wood panelling and mosaic tiled floor dimly illuminated through the dull greenish glass of the windows, it was rather like being in a neglected aquarium, the cold air seeming to impede movement as water would.

Reluctantly, Mary shed her coat, rain-dampened from the short dash from the car to the front door where, as always, she had struggled, with cold fingers and rain bombarding her unprotected head, to turn the key in the stiff and antiquated lock, the knack of which only the Professor seemed to possess.

'We'll have a cup of coffee,' announced her father, ignoring her struggles with the wet coat and striding to the door that led to the kitchen. Mary followed him with alacrity. The kitchen was one of the few comfortable rooms in the house. It had once been the morning room, a small, south-east facing parlour used by its original owners for breakfast, and as a sitting room for the females of the house where they could be private and warm. Mary's mother, newly married, had (as she subsequently related) thrown up her hands in horror at the sight of the original basement kitchen, where the smell of damp vied with the lingering effluvia of boiled cabbage and tom cat, and the only daylight came dimly from above, by means of a dismal courtyard known as The Area. Her Southern American blood already chilled by the English climate – they had met and married, inexplicably to Mary, on a cruise – she had threatened to go straight home to Mother unless Something was Done.

The Professor, wildly in love with his exotically beautiful young wife and, for the first time in his existence, coming up against a will even more forceful than his own, had capitulated. The basement was left to be a laundry room – Mary's mother had no intention of seeing to the washing and ironing and was quite prepared to pay someone else to do it – and the old morning room was enlarged and transformed into a kitchen that became, for a few years, the hub of the house. Mary's mother painted the walls a brilliant sunshine yellow, and made curtains and tablecloths out of red checked gingham. A huge refrigerator, looking startled to find itself in north Oxford, was sent from the States, and parcels of exotic foods like popping corn, or angel cake mix, would arrive at frequent intervals.

Some of Mary's earliest memories were of watching her mother, her clothes decorated rather than protected by a frilly apron, frying chicken, or sweetcorn fritters, or simmering golden pumpkin for pies, cursing as the plopping bubbles spat hot globules, and complaining endlessly about the post-war shortages of such things as spices and brown sugar, and about the impossibility of obtaining proper ingredients in the country she referred to, increasingly, as 'this God-forsaken hole'. When, soon after Mary's sixth birthday, her mother had run away with a jazz musician, the kitchen lost its exciting fragrances, but its colours were still bright and cheerful, and though in later years they faded Mary was still inclined to think that she had something to be grateful to her mother for, even if it were only the kitchen.

Mary made the coffee. As she measured and ground the beans and warmed the jug, her eye fell on a large jar of instant coffee standing on the worktop, conveniently near the kettle. It was half empty. Mary blinked at it, almost wondering whether she were imagining it, but it stayed solidly there and felt, when she allowed her hand, as if accidentally, to nudge it, reassuringly solid. It was the same brand that she used at home and next to it, in an empty jam jar, were white packages that she had no hesitation in identifying either. Tea bags.

Instant coffee, like tea bags, was something the Professor had never permitted in the house, regarding it as a pernicious American influence (he had never altogether forgiven America for producing his wife), and as morally suspect. A perfectionist in this as in all things, he regarded any deviation from his exacting standards with all the horror of a vampire encountering a crucifix. A succession of housekeepers and cleaning ladies, most of whom regarded the labour of making proper coffee unnecessary and messy, and who in any case found it too bitter for their taste, had been driven to bringing their own supplies, something which they regarded with resentment bordering on hostility. The Professor, who would not have grudged them twenty cups a day of the expensive, fresh-roasted beans, refused to contemplate spending a penny of the housekeeping money on instant granules.

Thoughtfully, Mary allowed the water to go off the boil and then poured it over the grounds in the warmed jug. The smell, warm and delicious, surrounded her with an illusion of warmth and safety. She stirred it with a wooden spoon (another of her father's foibles was that metal should never be allowed to come into contact with coffee) and covered the jug to stand while she fetched two cups and saucers, and a jug of milk. One of the few things her father had in common with John was their abhorrence of milk bottles; milk for tea and coffee must always be in a jug, just as the drink itself must be in a cup (and, of course, saucer,) rather than a mug. At home on her own, Mary derived considerable pleasure from pouring milk straight from the bottle into a battered mug that she kept for her own use.

While fetching the milk, Mary opened the other door of the fridge freezer. The monstrous American refrigerator of her childhood, all voluptuous curves and rich, cream-coloured lacquer, was long gone, but the modern combination filled its space well. Once every six weeks or so she came and spent a day shopping and cooking, filling the freezer shelves with neatly labelled meals that were the nearest her father was prepared to come to convenience food. Convenience, for him, meant his own time and effort being saved, and it was fortunate for Mary that she enjoyed cooking, and gained considerable pleasure from concocting interesting meals that he could heat up in the microwave. In the past he had travelled widely, always making it a point of honour to eat only the local food wherever he might find himself, and as a result he enjoyed the kind of exotic meals that Mary found interesting, but could never cook for John. Cooking, or rather eating, was the thing that brought them closest together, though Mary often thought how unfair it was that her father, even at eighty, could eat as much as he liked of anything without adding a millimetre of fat to his tall, spare frame.

Now, eyeing the empty shelves that she had filled only four weeks earlier, it occurred to her for the first time that John's worries might after all have some foundation in fact. If, as on previous occasions, her father had left the freezer door open for long enough for everything inside to thaw, he would have swept the entire contents out into the dustbin and summoned her at once, blaming the freezer, naturally, for not working properly. This time, however, there were still several plated meals and six or seven cartons left, apparently unchanged.

Mary always, when re-stocking, cooked enough for guests, since the Professor, though he had no close friends, had several old colleagues and sparring partners who would come to talk and stay to eat. Either he had taken to eating two or three full meals a day, or he had been inundated with argumentative intellectuals, for the amount remaining was far too little. More significantly, there was the food equivalent of the instant coffee on one otherwise empty shelf, in the shape of several boxes of frozen pizzas. While he might at a pinch have condescended to eat a freshly made pizza in Italy, as long as it had been made with the traditional ingredients and baked in a wood-fired oven, under no circumstances would he have entertained the idea of eating a Mister Freezee ham and pineapple pizza.

'You haven't lost your appetite, I see,' she said mildly, shutting the freezer and coming back to the table with the jug of milk. The red and white gingham of her childhood curtains and tablecloths had long since faded and been turned into polishing rags, and Mary had replaced them from time to time, keeping to the red and white theme but changing the fabric. The present tablecloth, red spots on a white background, with a wide red border, seemed to have sprouted some new spots, and as she came closer she saw that they were not spots but holes. Burn holes, to be more accurate, as from carelessly flicked cigarette ash, or larger, speaking of a cigarette falling from the edge of the big ashtray that had never before been known to sit like this on the kitchen table.

'Irony, to be at all amusing, should always attempt to be s-subtle,' said her father acidly. 'If the effort of making a few frozen meals for your father is more than you can manage, I am sure I could make other arrangements.'

'All right,' she said mildly. 'I don't mind making them, but I expect you'd prefer a change.' Her only defence against him was to appear to go along with whatever he suggested, however outrageous, and it never failed to disconcert him.

'Change is very bad for people like me,' he said petulantly.

'People like you? There are no people like you, Pa.' Mary spoke seriously and without malice. He was flattered, and once again his hand came up to run his fingers through his hair. Mary hoped she was the only person who had noticed that he performed this gesture far more frequently when John was there. She hoped, too, that this was unconscious.

'People of my advanced age,' he articulated carefully. 'Old people.'

The adjective, as applied to him, seemed incongruous. It was true that his hair was white, his leathery face seamed and lined and his speech, since the mild stroke six months earlier, occasionally hesitant as he searched for the correct word. His walk, too, was slower than before and, when he was tired, slightly uneven as he favoured the side of him that the attack had left slightly weaker, with tingling in the fingers and toes that irritated him. His eyes, however, beneath the fierce bristle of his white eyebrows, were the same vivid blue as ever, penetrating and blazing with intelligence, so that the lined and folded skin round them seemed irrelevant, a leathery construct hiding the youthful inner man.

Mary knew that she was supposed to display horror at the use of the word 'old', but though she might humour him in most things she was not prepared for that degree of sycophancy. She was aware, also, that he knew it, but that he could not resist trying to catch her out. She gave him a bland smile, and sipped her coffee.

'Any particular preferences, while I'm cooking?' she asked. 'I'll go down to the market in a minute and get some fish, and something for our lunch. What would you like?'

'Not fish,' he said decisively. Mary raised her eyebrows. He loved fish, and they invariably ate it when she visited, since he was convinced that even when cooked into meals or dishes it lost its flavour when frozen.

'Why not?'

She saw from the raising and lowering of his eyebrows that he felt he had scored a point by pushing her into asking a direct question. Mary stifled a sigh: these contests with her father were hard work, and she knew beforehand that he would always win since he set, and changed, the rules to suit himself.

'Come on, Pa. Spit it out.'

'What a disgusting expression. I don't spit, do I?' A look of unaccustomed anxiety crossed his face. 'False teeth are the devil. Nothing tastes the same, and you can never be sure they're not going to let you drown. Down.'

'No, Pa. You don't spit.' She could never quite decide whether these sudden insecurities were not another manipulative ploy, but she felt compelled to reassure him.

'Good.' He finished his coffee, and pushed his cup forward for more. 'Good coffee,' he said. 'If nothing else, Mary, at least I've taught you to make coffee properly.' His words of praise were so rare that, on top of the momentary softening induced by his worry over his teeth, she felt quite affectionate towards him. She poured him a second cup, added milk, and stirred it for him. Then she glanced up, and saw his eyes fixed on her. Their vivid blue, made even brighter by the whiteness of hair and eyebrows, was startling even to her. They were intent, with the fixed regard of a dissecting biologist, or of a hunter stalking its prey. She shook her head, half in admiration.

'Come on, Pa,' she said again. 'What's going on?'

Satisfied, he leaned back in his chair.

'Nothing is "going on", as you inelegantly phrase it. I have a house guest, that is all.'

A house guest. Ah.

'That's nice,' she said inanely. 'Um, where is she?'

His eyes glinted. Damn, she thought. Damn and double damn, when will I ever learn? Too much to hope that he would miss her careless slip of the tongue.

'My spies are everywhere.' She tried to sound composed.

'So, this caring visit from my loving daughter is to check up on me. How charming.'

Wisely she said nothing, but looked at him steadily. She would not allow him to make her feel guilty. To her astonishment, his eyes dropped.

'You don't need to worry,' he mumbled.

'Worry? Who said anything about worry?' He seemed to have nothing to say, a state of affairs so rare that she thought she might attempt to put her cards on the table. 'John met one of your old students – Rupert Greenwood, do you remember him? – on Thursday and he took great delight in telling John he'd seen you in the Botanic Gardens with a young girl. He . . . um, he described her quite vividly. To be quite honest I didn't take much notice. I thought he'd been winding John up, actually, but I said I'd come over just to keep him happy, and also, *also* mind you, because I wanted to come. I thought I'd like a day in Oxford, and to have lunch with you – though I can't, now, think why. And that's all. I am not spying on you. If you are having a torrid affair with a girl rather younger than your grandson, that's your business.'

'I might marry her. I might make a new will and leave her all my money.'

Mary laughed. 'So you might!'

His lips twitched reluctantly, his nearest approach to a grin.

'One thing I will say for you,' he said in the tones of one handing out a bouquet of gold-plated orchids, 'you're not grasping.'

'If that's the only good thing you can find to say about me, I might as well go home now and forget about lunch. And the freezer, of course. I dare say you can manage on ham and pineapple pizzas.' She made no attempt to move, and her voice was quite cheerful, but he looked at her in amazement. Mary quailed inwardly. She had never spoken to him like that in her life before. With an effort she held his gaze, schooling her face to impassivity.

'Ha!' She jumped, but incredibly it was a bark of laughter. 'Ha! Good girl. Very well, I admit that your cooking is second to none. Just because dear John is anally retentive and has never progressed beyond pap, doesn't mean you can't cook. There, does that satisfy you?'

Mary felt herself blushing like an adolescent.

'Pa! I'm overwhelmed! I'd better get out and shop before the compliments go to my head.' She stood up.

'Don't you want to hear about her? Meet her?'

'If you want, but I suppose that can wait until later. Will she be here today?'

'She's here now. She's asleep. You know what these young things are, awake half the night and asleep all morning.'

'Then I'll meet her later. If you want the freezer filled up I'll have to get a move on. Is the no fish rule still in operation?'

'She doesn't like fish.'

'That's no reason for you to go without. What does she like?'

'Most things. Not offal. Spicy food, she likes. Or steak. Get her a steak, and some scallops for us, if they've got them.' He stood up also, thrusting his hand in his pocket and withdrawing a handful of notes. 'Here.'

Mary took the money. Professor Hill, though he naturally did not know that his son-in-law was unemployed, would never have contemplated allowing him to subsidise his own housekeeping expenses.

'Fine,' she said cheerfully. 'I'll see you later.'

'Tell you what,' he said as he headed for the door, 'I'll come with you. I've a book to pick up at Blackwell's.'

'Of course, if you like, but it's pouring with rain. Tell me what it is, and I'll get the book for you.' She quailed inwardly at the extra effort, but sternly told herself that her father was eighty, and less than robust.

'No, no.' He sounded irritable, and was already struggling into his overcoat. 'That's not the point. I've got a disabled badge. For the car. Means you can park anywhere.'

'Good God!' Coming to a halt, she stared at him in astonishment. For him to have applied for a disabled badge, not just an admission but an advertisement of the fact that he was less than fit, was astonishing enough, but that he should think of using it to save her from the hideous struggle of finding somewhere to park within even reasonable distance of the market was so startling that she scarcely knew what to say.

'Well, don't just stand there,' he said crossly. 'Help me with my goat. Coat, dammit. And my hat, where's my hat? If she's been borrowing my hat again ... Oh, there it is. Right. My scarf, girl. Give me my scarf. Come along, now. We haven't got all day.'

'Er ... should you write a note to your ... your guest? To tell her where you've gone, in case she should be worried?'

'Worried? About me?' He considered the possibility, and dismissed it. 'She won't be worried. It's not like that. No responsibilities. No ties.'

'Right.' Rather breathlessly, Mary found herself swept out to her car.

The disabled badge was a revelation. Mary was better off than most, since she knew all the secret places where a car might, with luck, be left for an hour, but even so she was used to allowing at least an extra half hour for parking. Now, with the orange cardboard disc displayed on the window, she was able to pull up in new and convenient places and smile smugly at the cars that hovered, eyes desperately scanning, near the few available spaces. Her father, to her continued amazement, came with her to the market and entered into a long and mutually satisfying sparring match with the fishmonger, which ended in him getting a bargain in the shape of extra scallops for the same price and a large salmon head, since so many people stopped to listen to the battle of words and stayed to buy a piece of fish. Mary left him to potter while she found the vegetables and the meat she needed, and they made their way back to the house in better charity with one another than Mary could ever remember.

Back at the house, Mary swiftly chopped onions and meat, and set casseroles and mince simmering, as well as bones for stock and the salmon head. By the time the mince and the casserole were gently cooking in the oven the kitchen was full of savoury steam, and Mary opened the windows for a moment, not so much to get rid of the steam, for the air outside was even more saturated with water, but to take a breath of fresh air and cool her flushed face. There was a howl of dismay from behind her, accompanied by a delicate chiming that she connected with Peter Pan's Tinkerbell.

'Aah! Shut the bloody windows, can't you? It's bloody February!' Mary turned round.

Rupert Greenwood, she saw at once, had not lied. If anything he had rather played down his description of the Professor's house guest. Framed in the doorway, glowing against the dark hall behind her, stood a small, spiky figure. Her hair, which Rupert had described as sticking up like a cockatoo's, was still multi-coloured, but had been twisted painstakingly into hundreds of little plaits, each one ending with a bright glass bead or, in some cases, a small bell. A large, bright jewel – surely not a diamond? – flashed in her nostril, and each ear (though not, Mary saw with relief, her eyebrows) was pierced with several studs and rings. Framed within the technicolour tentacles of her hair, the girl's face was small, pointed and white with a natural pallor beneath a thick layer of white make-up, and the heavy black eye pencil ringing her eyes failed to disguise the dark shadows beneath them.

Her pregnancy was very apparent, her swelling stomach made still more obvious by the stick-like thinness of the rest of her. The legs of a skinny ten-year-old protruded from beneath the short black skirt that was not quite long enough to cover the red suspenders holding up her black stockings, and was topped by a short-sleeved purple tee-shirt that had been raggedly chopped off at the waist. This skimpy collection was partly covered by a long sleeveless jerkin crocheted, as far as Mary could make out, in tarred twine.

Transfixed by this vision Mary failed to close the window. The girl started forward and brushed past her to slam the casements shut. She smelled, disarmingly, of baby powder. On her feet, Mary was fascinated to see, she wore calf-high buttoned boots of the kind Mary associated with Edwardian governesses. Then she stood, clasping her goose-fleshed arms across the mound of her stomach. Her lips, painted a glossy damson, drooped like a sad child's.

'Oh, I *am* sorry,' said Mary. 'I only meant to open them for a minute. Shall I make you a cup of coffee, or tea? Lunch will be ready soon, so it's not really worth offering you breakfast.'

'Who are you?' The girl did not move. Her voice was high and childish.

'I'm Mary. Mary Marsh. I'm Professor Hill's daughter.'

'Oh.' A moment's thought. 'I don't do drugs.'

'Oh, good,' responded Mary weakly. 'Very good.'

The girl's back was up against the sink. She unwrapped her arms and clutched at the edge of it. Her nails were bitten short, and her small fingers were loaded with grubby silver rings.

'I haven't taken nothing. Anyfing.' She dipped her head with effort, like a chicken pecking at corn. 'Anything,' she finished, offering the correct word, as it were, on a salver.

'Of course not.' Mary, embarrassed, turned away and lifted the lid of

47

the pan to check the salmon head. A waft of fishy steam gushed up. It looked ready, so Mary took the pan off the heat and set it on the draining board to cool.

'What's that?'

'A salmon head. Don't worry, I know you don't like fish. I'll make it into soup for my father's supper tonight. He only has fish when I'm here; he doesn't like it frozen.'

'Let's see.' The girl lifted the lid, and peered into the saucepan. 'It's got its eyes in! Gross!' With horrid fascination she tilted the lid again. 'Ugh. How can you make soup out of that?'

Mary chose to take the question literally.

'When it's cool, I'll take the bits of fish out of the head – there's quite a lot – and strain out the bones and skin. Then I'll put in salt, and lemon juice, some lime leaves and lemon grass if there is any, some sliced mushrooms and spring onion and perhaps a bit of finely cut up fresh ginger. Then all he needs to do is simmer it for a minute or two this evening, and put some chopped coriander in when he comes to eat it.'

There was a considering pause.

'Opening a tin's easier.' The tone, however, was not so much critical or dismissive as surprised.

'Yes, but I don't like tinned soup, and they don't make this kind in tins anyway.'

She nodded, accepting a rational explanation.

'I'll go.' Her voice held a kind of hopeless patience. Mary turned and considered her.

'Just as you like, of course, but it seems a pity. There's a bit of steak for your lunch. You like steak, don't you?' The girl shrugged, defiance struggling with hunger that was not, Mary saw, for the steak. 'I haven't come here to turn you out,' said Mary gently.

'Straight up?'

'Straight up,' answered Mary seriously. 'Now, if you want that cup of anything, put the kettle on, will you? I wouldn't mind a cup of tea myself. And you can tell me how you like your steak.'

There was a long pause. Then, moving slowly, the thin arms and hands reached for the kettle and picked it up. Holding it to her, resting it against the curve of her stomach, she looked at Mary.

'I'm Zen,' she said.

'Like the Buddhists?' hazarded Mary.

'Short for Zenobia,' corrected the girl. 'She was a queen, in some place in the desert. She rode on a camel, and fought against the Romans. The Prof told me. He's learning me things. Teaching me.'

Her self-correction held, for Mary, the vivid echo of her father's voice. The germ of an idea sprouted in her mind.

'Is he, indeed.'

Her tone was grimmer than she had intended. Zen slammed down the kettle, spilling water as she did so.

'You gotta problem with that?' she asked aggressively. Mary reached for a cloth, and wiped up the water automatically. 'Here, I can do that.'

'Thank you.' Mary surrendered the cloth. 'No, Zen, I don't have any problem with that.'

'There's nothing funny going on. I mean, he hasn't made a pass at me or nothing. Anything.'

'No, no, I'm sure. It's all right, Zen, I don't think there's anything wrong in your being here, if it's what you want. But is it really what you want?'

''Course.' Zen looked at her pityingly, as if she were mad. 'Yeah, 'course it is. I like it here. Lovely, it is. Tell you what,' she offered, 'tell me what to do, and I'll give you a hand. You'll have to explain what you want; I never learned no cooking.'

Chapter 5

O ver lunch, while enjoying her scallops, Mary at last had an opportunity to observe her father and Zen together.

She was secretly rather relieved that she could find no symptom of the kind of elderly infatuation John had obviously feared. There was nothing lover-like in the way the older man spoke to the girl. If anything he behaved as if she had been one of his students, but more gently, whether in deference to her condition or her youth Mary could not decide. He treated her, in fact, as he might have done a bright child; rather as he had once treated David when, as a small boy, he had shown signs of a precocious intellect. Certainly he was perfectly sure of himself in his dealings with her, and there was no sign of the discomfort he had so often displayed when talking to Mary in her childhood.

He was, as he had been with the most promising of his students, demanding, critical and exacting. He corrected her grammar, her pronunciation and her table manners with equal impartiality, making her repeat some words and phrases until he was satisfied, and instructing her meanwhile on the subject of scallops – their habitat, lifestyle and historical connections being laid out succinctly and amusingly. He even insisted (in the face of her obvious distaste) on Zen trying one – from Mary's portion, naturally. He was extremely fond of scallops, and these were particularly succulent in the delicate white wine sauce Mary had made.

What Mary found fascinating was that Zen, whose appearance positively shouted rebellion against adult values and who might as well have had 'So What?' in neon lights over her head, accepted everything – criticism, instructions and the eating of a strange and (to her) repulsive-looking shellfish – without protest and even, apparently, with gratitude. Meekly she held her knife with its handle beneath her palm and her fork

51

with the prongs downward. She made an obvious effort to keep her mouth closed when chewing, and listened to the life cycle of the scallop and its significance as an emblem of pilgrimage with what seemed to be equal interest. Only at the prospect of eating one did she balk for a moment, before obediently putting it in her mouth where she agonised over chewing it but admitted, afterwards, that it was 'all right'.

Mary herself said little, content to observe and to enjoy her meal. The niggling suspicion of earlier was growing, however, into a recognisable shape, and by the end of the meal even the mango *crème brulée*, one of her own favourite desserts, was beginning to slide unnoticed down her throat, as if it had been John's favourite rice pudding with jam. The Professor regarded desserts as unnecessary and even morally suspect – a good selection of cheese, or a piece of fruit, was all the rounding off a good meal needed, he maintained – but he ate the half mango Mary had prepared for him, and seemed to take pleasure in watching Zen enjoy hers.

After the meal he retired, as always, to his study with a cup of coffee.

'I shall meditate for a while,' he said. 'You can bring me another cup of coffee when you've finished the washing up.' An unreconstructed man of his generation, it would never have occurred to him that he might help. In the normal course of things, when Mary was not there, he would go so far as to stack his used crockery and cutlery in the dishwasher, but he never switched it on or emptied it. During the weekend, when his housekeeper (as his cleaning lady liked to be called) did not come, he put things in the dishwasher until it was full, then left the remainder beside it. 'A fresh pot, mind. I won't have it stewed and tepid.'

'As if I would, after all these years,' muttered Mary as he stalked from the room.

'My mum was just the same,' said Zen, uncritically. 'Treat you like a halfwit, parents do.'

'You don't get on with your mum?' Mary rinsed the plates, careful not to look at Zen. David had never really been into teenage rebellion. Unfailingly polite, he had simply withdrawn into his own life and interests. Mary felt completely out of her depth, wondering whether such a question might not provoke an angry response.

'Mum's all right,' Zen answered, without much interest. 'Bit bossy, but that's where it's at, I s'pose.'

'But you don't live with her any more?'

Zen stared at her in astonishment. Her upper lids were caked with black, her lashes matted and unnaturally thickened with endless layers of mascara, but within them the whites had the bluish clarity of the very young, and her irises were a true, deep grey. Irish eyes, thought Mary suddenly.

''Course not. I'm here, aren't I?'

'But she knows where you are?' Mary pursued relentlessly.

'Yeah. I rang her, didn't I? The Prof made me do it. I told him there was no need, she wouldn't be worried, but he went on and on – you know how he does.'

'Yes, I know how he does.' Mary spoke with feeling. 'But wouldn't she be worried? How old are you? And besides . . .' she indicated, with a sweep of her hand, Zen's pregnancy.

'I'm seventeen. Eighteen in the summer. I just look like a kid because I'm so small. Mum don't worry about me, she knows I can look after myself. Done it all my life, haven't I, and kept an eye on the younger ones besides. Oldest of seven, that's me. Nothing much I don't know about having a baby, or how to look after one. The Prof, he took me down the clinic, made them check me over good and proper. They wanted me to go to some class or other, relaxation and all that, but I said, why bother? I never been so relaxed in all me life. Lovely, it is.' She glanced anxiously at Mary, still worried that she might evict her from this haven.

'What about your father?' Having embarked on her interrogation and not been rebuffed, Mary felt emboldened to go further. Zen shrugged.

'Went off, didn't he. Just after I was born. Irish, he was.' Aha, thought Mary. Clever me. 'I never knew him. Mum had boyfriends after that. She never bothered to divorce him – Catholic, wasn't he, they don't hold with that kind of thing – but as Mum says, nowadays who cares about a bit of paper? Men, they go or they stay, according, and it don't make no difference if they put a ring on your finger or not. That's what Mum says, and she's not far wrong, I'd say.'

Mary found her casual acceptance of such a state of affairs breathtaking.

'And your, er, boyfriend?'

Zen gave her a wry look. 'He was one that went. I don't mind no more. Anymore. Not now. He said he'd look after me, but he went off with a slag from Liverpool. Better off without him, we are.' She patted her stomach, and grinned. 'CSA can chase after him, if they want.'

'CSA?'

'Child Support Agency.' Zen looked at her pityingly, as someone slightly simple. 'They goes – go – after fathers what don't support their kids. All very well, and he deserves a bit of hassle, but the money they screw out of him don't – doesn't – come to me. Them bastards in the government nick it all, don't they?'

'Probably. I had heard of them, of course,' said Mary defensively. 'It's just I've never had anything to do with them.'

'Well, you wouldn't have, would you?' What, Mary wondered, was Zen's image of Mary's life? It must be as strange and difficult to imagine as Zen's was for her. It was hard to see how there could be any point of contact.

'My parents did it the other way round,' she offered tentatively. 'My mother went off, when I was six. With a jazz musician. I never saw her again.'

Zen looked at her dubiously. Mary supposed she was finding it hard to imagine Mary as a six-year-old. Her response, however, was surprisingly puritanical.

'That's bad, a mum going and leaving her kid. My mum don't hold with that, never has. Kids don't ask to be born, she says, so the least you can do is to stick by them when they're little. I mean, I know you had the Prof, but it's not the same, is it? A man, I mean.'

'No,' said Mary. 'No, it's not the same at all. Though to be fair, she did say she'd send for me when she was settled. The jazz musician was always on the move, they went back to the States – my mother was an American – but it didn't last. He wasn't really a very successful musician by all accounts, more of a drifter than anything. She moved on to a Texan oilman for a while, and he had plenty of money but was dull as ditchwater, so she went off again with a pilot. The oilman's pilot, in fact, and they took the oilman's private plane with them.'

Zen was gaping at her. To Mary it was ancient history, something distant and as unconnected with herself as if it had been the plot of a soap opera. Zen, however, was obviously having difficulty meshing this dramatic story with the staid, middle-aged figure before her, and from her expression was wondering whether this was not simply some kind of bizarre joke against her.

'It's true,' said Mary, rather amused. 'I know it sounds wildly unlikely, when you look at me, but my mother wasn't at all like me. She was small and slim and lively, and very much a Southern Belle, if you know what that means.'

'No, I don't. What does it mean?'

Looking at her, Mary saw that Zen really wanted to know. Her heart sank. She saw, all too clearly, the appeal this girl had for her father.

'I'll tell you later. Anyway, my mother and the pilot flew off, heading for South America, but they didn't make it. The plane crashed and they were both killed. The oilman was furious.'

'Because of the plane?'

'Because of the pilot. The plane was well insured, but the pilot was a good one and had been with him for several years.'

Zen glanced at Mary, to see what response was allowed. Mary grinned at her, and Zen relaxed and laughed.

'You sure you're not making this up?'

'Cross my heart.'

Zen laughed, then sobered. 'Poor you. And the poor old Prof. Bit of a downer, that.'

'Yes.' Mary had never had any idea what, if any, had been the effect on her father of her mother's disappearance and death. That they had been a wildly mismatched couple had always been clear, but that in itself argued for a powerful attraction between them. Mary remembered rows, and shouting, but she also remembered reconciliation and laughter, and certainly their involvement in one another had seemed to preclude any close attachment to her, their daughter. Mary had been a solitary child, content in her little world of books and toys. It seemed to her that she had learned very early that she was not altogether the child either of them would have expected or even wished for, and she had retained ever since a deep-seated feeling of inadequacy, of apology for being the kind of person she was.

Mary gave the grillpan a final rub and wiped it dry with a wrung-out dishcloth.

'There, that's done,' she said briskly. 'I'll make some more coffee. Do you want anything?' She indicated the jar of instant, and the tea bags.

'No, thanks.' Zen yawned, her clean, pink tongue curling like a cat's. 'Aah. I has – have – a sleep after lunch these days. Doctor's orders. If I have a drink now, it makes me want to pee the minute I lay down,' she said frankly. 'You busy? I'll stay and help if you like.'

'No, you go and have a rest, you look as though you could do with it. When is the baby due?'

'June, May perhaps.'

Mary counted on her fingers.

'You're very big for five months.' No wonder her father had taken Zen for a check-up.

'Yeah.' Zen sighed, patting the bulge. 'It's twins, innit. Double trouble, my mum used to say.'

'Goodness. Then you must definitely go and rest. I'm quite happy with the cooking, and if you want to help when you come down I'm sure there will still be things to do.'

'Righ'.' Zen yawned again. 'Right,' she repeated, without the glottal stop. 'See you later, then.'

Alone in the kitchen, Mary checked the oven with only half her mind on what she was doing. Frowning, she refilled the kettle and rinsed out the coffee pot. While the kettle boiled she laid a tray with two cups, the little milk jug and a small plate of the bitter chocolate pastilles that were one of her father's few sweet indulgences.

'Not that he deserves them,' she apostrophised the sweets. '*Wretched* old man. He deserves – what does he deserve? *I* don't know.' Nevertheless she made the coffee with care, then carried it through to the study.

The book-lined room was warm. Her father had always had a fire in the grate, except on days of absolute heatwave when he still refused to allow the fireplace to be cleared.

'Leave the ashes alone, woman,' he would thunder at the current housekeeper. 'Nothing wrong with ashes. No, I don't want a nice arrangement of leaves. Nor do I want a pleated paper fan, or any other genteel substitute. This is a hearth, and hearths contain fires. Fires make ash. A good fire needs a bed of ashes to sit on, surely you know that.'

Another of his foibles was that he insisted on burning, not coal or wood, but peat blocks because, he said, he liked the smell of them. They were difficult to obtain, even more difficult to light until you had learned the knack, they dropped fine brown dust, and the ash they left was so feather light that it floated out into the room on every breath, filming every book, every paper, in short, every surface with a bloom not unlike that on a ripe sloe.

John had tried, against Mary's advice, to persuade him to have a gas effect log fire fitted.

'It's clean, and easy,' he pointed out earnestly. 'Instant warmth whenever you want it, and you can turn it out when you leave the room. Much more economical.'

'You sound like some ghastly advertisement. I have always had a peat fire. A peat fire is what I like. A peat fire is what I will continue to have, until they carry me out in a box or shoot me.'

'But the expense...'

'Bugger the expense.'

Offended, John gave up, as Mary had known he would have to.

Now, her entrance with the tray set up a movement of air that wafted a fine mist of peat-scented ash from the glowing fire. Mary breathed it in with pleasure. Her father, stretched out in the rubbed leather armchair he always used, opened his eyes.

'There you are,' he said, for all the world as if he had been waiting hours instead of dozing for a few minutes.

Mary pushed the door shut with her back, then put down the tray. As usual, his desk was covered with piles of books, each with its slip of paper to mark a page, and heaps of papers. Professor Hill still contributed regularly to learned journals in his field, History, and was currently engaged in writing a book on the Crusades. John found it strange that a man of eighty, who had retired from active teaching and lecturing several years earlier, and who had moreover had a stroke which made it difficult for him to express himself, should still be working.

'Shouldn't he be relaxing more? Enjoying himself?' His concern was genuine, but Mary wondered how she could explain to someone to whom work was a necessary duty, carried on conscientiously between the hours of nine and five-thirty, that to her father relaxing meant reading a book, and that his truest enjoyment came from putting forward a new, preferably controversial theory concerning the period that currently engrossed him.

Mary nudged a pile of books over to one side, and put the tray down with care on a heap of manuscript, neatly written in ink in her father's crabbed handwriting. He hated typewriters, and the advent of word processors had entirely escaped his notice. She poured the fresh coffee into a clean cup, added milk, and put it on the stool beside him, taking away the empty cup he had brought through earlier.

'Your coffee, Professor Hill. Or should I say, Professor Higgins?'

'What? I don't know what you're talking about.'

That her father, generally so painfully direct, should prevaricate in this feeble way showed that his conscience was far from clear. Mary poured her own coffee and sat down in the chair opposite, the one used by his students when they came, nervously, to read their essays to him. It was of course a shade lower than his chair, so that he could if necessary tower over even the tallest of them, though it was seldom that he used such obvious tactics. A look was usually enough. He tried it now. Mary glared back at him, taking off her glasses, which were smeary from kitchen steam and washing up, and polishing them. She had felt she needed to see him as clearly as possible, and had put them on specially.

'You know perfectly well what I mean! What do you think you're doing with that child? She's a human being, not a laboratory animal, or a toy for you to amuse yourself with!'

'I've never so much as laid a finger on her!' He was blustering, his blurred image looked trembly. Hastily she resumed the cleaning of her glasses, and focused her eyes on him.

'Of course you haven't, I know that. But there's such a thing as mental violation too, you know. Don't think I can't see your footprints where you've been trampling all over her brain.'

He drank, his blue eyes regarding her warily over the rim of his cup.

'But that's just it, don't you see? That's just it. Her mind is a blank page, a field of new-fallen snow. That's *why* you can see my footprints – though I'd prefer to think of them as fingerprints, or writing – because there's *nothing else there*! Educationally speaking, her mind is completely virginal. She can read, she can write, she can perform simple mathematical functions, but other than that she knows nothing. Nothing of the world she lives in, except what she has seen on the television. Nothing of the past, of the present, of ideas, of inventions, of art or of philosophy. A child raised by wild animals could scarcely know less. What an opportunity! For a teacher – and you know that, unlike some of my esteemed colleagues, I have always regarded myself primarily as an educator – what a chance!'

'But Pa,' Mary broke in on the flood of his enthusiasm, 'think a minute. She isn't a child, or an animal. She's a young woman who has to live in the real world. In four months' time, or probably less, she's going to have two babies who will depend on her to provide them with everything they need – a home, warmth, food, stability. She doesn't need theories, or history, or art galleries. If you could teach her something that would help her get a job ... but what? You know yourself that half the graduates who leave here can't find work. The man who told John about Zen, Rupert Greenwood, he's running a sandwich bar.'

'Nothing wrong with a sandwich bar, if they're good sandwiches. Are they good sandwiches?'

'Yes, John said they were. But—'

'There you are, then.' He leaned back, with the air of one who has proved his point. 'I think, just this once, I'll have another cup of that excellent coffee.'

'No.' Mary was not going to allow herself to be sidetracked. 'No, Pa, it won't do. I can't allow you to do this. It isn't right, and it isn't fair. You're *not* Professor Higgins – who was a monster, anyway – and there's no way you're going to turn Zen into some kind of experimental creation of your own, who won't fit in anywhere.'

'But it's what she wants!'

'It was what Eliza Dolittle thought she wanted, too. But this is the nineteen nineties, Pa. You can't impose your own standards, however high they may be, on someone else. Particularly not on someone as vulnerable as Zen. Of course she wants to be here! It's comfortable, and warm, there's plenty of food, and it's free! She thinks she's in heaven!'

'You think she's just after a meal ticket? You're wrong, Mary. If that was all it was, I could fill the house a hundred times over, every day of the year. But that child, woman, whatever you call her, has something that three-quarters of the so-called brilliant students who pass through the university every year don't possess – she wants to know! She has curiosity; true intellectual curiosity. And she doesn't just take the answers on trust, either – she wants to know the why and how of them, too, before she'll make up her mind. And that's worth any number of A levels, in my book. She wants to learn, she's hungry for information and better still she has no preconceptions, no set ideas or received wisdom, to blinker her. Her mind is free to travel down any path, to make connections and draw inferences that would never occur to the "educated".' His fingers sketched quote marks in the air. 'Do you see? It's the most wonderful thing that's ever happened to me!'

Looking at him, Mary felt a pang. Ashamed, she diagnosed envy. Envy of Zen; that in his eighty years of life this girl, and not his own daughter, should have provided this wonderful thing. Envy, too, of her father, because she could think of nothing in her own life that had ever illuminated her as he was now lit up. Even the birth of David, marvellous though it had been at the time, had not affected her as deeply as this.

She poured herself an unwanted cup of coffee to give herself time to get her emotions under control.

'OK,' she said, disregarding her father's wince as the affectation she knew it was. 'I will grant that Zen wants to live here and that, more importantly, she wants to learn what you have to teach her. I accept that she will gain tremendously from your teaching. In terms of mental and spiritual resources, in self-esteem and self-confidence, in the ability to rationalise, to study, to learn . . . all of that will make her what she would never, in other circumstances, have had the opportunity to be. That, in turn, may enable her to give her babies a better start in life. How can I deny her all this, or you the chance to give it to her? But, Pa, we must be *practical*.'

'I am being *practical*.' He mimicked her tone with cruel accuracy. 'I have ensured that she is getting proper medical supervision. I have persuaded her, which you may not know, to give up smoking, because it can harm her unborn children.'

'And because you dislike the smell of it.'

'And because I dislike the smell of it, which may have been a more deciding factor in her mind. It is very much in her interests to please me. Does the motive matter? The result, in the improvement of her own and her babies' health, is good. Is not this *practical*?'

'Yes, as far as it goes.' Mary hesitated only a moment. 'You should perhaps consider, though, that you are a man of eighty. You have already had one stroke, fortunately a mild one. Your health is good, but you can't deny that you could drop dead today, tomorrow, at any time.'

'So could anyone. So could you.'

'Of course. But if I were to drop dead, I have no one who would be unable to manage without me. No one who would suddenly become homeless and without support. If you take on the pleasures of teaching Zen, you must also take on the responsibilities. Are you really intending to keep her here, once the babies are born? She will have no time for learning, and the house will be full of nappies and sterilisers and damp washing. They will scream in the night, and when they grow out of that they will start crawling. They will be at your desk, your books, your papers. And if your experiment goes sour on you, begins to bore you, will you not just end it as suddenly as you began it ? Because if so, you had very much better not start.'

He nodded. 'You're right,' he said unexpectedly. 'I had not looked that far ahead. I can see that I must plan for the children. I will certainly not have them in here. But this is a big house, there should be room for them to co-exist.'

'And if you are ill?'

'If I am ill surely I am better off with someone else living in the house? Isn't that what you wanted before, when you suggested I have a live-in housekeeper?'

Mary could not deny the truth of this. Her nightmare was that her father should have another stroke, or a heart attack, and be unable to call for help. He had flatly refused to have a nurse or housekeeper on a full-time basis, and the most she had been able to get him to agree to was to have extra telephones installed, with an alarm system.

'And if you die?' she continued relentlessly. His bright blue eyes contemplated her.

'I could change my will? Leave her the house?'

'You could, of course,' said Mary levelly.

'I'd like to see dear John's face if I did.'

Mary did not allow herself to think of that, or to respond to the implied criticism. She looked him in the eye.

'Your will is your own affair. I would rather you changed your will than that you should leave Zen high and dry with two small children and an awareness of things in life that she will have no means of achieving.'

He had the grace to look ashamed. 'I'm not going to change my will, stupid girl. This house is for you, and whatever else I may still have by the time I kick the bucket as well. So, what to do? I know, I'll leave her to you.'

'To me?'

'Yes. Along with the house, and all the other bits.'

'You can't dispose of people like that! She's not a cat!'

'House ownership carries responsibilities, you know. Think of this as another responsibility, like having to do something about the damp in the basement. You can take her on.'

'And what am I supposed to do with her? I can't carry on where you left off. I can't educate her.'

'I think she could learn a lot from you. How to put up with difficult men, for example. You've had plenty of experience in that line.'

Mary stared at her father. Never before in all her life had he said anything to her that gave any indication that he noticed her as a real person. Was it an apology, or a dig at John? Mary wished she could understand her father better. This was the longest, most personal conversation she could ever remember having with him. If nothing else, she could be grateful to Zen for that.

'I don't think that's something that can be taught,' she said wryly. 'You either do it, or you don't.'

'Teach her to cook, then. Now that's something you know you can do, and it's useful, too. Think of Rupert Greenwood. There you are – you can teach her to make good sandwiches. That ought to give her a start in life.' He said it cheerfully enough, but Mary thought she detected something she had never seen in her father before: a kind of vulnerability. Even after his stroke, when he had been forced to rely on her for so much in terms of physical care, she had never felt that. Physical weakness had made him angry, even ashamed, but never vulnerable. She was moved, and then found herself wondering cynically whether he had calculated just such a reaction. She dismissed the thought, rather ashamed. Her father might be self-centred and arrogant, but he had never been manipulative. Probably because he seldom saw other people's opinions and actions as particularly important to him.

'Really, Pa, you are quite impossible.' And I've never said anything like that to him before, thought Mary. Are we, after all these years, going to get to know one another, have what is now called a relationship? What an extraordinary idea.

Chapter 6

The drive home was even more unpleasant than the journey in the morning had been, since it was dark by the time Mary left Oxford, and she found the combination of headlight dazzle and driving rain difficult to deal with. Her head felt tight, not so much with an incipient headache as stuffed with the events of the day, and having spent so much time in the kitchen she now felt faintly greasy, aware of the smell of cooking that hung around her clothes and hair. What I want, she thought longingly, is a relaxed soak in a hot bath with plenty of bath oil in. Perhaps, if John has met up with a friend in the clubhouse, he'll be late enough. John. Oh dear, what am I going to tell John? Thank goodness David's gone out with Alison; at least I won't have both of them being shocked.

The thought of explaining to John that her father, in his old age, was proposing to take in and educate a pregnant (with twins) seventeen-year-old was rather more than she could contemplate with equanimity, and as for her father blithely suggesting that she, Mary, should take on the responsibility of continuing his mad scheme if he should die sooner than he hoped, her imagination boggled at the idea of Zen moving in with them. Zen and, of course, the twins. It was impossible, naturally. And yet the thought was oddly exhilarating. Or was that merely the effect of having come closer to an understanding with her father than had ever happened before?

The trouble was that her father saw nothing in the least eccentric about his behaviour; and such was the strength of his will that Mary found herself going along with him while she was there, under the spell of his enthusiasm. He and Zen, in her way, were larger than life characters, while Mary for all her height and build felt herself to be insignificant in the general scheme of things.

Lonely, she allowed herself to put her lover in the passenger seat, and told him all about it. He was, naturally, interested, supportive and amused, and it was comforting to put the events of the day into narrative form for him, but for once she felt that he was no help to her. Was it her imagination, or did he seem rather more two-dimensional than usual, even slightly transparent? Usually when they were alone together he was so real to her that she was aware of him with every sense. His appearance of course, that went without saying, but also the sound of his voice (deep), the texture of his skin and hair that her fingers thought they knew, the faint smell of some unknown aftershave, smelled once or twice on well-dressed men in London and stored away for her private pleasure – all these seemed less real than usual.

'Don't worry about it for now,' he said soothingly. 'Tell John as little as possible, make it sound trivial, and wait and see what happens. It may well all blow over as quickly as it came: your father could lose interest, Zen could meet a man she wants to move in with, or she might just find the pressures too great and move out. It will sort itself out, you'll see.' It was comforting, it was what she wanted to believe, but could not, and it sounded suddenly too honey smooth in her ears, irritating, even . . . patronising? She blanked him out, her eyes prickling with tears. It was coming to something when one was patronised by one's own creation. Her lips set, frowning through her glasses at the windscreen on which oncoming headlights splintered and refracted, she drove grimly home.

It was after six o'clock when Mary finally parked her car in the double garage and climbed wearily out. John's car was there, but the rain on it was still standing in drops, and when she put her hand on the bonnet it was still warm. He had not been home for long, then. Good. John had a violent dislike of coming home to an empty house, even when he had been out playing golf rather than supposedly at work. She went to the boot to fetch the carrier bags of shopping: such an opportunity could not be wasted, and she had taken advantage of it to stock up.

She was thankful to have bought Dover soles for their evening meal. Having spent most of the day cooking she was daunted by the prospect of more, but she was strongly of the opinion that anything as delicious as a Dover sole needed nothing more than grilling with butter and lemon juice. The vegetables to go with them she had prepared while doing the Professor's, so there would be little to do. She would be able to relax with a drink for half an hour, and find a tactful way of explaining to John just what was going on at her father's house.

Unlike John, she went in through the door that led directly from the garage to the lobby outside the kitchen. The lobby was dark: disapproving of her habit of entering the house this way, it would never have occurred to John to put the light on for her. With her hands full of bags she stumbled over John's discarded boots and felt with her elbow for the handle of the kitchen door, pushing it down and giving the door a good shove with her hip. It was inclined to stick in wet weather.

The kitchen, too, was lit only by the light spilling in through the open door to the hall. Warm from the car, and still wrapped against the cold and wet of the day, she did not at first notice the chill. It was not until she had dumped the carrier bags on the worktop and pulled off her coat and scarf that it struck her that the air, which should have been warmed by three hours of central heating – even at weekends the radiators were off from ten until three – was unpleasantly cold. Switching on the lights she put her hand on the radiator. It was icy.

'Blast it,' she muttered, remembering that the boiler was due to be serviced, and that it was unlikely that anyone would come out before Monday. 'John? John, I'm back.'

At her call the sitting-room door opened, letting out a gush of television noise and a puff of smoke that looked like the physical manifestation of the garbled voices. John, though very practical and able to mend the washing machine when pressed, was hopeless at lighting the fire.

'Where on earth have you been?' he asked crossly. 'The house is like an igloo, there's no food and those logs must be damp, or else the chimney needs sweeping.'

He was still in his golf clothes; sturdy corduroy trousers, brushed cotton shirt and golfclub tie under a V-necked pullover, with a thick padded waistcoat that masqueraded under a knitted outside. He was holding himself in the stiffly upright position that meant, Mary knew, that he was wearing his surgical corset. A very bad sign. John, tall and thin, had always suffered with bouts of 'bad back'.

'Darling, I'm so sorry! That wretched boiler – I'll have a fiddle with it, but I'm afraid it needs servicing. Let me have a go at the fire.'

'I can light a fire, you know,' he said petulantly, choosing to take it as a criticism.

'Of course you can, but your back's bad, isn't it? You don't want to have to stoop, it's bad for it. What happened? It wasn't the golf, was it?' Heaven forbid, she thought. The prospect of John giving up his Saturday afternoon golf was rather daunting.

'I don't think so,' he said, slightly mollified by her sympathy. 'The wheel of the trolley got caught in a rut, and I tried to give it a sharp pull to free it. I felt a kind of twinge, and it seemed a bit sore, so I thought I'd put the corset on when I got home to give it some support.'

'Oh, good. I mean, I'm glad it's not serious.' Swiftly, Mary dismantled the heap of large logs he had built over far too little newspaper and scarcely any kindling, and relit it. 'There. You sit and have a drink, while I get going on the supper. I bought some soles,' she offered. 'And Pa sent you a bottle of his malt – you could have some now. Medicine for your back,' she smiled, and to her relief he smiled back. Professor Hill, who never did anything by halves, went to Scotland for a week every year and indulged his interest in single malt whiskies by embarking on a tasting tour, returning with a year's supply which, now that his stroke had forced him to cut down, was more than adequate.

John followed her stiffly into the kitchen while she disinterred the bottle. He poured himself a healthy slug, raising his eyebrows in a question to her. Mary shook her head – the only way she really enjoyed the taste of whisky was to disguise it with ginger ale, and she was aware that to do that with a single malt was as criminal an act as smothering the Dover soles with HP sauce.

'How was the Professor?' John perched on the edge of the kitchen table, first checking its pristine formica surface. For once he seemed to want to be sociable, perhaps because the sitting room was still rather smoky. Smartly stifling the thought that it was her lover's sitting place, and how much rather she would have him there than her husband, whose long legs would certainly be in her way, Mary switched on the grill – it was too soon, but at least it would warm the room a little.

'Oh, fine,' she said heartily. 'Very well indeed. I'll tell you all about it, over dinner. Could I change my mind about the drink, darling? It's so cold, a small whisky would be warming.' She hurried out of the door with a handful of cutlery as she spoke, to lay the dining table. She badly needed more time to think. During the journey home she had tried to work out how she could make Zen's continuing presence in her father's house seem more acceptable to John, but so far it was an uphill struggle.

As she put the potatoes to boil, and laid the fish in the grillpan, she managed to distract him by asking about his golf. As she had rather expected, he had not had a good afternoon. His careless tug at the trolley had warned her of that – usually he was wary of any sudden action that might hurt his back.

Mary was prodding the simmering potatoes with a narrow-bladed knife when the doorbell rang. John, who was mellowing under the combined influence of his second malt and the sight of a large plump sole waiting to go under the grill, made a token stirring movement but did not stand up. He had achieved a comfortable position and was reluctant to lose it.

'I'll go,' said Mary hastily, putting the knife down on the table. The outside lights were still on, and when Mary peered through the spyhole (John insisted she must always do this, and when he was at home she invariably remembered) she saw the glow from the twin carriage lamps lighting up a head of blonde hair and a small feminine figure. She opened the door.

'Does John Marsh live here?' The voice was high pitched, with anxiety perhaps? A woman a few years younger than Mary but carefully – presented was the word that came to Mary's mind. From Mary's larger perspective she seemed diminutive, almost doll-like, her figure slim with none of the adolescent skinniness of Zen but the product of a strict regime of diet and exercise. She wore tapered black trousers so tight they were almost leggings, and the green turtle-necked pullover that showed fluffily above a smart black coat exactly matched the green of her high-heeled shoes. Mary, who found high heels uncomfortable and particularly disliked them with trousers, supposed that if you were very small you might well prefer to wear them with everything.

The blonde hair was piled with artless care over the kind of face Mary had always thought of as 'pussy cat' – a wide forehead and upper cheeks tapering to a little chin, the nose small and the eyes far apart and wide. Her little hand, clasping a black umbrella lined with green and frilled at the edges, was laden with a positive knuckle-duster of gold rings, matching the equally large gold earrings and the buttons on her coat. Heavy, musky perfume came in on a waft of cold damp air. She looked, if not precisely a soulmate, at least prosperous, familiar in type, and harmless.

'Yes, he does,' said Mary, stepping back. 'Won't you come in out of the rain? I'm Mary Marsh. My husband's in the kitchen. I'll just call him.'

The visitor closed her umbrella with a snap as she stepped onto the mat, giving it a brisk shake outside before leaning it up next to John's in the stand by the door.

'John!' called Mary. 'Someone to see you . . . ?' She looked hopefully at the woman, expecting to be given a name.

'Don't bother,' she said crisply. 'I'll find him.' She brushed past Mary as if their relative sizes were reversed and Mary fell back. Before she could say anything the woman was at the open kitchen door, her high-heeled shoes clattering a sharp tattoo on the parquet flooring of the hall. Mary trailed after her, like a liner after a tug. She came to a halt, unable to go into the kitchen because the visitor was standing firmly in the middle of the doorway.

'Excuse me,' muttered Mary, 'if I could just come by . . . Can I get you a drink?'

She was ignored.

'John Marsh?' Surely an unnecessary question, since there was no one else there.

'Yes?' John's voice was wary, his face, seen over the woman's shoulder, affronted. 'I'm afraid I don't quite remember . . .'

'I,' said the woman with some emphasis, 'am Elaine Brantridge.'

'Oh . . .' John was evidently none the wiser. 'Um, how do you do? You wanted to speak to me?'

'You don't remember, do you? You don't bloody well even *remember*!'

'Er . . . the name rings a bell . . .'

'Rings a bell, he says. Rings a bell! I should think it ought to ring a whole peal of bloody bells! My husband's name is Euan Brantridge. Does *that* ring any bells?'

'Euan Brantridge.' John pursed his lips, looked at the ceiling for inspiration. 'Euan Brantridge,' he repeated, in tones of relieved recognition. 'I remember. Euan Brantridge, of Brantridge's. I did his accounts for several years.'

'That's *right*. You were his *accountant*. How *clever* of you to remember.'

'Well, it was a long time ago.' John was beginning to look worried. Of all things in the world he most disliked what he called, with distaste, 'a scene'. Particularly where the scene involved a woman. John could never quite decide how he felt about women. Brought up to treat them with respect, to open doors for them, help them on with their coats, he tended to dismiss them as real human beings. Angry women, argumentative women, terrified him because he did not know how to answer them. His instinct to shout back, his feeling of innate manly dominance, was sharply at war with his self-image of being 'a gentleman'.

'I can't imagine why you would suddenly want to speak to me, after all these years,' he now said pompously.

'No, I don't suppose you can. I expect you thought you'd got away with it, didn't you? Why Euan didn't . . . why I didn't have a go at you before now, come to that, but . . . Anyway, I'm here now.'

She sounded, thought Mary, distinctly threatening. John obviously thought the same, because he stood up. His tall thin figure, padded out by clothes, looked quite astonishingly large next to the visitor's tiny person.

'This is ridiculous,' he said, with a creditable firmness. 'It must be three or four years since I did your husband's accounts, and if he had any complaints they should have been raised then. You can't expect me to remember what was done all that time ago and besides, this is neither the appropriate time nor the appropriate place. I don't know how you managed to get my home address, but I must say that I take grave exception to being confronted in my own home, and at a weekend, too! I'm afraid I must ask you to leave at once.'

Mary stepped back, expecting the visitor to go. Elaine Brantridge, however, stood her ground. Her small body seemed to vibrate with the energy generated by her fury.

'Leave! I'm not leaving until I've told you exactly what I think of you, you pompous, stupid, self-satisfied *shit*!'

'Now, really!' John protested. He disliked coarse language, particularly from a woman.

'Yes, really!' Her voice was rising to a shout. 'My God, you think you can ruin our lives like this, do away with everything we've worked for over the years, and that we'll just sit there meekly and thank you for it! And yes, I'll do this here, in your house – and why should you have a nice house, when thanks to you ours will have to be sold? – and in front of your wife, in front of the whole world if necessary. In fact I'd prefer it. I want everyone to know what a useless apology for an accountant you are. But then I suppose they've already noticed that, haven't they? At your old firm, I mean? I went along there first, looking for you, and . . .'

'Mrs Brantridge!' John broke in desperately. His hands made unconscious silencing motions; his eyes flickered from her to Mary and back again. Mary wondered if it would be kinder, more tactful, if she were to go away, but there was nowhere in the house out of range of that sharp, angry voice. Besides, she had to admit she was riveted. For once in her life, reality was more exciting than fantasy.

'Don't *Mrs Brantridge* me! You won't shut me up that easily, you know. What's the matter – don't you want your wife to know what a pathetic little creep you are? Or does she know already?' Abruptly she swung round, the wide eyes in the kittenish face turning their glare on Mary.

'If you mean that my husband no longer works for Henderson Rideout, then of course I know all about it,' said Mary calmly. John gave a noise that could properly be termed a whimper, but she looked at him with a faint smile, trying to make it easier for him. 'There's no shame in redundancy nowadays, Mrs Brantridge. My husband now works on a private consultancy basis.' In the library, she thought. Advising on re-arranging the books. John was gaping at her blankly. Mrs Brantridge glared at her in silence for a moment, and Mary held her gaze. Then she turned back to John.

'You don't even know, do you? You don't even remember what you did to us! Do you ruin people's lives all the time, then? One a week? One a day? Why not? It's all just on paper to you, isn't it? Profit and loss and double entry and spending two hours to find a discrepancy of two pounds that costs us two hundred pounds in fees? And he trusted you! That ought to give you a good belly laugh. He trusted your advice, even when it went against his own instincts.'

'I can't be held responsible for what is in the accounts,' blustered John. 'I can only prepare them from the figures shown me. If your husband was cooking the books—'

'Cooking the books! How *dare* you?' She was screaming, and he fell back a pace. 'He wasn't cooking the books! Things were going well, we were making money, the business looked a good proposition. Why else do you think they wanted to buy us out?'

'I don't know what you're talking about. Who wanted to buy you out?'

'What does it matter! They would have given us a lump sum, and employed Euan for two years, and everything would have been all right, but you – *you* – stopped him! It was all agreed, he was due to sign the contracts the next day, and you rang him up and told him you'd just worked out the tax implications, and you didn't think it was a good idea. *You,*' she repeated, stabbing at him with her forefinger, *'didn't think it was a good idea.* So, because you were supposed to know what you were talking about, he didn't sign. Made him look a proper fool when they turned up the next day, but *nothing* to the kind of fool he's looked since, with the market collapsing and the business going down and down so no one in their right mind would buy it unless you paid them to take it off our hands! And now the receivers have been called in, and Euan went off to kill himself, and it's all thanks to *you!* Oh!'

She shook all over convulsively, unable to find adequate words. Her hands clenched into fists and she lunged forward, beating against his chest, arms flailing. John, seemingly stunned by this sudden violence, stood without moving. Frustrated by his lack of response, Elaine Brantridge looked wildly round, snatched up the knife with which Mary had been testing the potatoes and which she had abandoned on the table when going to answer the door, and before either John or Mary, shocked into immobility, could do anything to stop her, struck out at his chest in the general area of his heart.

The knife went in a little way. Her hand dropped and the knife stayed, quivering gently, sticking from John's chest. They all stared at it as it vibrated there. This isn't happening, thought Mary. It can't be. People don't do things like this to people like us. Mugging, yes. Robbery with violence even. But not walking into our house and stabbing my inoffensive husband with a kitchen knife. Oh God, is he going to die? There's no blood – is that a bad sign, or good? Does it mean he's bleeding internally? She must be mad. I must do something, grab her, before she does anything else.

She stepped forward, feeling that she was moving in slow motion, her limbs hampered as though she were moving through treacle. As she did so John, still looking down at the knife protruding from his chest, brought up his hand and grasped the handle. Mary, who remembered reading (in a book by Dick Francis, her mind told her with its usual tendency to come up with something irrelevant) that you should never pull out knives as doing so could do more harm, opened her mouth to protest. Before she could do so he gave a swift jerk and held the knife up in front of his face. No gush of blood followed its exit, and the blade seemed scarcely discoloured. Elaine Brantridge gave a whimper. Her arms, that had only moments before been flailing with purposeful violence, lifted aimlessly like paws. Then she collapsed soundlessly, not with the graceful crumpling fall of a stage faint but into the ungainly sprawl of true unconsciousness. Her face, beneath the carefully applied make-up that suddenly looked as obvious as a clown's, was greenish, and a crescent rim of white glistened beneath caked mascara on the not quite closed lids.

Mary stepped over her as she rushed to John, who still stood staring at the knife; for all the world, thought Mary hysterically, as though he was going to break into 'Is this a dagger that I see before me?'. Certainly the whole scene was so theatrical that it seemed completely unreal, and for a moment Mary wondered whether her imagination had finally taken over and she was actually experiencing some kind of unwanted fantasy. But not even in her most desperate moments had she ever imagined any harm coming to anyone, and she tried to pull herself together.

'John!' she said. 'John!' His eyes fixed on the knife, he seemed not to hear her. Gently she took his hand, tugged at it, finally loosened his fingers one by one and took the weapon from him. At the last moment he seemed to come back to himself and tried to stop her, but he was too late.

'You shouldn't touch it,' he said testily.

'Why not? Sit down, John. I'll call an ambulance.'

Obediently he sat down again on the corner of the table.

'Fingerprints,' he said. 'Her fingerprints will be on it. Now they'll be yours.'

'And yours,' she pointed out. 'For goodness' sake let's not worry about that. Sit there for a minute while I go for the phone. Are you in pain? Can you breathe all right?'

He drew in an experimental breath, and winced.

'I feel all right,' he said, surprised. 'My back still hurts,' he added as an afterthought. Mary looked at the knife, lying now on the table and looking so familiar. It was the one she used every day for preparing vegetables. I'll never be able to use it again, she thought with a shudder.

John unzipped his padded waistcoat. The thin blade had passed through the knitted outer surface without doing any damage, but there was a small slit in the nylon lining through which a few wisps of the thick wadding inside protruded, stained with red. Mary shuddered. John looked at her helplessly, and with careful tenderness she lifted up his thick pullover and unbuttoned the brushed cotton shirt. Beneath it, forgotten in the tension of the moment, was the solid canvas-like fabric of the surgical corset. The overlap of the fastening, held together by velcro, was just where the knife had been, she realised. There was a little red mark on the fabric, but she knew from having had to re-stitch the velcro, how very tough the combination was. The rush of relief made Mary feel for a moment as though she too might faint, and only the thought of how ridiculous it would be for the pair of them to be heaped up unconscious at John's feet made her able to draw in a long breath, and still the grey buzzing in her head.

She tugged at the velcro fastening, still gently but without the wrenching anxiety of earlier. John shuddered as it ripped open, then they both stared down at the small cut, about half an inch long and with the little oozing of blood already dry round it, in his chest. He prodded at it with fingers ready to wince away, then more firmly.

'It doesn't hurt,' he said. 'It just stings.'

'I don't think it's very deep.' Mary fetched the first aid box, opened a sealed package of sterile wipes. She dabbed at the cut. The skin parted, revealing a small slicing incision less than an eighth of an inch deep. 'It's just a scratch,' she said. 'Oh, John, thank God. It's just a scratch.'

'Ow!' he said, as the antiseptic stung. 'That hurts. Are you sure?'

'Yes, look.' He looked down, turning his head slightly sideways.

'Yes,' he agreed, with what sounded like reluctance. 'Yes, you're right. It's only a scratch. Nothing to make a fuss about.'

'Do you think I should run you to Casualty, just in case?'

'On a Saturday night? We'd sit there for three hours, and then be laughed out of the place. No, just stick a plaster on it so the corset doesn't rub.'

'Should we ring the police?' All Mary's instincts were against it and John's too, for he immediately shook his head.

'No. All that fuss, and explanations, and .. No. I don't think she's really dangerous, do you? Just overwrought.'

He looked down at his attacker as he spoke and Mary was stunned to see in his face neither anger nor disgust, but a kind of approval, almost pleasure. He straightened his body, pulling back the shoulders that were usually slightly hunched, and lifting his chin. Astonished, Mary realised that he was enjoying the drama of the situation, seeing himself for a moment as a hero, a kind of James Bond figure. Goodness, she thought. And I thought I was the one with the fantasies.

At that moment Elaine Brantridge moaned, her head rolling on the floor.

'For God's sake get rid of that knife!' said John, shuddering at the sight of it. Mary snatched up a tea towel, (plastic bags destroy fingerprints – Dick Francis again), picked the knife up by the blade and wrapped it gingerly, then tucked it into a drawer. As she closed the drawer she looked up and saw the array of kitchen knives, all good quality steel, well sharpened, on the magnetic rack on the wall.

'We must take her out of here,' she said firmly. 'We can't leave her lying on the floor like that, anyway. We'll put her on the sofa in the sitting room, that's warm at least.'

She bent and straightened the tumbled limbs. One of the high-heeled green shoes had come off and she attempted to replace it – surprisingly difficult, with a limp foot on a flaccid ankle – then thought that she didn't want them on her sofa, and removed the other one. John bent to lift her, and groaned.

'My back!' he said, straightening carefully with his hand pressed to the small of his back. 'You'll have to move her, if you want her moved.'

'Of course. Sorry, darling.' Mary thought that she could probably have lifted the small body as easily as a child's, but she felt a reluctance to hold in her arms someone who was after all almost a murderer. She put her hands under the woman's arms and half lifted her, pulling. She slid easily across the parquet of the hall floor, her legs trailing. When they reached the carpet it was slightly harder, but not unduly so, and soon Mary had her lying on the sofa. She disposed her limbs tidily, lifted her head to put a cushion beneath it, and glancing swiftly round removed a heavy glass ashtray from within reach. There did not seem to be anything else that might be used as a weapon, barring the poker. She stood back, watching as Elaine's eyes flickered open and shut, and her lips worked and parted stickily. Grimly, Mary went for a glass of water and, on second thoughts, a bucket. It's bad enough having her stab my husband, she thought crossly. I'm not having her being sick on my carpet as well.

Chapter 7

Elaine Brantridge opened her eyes. They settled on Mary who was standing next to her, leaning over and ready to offer the bucket if necessary.

'Who are you?' she asked. Her eyes wavered round her. 'Where am I?'

Really, thought Mary, how corny can you get?

'It's all right,' she said soothingly. 'You fainted. Er, how do you feel?'

'Not very well,' was the plaintive answer. 'My head's going round and round. Can I have a drink?'

'I've got some water here.' Mary didn't see why she should waste spirits on this woman. She bent to pick up the water – prudently in a plastic picnic mug – and as she did so John stepped forward to peer over her shoulder. The woman's eyes, still wavering round the room, fell on him and she shrank back.

'Go away!' she shrieked. 'Go away! You're dead! You're dead!'

The horror in her face was real, and Mary instinctively glanced over her shoulder. Wreathed in smoke – the fire was still not drawing properly, she thought – John's thin body and sallow face did look rather like a phantasm. He put out his hand, and the visitor cringed back still further, as though she would have disappeared into the cushions if she could. Her hands came up, so that with her little triangular face and pointy nose she looked, Mary thought, like an animal that had been run over.

'No! No!' she wailed. 'No, you're dead, you're dead, oh, ha ha ha, you're dead, ha ha ha!' The laughter was clearly hysterical, her bare feet were drumming on the sofa, her hands pawed at the air like someone trying to free herself from a smothering cloth. Mary looked at the mug of water in her hand, then thought of the sofa cushions and put it down before giving her a sharp slap on the cheek.

'Uh!' A whimper of protest, echoed from behind her by John who disapproved strongly of any kind of physical violence. 'You hit me! Oooh!'

'Well, I'm sorry,' said Mary entirely without apology, 'but you were getting hysterical. There's no need for all this fuss, my husband's not dead at all. He's not even hurt.'

'But I stabbed him!'

'I am hurt! I have a nasty cut!'

The two protests came at the same moment.

'You tried to stab him, yes, but he only has a cut. Quite a nasty cut,' Mary amended, feeling John's outrage.

'But the knife! I saw the knife, it was sticking into him! Oh!' It was almost a shriek again.

'For heaven's sake show her, John,' said Mary crossly. 'Show her you're not some kind of zombie with a knife in your heart, or she'll never stop.'

'Oh no, please don't worry!' Apparently reassured by this exchange, Elaine Brantridge was pulling herself upright. 'Of course you don't want to show me ... and I don't want to see it. Oh!' With brimming eyes she looked piteously up at him. 'What must you think of me? Oh, Mr Marsh, I'm so terribly, terribly sorry! How I could have done such a thing ...' She gave a sob, and buried her face in her hands. Her eye make-up, Mary noticed, had survived the hysterics without a smudge, and she could not help seeing how carefully the ringed fingers were placed now. Not only did they not smudge at her eyelids, but they left little gaps through which she could peep at her victim.

John drew himself up.

'It's all right,' he said magnanimously. 'I understand. I can see you're very upset.'

'I am! But those dreadful things I said! Please, please say you forgive me!'

'He's not going to press charges, if that's what you're worried about,' said Mary acidly.

'Really, Mary, that's scarcely sympathetic,' said John.

'I don't *deserve* any sympathy,' wept his attacker. 'I deserve to go to prison! Call the police!'

'No, no,' soothed John. 'No one's going to call the police. Now, try not to be so upset. I'll get you a drink, and you'll feel much better, and then we can talk about it calmly.'

'You're very kind.' Mrs Brantridge raised her face – still with make-up unsmudged – from her hands and smiled tremulously up at him. 'And so brave, too. I'm sure you must be in a lot of pain, and no one's thought to take you to the hospital.'

They both looked reproachfully at Mary.

'I did suggest . . .' she started to say, then: 'oh, never mind. Though we should have called the police. Anyway,' she continued hurriedly, as the woman shuddered and John glared towards Mary as though she had been the one who had stabbed him, 'let's have that drink. I'll get some glasses.'

As she went to fetch them she wondered why John was so angry and hostile towards her. His eyes avoided hers, as they always did when he was annoyed with her. Thinking back, she remembered that before the stabbing she had betrayed her knowledge of his unemployed status.

Mary leaned against the worktop, and thought over the events of the last half hour. John, quite obviously, was stimulated by his brush with death, and from the complacent way he had looked at his attacker was inclined to admire rather than resent her. What he did resent, as she should have foreseen, was that Mary had found out about his work, or rather lack of it. Knowing John, she suspected that what he really minded was not that she knew, but that she had revealed her knowledge.

Her instinct to hide it had, she knew, been correct. Where her own fantasy world required only her own participation, his was the reverse, and depended on the belief of everyone else. Her awareness, and the possibility that she might have spoken of it to others, shattered his fantasy. Elaine Brantridge, on the other hand, had provided him with a little moment of excitement, of glory even. Behaviour which would have appalled him in his wife became, in Elaine, acceptable and possibly romantic.

Mary returned from the kitchen to find that John was standing beside the sofa looking brave, while his attacker sat curled like a kitten in the corner of the sofa and gazed admiringly up at him. He poured the malt with a generous hand and it was received, by Mrs Brantridge at least, as if it had been the holy grail.

'There,' he said. 'Drink that up, it will do you good.' He spoke in the indulgent tones of an adult to a fractious child. She sipped at the glass, pulled a face and coughed a little.

'It's very strong,' she said, looking at John as though he and the whisky shared this admirable quality.

'It's good for you,' he repeated. Mary took a healthy swig, feeling that she, too, had had a shock. The pungent spirit went up her nose and she choked, feeling her eyes and nose fill with water and her face go red as she gasped for breath.

'Oh dear! Are you all right?' Elaine made no move to rise.

'Whisky is wasted on my wife,' said John. 'Now, are you feeling better?'

'Oh, yes, and I'm so very, very sorry! I don't know how you'll ever be able to forgive me. I know I'll never forgive myself.'

'Now there's no need for that. You've obviously had a terrible, terrible shock. And while of course I can't take any responsibility for what has happened,' he added, his usual caution reasserting itself, 'I can assure you that you have all my sympathy.'

Somehow she produced a wispy, lace-edged handkerchief that seemed to materialise from nowhere, and dabbed carefully at her eyes.

'It's all been so dreadful,' she confided mournfully. 'And it looks as though I might lose the house and everything! I just don't know what to do!'

'Dear me,' said John. Mary thought that as a response it was somewhat inadequate, but it elicited a grateful look.

'Why don't we all sit down?' suggested Mary. She wondered, briefly, whether she should get a bowl of nuts, or some olives. It seemed to be about to turn into a social occasion. She sat on the sofa next to Elaine, and after a moment's hesitation John sat in his usual armchair. There was a short, awkward pause. Perhaps sitting down hadn't been a very good idea after all.

'I'm so sorry to hear about your husband,' said Mary at last, in what she hoped were suitably sympathetic tones. She wondered straightaway whether this was a mistake, and might set the other woman weeping again, but instead she sat up straighter.

'Yes,' she said fiercely. 'The bastard! He's the one responsible for all this. I was mad to come and blame you. Quite mad.'

It seemed rather an extreme reaction for a newly widowed woman, but Mary told herself that anger was said to be an emotion frequently found in the recently bereaved.

'Of course, I can't take any responsibility for what has happened,' said John cautiously, 'but with hindsight it is a pity he didn't sell when he had the chance. Not that my advice was wrong,' he added quickly. 'At the time it was the right thing, and no doubt the tax implications were a serious hindrance. No, it's only with hindsight that one could say he might have done better to sell. But then, it's always easy to say what we should have done. Not so easy to foresee what we should do in the future, though, eh?'

Mary found herself wondering how all the other businesses that changed hands every day managed to deal with the tax implications, but it didn't seem the moment to ask. She nodded, sipping at her drink to give her an excuse not to say anything.

'Oh, I do so agree!' gushed Elaine. 'And in any case, it was his decision, not yours. I mean, he should have gone ahead anyway, like he wanted to, instead of letting himself be put off. Stupid bloody man! I could kill him! Oh dear, I shouldn't say that, should I? Not when I've just nearly killed you, and you've been so nice about it. But I didn't mean to hurt you, not really. It was just a – a moment of madness. But him! I could really kill him, and he'd deserve it too!'

Mary blinked at her. 'But I thought...'

Elaine looked at her blankly, as if she had scarcely noticed her presence and was astonished to find that she could speak.

Mary continued, undaunted. 'I thought he was dead already. Didn't you say he had killed himself?'

'Killed himself? Did I say that? Maybe I did, in the heat of the moment. No, I thought he did, but it's worse than that. Much worse.'

What, Mary wondered, was worse than one's husband committing suicide?

'He didn't really kill himself. He just pretended to. And went off,' said Elaine with venom, 'with his secretary.'

'Oh!' Mary gave a snort of laughter, and buried her face quickly in her glass. John glanced crossly at her.

'How dreadful,' he said, with evident sincerity. Elaine looked at him gratefully.

'Well, it *was*,' she said. 'It was all such a shock! First of all I had the police on the doorstep, breaking it to me that he was dead. Or at least that they thought he was, because of course they didn't find a body. Naturally.'

'How did he, er, do it?' Mary could not resist asking. John frowned at her again, but Elaine was only too ready to tell her story.

'That's just it, he did it so badly! He drove to the seaside and parked his car and left his clothes on the beach. I mean, it's so corny, isn't it?' Reggie Perrin, thought Mary, feeling the laughter bubble inside her. Oh dear. 'And a note on the clothes, pinned down with a clothes peg, saying he couldn't go on. At least, that's what they thought it said, only he wrote it with an ink pen, and it got rained on for hours before anyone found it so all the ink had run, and the paper was practically pulp. He couldn't even think to put it in a plastic bag or something! He just couldn't do anything right, the stupid fool.'

'I suppose,' said Mary tentatively, 'he wanted to give the impression of someone at the end of his tether, out of his mind with worry. I mean, I don't suppose genuine suicides think of things like plastic bags either.'

Elaine gave her a blank look.

'But he wasn't a suicide, was he? So he should have thought of it. Anyway,' she continued, dismissing the interruption as irrelevant, 'he'd taken on a lot of new life insurance only the week before, so that made them suspicious. And he may say,' she added viciously, 'that he meant me to have all the money, so I wouldn't have any worries, but you can be quite sure he'd have been on to me later to share it with him! Not that I would have done, of course.'

'Of course not,' murmured John. Mary could see that he thought she meant she would have given it back to the insurance company, but she, Mary, wasn't so sure of that. Elaine Brantridge didn't strike her as the sort of person who would easily give up something once she had hold of it.

'So the next thing I knew, I had some man on the doorstep saying he was an insurance fraud investigator. I mean, there I was, just getting used to the idea that Euan was dead and gone, and I was all alone in the world.' Somehow she contrived, without moving, to look fragile and helpless. 'And then there he was, actually accusing me of colluding with my husband to defraud the company! He was quite abusive, and I found it very upsetting indeed! He didn't seem to believe anything I said!'

'Dreadful!' breathed John. 'How could he think such a thing? You obviously had no idea!'

'Of course I didn't! Well, at least, I may have wondered a bit...'

'He wasn't the suicidal type?' Mary, against her will, could not help being fascinated.

'Oh, yes, he was a great one for giving up, was Euan. But he was terrified of the water, you see. Couldn't swim. He got pushed in at the deep end at a school swimming lesson, something feeble like that, and he wouldn't even paddle, let alone go near deep water. So I did think it was a funny way for him to choose. But it wasn't for me to say so, was it? Only, of course, not knowing the coast and being a complete *fool* into the bargain, he chose a bit of beach where the current *always* brings things back within a few days, just a few miles along. And when his body didn't turn up, well . . .'

'And when his secretary went missing?' Mary could not refrain from mentioning.

'That bitch!' Her fingers curled round the glass.

'A young girl?' suggested Mary sympathetically. 'They call it a mid-life crisis when men do things like this, don't they?'

'Crisis? I'd give him crisis! She's the same age as I am, and she's fat, and ugly with it!' Mary felt herself pulling in her stomach defensively. She let it go again. Nothing in the world was going to disguise the fact that she was twice the size of Elaine Brantridge. And ugliness, she thought, was definitely relative. She certainly had no wish to look like her visitor.

'He must be mad,' said John decisively. Elaine, Mary was fascinated to see, looked at him coyly through her eyelashes. Mary had never seen anyone do that before, only read about it in books. Was it attractive? She found it ridiculous, but John was clearly captivated. It seemed extraordinary to Mary that he should be sitting there admiring someone who had, even without premeditation, come close to killing him; but perhaps it created a bond? She supposed she should mind, should feel jealous, but all she really felt was surprised. And, she thought suddenly, rather sick. The potatoes! She leaped to her feet.

'Excuse me,' she murmured. The other two ignored her, and she sidled out of the room and into the kitchen. A waft of scorched potato, acrid and unpleasant, met her on the threshold.

'Blast it,' she muttered to herself, snatching up the pan and examining it in the vain hope that something might be salvageable. One sniff told her that the contents would all be inedible. When she ran cold water into it there was a hiss and a gush of evil-smelling steam that blinded her for a moment. 'Damn, damn, damn.' She knew that the thing she minded most was that Elaine Brantridge would smell the potatoes and know that she had burned them. She longed, with an almost physical ache, to have her lover there, to be able to tell him about it and share both the horror and the humour, but she knew it wouldn't work. From the very beginning she had made it a firm rule that she would only allow him to be there when she was alone in the house. Anything else felt vaguely dishonourable. And although of course she could make him be there now, she knew he would have no reality, and it would never work.

She couldn't face doing more potatoes, especially since the knife she might have used was still hidden in the drawer, faintly smeared with John's blood. Rice would do, though John didn't really like it except with a mild English curry made with leftovers from the Sunday joint and rendered exotic, in his eyes, by the addition of a spoonful of marmalade and, if he was feeling very daring, a sliced banana. Mary measured out rice and water and put it in the microwave. The grill, still on, was red hot and radiating heat – she turned it down, then went back to stand in the doorway of the sitting room.

The smoke had finally dissipated and the fire had warmed the room, so that it now seemed quite cosy. The emotional atmosphere, too, seemed to have cleared. John and Elaine were drinking from glasses that must have been topped up, and chatting without constraint. Mary wondered whether she was supposed to invite her husband's near killer to stay for dinner. There were only two soles, of course, difficult to share and not really sufficient for three. Damn it all, she thought, she's had plenty of Pa's whisky. I'm not feeding her as well.

After Mary had stood in the doorway for a few minutes, her stillness attracted Elaine's attention. She glanced at her watch – a Rolex, Mary had noticed – and put her feet to the floor.

'It's getting late, I had no idea,' she said. John glanced at Mary, who was careful not to catch his eye. He rose with reluctance.

'It's such a nasty night. Will you be all right going home by yourself?'

'Oh yes. I have to get used to managing on my own now, don't I?' Her voice was bright and brave. 'If you could just tell me where my shoes are?' Silently, Mary fetched them and the small handbag, with its large gold clasp, that was lying on the telephone table where the visitor must have placed it when she came in.

'You've been so very kind,' Elaine said, blinking up at John. 'I don't know how to thank you enough.'

Mary brought the frilly umbrella, but John insisted on fetching his large golfing umbrella and seeing her out to the car. Mary heard his voice murmuring soothingly, and the woman's high-pitched replies as she stood at the open car door. The rain had eased to a slight drizzle that hung in the air like mist. John came back, his free hand smoothing the long lock of hair that covered his bald patch in a self-conscious gesture.

'Poor thing,' he said awkwardly. He never knew how to refer to females – 'woman' he thought impolite, 'lady' too subservient, and 'girl', in this case, scarcely apt. 'She's had a terrible time. Terrible.' He shook the umbrella and wiped his feet carefully. 'I did wonder whether we should have invited her to stay for a meal?'

'So did I,' admitted Mary, 'but I just couldn't face it. You're being wonderfully forgiving, but she did try to kill you, John! I don't want to sit down and eat with someone who's tried to kill my husband!'

His face cleared at this evidence of wifely solicitude, and Mary despised herself. Still: 'How is your cut?' she asked sympathetically. 'Shall I have another look at it, just to make sure it's all right?'

Mary fetched the first aid box, and brought it back to where John sat complacently in his armchair. She looked at the cut, which was dry and clean, and put a fresh plaster over it, smoothing it down with gentle fingers.

'There. I don't think it will give you any trouble.' She sat down again, feeling suddenly rather weak.

'I'll do supper in a minute,' she said. 'I just want to sit for a moment. I'm afraid the potatoes burned, but I'll do some rice instead, it won't take very long. I just can't face it for a moment.'

'Aren't you hungry?' He sounded surprised.

'Not very.' Mary spoke rather shortly.

'I expect you found it all a bit upsetting,' he said smugly.

Upsetting? she pondered. Yes, it was a bit upsetting seeing some strange woman stabbing your husband with your own kitchen knife. And perhaps just as upsetting to have to watch him getting on so well with her afterwards. She thought how much she preferred Zen's appearance, unnatural though it was, to Elaine Brantridge's gold and high heels. She dismissed the thought of Zen. After all that had happened, she certainly couldn't face explaining to John just what was afoot in her father's house in North Oxford.

John looked up at Mary with a little frown.

'*I* was upset too,' he said.

'Well, of course you were!' said Mary eagerly. 'Anyone would be.'

'Upset,' he pursued relentlessly, 'by *you*. You haven't been very honest with me, have you, Mary?'

Guiltily, Mary wondered if he had picked up the thought of Zen from her mind.

'There hasn't been any opportunity to talk to you about it . . .' she said weakly.

'No opportunity? I find it hard to believe that there could not have been any opportunity – unless it was only today that you started spying on me?'

Mary stared at him.

'My spying on you . . . ?'

'Come now, Mary, don't pretend you don't know what I'm talking about. You made it quite clear, earlier on, that you knew that I'm no longer with Henderson Rideout.'

'Oh, that!' Mary was relieved. 'No, I've known about that for quite a while. I saw you one day, when I had to go the library on one of my office days.'

'To the library? Why would you be going to the library during your working hours?'

Mary stared at him. His anger, obviously, was because she had found him out. That having done so she had not spoken to him of it seemed not to matter at all. What he minded was that she had made the discovery.

'I had to look something up,' she said. His look expressed disbelief. 'I did! You can't really think I would spy on you, surely?'

'I suppose not.' It was a grudging admission, but sincere. His anger dissipated. He looked down, and was silent.

It seemed odd to Mary that he should see her as a fragile little woman to be shielded from the cold winds of reality. Her size and build were so much part of her self-image that she had always felt obliged to hide her insecurities from the world. Was John, then, more perceptive than she had believed, or did he simply create her in the image he found attractive? Certainly Elaine Brantridge's fragile helplessness had roused in him a protective instinct of chivalry that easily overrode his resentment of her attack, both verbal and physical.

She could not deny that she had found John's refusal to admit that he had lost his job a touching evidence of weakness that had awoken her affection and the powerful maternal instincts that had had so little outlet since David had left childhood behind. Believing that she was giving him what he wanted, had she, Mary, failed in this as she felt she had failed with her parents and with her son?

'I'm sorry,' she apologised gently. 'I meant it for the best.'

'I suppose you did,' he said. He still did not look at her, and Mary wondered if he were still angry, but at last he raised his eyes from the carpet. 'You, er, you won't tell anyone?'

'Of course not, if you don't want me to.'

He drew in a deep breath, and looked at her.

'Thank you,' he said.

'Oh, John!' Moved almost to tears, Mary went to him. When she tried to hug him, however, he withdrew stiffly from her embrace. The little moment of closeness was over, and she knew he would not refer to it again. Her mind went back to dwell on the look she had seen in his eyes in that brief moment. Gratitude, relief and, if she were not mistaken, a kind of appeal that went straight to her heart. In that moment it seemed to her that he needed her, that her collusion in his own make-believe was necessary to him.

Mary sighed, and sat back in the armchair. It was at least warm, the fire was now burning well and giving off an almost visible blast of heat. Was it her imagination, or could she still smell the heavy scent of Elaine's perfume through the clean lingering tang of smoke? Mary stood up and went to the sofa. She plumped up the cushions, then sat where Elaine had sat, obliterating the slight presence with her solidity.

John switched on the television, and Mary was glad of it. She let her eyes rest on the screen as they might have done on the shifting coloured patterns of a kaleidoscope. It was the usual Saturday evening diet of game shows, but at least it gave them an excuse not to talk. Mary felt she needed time to evaluate this subtle shift in their relationship. She could not recall him ever having looked so grateful to her – in the past it had always seemed the other way around. She remembered the astonished gratitude with which she had reacted on realising that this man, this tall, not unattractive, suitable man was actually interested in her.

After years of her father's students, of half-heard murmurs and stifled giggles, of hopeless passions and endless small, hurtful rejections, he had seemed to shine with an unearthly angelic light. He liked her, he wanted her, above all he seemed to need her. Gratitude and relief had been all too easy to interpret as love, and in the belief that he loved her she had vowed, with youthful fervour, to do everything in her power to make him happy. In the early years she thought she had succeeded. Lately she had begun to wonder whether they had not both been mistaken in each other. Certainly she doubted that she was the wife that John wanted, though out of guilt and a stubborn sense of loyalty she still struggled to please him.

And there was David. If in nothing else, surely by producing David she had repaid what she still saw as her debt to John? For David, in his character, his likes and dislikes, his habits, and even his appearance, was utterly John's son. It was almost as though she, his mother, had had nothing to do with his creation, had been no more than the nurturing receptacle for John's cloned DNA. She loved him, of course. He was her child, and she would cheerfully have died for him, but in her heart of hearts she knew that he was far away from her, as separate and distant as if he lived in Australia, or Alpha Centauri. With John, David could communicate in the kind of shorthand she had heard between couples married so long they were practically telepathic. With her, though each tried hard to explain and describe, conversations were like tennis played between two inept beginners – the ball of words and ideas was served, but rarely came within reach of the other and was never returned.

As if she had summoned him by the thought, there was the sound of a key in the front door, and voices in the hall. She glanced at her watch – half past nine. Early for David and Alison to be coming back. Mary stood up to go and greet them, but with uncharacteristic ebullience the door was flung open and they were in the room.

'Goodness, Mum, the house feels cold!' exclaimed David cheerfully. 'Nice and warm in here, though,' he added approvingly.

'I'm afraid the boiler's broken down,' apologised Mary. 'Do come to the fire, Alison. Is it still raining outside?'

'Only drizzling, thanks, Mrs Marsh.' Alison, however, did not leave David's side. She was a mousy little creature, thought Mary sadly. Polite to the point of inanity, she never managed to call Mary by her name although she had several times been asked to. It was not that she was frightened of Mary, but that she saw her as unimportant. In spite of all Mary's attempts to be friendly and welcoming Alison largely ignored her, simply agreeing as a matter of course with everything Mary said.

'You're back early,' said John. 'Want a drink?'

'I certainly think we ought to have something,' said David unexpectedly. He was not a great drinker. 'Guess what, everyone! We're engaged!'

Chapter 8

'Darlings! How lovely!' Mary trusted that the fraction of a second's hesitation before she spoke had gone unnoticed. 'Have you just decided this evening? Wonderful!' She went up to David to kiss him. He bent for her kiss, though he was not so very much taller than she was, then put his arms round her and hugged her, which was unusually demonstrative. Mary felt the hot prickle of tears in her eyes as she hugged him back. 'Darling David,' she said. 'I do wish you all the happiness in the world.'

David released her and turned to shake his father's hand, while Mary leaned over to kiss Alison. She would so much have liked to hug her too, but Alison offered a satiny cheek, stretching her neck and keeping her body well back. Mary felt rebuffed, but stifled the feeling. The girl was shy, she told herself, that was all. At all costs, she must not start seeing faults in this young woman who was to be her daughter-in-law. John's inhibited little peck, she saw, was better received by Alison than her own enthusiasm. I must be careful, she thought.

Mary wished, not for the first time, that David had not chosen Alison as a girlfriend. It was difficult to feel warmly disposed towards someone who invariably ignored her. Mary had met her parents at a golfclub dinner. Both were doctors, dedicated GPs whose life revolved around their practice and their patients; one had been called away in the middle of the dinner. Alison's lips had tightened with irritation, and Mary had wondered whether her parents' selflessness had driven her to the opposite extreme. She suspected that saints might be as difficult to live with as their opposites, and certainly Alison appeared to have rejected her parents' life of service to others and headed for single-minded pursuit of financial success.

Over the months Mary had struggled to find some interest they could share, but her tentative mentions of music, books, cinema, cooking and even, stretching her own horizons, sport, met with blank disinterest. None of these things, it seemed, appealed to Alison unless they led to a new client or an expansion of business. Mary couldn't help blaming her for David's current obsession with golf, a game which he had hitherto disliked.

John went to fetch the bottle of champagne that he always kept in the refrigerator, though there was seldom any call for such debauchery. The wine tasted cold and thin, the bubbles prickling almost painfully against the back of Mary's throat and up her nose, so that she was afraid she would do a nose-trick again.

'The happy couple!' said John, raising his glass.

'David and Alison,' murmured Mary. They all drank, and there was a little pause while the fire crackled. The television mouthed silently – John had pressed the sound-off button on the remote control – and Mary noticed how all their eyes were drawn to the unintelligible screen. She walked over and switched it off.

'So, when are you planning to have the big day?' she asked, falling into cliché and despising herself. 'In the summer, I suppose? You must tell your parents we'd be only too happy to help, of course, in any way. I mean, weddings are so expensive, and nowadays . . .' She realised she was gabbling, and tailed off. Alison was looking at her blankly.

'Oh, we're not planning the wedding yet! Not this summer, certainly – perhaps next year, or longer, it depends. It's not as if there were any financial advantage to being together. We want to get some more money saved up for a house, you see, and of course David wants to establish himself.' She looked sternly at David, who nodded seriously.

'Marriage is a big commitment,' he informed them. 'Buying a home, furnishing it, all that kind of thing. We don't want to be rushing into anything, and overreach ourselves. Look at all those people who bought a few years ago, and are stuck with negative equity.' He shook his head. 'Dreadful position to be in.' His voice was solemn and condemnatory, that of a fervent believer describing the ultimate sin.

'It was awful,' Mary told her lover the following week after work, when she was getting supper in her kitchen. 'At his age he should be so madly in love that he'd be suggesting getting married next week and living in a cardboard box, or just living together!'

'You'd hardly be glad of that,' he pointed out. He sat in the rocking chair, and the cat was stretched out across his knees. 'The cardboard box bit, I mean. The living together would be all right.'

'Well, it would be normal, at least. And I don't think it's a bad idea, anyway, to get to know one another properly before making a final commitment. Nothing like sharing a bathroom with someone to really get to know them.'

'Or a kitchen?' His eyebrow quirked up as he gave her a laughing glance.

'Especially a kitchen! Oh dear, of course I wouldn't want them to rush into anything, but this was more like a business proposition than two people who love one another. I know I should be glad he's so sensible, but I just wish it could be a bit more romantic.'

'I know, love. But it's just not in them, is it?' He did not say, and nor did she, that in this, too, David was his father's son. John never forgot her birthday, nor their anniversary, or even Valentine's day. On each occasion he brought her flowers: long-stemmed red roses in February, and mixed florists' bunches for their May anniversary and her October birthday. There would be large pink carnations like marshmallows, spray chrysanthemums, bits of gypsophila – all of them unscented, all looking as if they had been manufactured rather than grown, and all, to John's satisfaction, lasting for weeks before she could throw them away and go back to what she preferred, the garden flowers and leaves that looked untidy and lasted only two or three days but which she grew for their scents and the subtlety of their colours.

Like the house, like the furniture, the flowers were bought because that was the appropriate thing to do. At the beginning, Mary had searched out little intimate gifts, jokey or sentimental, to give him on special days, but although he thanked her politely he always looked at them in surprise and dismay, and the things were always put away in a drawer or a cupboard in case anyone should see them. After a while she learned that he actually preferred to be given something useful, like socks or a drill bit. David, she could see, would be just the same. The difference was that Alison, presumably, would welcome the dull flowers and the gift of a sensible jumper. And Mary was grateful; she knew only too well that many men did not bother with such things, but she wished he were the kind of man who took the trouble to find out what flowers she liked. Unreasonable, of course. In this, too, she had failed John. Or was it David she had failed, in not managing to teach him anything beyond the sensible and practical?

In his early childhood she had bought so many books for him – fairy tales, and nursery rhymes, and beautifully illustrated books of nonsense verse and fantasy. His Christmas stockings had been crammed with the kind of toys she hoped would seize his imagination and stretch it. He had sat quietly while she read to him, enjoying the attention and the closeness, but as he came up to school age she noticed that the fantasy and magic she loved both bored and embarrassed him.

'That's not *real*, Mum,' he would say, wriggling away from her. 'There's no such things as dragons' (or unicorns, or animals that talked).

'There might be,' she had found herself pleading with him. 'Somewhere. In some other time, or on another planet.'

His look expressed the feelings he was too young to have the vocabulary to express. By the time he was eight she had learned to choose him practical books and toys – science or natural history were all right; so were books about other countries or straightforward adventure stories. Dutifully she read them with him: together they collected frogspawn and caterpillars, and made mechanical toys out of rubber bands, cotton reels and cardboard rolls. She took him to museums, zoos and the Planetarium; he was fascinated by space for a few years, but thought *Star Wars* films silly. Mary, who thought of science fiction as a modern form of fairy tale and rather enjoyed it, went to the cinema on her own, in the afternoon, and felt as guilty as though she had been having an illicit flirtation.

The level in the champagne bottle dropped rapidly. When it was nearly empty John, to Mary's astonishment, fetched another bottle from the fridge. Not champagne, of course – there was never more than one bottle in the house – but quite a good white wine that they had been brought as a gift by one of John's golfing friends who had visited them for a meal the previous week. John's eyes were sparkling and his cheeks were stained with pink; the result, Mary presumed, of champagne and whisky on an empty stomach combining with the relief of his escape and pleasure at David's engagement. Normally his face never varied from its indoor whitish beige which no amount of golf ever seemed to tan, and it had sometimes seemed to Mary that the thin covering of flesh over the bones of his skull was isolated from the normal circulation of blood, so rarely did it show any colour.

Uncorking the bottle with a flourish John refilled their glasses with abandon, splashing the wine in carelessly. Mary, whose head was beginning to feel as though her brain had been lagged with fibreglass, tried to put her hand over the glass to stop him giving her any more but was too late. John's reactions were sluggish, and he continued to tilt the bottle so that the wine sloshed over her fingers and dripped on to the sofa cushions. They landed, Mary noticed, just where Elaine's head had rested, and in her fuddled state it seemed somehow significant. She looked at the dark spreading stains, then brushed ineffectually at them with her other hand.

'You shouldn't have moved,' said John reprovingly.

'Oh, dear,' said Alison, 'you don't want that to stain. I'll get a cloth.' She bustled out to the kitchen. Mary, who had had the same idea but not as quickly, subsided back into the sofa. She suddenly felt exhausted, her limbs like blocks of wood. Alison came back with a dampened tea towel and rubbed industriously at the spots on the cushions. She looked embarrassed, as though she had found a packet of condoms on the kitchen table. 'I'm so sorry,' she said to Mary in hushed tones. 'I've only just realised. It never occurred to me you wouldn't have had it yet.'

Mary blinked at her.

'Had what?' Was it her voice that was indistinct, or were her ears full of fluff? She sat up straighter and made an effort. 'It seems to me that I have had it. Completely.'

The little joke was lost on Alison.

'But it's still sitting there! The fish and everything! And the potatoes seem to have burned . . .'

'Oh, the *supper*! I'd forgotten all about that.'

Alison was looking at her oddly again. Mary saw her glance at the clock on the mantelshelf, and was herself astonished to see that it was after ten o'clock. In a house where the meals, in general, ran to a timetable as strict as the Swiss railways, it was an unheard of event and she could understand why Alison was looking at her with such nervous anxiety.

'We had a bit of a crisis,' said Mary vaguely. 'Someone turned up . . .'

'Just before your meal? People can be so inconsiderate.'

Her smugness was suddenly unbearable. Mary made an effort and stood up. She was only two or three inches taller than Alison, but somehow she always felt as though she towered over her. Perhaps it was because Alison was so slightly built. She was nearly as thin as John, thought Mary suddenly, narrow-hipped as a boy, her small breasts scarcely lifting the fabric of her blouse. It was not so much that she lacked femininity as that she was somehow sexless. Mary had seen her

91

withdraw, with something like disgust, from babies and small children. It was hard to imagine her giving up her career, even for a few months, in order to start a family. Would the grandchildren Mary longed for be carried within that spare body, be born from that narrow pelvis? It was difficult to imagine. Mary felt unreasonably annoyed, as though Alison had somehow cheated her.

'I don't think she was much worried about disrupting our meal,' she said. 'She wanted to have a go at John. If you're intending to marry an accountant, you'd better be warned that it can be a high risk activity.'

'Not just marry one,' Alison pointed out. 'I'm one myself, don't forget. And of course I know that there's very little security in any job these days, but still . . .'

'Of course you're one too. A whole family of accountants. Well, nearly. If you count my book-keeping course.' Alison looked as though she certainly didn't count mere book-keeping, but Mary continued. 'Just think, the two of you, balancing the books together, cash-flow forecasting, perhaps even a bit of double entry when you're feeling frisky . . . Good Lord, I'm sorry. I must be a bit tipsy, I'm afraid.'

'It's drinking wine on an empty tummy,' said Alison condescendingly. 'Why don't we go and finish the cooking, then you can eat? I'll come and give you a hand.'

She steered Mary towards the door. Mary felt less like a liner being pulled by a tug than like a large woolly sheep being directed by a sharp-nosed collie.

'One Man and his Dog,' she muttered to herself.

'That's right,' soothed Alison. 'Off we go.'

Is this how it's going to be? Mary wondered as she leaned against the kitchen sink and watched Alison turn on the grill again. Am I going to be cursed with the perfect daughter-in-law? Is she going to organise me, when I get old and infirm, and chivvy me into some kind of ghastly sanitised sheltered accommodation? And be irritated when I forget things, and interrupt me when I repeat the same old stories? Am I going to have to spend the rest of my life being grateful to her?

'Thanks,' she mumbled ungraciously. 'It's very kind of you.' The fish, she saw crossly, was being cooked far too long and would be dry, and she was afraid she had put too much water in with the rice which would, conversely, be soggy.

'It's the least I can do,' said Alison. 'Besides,' she added with a coy look, 'I'm almost family, now, aren't I?' She peered into the microwave. 'The rice is nearly done, I think. How does Mr Marsh like his vegetables?'

'Thoroughly cooked,' said Mary sadly. She was, she knew, being unfair to Alison. She should be thankful that David had chosen such a nice, sensible, suitable girl. After all, he could have come home with someone like Zen ... Mary tried to tell herself that she wouldn't have liked that at all, and certainly John would probably have fallen down and frothed at the mouth. 'You must call us Mary and John. Now that you're family.'

'Oh, thank you, Mrs – um, *Mary*,' she said with an effort. Goofed again, thought Mary. She'll be so uncomfortable she'll end up calling us nothing. I bet she calls all her mother's friends Auntie. Oh dear, why am I being so critical? What's the matter with me? It must be shock or something.

'What was she angry about, then?' Alison took the pan to the sink to drain off the vegetables.

'Who?' Mary, confused, wondered whether Alison was referring to her, Mary, in the third person. Surely she hadn't been able to tell that Mary was annoyed?

'The visitor,' answered Alison patiently, turning off the grill and opening a drawer. 'You said she wanted to have a go at, um, at John. Where's the fish slice? Oh, there's something sharp ... what's this kitchen knife doing in here with the mats and napkins?'

She turned round, holding up the knife which Mary had hidden there – was it really only an hour or two ago?

'"Is this a dagger that I see before me?"' murmured Mary. 'You probably shouldn't have touched it. It'll have your fingerprints on it now. Oh well, he wasn't going to do anything about it anyway.'

Alison looked at the knife in her hand, holding it further away from her as if it might spit venom, then stared at Mary.

'Dagger? Fingerprints? I don't understand. I don't think you're very well. Wouldn't it be better to go upstairs and have a nice lie down?'

Her tone was, just faintly, patronising. Mary, who knew that she was in fact drunker than she wanted to appear, was unreasonably annoyed.

'No, it wouldn't.'

A look of steely determination came into Alison's eyes. Mary was astonished. Was this the girl she had thought so meek and inoffensive? Had David ever seen her look like this? Alison came towards her.

'Now, we don't want any embarrassing scenes today of all days, do we? Not on our engagement day. I'm afraid the champagne and the excitement have all been a bit too much for you.'

'Alison,' said Mary in a carefully controlled voice, 'I admit I may have had a bit too much to drink, but I am not drunk, nor am I off my head, and I'm certainly not going to make any kind of embarrassing scene. And I'd be grateful if you'd stop waving that knife around in my face. I hid it in the drawer because our visitor – the one who interrupted our meal, you remember? – tried to stab John with it.'

Alison's mouth fell open. She looked from the knife in her hand to Mary's face, the expression of outraged disbelief changing, after a few moments, to horror. With an exclamation of disgust she half dropped, half flung the knife from her. Perversely it did not fall on its handle or bounce flatly, but flew like a dart to stick, quivering gently, in the cushion flooring about two inches from Mary's feet. Alison's hands went to her still gaping mouth and clasped over it as if holding back a scream.

'You know,' said Mary, looking down at the knife, 'I really think I'd better get rid of that knife. It seems to be harbouring some kind of grudge against us, I can't think why. Perhaps it's got a taste for blood. In any case, I don't really think I could bring myself to use it again, after seeing it . . . well, you know.'

Alison peeled her hands off her face.

'You're . . . you're joking, aren't you? It's not really true?' She was once again the mousy girl Mary had always thought her, but Mary knew she would not forget that implacable look. She bent and picked up the knife, then wrapped it in a sheet of newspaper and pushed it into the bin so that it was beneath some other rubbish. Alison watched her with the quivering intensity of a rabbit facing a weasel.

'There,' said Mary briskly, washing her hands, 'that's out of the way. Now, we'd better get that fish onto the plates before it's completely cold.' Back in control, she slid the fish onto the warmed plates and spooned out rice and vegetables. 'Just call the men, would you, Alison? And what about you and David? I know you've had a meal, but what about something to keep us company? Cheese and biscuits, perhaps?'

'That would be very nice, thank you, Mrs Marsh.' Meekly Alison went to fetch David and John, and Mary quickly laid two extra places and put out cheese, biscuits, butter and celery. The men came through, talking golf, and they all sat down.

The fish, as Mary had feared, was dry and tasteless, and the rice had congealed into a doughy mass. John, however, ate with enjoyment.

'Nothing like a game of golf to build up an appetite, eh, David?' His moustache twitched as he chewed. Alison, who had shaken her head at the cheese and was nibbling on a biscuit, looked at him in awe.

'Oh, Mr Marsh, I do think you're brave!'

He looked at her in surprise.

'Brave, my dear? I'd say you were the brave one, taking on young David. Eh?' The wine, Mary thought, was still making him unnaturally jocose.

'What about me, then? Don't you think I'm brave?' David looked puzzled. He couldn't see why Alison should think his father brave. Alison ignored him.

'But – that woman – and the knife...' She glanced at Mary, obviously wondering whether it had all been some kind of elaborate tease.

'I'm afraid I told Alison about what happened,' said Mary apologetically. 'It just slipped out.'

John, however, had the kind of modest look on his face that people wear when they are secretly glad something has come out into the open.

'What just slipped out?' David was pursuing this with his customary tenacity. 'What's been going on, Dad? Mum?'

Mary and John looked at one another.

'One of your father's ex-clients turned up – or rather his wife did. Poor thing, she was pretty much off her head: her husband had gone bankrupt, then faked a suicide and gone off with his secretary like that politician, you know, John whatever, only he didn't do it very well and they caught up with him almost straightaway.'

'The insurance companies are on to that one,' David nodded seriously. 'Nobody gets away with it.'

'How do you know?' Mary was easily sidetracked after a few drinks. 'I mean, if they'd got away with it nobody would know, would they? Like the murders that nobody knows about...' She saw that John was looking annoyed. 'Sorry, of course that's nothing to do with it. Anyway, this woman was in a state, as I said, and for some reason she'd decided it was all your father's fault, so she came round here to have a go at him. The knife was lying there – we were in the kitchen – and she just snatched it up and stuck it into him. It was awful.'

'Good God!' David was staring round-eyed at John. 'But you're all right? Shouldn't you have gone to hospital or something? And what about the police? I suppose they took her away.'

'No, I didn't call the police,' said John. 'All that publicity, you know, local papers and all that. Besides, she didn't hurt me.'

'But the knife . . . Mum said she stabbed you!'

'Tried to. Luckily it stuck in the Velcro fastening of my back thing.' John hated the support to be called a corset. He thought the word effeminate.

'But Dad! Just because she didn't hurt you doesn't mean she didn't try! She might have killed you! I think we should call the police right away!'

David was actually getting to his feet, but John waved him down again.

'No need to make a fuss. She's not dangerous. She was just upset, acted on an impulse. When she saw what she'd done she fainted, poor thing.'

'Easy enough to fake a faint.' David wasn't going to give up too easily.

'Not at all!' John's voice was quite sharp. 'As a matter of fact she was rather a nice woman, I thought.' He noticed that they were all staring at him in astonishment. 'Well, she was,' he said defensively. David opened his mouth to argue and John, knowing how tenacious he was, decided to change the subject. 'Anyway, you've heard all the drama, it's all over now with no harm done. But your mother's had a busy day too, haven't you, dear? You never told me how you found the Professor, and whether it's true about the girl he was with.'

The two pairs of eyes swivelled in Mary's direction. Caught out – she had really thought she was safe from being asked about Oxford – she looked helplessly back at them.

'Girl?' said David, as though this was some new species he had always thought to be mythic, or extinct. 'What girl? Surely Grandprof hasn't got a girlfriend, at his age?'

'I should certainly hope not,' said John grimly. 'That's just what your mother went to find out. I expect it was all a mistake, wasn't it, Mary?'

'Of course it was!' said Mary crossly.

'I thought so,' said John. 'I didn't think the Professor would do anything so foolish as to get tangled up with an unsuitable girl. Not,' he added, with heavy humour, 'that any girl would be exactly suitable, at his age! Well, I'm glad that's all cleared up. And how was the Professor? You must take Alison over to meet him, David.'

Mary had a sudden vision of Zen and Alison face to face. She gave a snort of hysterical laughter.

'When I said it was all a mistake,' she said cautiously, 'what I meant was that my father hasn't got a girlfriend. Not in that sense of the word, anyway.'

John looked at her suspiciously. 'But there is a girl?'

'Yes,' admitted Mary. 'Yes, there is a girl. He's teaching her.'

'Ah, a *student*! I thought he wasn't taking any more students now, since his little turn?'

'Since his stroke. No. She's not a student, except in the sense that she's learning from him. Not at the university. She's quite young – only seventeen, in fact.'

'So what is he teaching her? And why?'

What, Mary pondered, was the answer? That her father was teaching Zen about the life cycle and history of the scallop, and how to eat properly?

'He's teaching her ... well, everything really. As I say, she's very young, and almost completely uneducated. It's a kind of ... of experiment. In social adaptation.'

'What on earth's that?'

Mary, who had made up the term on the spur of the moment, was hard put to answer.

'He's fascinated by the fact that she knows so little. She's very intelligent, he says – well she must be, or he wouldn't be wanting to teach her.'

'If she's that intelligent, why doesn't she know anything?' John sounded far from convinced. 'I know our education system isn't perfect, but I'd have thought any school would encourage a clever child.'

Mary shook her head.

'I know. I thought it was odd, because you can see how bright she is. But when I asked her, she said she was bored at school, and always in trouble. I think that sometimes happens with these very bright ones. If no one realises when they're quite young how clever they are, they tend to get so bored that they switch off and start playing up. She said they did some tests on her when she was nine, but she messed them up on purpose.'

'Silly girl.'

'Yes. Anyway,' Mary laboured on, 'Pa wants to see whether he can't help her to find some kind of place in the world, in society.'

'Get a job, you mean?' David, as always, went for the basics.

'Yes, that too. But more than that really. I'm not expressing it very well. He sees her as a kind of embryo, an egg, if you like. He wants to hatch her out to see what she'll turn into.'

'Sounds potty to me,' said David cheerfully.

'One wonders,' said Alison austerely, 'whether people like that really appreciate being helped.'

Mary, who disagreed profoundly with all those remarks (though she had to admit that there was a kernel of truth in David's), kept quiet.

'And where is this girl living?' John's frown was growing deeper.

'Oh, in the house. It's company for him – safer, really, if he should have another stroke – and of course there's plenty of room. Besides, she hasn't anywhere else to go.'

'You mean she's some kind of drop-out?'

'Oh no! Just . . . just homeless, at the moment. You know how it is, so difficult for these young people. Her mother's on her own, with several younger children to look after, and there's not much room for the poor girl. Because,' finished Mary, who thought she might as well get the whole thing out in the open now, 'she's pregnant.'

'Pregnant!'

'Yes, pregnant. With twins.'

'Twins.'

'Yes, twins. Quite soon.'

'Are you telling me,' asked John in the quiet tones of one about to explode, 'are you really telling me that your father, Professor Hill, has taken into his house some kind of little tramp who's been thrown out by her parents and is about to produce not one, but two fatherless children; a parasite who is doubtless claiming vast sums in social security and income support while she battens on his helpless state? And you have done nothing about it, not even spoken to me?'

Mary drew in a breath, calling on the deep well of patience she had created over the years.

'No,' she said calmly, 'that's not what I am telling you. I am telling you that my father, who though he may have had a stroke is still far from helpless, has decided to let an intelligent girl, a girl who he feels has been betrayed by the educational system of this country, stay in his large empty house so that he can go back to doing what he likes best, which is educating. I was as astonished as you are, and I was also worried – not so much for him, because I know he is more than capable of taking care of himself, but because I thought it was unfair on her. We talked about it, and although I can't say I'm completely happy about it I don't see that there's any need to make a fuss.'

David and Alison, who were sitting opposite one another between Mary and John, watched the conversation in silence, their heads slewing from one to the other as though they were watching slow motion tennis.

'Ridiculous!' spluttered John. 'Utterly ridiculous! I shall go to Oxford tomorrow and insist that she leaves at once!'

'You'll get a flea in your ear if you do,' said Mary. 'He doesn't take kindly to anyone interfering with his arrangements, as you should know by now.'

'But she'll get a hold over him! Old men can be very peculiar when it comes to young girls. She'll make him change his will!'

'My father doesn't need a young girl to make him peculiar, he can manage it all on his own. And if you're talking about changing wills, nothing is more likely to make him do that than trying to make him do something he doesn't want to do.'

'Mum's right, Dad,' put in David unexpectedly. 'Nothing's more likely to make Grandprof fly off the handle than you telling him he can't do something. He'd be just as likely to change his will and leave everything to this girl, just to show you.'

Mary and Alison waited. John looked thoughtful.

'Hmf,' he said, snuffling down his nose. His moustache twitched.

'It's probably no more than a passing phase,' said Mary. 'He'll begin to find her irritating, or more likely she'll get fed up with his constant lecturing, or he won't be able to stand it once the babies are born. It'll sort itself out, given time.'

'Least said, soonest mended,' put in Alison, offering up her mite like a little dog frisking up with a newspaper in its mouth.

'Why don't I make some coffee?' asked Mary brightly. 'It's chilly in here. We can leave this for the morning, and go back to the fire. After all, this is David and Alison's day, isn't it? Let's forget about the problems, and concentrate on that.'

Chapter 9

Mary woke on Monday morning with a feeling of impending doom that seemed to fill her whole body with leaden blackness. It was like the kind of irrational anxiety left behind by nightmares and she lay still, eyes closed, searching for the memory of the night's dreams. She found nothing, which was unusual. Mary generally dreamed in vivid colour, exciting and often entertaining dreams that she usually remembered the next day. In the early days of their marriage she had sometimes recounted the more amusing ones to John, but she had found that he resented her busy dream-life and had soon abandoned the attempt.

Now her dreams evaded her, but in looking for them she found instead the memory of the weekend's events, and her anxiety was instantly explained. Then she remembered that it was Monday, and the black cloud lifted and dissipated. The weekend was over: on Mondays she went to work, and she would be able to escape, for a few hours, into the relative simplicity of Naseby's.

With a lighter heart she showered and dressed, then went downstairs as usual to make breakfast while John was in the bathroom. As she laid the small table in the kitchen – mercifully John did not insist on eating breakfast in the dining room – it suddenly occurred to her that things were not, after all, quite as they had been. Among the welter of discoveries and events of the previous two days lurked the small though significant fact that she now knew, as it were officially, that John was unemployed. He knows I know, she said to herself, and I know he knows I know, and he knows ... stop it! This is no time, she told herself severely, for playground humour. When was it ever?

The chill of the house, slightly mitigated in the kitchen by warmth from the grill where she was making toast – Mary had a theory that toast

101

didn't taste right when made in a toaster – reminded her that there should be an engineer coming to look at the boiler. She knew that Mr Naseby, the most indulgent of employers where she was concerned, would not mind her coming home for an hour to let him in but now, surely, there would be no need? John, after all, could easily stay at home all day if necessary and see to it. The saucepan of water for John's egg was coming to the boil, and as she did every weekday morning she listened for his footsteps on the stairs, ready to lower the egg in. By the time he had sat down, buttered his toast and poured his coffee, it would be ready for him.

Mary waited until he had, with finicking patience, picked the top of the shell off and satisfied himself that the yolk was still runny. She herself was a decapitator, preferring to slice the top off with one swift blow, and it irked her to watch his painstaking technique. She had frequently offered to slice the top off for him, but he had refused.

'I don't want any bits of shell getting into the egg. You know how it sets my teeth on edge to chew a bit of shell.'

'But you don't! Get bits of shell, I mean. It's a bit like that trick with the tablecloth, when you whisk it away and leave all the glasses and china still on the table. If you do it with enough conviction, it works. So they say.'

'Well, "they" say a lot of things that I've yet to see proved. No, thank you, Mary. I prefer to do my egg in my own way.'

Mary knew there was no use in continuing. She remembered the Big-Endians and the Little-Endians in *Gulliver*. She suspected that more marriages foundered on such trivia than was commonly known.

The egg, fortunately, was perfect. As it should be, thought Mary, since John had eaten a soft boiled egg for breakfast for more years than she could remember. She ate a few spoonfuls of muesli while he carefully spooned up the yolk, accompanying each drippy mouthful with a bite of buttered toast. Would I love him more, she wondered, if he cut his toast into soldiers and dipped them in? She decided, sadly, that she probably would.

Once he had located and removed the stringy bit from the white, Mary thought that it was safe to speak to him.

'Um . . .'

He looked up.

'Yes, dear? Was there something? I haven't dripped egg yolk on my tie, have I?' Anxiously he squinted downwards.

'No, no, not at all. No, I wanted to ask you about the boiler. You know, the repair man.'

He looked puzzled.

'Surely you telephoned yesterday, and left a message? I thought I heard you doing it.'

'Yes, I did. He'll probably ring soon. But he'll need to be let in, and I wondered...'

His puzzled expression had not abated and seemed, as far as she could tell, to be genuine.

'You wondered what, dear?'

'Well, whether you could be here. To let him in. As it's my day for going to Naseby's.'

His face, suddenly, was as blank and expressionless as the egg in its eggcup had been.

Mary hurried on: 'I mean, it just seemed sensible. I know Mr Naseby would let me come back for an hour, he's always very good like that, but it seems a bit silly, doesn't it? For one thing, you can never be sure the engineer will turn up at the time he said – not his fault, poor thing, it must be difficult to work out how long each job will take him – and of course I don't really like to take advantage of Mr Naseby's kindness unless I absolutely have to. This is such a busy time, with the VAT and the end of the tax year coming up...'

His eyes slid away from her.

'It's not very convenient,' he said. 'Monday is a very busy day for me.'

'But surely...'

'A very busy day,' he repeated firmly. 'I have an appointment.'

'Oh, of course. An appointment. Of course, that's different. What kind of appointment?' It could not be with the dentist or the doctor – such matters were always left for her to arrange. Could it perhaps be a job interview? She hoped very much that it was. Now she came to think of it, did she really want to encourage John not to go off to the library each day? Today was a working day, of course, but there were two free days left in her week, Tuesday and Thursday. Did she really want him at home on those days? Of course not. Even the most affectionate of wives found it difficult, when their spouses retired or lost their jobs, to have them hanging around the house, upsetting routines, wanting conversation and coffee and lunch or, worst of all, trying to help with the chores. John avoided her eye, peering into his empty eggshell.

'Just an appointment,' he said in an offended tone. 'Nothing you need to worry about.' It was the nearest he would come to telling her to mind her own business. Mary saw that the appointment was probably non-existent. His concern was with keeping things as they had been. He wanted to continue the pretence, to act as if she was still unaware of his circumstances. She bit her lip to quell angry words. They would do no good, and any kind of confrontation would make him even more stubbornly determined not to change anything.

'Not to worry,' she said stiffly. 'I'll fit it in with Mr Naseby and stay a bit later on Wednesday if necessary to make up the time.'

'That's the ticket.' He pushed his egg plate to one side, buttered another slice of toast and spread it carefully with marmalade. 'Is this the batch you made this year? It's very good. A very good set,' he said approvingly, lifting the jar up to the light and squinting at it. 'Nice distribution of peel,' he nodded. 'Well done, dear.'

'Thank you, John.' Mary tried hard to put some enthusiasm into her voice. This was, she knew, no more than a sop to keep her happy, though she had to admit – looking herself at the marmalade jar that John was still holding up – that it was as near perfect as any she had ever made. 'I expect I could win prizes with it,' she joked.

'I'm sure you could,' he replied seriously. 'I've often told you that you ought to join the WI.'

'Yes.' Mary put a large spoonful of muesli into her mouth, so that she would be unable to talk for chewing its fibrous bulk. She had in fact joined the WI during their short stay in the old house. She had loved it, too, not least because it represented to her a way of life that she thought had long vanished but that she yearned for. When they had moved back to suburbia she had not wanted to continue with the local branch, although they had contacted her. Somehow that kind of activity was too poignant a reminder of what she saw as her failure.

John left exactly as he had always done, with his briefcase and umbrella. The engineer had promised to make the house his first visit of the day, and in the end Mary was only half an hour late for work.

'Sorry, Mr Naseby, sorry I'm late.'

'No problem, Mrs Marsh. No problem at all. Heating all sorted out, is it? You should have told me, I could have come and had a look at it for you yesterday, saved you having to put up with a cold house all Sunday. Unless you don't trust me with your boiler, that is?'

Mary, who had seen him put right a client's car and repair a child's complicated electric robot, gave this sally the smile it deserved.

'I'd trust you with anything,' she said seriously, 'but I wouldn't dream of disturbing your Sunday, Mr Naseby. We had a couple of electric heaters, and the fire in the sitting room, so we didn't suffer at all.'

He shook his head.

'It's not the same, not the same at all. This early spring weather can be very treacherous. It isn't right for a lady like you, used to everything being just so. Not right at all.'

'A lady like me!' Mary laughed. Her image of herself was poorly developed, but on the whole when she thought of herself (something she tried not to do) it was as a large, amorphous creature, rather vague and woolly in outline and detail. The word 'lady', encrusted as it was with social implications, was not one she would ever have thought of in connection with herself. Other women of her age, she knew, referred to their female friends as 'girls', but this too had always struck her as ludicrous and faintly pathetic. If pushed, she would most likely have described herself as a housewife, aware that the term evoked pity or derision, and accepting these reactions as, if not appropriate, at least expected.

She became aware that Mr Naseby was still standing beside her. Her face still creased with laughter she looked up at him, and saw to her dismay that she had hurt his feelings. It was a shock: she had not thought him so sensitive. His round, slightly doughy face was set into sorrowful creases, and his brown eyes – as she had noticed but tried not to see before – had a spaniel quality as they fixed themselves on her face. Mary leaned back in her chair and let the smile fall from her face.

'Oh, Mr Naseby,' she sighed, 'I do beg your pardon. I wasn't laughing at you, truly I wasn't. It's just that if you only knew...'

'Of course, Mrs Marsh, of course. Of course it's not for me to say, and naturally I wouldn't dream of coming to your house unless you asked me. I just thought, if I could be of service...'

Mary put out her hand and clasped his, which were folded over the gentle swell where his stomach pushed against the brown overall coat he wore, clean every day, in the workshop.

'Dear Mr Naseby,' she said, 'if you only knew how very much I would have welcomed you in my house this last weekend. Not because of the boiler, but as a friend.'

A little blush suffused his round cheeks and his eyes lost their sadness.

'That's very nice, Mrs Marsh. I don't know when anyone's ever said anything nicer to me than that. And I wouldn't like you to think that I'd ever take advantage of your kindness . . .' Mary stifled another laugh. Emotion was making him even more old-fashioned than usual, and Mary had often thought that he would prefer to end his business letters with 'Assuring you, Esteemed Sir, of our prompt attention at all times'. There was no other chair at her desk, but she shuffled her own to one side, moved a pile of receipted invoices to the other end of the desk, and patted the cleared space invitingly.

'It really was the most extraordinary weekend,' she said. 'I think I must still be a little hysterical. Can I tell you about it?'

He hesitated.

'Of course, if you want to, Mrs Marsh. And don't think I don't appreciate the honour. But my wife always used to say,' he paused reverently, as he invariably did when speaking of his late wife, 'that you should be as careful what you hear as what you say. People tell you things, she said, and then afterwards they wish they hadn't, and somehow they blame you for it, and take against you. I don't know so much about that, but that's what she always said.'

'And she was quite right, Mr Naseby. Mrs Naseby must have been a very wise woman.'

'She was that, Mrs Marsh. She was that.'

'But I'd still like to tell you about it, if I may. I can't imagine that there would be any reason for me to take against you, under any circumstances. And . . . I'd really like to talk about it.'

Having started with the intention of soothing him, his reluctance had the effect of making her feel that it really would be a relief to be able to tell him about it. Her face must have convinced him, for he pushed shut the door between her little office and the passage that led between the front shop and the workshop, then perched neatly on the edge of the desk and fixed his eyes on her face.

Mary told him everything, starting with her visit to her father. She left nothing out, not even John's redundancy and his attempts to keep it a secret from her. He was a good listener, nodding and grunting in the right places but saying nothing. When she described the stabbing his eyes widened, and at its aftermath narrowed and crinkled with amusement.

'The funny thing was,' said Mary, 'that John seemed quite taken with that Elaine woman. I mean, you'd think he'd be furious with her, but he seems to admire her.'

'You get some men like that. My cousin, now, he married a woman with a temper like a steam engine. She'd build up and build up, and then it was as though she had to let rip, or explode. Laid him out with a frying pan once, she did. None of us could see why he stuck with her, but when she upped and went off with the chap next door he was broken-hearted. He married another one just the same. Said he liked a woman with spirit.'

'Oh dear, maybe that's what John's been missing all this time. I've never wanted to stab anyone in my life, or lay them out with a frying pan either.'

'I should think not indeed!' He was shocked. 'And that's not spirit, anyway, that's just temper tantrum if you ask me. Spirit? Why, you've got spirit like . . . like . . .'

'Like a tramp on meths?'

'No! Now you're teasing me, that's good, shows you've cheered up. No, you've got a different sort of spirit. The quiet, enduring sort.'

'Oh, Mr Naseby, do you think so?'

'Think so? I know so. It shines out of you, like a lamp.'

A lump came into Mary's throat.

'No one's ever said anything like that to me before. I'm not sure I believe it, but thank you, Mr Naseby.'

'You don't have to thank me for telling the truth. So, was that the end of it? Did you tell Mr Marsh about your father, and the girl? He'd have been upset, I suppose.'

'Yes, he was. And my son, too. That was the other thing. Just after the . . . the incident, he turned up with his girlfriend, and announced that they were engaged.'

Her tone was lugubrious, and Mr Naseby did not attempt to pretend that he thought this might be good news.

'And you don't like her?'

'Well, I don't dislike her. At least, I used not to. And it's not that I'm a possessive mother and all that kind of thing. It's just that I always thought she was such a mouse – no spirit in *her*! – and she's so very thin!'

Put like that, it sounded absurd. She tried again.

'I just don't feel comfortable with her. And I *think* she's going to patronise me.'

'That won't do,' said Mr Naseby firmly. 'That won't do at all.'

'I suppose not. At least, I suppose I wouldn't mind very much if I really thought she would be good for David. Until this weekend I suppose I might have thought she would be, but now ... I'm not so sure. Not that there's anything I can do about it.'

He shook his head.

'Seems to me there isn't much you can do about any of them except wait and see. And be ready to pick up the pieces.'

'Of me, or of them?'

'Of them, of course. You won't go to pieces. You're not the type.'

'I wish I could be as sure of that as you are.'

'Well, time will show.' He smiled comfortably at her, and there was a warm glow in his eyes that she had never seen there before. He likes me, she thought. If it weren't so unlikely, I'd have said that he *fancies* me. Well I never did! As he might say. Do I mind? I think I feel rather flattered. And it's not as if he'd ever *do* anything. No sexual harassment in the workplace. No shenanigans. No chasing me round the lathe or cornering me by the welding machine.

'I feel much better now,' she said truthfully. 'Thank you for letting me bore you with it.'

He shook his head, his chins wobbling gently. She knew he had not been bored. He sighed, and stood up.

'Best be getting on. Those lads will be getting into mischief.'

'I thought they were in college today?'

'They are. I was talking about Dad and Uncle.'

They exchanged a smile.

'Relatives, eh?' said Mr Naseby. 'Can't be doing with them. Can't be doing without them.' He trotted through the door, and Mary returned to her books. She was amazed to find how much better she felt. It was quite a new experience for her. Her life having run, for the past few years at least, along placid and tranquil lines, she had not felt the lack of someone to tell things to. Generally, of course, she told them to her lover, and although she realised that this was scarcely more than telling herself, still he had acquired enough of a personality of his own that his sympathy, encouragement or advice (which was naturally always what she wanted to hear) were enough for her.

Mary had few close friends. She liked to think that this was not because she was inherently unlikeable, but because she made so little effort to acquire new friends. One good schoolfriend had gone to

Australia with her husband; another had changed so much after her marriage that Mary found they literally had nothing to say to one another. The neighbours of her early married years had been pleasant but alien, and it was only during the short time they had lived in the village that she had made a real effort to get to know people. On leaving, it had seemed pointless and irrelevant to try to keep these new relationships going, built as they had been on local interests. Other than that, she was still friendly with the mothers of two of David's schoolfriends, though since she had been working, and had dispensed with the services of Mrs Woodend, she had curtailed their former meetings for coffee, tea and a chat.

It suddenly seemed to her that she had been very wrong to do this. Her introversion, her retreat into the world of fantasy she had created, seemed suddenly unhealthy and self-indulgent. She resolved that she would make more effort in future, and made a decision to telephone one or two of her women friends as soon as she got home from work.

Even as she thought it, the telephone on her desk rang. This was rare; the main telephone rang in the shop, and although calls could be transferred through to the workshop or her office, it was rare for anyone to ring her at work. She picked up the receiver.

'Hello?'

'Mary.' Her father's voice came strongly down the line. He never said who he was, assuming – as was invariably the case – that his listener would recognise his voice.

'Pa! I didn't know you had this number!'

'Directory Enquiries,' he said succinctly. 'Remembered the name of the company, of course. Battle of, 1645.'

'What's wrong?' It was rare for him to telephone her at all. 'Has something happened? Is it Zen?' Presumably he could not have had another stroke. His voice sounded quite normal.

'Wrong? Why should anything be wrong? Don't panic, girl. Why assume something's wrong, just because I telephone you? I just wanted to have a private word with you. Without any risk of John overhearing, that is. I thought you might not have told him about my arrangements.'

'Of course I've told him,' said Mary, ignoring the fact that she had done her best not to. 'And why would you think he'd be at home at this time of day, during office hours?'

'Out of work, isn't he? That's what I heard, anyway. Glad if it's not true, of course.'

109

'Well, as a matter of fact it is, though I can't think how you found out. I only learned about it myself a few months ago.'

'One hears things,' he said grandly. 'In any case, that isn't at all what I have telephoned you about. Why must you always distract me with irrelevances? You have made me forget what I wanted to say to you. Wait.' There was a crash, which Mary correctly interpreted as the sound of him letting the receiver fall. A slow, rhythmic knocking signified that it was swinging gently on its spiralled cable, banging against the desk drawers as it did so. Professor Hill's memory, even before his stroke, had been erratic when it came to the affairs of everyday life (though capable of tremendous feats of retention when it came to the minutiae of his subject). Since his stroke his grasp on practical matters had failed still further, and he frequently found himself somewhere, knowing that he had gone there for some purpose, but unable to recall what the purpose was.

His solution, typically, was to return at once to the place he had come from (if he could remember where it was), on the assumption that there would be some clue there to remind him. Since this method worked more often than not, Mary had become accustomed to conversations with him being punctuated with just such a hiatus as this. She waited, shuffling bits of paper with the other hand and half hearing the slowing of the knocking as the other receiver ceased its swing. The sound of the grandfather clock in the hall chiming the hour came to her clearly, and for a moment she was a little girl again, smelling the damp raincoat smell of the hall as she peered up at the clock face, trying to decipher the Roman numerals.

The shuffle of footsteps and a returning voice warned her he was coming back.

'Of course I'm all right, girl. Don't *fuss*.' Zen's voice, expostulating, was clear although Mary could not make out every word. She smiled to herself.

'Mary? Yes, of course I'm going to sit down. Are you there, Mary?'

'Yes, Pa. I'm here.'

'There's a book I want. Or several books, if possible.'

'Of course. You want me to come to Oxford and get them for you?' Mary was surprised, and let it show in her voice. Professor Hill might have retired, but he was still more than capable of ordering books from Blackwells, and of making some overworked assistant bring them to his house within the hour.

'Yes. That is, I don't know exactly what I want.' He sounded embarrassed, if such a thing were possible. Mary tried to imagine what kind of book it might be that he would hesitate to order for himself. Pornography? That was positively respectable nowadays, surely. Enid Blyton? Light romantic fiction? He might hesitate to ask Blackwells to send him an assorted bundle of Mills & Boons, but Mary could not believe that he would want them.

'You'll have to give me a clue, Pa,' she said. 'What sort of books? On what?'

'I want something on gravidity.'

'On gravity? Physics, you mean? Or the historical aspects. Newton?'

'Don't be a fool. Gravidity, I said. Gravidity!' He rolled the R extravagantly, and gave the D and the T a clarity worthy of Olivier. 'And parturition,' he added.

'Oh!' cried Mary, enlightened. 'Of course. Zen's there with you?'

'That is correct. I find myself in a state of ignorance, and it seems the appropriate moment to enlighten it. After all, you never know.'

'No, you don't. Um, she's not proposing to have them at home or anything dotty like that, is she? It would be most unwise, particularly with twins, and her being so small.'

'Nothing like that. My interest is intellectual rather than practical. I have never been at close quarters with it before. I find it extraordinarily interesting.'

'What do you mean, you've never been at close quarters with a pregnant woman before? Where did I come from, then?'

'That,' he dismissed, 'was entirely different. I was busy. I had my work, my students, my time was not my own.'

It wasn't mine, either, Mary thought rather sadly.

'Things were different then,' he said brusquely. 'Fathers weren't allowed to be involved in that kind of thing.' Mary was astonished. Very occasionally her father would abandon his complete self-absorption and display an almost psychic awareness of her feelings. Mary found it touching but alarming, as though he had been able to read her mind all along but had never bothered to mention the matter.

'I know, Pa. And I'm glad you're finding it interesting. I've still got a couple of books I had when I was expecting David. I'll dig them out for you. They'll be a bit out of date, though. I'll pop into the bookshop and see what I can find. Do you want them soon?'

'Yes. I thought you might like to come over tomorrow.'

It was more or less an order, but Mary was too accustomed to that to mind.

'All right, Pa. Do you want me to do some cooking? And have you heard from David?'

'Yes. And yes. It sounds as though she will suit him very well. A thoroughly boring girl.'

Mary could not help resenting this slur on David, although she was honest enough to agree with it.

'I believe she may have hidden depths,' she said carefully.

'Oh dear.'

'Quite. Pa, I'll have to go. I was late getting here today, and I've hardly done any work yet. I'll see you tomorrow.'

'With the books?'

'With the books.'

As usual, he rang off without saying goodbye. For once Mary found this reassuring rather than annoying. Professor Hill, at least, was still the same. Even his demanding arrogance could be comforting at times, she thought.

Chapter 10

Driving to Oxford on Tuesday morning, Mary could scarcely believe that it was only three days since she had last made that journey. For one thing, the weather had performed a classic *volte face*, the sun smiling with gentle warmth from a sky that boasted just enough floating puffs of white cloud to set off its limpid blue. The early daffodils, slightly battered by the rain and wind, seemed to be recovering almost visibly, and the hedgerows that had looked as drab as old sepia photographs were suddenly fat with buds.

Regeneration, thought Mary. The eternal miracle, the eternal frustration. That gnarled old tree can do it, why not me? That is, not me, but people generally. The advertisements are full of miracle cures – younger-looking skin; slimmer thighs; hair restored (for men) or removed (for women). Mary had never taken much notice of any of them, barring a fleeting astonishment that anyone would be taken in by them. Her dissatisfaction with her own appearance was so much a part of her that it had never occurred to her that she might do anything about it. Now, however, she wondered. Not about changing her appearance, but her inner self.

I am not the person who drove down this road on Saturday, she thought. Have I changed, or has everyone else? Or rather, is it that my perception of them has changed? The three most important people in my life – Pa, John, David – I've seen them all so differently over the weekend. It's disturbing, like getting a new pair of spectacles and finding that the ground isn't quite where it used to be.

The usual struggle to get into Oxford and to find a parking space effectively distracted her from her introspection. She bought the books first, choosing a heavyweight version that was practically a medical textbook for her father, who never did anything by halves, and a more approachable paperback with plenty of cheerful illustrations that she thought Zen might find useful. Professor Hill, typically, had not mentioned the possibility of Zen wishing to look at the books. Presumably he intended to study them and then reinterpret them for her. Once a teacher, always a teacher, Mary thought. It was quite possible that at the moment Zen knew far more, in the practical if not the medical sense, about pregnancy and childbirth than he did, a situation that would be unbearable to him. The rest of the shopping was easy. Having cooked for the freezer on Saturday she did not need to worry too much about buying a lot. She reached her father's house earlier than she usually managed, and found him in the kitchen drinking coffee with Zen.

'There you are,' he said, as if she had kept him waiting for hours.

'Here I am,' she agreed placidly. 'Good morning, Pa. Good morning, Zen.'

He grunted, and Zen gave her a flashing smile and started to heave herself to her feet. She looked pale and slightly drawn, Mary thought.

'Don't get up. I'll get myself a mug. How are you feeling?'

Zen grimaced.

'Tired. These little darlings thump around all night, kicking at me bladder so I'm up and down every half hour peeing. OK otherwise.'

'Good. I've brought you a book. I looked out my old ones, but they're a bit out of date now.'

Her father was glaring at her, but Zen looked pleased.

'Thanks! That's really kind of you! My mum always said there was no point knowing too much about what's going on and what might happen, it'd only put you off and get you worried. Them up the 'ospital know it all, let them do the worrying, she said. But I dunno. I think I'd rarver – rather – know what's happening. It's my body, after all, ennit?'

'It certainly is. And your babies, too.'

'Yeah.' Zen flicked through the book. 'Gawd, look at that,' she muttered, but she was soon engrossed. Mary returned her father's look blandly, and drank her coffee. He emptied his mug and stood up.

'I shall be in my study,' he announced austerely, and left the room with the air of one quitting the mundane for the purer air of scholarship. Zen grinned at his departing back.

'Likes to be the boss, don't he?'

'I expect he thinks I should have given it to him, to give to you. To be fair, it was his idea that I should buy some books for him – which I did – but I thought you might like to have one of your own.'

'Mm.' Zen stroked the shiny cover of the book. 'I never thought about books before. Nothing to do with me, were they. Just something the teachers made you read, when you couldn't get out of it. Now I got some of me own. My own. And bookshelves. Nice, that is. Is it to keep? Can I write my name in it?'

Mary was touched.

'Of course you can. What sort of books do you like best? I go round junk shops quite a lot, on my free days. I'll keep my eyes open for you, if you like.'

'Would you?' Her eyes clouded. 'I ain't – 'aven't – got much money. I got to put by what I can, for the little 'uns. Things they'll need, like.'

'Of course. Come to think of it, I've still got some of the things I had for David, up in the loft. A cot, and a baby bath, and quite a few baby clothes. There's a pram too, I think. Rather old-fashioned, but it was a good one and very large. Not made for twins, of course, but big enough for them to use for a few months at least. I'll fish them out for you.'

'David? That's your son, isn't it? And he's getting married, the Prof said.' Zen glanced swiftly at Mary, then lowered her eyes to the book. Mary laughed.

'Yes, I can imagine what he said. I'm afraid they're not exactly soulmates, and his fiancée ... well, she's David's choice.'

Zen nodded. She had no difficulty picking up the subtext of a conversation, Mary noticed.

'So don't you want to keep the pram and that for them, if they're getting married?'

'Not really. I rather think Alison is the sort of girl who would want everything new. Besides, they're only engaged. They're not going to get married for ages, until they've saved a good deposit for a house. And I don't suppose they'd want to start a family for several years. They've probably got it all timetabled out.'

'Never mind,' said Zen, once again effortlessly understanding what Mary was being careful not to say. 'They're only human, after all. Chances are they'll have a little accident, and you'll be a grandma in no time. You want me to help you with that?' Mary had finished her coffee, and was unpacking the food.

'You could check these fillets for bones, if you don't mind handling raw fish.'

'I don't mind. That's pretty. What is it?'

'Salmon. I'll look for some cookery books for you, if you like. My father suggested that I teach you to cook.'

'I'd like that. And I'd like the books. Any books, really. I just like them, you know? The way they feel. And the smell, specially those old ones in his study. Got a special smell, they have. Sometimes I think I learn something, just breathing it in.' She inhaled with a long breath, her nostrils widening. Mary was relieved.

'You really do like learning from him, then? He's not boring you, or bullying you?'

Zen looked amazed.

'No, course not! I wouldn't stop here if I didn't like it, would I? I mean, don't get me wrong, this house is great, I never had so much room before, and all this food, and all – ' she lifted her eyes from the fish she was examining with look and touch ' – but I wouldn't stop here just for that. I can look after myself. I could find somewhere, not as nice, but somewhere I could live, if I had to. It's the books and the teaching keeps me here. I'd stay even if it was mould up the walls, and cockroaches, and bread and ketchup every meal. I never knew I wanted it, but now I do I can't do without it, like a junkie. That sound mad to you?'

'No,' said Mary. 'No. I envy you. I thought my father had gone off his head when he took you in, but as usual he's right and I'm wrong.'

'Don't worry, I won't tell him.'

'You won't need to,' said Mary in mock despair. 'He'll know.'

After lunch Zen went upstairs for a rest, and once again Mary took a second pot of coffee through to her father's study. When she gave him a fresh cup, she laid the book she had bought him in his lap. He opened it at random, and studied the page.

'Good,' he said decisively.

'Zen looks tired,' said Mary. 'You mustn't work her too hard.'

He snorted.

'A lot you know! I'm the one who tries to stop her! She's like a greedy child let loose in a sweetshop; she doesn't know when to stop.' His eyes burned with the light of a true fanatic. 'That girl could do anything, go anywhere. If she carries on like this I could get her a place in college in a year or two. And she'd get a first, too. The waste of it! Criminal!'

'Well, you read the book I've bought you. She's small, she's probably never had an adequate diet, and she's expecting twins. I know she's being monitored by the midwife but you still need to be aware of the possible problems, and the signs of them. Swollen hands and feet, for

116

instance. Headaches. And by the same token,' she continued firmly, 'you must tell her *your* warning signs. What to do if you have another stroke, or a heart attack.'

To her surprise, he nodded.

'Fair enough. Though if it's a stroke there's not much she can do except dial 999, and she's got enough sense to know that anyway. Still.' He sipped at his coffee. 'You look tired too,' he said abruptly. 'That husband of yours making trouble, is he? Worried about Zen, I suppose.'

Mary sighed. Loyalty to John would not allow her to say too much, but her father was uninterested in such niceties and was capable of continuing to niggle at the subject for hours; and he was likely to move from that to the possible shortcomings of David's intended bride.

Distraction, she knew from past experience, was the only solution. Setting her mind to making the story as amusing as possible, she told him about Elaine Brantridge and the stabbing. He was amused, and showed it not merely by his sharp coughs of laughter, but by the lack of his usual interruptions.

'You want to watch out for her,' he said, when she had finished.

'Do you think so? I don't think she's really the murdering type.'

He grunted, glanced at her swiftly, and shook his head.

'Never mind.'

Mary swirled the dregs of coffee in her cup. Once, she remembered, John had had an Armenian client who had invited them for a meal, and his wife had read the coffee grounds as English people, in the days before tea bags, had looked for the future in the tea leaves. You are going to have a baby, a little girl, she had said to Mary and Mary, who was just pregnant and had told no one but John, had been impressed. She had never admitted it to anyone, but the idea that she was carrying a daughter had delved deep into her subconscious so that her first emotion, when David was born, had been astonishment and even the conviction that there must be some kind of mistake. Now, smiling at the memory, she gave the cup three swirls, put the saucer upside down on the top, and swiftly turned them both over.

'Won't work,' said her father. 'Not enough grounds when you make it like this. You want that thick Turkish coffee for that.'

Mary, who had momentarily forgotten his presence, upturned the cup and peered into its depths that were innocent of any significance at all.

'One of the most unbearable things about you, apart from the fact that you're always right, is that you always know everything. How did you know what I was doing?'

'Sickening, isn't it?' he agreed smugly. 'You forget I was out in Cairo during the war. See anything significant?'

'Not unless a complete blank is significant, which I suppose it could be. And speaking of knowing everything, how did you know about John's work?'

He frowned.

'I don't recall. Heard it on the grapevine, I suppose. No, I remember. He does my accounts for me, and I send everything off to him the minute it arrives, so nothing gets lost. You know how I hate all those nasty little forms and things. And a while ago he told me not to send them to the office any more, but direct to him at home. Said something about a reorganisation of the office, but I thought it a bit odd. I know he never likes taking work home. So I asked around a bit, and when nobody seemed to know what was going on I rang the firm. Didn't give my name, said I was a client and I wanted some advice. They told me he'd gone, offered me someone else, so I said no thanks and hung up.'

'He always told me not to ring him at the office, so I never did,' said Mary. 'You didn't say anything to me?'

'Well, you hadn't mentioned it, so I thought you didn't want to talk about it. I assumed he'd get another job somewhere. He's good enough at it, in a nit-picking, unimaginative sort of way. I knew you'd come to me if you were in difficulties.'

He spoke with the calm tones of absolute conviction. Mary looked at him for a moment as if she had never seen him before in her life, then dropped her eyes to the cup she still held. The saucer was slopping with coffee dregs. Carefully she set it down on the tray.

She was astounded. *I knew you'd come to me, if you were in difficulties.* The words rang in her head, reverberating as if against the polished inner surfaces of her skull. *I knew you'd come to me...* When, she wondered, was the last time she had done that? Had she ever done it? Before her mother's departure he had been a distant figure, approached only via her mother and viewed, always, with awe bordering on fear. All she really remembered about him from that time was his highly polished brown shoes, the leather buffed to a shine like the gloss of newly opened conkers, and his voice that seemed to come from somewhere unimaginably high, and which always said things she found quite incomprehensible.

After her mother had gone he had made an effort, she now realised, to help her. She remembered walks, her hand firmly clasped in his which he had kept rather high so that her arm was always uncomfortably raised. He would talk to her, telling her about his work which meant nothing to her but which she found flattering, but in the telling he would become drawn into some current line of research until his words became a monologue, declaimed as it were from the lecturer's desk. He would start out slowly, but gradually he would forget and his stride would grow longer and faster until she was almost running, three steps to his one. In the end he would come back from whatever academic reverie had engrossed him and become aware that she was lagging behind, her weight pulling on his arm. Then he would scold her, though not angrily, for not telling him that he was walking too fast, and Mary would hang her head, unable to tell him that she had not enough breath to make herself heard on his Olympian heights.

At first, Mary had assumed that she too would be going to America. In her world, children were looked after by their mothers – no matter that hers had not been very good at it – and she had thought it only a matter of days or weeks before the summons would come. The thought of the journey was both alarming and exciting. She did not expect her mother to come and fetch her. Even the short trips to nursery school had been seen as a dreadful chore and her mother had always arranged for someone else to do them. She supposed that some friend of her mother's would be cajoled into taking her across the Atlantic – her mother had always been very good at persuading people to do things for her – and the thought of the crossing absorbed her thoughts far more than the parting with her father, which she regarded as inevitable and assumed that he did too.

Even when several months went by it did not occur to her that this would not happen, and it was not until her father took her into his study to tell her that her mother was dead that she finally realised she would be staying with him. The news was in any case difficult to comprehend. She had been aware, as children are, that the current housekeeper was strongly opposed to something her father wanted to do. Snatches of low-voiced conversation drifted up stairs and through half-opened doors. 'No point in upsetting her . . . too young to understand . . . let her go on as she is' came hissing from the housekeeper's lips. Her father's replies, louder and clearer, were about honesty, telling the truth, facing up to reality, and her being old enough to understand. She had felt obscurely flattered by this, and had gone with more confidence than usual when he took her by the hand and led her to the study, closing the door firmly in the housekeeper's face.

He had, unusually, sat her on his knee. He had never been a cuddly father, and although he kissed her goodnight every evening and frequently stroked or patted her head, he had never been particularly demonstrative. Mary, even at six, had already noticed that she was larger than other children her age. It did not bother her particularly – she was not so fat that the other children made spiteful remarks, and adults had been known to remark how well-grown and sturdy she looked – but she saw from his face that he had required some effort to lift her on to his knee, and it made her anxious. He was so tall and thin that his thigh beneath her was bony. Was she too heavy for him, she wondered? Would she hurt him? She breathed in and held her breath as she did when she had her swimming lessons at the baths, willing her solid body to be lighter, to float on the air. As a result she did not take in what he was telling her at all.

Never a patient man, the re-telling of what was already so difficult to put into words must have been painful, but he explained it again. His command of language, as always, was precise and he had chosen his words carefully. Even so, the concept of death and its utter finality had been a hard one for Mary to grasp. Mummy had gone – of course she knew that – and had gone a long way away. She would not be coming back; but Mary had not expected her to come back. Professor Hill did not believe in God, and even to comfort a child he was not prepared to embark on soothing platitudes of Jesus and heaven and angels. Mary was left with the impression of immense distance, that her mother had gone so far away that it was impossible for Mary, or anyone else, to join her. She did not cry, for she had never been a tearful child, but when her father asked whether she had understood she nodded solemnly and he seemed relieved.

After that he had been almost gentle with her for a few months, and although she was mainly looked after by housekeepers it was always clearly understood that she might interrupt him at any time if she needed to – a privilege not even her mother had been awarded. A placid child, her small problems had seldom seemed to her important enough to bother him with, and she had besides an underlying fear of him taking her on to his knee again. The housekeepers were, in the main, the kind of women who classed themselves as 'good plain cooks' and, with memories of wartime rationing still fresh in their minds, there had been an over-emphasis on carbohydrates and an insistence on eating everything on one's plate.

To go to her father if she had a problem was, therefore, a habit that Mary had never developed. She tended to keep her problems to herself, regarding them as too private to be spoken of to others. It had sometimes occurred to her to wonder whether this were not why she never really progressed beyond a certain point in her friendships. Other women, she knew, poured out their feelings and worries to their friends in a way that she was quite unable to do. Even to be the recipient of confidences made her uncomfortable, and although she was always delighted to help in a practical sense, being endlessly ready to mind children, to cook or shop or look after the sick, she could feel her own withdrawal when friends, people she liked and was fond of, made chance references to marital problems or emotional difficulties.

'You're not in difficulties, are you?' he asked her now. 'About money, I mean? I assumed that John had money put by, and I suppose the income from what his mother left him, poor old thing.' John's mother had, in fact, been younger than Professor Hill, but it was true that her timid demeanour and apparent inability to make up her mind about anything had given an impression of age far beyond the Professor's years. 'Anyway, I've got a bit put by. Quite a bit, in fact, one way and another. You've only got to say. Better, anyway, to have it now and try to beat the old death duties, or whatever euphemism they've given it now.'

'You don't have to . . .' Mary was incapable of finding the words she wanted.

'I know I don't. If I had to, I probably wouldn't. You know me, always was an awkward old bastard.'

'Yes,' she said, humouring him. 'We're managing. But thank you.'

'So,' he said after a moment, 'he didn't tell you he'd lost his job? Doesn't surprise me, now I come to think about it.'

'He wanted to protect me,' said Mary, wanting to believe it. Her father gave a kind of barking grunt, such as she had heard him use when one of his students said something particularly fatuous. 'Well, I think he did. It's difficult for a man like him.'

'Everything's difficult for a man like him,' he growled.

'Really, Pa, you're not being very fair. You've never spoken about John like this before. I thought you liked him . . . well, I didn't think you *dis*liked him, anyway. You didn't say anything when I married him.'

He stirred uncomfortably.

'He was what you wanted. I thought you knew what you were doing, you always seemed so certain about things. And I don't dislike him. I can't see much there to dislike. Or to like, come to that. I suppose I'd always hoped he'd improve with age, get a bit of depth, a bit of character. Didn't hope for intellect, but . . . there should be *something* by now. Thought he'd learn from you.'

'From *me*?' For the second time in an hour Mary stared at her father in astonishment. 'What could he possibly learn from *me*?'

Now it was his turn to be surprised.

'If you don't know, how can I tell you?' he asked testily. 'All I know is, you wouldn't be sneaking around picking up gossip about other people and using it to make trouble.'

Mary frowned in thought, then laughed out loud.

'You're cross with him because he found out about Zen! Really, Pa, how childish! As if I wouldn't have found out about her anyway, next time I came over! And it hasn't made trouble, has it? That's just paranoia!'

He smiled reluctantly, the thin layer of flesh over the bones of his face creasing into lines that an actor might have drawn in when making up for an older part.

'I don't care to be the subject of *gossip*,' he said with mock austerity.

'Then you shouldn't behave in a way that gives rise to it. Come to that, it wasn't so much John gossiping as that other man, your old student. He was the one who saw you, and told John.'

He gave his grunt again. 'Rupert Greenwood. Second-class brain.'

Mary was aware that this related solely to her father's assessment of a student's probable degree potential (in which he was rarely wrong), and that what to him was second class would probably fall within the top ten per cent of the country, intellectually speaking. 'Nice chap, though,' her father added, astonishing her still more. It was almost unheard of for him to remark on any attribute other than intellectual ability. He had spoken to Mary for almost a year about one particularly brilliant young man, without ever thinking to mention to her that he was a paraplegic, a fact that seemed almost to have escaped his notice. 'I liked him.'

He spoke as one conferring an honour, which perhaps it was.

'Goodness,' said Mary. 'I'm not sure I even remember him. Perhaps I should go and look him up next time I'm in Reading. Try one of his sandwiches.'

She was half joking, but he nodded.

'Yes, you should. Tell him to come and see me when he's in Oxford.'

'Well, I don't go into Reading very often. Not that bit, anyway. It's such hell to park, for one thing. But if I do, I will.'

Bother it, she thought. Now I'll have to make a special journey into Reading to see this wretched man or I'll never hear the end of it. And if I'm not careful I'll run into John, and he'll be offended and think I'm checking up on him. Why is everything so complicated all of a sudden? It may have been a bit dull, before, but at least it was peaceful.

Chapter 11

'I don't remember him at all,' Mary remarked to her lover as she prepared the meal that evening.

'Remember who?' He was sitting in the rocking chair because Mary was using the table. The details of her kitchen, she noticed uneasily, were harder to see. It was all there when she looked directly at it and concentrated – the dresser with its display of china glowing against the soft sheen of the wood, the hyacinth on the scrubbed wooden table, the Aga – but she had to make a conscious effort to keep it there, and the white melamine cabinets kept intruding into her peripheral vision, the cushion flooring coming through the quarry tiles like tidal water welling up through sand.

'That's the trouble. I can't remember his name either. The man with the sandwich bar. Pa's ex-student, who told John about Zen.'

'Oh, him. Rupert something. Rupert Greenwood.' He rocked gently, not looking at her. Mary felt annoyed and slightly alarmed.

'But I'd forgotten his name!'

'You'd pushed it to the back of your mind. It was still there.'

'So how come you can get at it, and not me?'

For a moment his image wavered, and she concentrated fiercely on bringing him back. This was always a problem area. She had always to be careful not to admit to him or to herself – which was after all the same thing – that he was a creation, that he came from her mind and knew only the things that she herself knew. Now he smiled at her lazily, and looked directly into her eyes.

'Because I'm in your mind, too. In some ways I *am* your mind. You couldn't recall his name because you thought you didn't want to. But beneath that, you had kept hold of it, and the keeping hold was stronger than the wish not to remember.'

'Too complicated for me. So, Rupert Greenwood, then. I may

remember his name, but I certainly don't remember anything about him. It's too long ago, and there were too many of them. I wish I didn't have to go and see him. I'm not sure I like the sound of him. He could be a bit of a troublemaker.'

'Your father said he liked him.'

'Well, he's a troublemaker himself. He likes troublemakers. He calls it "having a bit of spirit". He always loved it when his students argued back at him, though he pretended to be angry to see if he could put them off, and he used positively to encourage them to go against the college authorities.'

'I don't suppose they needed much encouragement.'

'None at all. But they could use him as an excuse if they got into trouble. It used to make the Master livid, but Pa just thought it was funny. Well, I suppose it was, but I didn't think so then. It used to frighten me.'

The cat was on his knee, and he stroked it. The sound of purring rose like the hum of bees on blossom in May.

'The rows, or the students?'

'Both. The students mostly, I suppose.' Her hands fell idle as she thought about it. So many young men and women coming to the house to see her father. He conducted his tutorials in his rooms in college, but occasionally he would summon particularly favoured individuals to the house instead. In her teenage years Mary had been the envy of her classmates, and she had found herself unusually popular with other girls who visited her regularly in term time though not, she noticed, in the holidays when the students were not in Oxford. When, at eighteen, she had left school and signed on for a secretarial course she had hoped perhaps her non-existent social life might burgeon. Certainly there was an almost unending supply of people her own age and a bit older.

The trouble was, the awkwardness she felt with her own father (who, though he had been careful never to express any disappointment that she was of no more than middling ability academically, was unable to hide his impatience when she did not instantly understand the subtleties of what he was saying), seemed to smother her like a blanket when she came face to face with any his students. Opening the door to them – and looking back she realised that her father had increased his home tutorials significantly during this time – she would find herself tripping over the mat, offering to hold and then dropping their books and papers while they struggled out of their coats, her tongue uttering banalities or, worse still, inaudible gibberish that made her giggle helplessly while they stood in embarrassed silence.

A few had made the effort to get past the barrier of her shyness. One in particular had invited her out. Maxim, she thought. Good lord, I haven't thought of him for years. He had been attractive, too, which had made it all the more astonishing. Tall, with long untidy auburn hair – Mary glanced with sudden awareness at her lover, who was looking down at the cat in his lap and whose hair glowed with the same reddish gleam – he had smiled down at Mary and his eyes had seemed warm, appreciative, friendly. Mary had felt her knees turn to jelly and she had clamped her lips together to prevent them from uttering anything to destroy that look. Oh, the pleasure of being able to look up at him, when so many men were her own height or shorter.

When he had invited her out she had been amazed and terrified in equal proportions, and when the time came for him to collect her – he had been meticulous in making this offer and, in her innocence, it had not occurred to her that he was making sure her father knew about him – she more than half expected him not to turn up. He was ten minutes early and she was still dithering in her bedroom wondering whether the ethnic skirt she was wearing looked ridiculous, so as he had doubtless hoped her father opened the door to him and invited him in for a drink.

As a companion he had been attentive and amusing. They had gone to see a Buñuel film which Mary had found completely incomprehensible. To her relief he made no attempt to kiss her or even hold her hand – her palms were sweating at the thought and she wiped them surreptitiously on the skirt as often as she could manage it. She had been achingly aware of him next to her, and equally conscious of her own body that seemed to be larger than ever, trying to overflow from the seat, her long legs cramped against the row in front so that she had to sit awkwardly sideways in a position that restricted the blood supply to her legs. For some reason she had been overwhelmed by the need to swallow. She did so, and thought that the gulp she made must have been audible three rows away. She tried to breathe slowly and deeply, but her mouth seemed to be filling with saliva and she knew that in a few minutes she would have to swallow again.

It had been a relief when the film ended, and she almost looked forward to getting home and being on her own to come to terms with the humiliation of the evening. Maxim, however, had had other ideas, and had whisked her off to a pub for drinks. It had been only half an hour until closing time, and when she had finished her first drink rather quickly – it had been a relief to be able to swallow normally – he ordered two more for each of them. Uncertain what to ask for she had said she would like wine, but in those days pubs seldom sold wine by the glassful and he had suggested Dubonnet, which she had found comfortingly sweet but which, by the end of the third glass, had gone straight to her head.

As a result when, in the cold dankness of the hall at home, he had kissed her, she had responded with a certain abandon that surprised herself more than him. His hands had started to roam and, conscious of her size, she had sucked in her stomach and withdrawn slightly from his hold.

'What's the matter? Don't you like me?' His voice had been a masterly blend of sympathy and hurt.

'Oh yes, I do! Of course I do! It's only that . . .' She had been unable to say the words.

'That what?'

'That I'm so . . . so big,' she had mumbled, on the verge of tears.

His hands had pulled her back to his embrace.

'I don't like small girls,' he said simply. 'You seem just right to me. After all, I'm not exactly tiny, am I?'

In a daze of love Mary swam back into his arms, and embarked on a few months of happiness during which Maxim relieved her, without difficulty, of her virginity. She did not even put up a token resistance, glad to be able to give him something he wanted and feeling, for the first time, part of her generation and of the Swinging Sixties.

The affair had lasted until the results of his finals came out. He got an upper second, and had been furiously, blindly angry. He stormed and raved, not at Mary but at her father, who had blandly informed him that he had never been in line for a first, and that he, Professor Hill, had thought that had always been clear.

'But I thought . . . I mean, there's Mary . . . and naturally I assumed . . .'

'You may keep whatever you may have thought and assumed to yourself.' Mary, in the hall, had heard the cold anger in her father's voice, and shivered. The implications of what Maxim had said had not yet penetrated her mind, but they soon became clear when, with some apparent regret but with implacable firmness, he had told her they would no longer be seeing one another.

'I'm sorry, too, Mary,' he said, 'but I've got to move on. Look, you knew I'd be leaving Oxford, didn't you? That was always understood. And now I haven't got a first, who knows where I'll end up? I'd hoped to go into the City, make some easy money, but now I think maybe the States is the place for me. Or Australia, even. Somewhere a guy can get on, use his initiative without being slapped down for it.'

'Is that what I was?' she asked bitterly, made brave by her misery. 'A bit of initiative?'

'Now come on, Mary, don't be like that. We've had some good times, haven't we? You were happy enough with what I had to offer. And if I hoped for a bit of something in return, was that unreasonable?' His handsome face had been open, unshadowed by any doubt or guilt. His self-assurance had shrivelled Mary. She felt like a salted slug; she thought she could have writhed on the ground from the pain of it. She had recovered, of course, pushed Maxim out of her mind and returned doggedly to her everyday life, but her confidence had been eroded to the point where she preferred to avoid people of her own age, and particularly her father's students, altogether. A year later she had met John at an evening class, and the year after that she had married him.

Looking back, she found that on the whole she was grateful to Maxim. It was true that he had given her a few months of the kind of happiness she might otherwise never have known, and certainly his love-making had been skilful enough to enable her, in her turn, to teach the unimaginative John so that their sex life, though lacking the incandescent excitement of the earlier experience, had at least been satisfactory. Maxim was, also, the foundation of her creation of her lover, and she now acknowledged that there were many resemblances between them beyond the colour of his hair.

'How could I have forgotten Maxim?' she wondered aloud to her lover.

'You haven't forgotten him. He's always been there. Here.' He lifted his hand to his hair.

'You're very perceptive this evening.'

'I always am. When you want me to be.' He smiled, stretching out his legs so that the cat, affronted, jumped from his lap. 'What are you going to do with that fish? Time's getting on,' he reminded her. Mary jumped.

'Goodness, so it is. Sitting here daydreaming . . . it's a good thing that cat . . .'

'Isn't real?' He finished the sentence for her.

'Don't!' she said, as his image blurred. 'Don't go! I still need you!'

'The fish,' he said gently. 'Tell me about the fish.' Mary relaxed. Cooking was safe. It was real, too, one of the places where she could carry reality into her fantasy.

'Well, I left most of the salmon for Pa – Zen's getting much better about eating fish these days – and I thought I'd do these pieces of fillet in individual foil parcels. That way I can do John's how he likes it, and jazz mine up. I got some new potatoes, and I'll do a salad. Nice and easy.'

'Sounds good. And afterwards?'

'Rice pudding for John. You know how he loves it, with a dollop of jam. I'll have fruit, make it a really healthy meal. Rice pudding's no temptation anyway. I always think it looks exactly like sick. Smells like it, too, come to that.'

'Sick with jam. Lovely.'

Mary twisted the edges of the second foil parcel of fish together, and set it on the baking tray.

'There. Potatoes are ready to cook, salad's done, rice pudding's in the oven. Just the table to lay.' She always left that until last. Going backwards and forwards from the kitchen made it difficult to maintain the fantasy.

'What are you going to do about Rupert Greenwood?' Her lover, sensing the end of their meeting, stood up.

'Who? Oh, him. Go and see him, I suppose. Better get it over with; Pa always expects everything to be done instantly. I could pop in tomorrow morning, even. I've got to go into Reading anyway to pick up some copy invoices. That way I've got an excuse to get away if he's ghastly.'

'Why should he be ghastly?'

'I don't know. I'm just sure he is. I feel it in my bones.'

The feeling returned even more strongly the following morning. The sunshine had gone and with it the illusion of spring. A chilly wind blew, the sky was overcast with a thick, dismal layer of cloud that looked as though it would hang there for ever without actually raining. Mary, perversely, had resisted the temptation to dress up and had put on an old and rather shapeless woollen skirt and a pullover in a shade of dingy green that she knew did less than nothing for her skin. In the same spirit she had put no more than a dab of powder on her nose, a quick brushing of mascara only on her eyes, and no lipstick. In her five-year-old winter coat she looked, she thought, rather less exciting than a school dinner lady.

I really don't want to do this, she thought. Why don't I stand up to my father more? I did about Zen, why not about this? Because it's the easy way out, the other part of her mind told her brusquely. You can't be bothered to make the effort, and where has it got you? Right here, stuck in a . . . no, not stuck in a traffic jam.

'Blast it,' she said aloud as the lights changed to green and the cars moved smoothly forward. 'Bugger it. Buggerbuggerbugger.' She caught a glimpse of a scandalised face in the car alongside her and giggled. 'Fake eff,' she said to the face with an exaggerated movement of her lips. It cheered her up, but not much. The traffic continued to deny her any reason to be irritated. Every light was green, nobody cut her up, other drivers hung back courteously to allow her out of junctions, and there was a space in the car park right next to the stairs.

'This,' she said severely to the dashboard, 'is a conspiracy. I must be on my guard.'

There was still a faint hope that she would have to wait so long for the copy invoices that she would have no time to go to the sandwich bar, but here again fate let her down. They had them ready for her. Ten minutes later, with the missing invoices tucked into her bag, Mary found herself hovering on the pavement outside the snack bar. It was very small, and not at all what she had imagined. For some reason she had envisaged something aggressively modern, all white tiling, mirrors and stainless steel. Instead it was part of a much older building in a narrow sidestreet. The small window housed an attractive display of growing herbs in pots and glowing jars of pickles and chutneys, and from the open door came a warm smell of fresh bread and newly roasted coffee, and a drift of music – Mozart, she thought. It looked unthreatening, friendly, welcoming, just as a sandwich bar ought to look. How unfair, thought Mary. She had been so sure that she would hate it.

She dithered at the window, pretending to be examining the jars. The labels were handwritten, the contents interesting enough to distract her. Thai chilli sauce with garlic and coriander; tamarind and ginger chutney; Japanese pickled ginger; spiced brambles . . . Mary became engrossed in the ingredients and completely forgot what she was there for.

'Mary!' A voice roared from the inside of the shop. 'Mary Hill!' A man erupted through the open door, a huge bear of a man who had to stoop as he came through the entrance and who then stretched up to a height that towered over her. It was not so much that he was tall – which he was – but that he was so *big*. His shoulders were broad as a navvy's, his chest had the barrel-like proportions of an opera singer's, and legs like young tree trunks supported a stomach that just avoided being a paunch, but which spoke of many good meals, robustly enjoyed. A huge and spotlessly white apron was tied round his middle in a businesslike fashion. He held out two large hands, and Mary, stunned and bemused, put her own into them.

If she had thought about it, she would have expected a kind of warm double handshake. Instead she found herself pulled towards him, and kissed on the cheek. Not a 'mwa mwa' kiss in the air, but a proper kiss, his lips warm against her skin that had chilled while she hovered on the pavement. Taken by surprise her lips moved in an automatic response but in the air only. He stood back, keeping her hands still within his warm grasp, and looked down at her in apparent delight.

'Mary, how lovely to see you! I'd have known you anywhere! You haven't changed a bit!'

Mary, who had been feeling a glow of pleasure that she was finding it hard to analyse, remembered her dowdy clothes and minimal make-up, and wondered whether this was altogether a compliment. That he meant it as such was plain; equally plain was his sincerity. It was, she found, impossible to resent his ebullience. It would have been like kicking a large, friendly dog.

'Hello, Rupert,' she said inadequately. 'I was just admiring your window display.'

'Great, isn't it?' he responded enthusiastically. 'All homemade, and they're selling well. But what am I thinking of, keeping you out on the pavement? Come in, come in and have a coffee, have a sandwich, have some cake . . .' He was gently pulling her through the door as he spoke.

'You must be busy . . .'

'Never too busy for friends. Besides, it's a quiet time – breakfast rush nearly over, coffee-break rush not quite started. Come on, tell me what you think of it.'

Inside it was a long, narrow room with a polished wooden floor and walls painted a soft green. A wooden counter, complete with high bar stools, along the left-hand wall was stained in a toning green, and the counter continued round the back section which was higher, up two wooden steps, and had a window overlooking a minute garden. Two women, obviously out for a day of shopping, were chatting over cups and crumb-strewn plates, and a young man worked his way studiously through the job pages of a newspaper.

On the right was a serving area fronted by an enclosed glass display containing plates of cakes and biscuits, dishes of fillings, cold meats and pâtés, and piles of flat Italian focaccia bread, and behind that a small, spotless kitchen.

'It's lovely,' said Mary with genuine pleasure. 'I like it very much.' It had, to her, precisely the right blend of old-fashioned and modern. The coffee machine on the serving counter was the latest in Italian design, the kitchen equipment and layout were to a professional standard, but the overall impression was of a place that had been well used, giving it a comfortable air of homeliness that just missed being shabby.

His smile was wide, showing strong, even teeth. His face was large but, like his body, not fat, and quite tanned so that his blue eyes, though lacking the piercing colour of her father's, looked bright against it. His pleasure in her praise was obvious as if, surprisingly, he really minded what she thought. He ushered her to a seat near the serving counter, seating her with as much of an air as a *maître d'* at a three-star restaurant. He gestured expansively.

'Now, what will it be? Tea? Darjeeling, Earl Grey, Orange Pekoe, Indian – not bags, of course. A proper pot. Or coffee? Cappuccino? Hot chocolate, nice and frothy?'

'Cappuccino, please.' Mary peered into the kitchen, but could see nobody there. 'You mustn't let me hold you up,' she said firmly. 'Do you run this place all on your own? How on earth do you manage?'

'On my own? Good heavens, no!' His laugh was as big as the rest of him. 'I've got a couple of lads. They share the day between them, one for the morning until the lunchtime rush is over, then they overlap at lunchtime and the other takes over until we close at seven-thirty. They take it in turn to do the mornings – week on, week off. You know what these kids are like in the mornings, dead from the neck up. I've sent him off for fresh salad. He's a good shopper, I'll give him that, and he's better out and about than stuck in the kitchen washing lettuce like a somnambulist.'

'Aren't they,' she said, with memories of the boys in the workshop. 'None of them seem to come alive before midday. And do you do the whole stint? It's a long day.'

'Long enough, but I enjoy it.' He lifted a flap in the serving counter and inserted himself neatly through a gap that looked scarcely wide enough for him. With what was obviously a movement so automatic that he was unaware of what he was doing he washed his hands at a corner basin, then pressed buttons on the coffee machine and assembled a mug-sized cup with matching saucer. While the machine hissed and hummed he considered the cakes, then with a pair of tongs he picked up a slice of something dark and luscious-looking, and put it on a plate. 'You're not going to tell me you don't eat cake, are you? This is a new recipe, and I'd really like to know what you think of it.'

'It looks lovely. Thank you,' said Mary weakly. He brought her the coffee and cake, then went back to a chopping board where he picked up a large kitchen knife and began to slice cucumber into wafer-thin circles. The knife moved so fast Mary could scarcely focus on it, but even so from time to time he lifted his eyes (without ceasing to chop) and glanced at her.

'So, what brings you to this neck of the woods?' he asked. 'You weren't looking for your husband, were you? I'm afraid he only comes in at lunchtime.'

'No, no, nothing like that,' said Mary hurriedly. 'He told me he'd seen you, of course. And ... what you'd said. About my father,' she enlarged in answer to his questioning look.

'The Professor! Yes, I saw him the other week. I was in a tearing rush or I'd have stopped and had a word with him. Wonderful man, isn't he?'

It was the sort of remark that Mary always found it hard to answer. Her father was, of course, wonderful in many ways. It was just that she sometimes found it difficult to see him like that.

'Mm,' she said non-committally. 'I'm afraid John was more con- cerned about the girl you saw him with.'

His look was comically guilty.

'Oh lord, I never thought! I didn't make trouble, did I? It's the last thing I would have wanted. Come to think of it, poor old John did look a bit pinched and tight-lipped about it. I'm afraid I just thought it was typical of the Professor. He never minded what anyone looked like, or how old or young they were, as long as they had a good brain. I was just so pleased to see that he hadn't changed. So many people fossilise as they get older, don't they?'

'Some of them are fossils from the word go,' said Mary rather unwisely. To keep herself quiet she took a mouthful of cake. It was delicious, light and spicy and tasting of banana and lemon.

'Well, it's different when it's family,' said Rupert tactfully. He scooped the cucumber into a dish and began to peel avocados.

'He liked you too,' said Mary. 'Father, I mean. In fact, that's why I'm here. He said to come and see you, and tell you to call in if you were in Oxford. He's retired now, of course, and he had a slight stroke a while ago, but he's still pretty lively.'

'I'd love to. This,' his hand swept out for a moment, indicating the sandwich bar, 'is partly thanks to him, in a way. I wasn't really up to his standards, academically, but we used to talk about food a lot. He used to encourage me to try things, to experiment with flavours. He was open-minded about that, too, and that's very rare.'

'You're telling me! John doesn't really even like onion, let alone garlic! So,' she continued hastily, thinking she must be more loyal, 'have you been cooking ever since?'

'Far from it. I married straight after Oxford, and I needed a secure job so I joined my father-in-law. Insurance brokerage. Very sensible, quite lucrative, deadly dull. I stuck it out for fifteen years, then one day I just couldn't stand it any longer. My wife and I had been drifting apart, and I knew she was seeing someone else. I got a job in the Middle East – very well paid, but a short-term contract. She came out with me, but she hated it, and we split up. The kids were at boarding school by then, and being abroad I got the fees paid by the company. They split their time between us during the holidays, and of course they're grown up now. They spend a lot of time with me – they helped me set up this place, actually. One of them has a friend who's training as a chef. By the time I came back to England I'd got a fair bit of capital put by, enough to keep me going while I had a go at doing what I wanted to do. So here I am.'

'What fun.' Mary felt quite envious. 'How do you make the pickled ginger pink?'

'A bit of beetroot in the vinegar.'

'And how do you stop the avocado going brown? I know they say lemon juice, but I never find it works all that well and if you put too much on it kills the flavour of the avocado.'

Before Mary knew where she was, they had embarked on a culinary discussion she enjoyed so much that she suddenly realised half the morning had slipped away.

'Goodness, I must go! I'm supposed to be at work!'

'Must you? I wanted you to try the curried chicken ... You must come back again soon. You didn't remember me, did you?'

The question was so sudden that Mary was unprepared for it.

'No, I'm afraid not. I'm sorry. I can't think why...'

He concentrated on his chopping.

'You were tied up with that bastard Maxim, in my first year. I don't think you could see beyond him to take in anyone else. I thought he was a bit of a shit ... but ... then you rather disappeared from view in my second year until you turned up with John in tow.'

'Oh.' What was he telling her? Surely not that he had fancied her? The thought made her want to giggle. She must be getting funny in her middle age, thinking every man she met was interested in her. First Mr Naseby, now Rupert Greenwood. Hastily she stood up and edged towards the door.

'I really *must* go,' she said, rather desperately. 'Work, you know, and ... but I will come back. I'd like to try your sandwiches. And some of your pickles and things. Next week. Perhaps. And thank you for the coffee, and the cake. It was lovely...'

He stretched up to his full height, and smiled at her.

'It's all right,' he said. Mary felt the anxiety leech out of her.

'Yes,' she said. 'Yes, it's all right. I must go, but I'll see you soon. And if you do manage to get to Oxford, do take Pa a pot of the tamarind, I think he'd love it. Or the Thai chilli sauce.'

'I'll take both,' he said. He leaned over to kiss her goodbye, and this time she was prepared for the gesture and kissed him back. His cheek, slightly rough although she could see that he had shaved that morning, smelled very faintly of aftershave. Of, more specifically, the aftershave she had chosen to give her lover. Embarrassed, Mary almost ran from the shop.

Chapter 12

'You are all coming to lunch on Sunday. I have arranged it.'
Professor Hill's voice was cheerfully brisk, and Mary experienced a feeling of helpless doom.

'All? All, as in, all of us?'

'That is, I believe, the generally accepted use of the word. Of course it might mean something quite different by now. Political correctness has a great deal to answer for.'

'What I mean is, all as in John and I – me? Or do you mean David and Alison as well?'

'Of course I mean David and Alison as well. I must meet my grand-daughter-in-law elect. And I assume, in the absence of any other family members, that she would be interested in meeting me.'

'Of course she wants to. David said so the other day. I told him to ring you.'

'So he did.' The Professor responded with awful patience. 'He telephoned me, and I invited him and – what's her name? Alice?'

'Alison.'

'Pity. Then I thought I'd make an occasion of it – to mark the event, as it were – and tell you and John to come too.'

'What you really want is for me to come and cook the lunch,' said Mary. Goodness, she thought. I'd never have spoken to him like that a few weeks ago. Has he changed, or have I? In the few weeks since first meeting Zen – it was now early March – Mary felt that she had become, if not a different person, at least a more open one.

'Not at all. Zen will cook the lunch.'

'Oh. Right.'

'I shall expect you at mud – midday,' said her father, and rang off. Mary replaced the receiver. The small lapse in his speech – something that rarely happened now that he was talking to Zen all the time –

137

reassured her that he was less relaxed about the planned meeting than he wanted her to think. Surely even he must realise that John, David and Alison were likely to be surprised, at the very least, by Zen. She rubbed the telephone thoughtfully with a duster where her fingers had left sticky smears.

It was a Tuesday, and she was polishing the hall floor. It was a job she rather enjoyed, the smell of the polish filling her with the rapturous pleasure some women get from air-dried washing or boiling marmalade. She was wearing rubber gloves (John preferred not to acknowledge that she did all the housework herself and was critical of stained or roughened hands), and now her hands felt hot and sticky. She started to tug the gloves off. It was better, in any case, to leave the polish for a little while before shining it up. She would have a soothing cup of coffee and sit down for ten minutes.

The telephone rang again, making her jump. Clumsily, with the gloves half off because they were sticking to her fingers, she picked it up.

'Did you go and see that chap Rupert Greenwood?' Her father's voice, without preamble, was speaking even before she had the receiver to her ear.

'Yes, I did. I told you. I went one morning, and then last week I went there for lunch. I brought you a pot of his chutney.'

'So you did. Well, I invited him too. He came over to see me – brought me some really excellent sauce he'd made. Nice chap. Got on well with Zen. So I thought I'd ask him.'

Mary was surprised.

'Did you?'

'No, I'm lying to you.'

'Just as well if you are,' she responded with a spurt of irritation. 'I thought this was to be a family event. I think Alison and David might be rather put out to find you've invited a complete stranger to join us.'

'Put out! Put out? They're not cats, girl. If you mean they'll be offended, then say so. Too bad if they are, anyway. It's my house, isn't it?'

'Undoubtedly. And David is your only grandson.'

'Well, it doesn't matter anyway. He said he wouldn't come. Said he's busy, but I don't believe him. He only remembered he was busy after I'd let on about David and Alison.'

'Then why are you ringing me about it, if he's not coming anyway?'

138

Mary, the phone held to her ear by one hunched shoulder, was pulling at the gloves.

'So that you can persuade him, of course. Go and see him again. You'll be able to make him change his mind.'

'Certainly not. He's got some sense, and some good manners too. He won't change his mind, and if I try to make him he'll be embarrassed. Ask him some other day.'

'I don't want him another day! I want him *that* day.'

'Then want must be your master,' said Mary austerely.

'I may have had a stroke but I'm not senile yet! Don't talk to me as if I were a child, my girl.'

'Then don't behave like one.'

'Hmf.' Mary's glove finally came free. The jerk as it did so dislodged the telephone receiver, which crashed to the floor. By the time she picked it up again, he had gone.

Oh dear, thought Mary. He'll think I hung up on him. What has got into me? I feel quite liberated, all of a sudden. Nevertheless, when the phone rang for a third time she jumped guiltily, and picked it up nervously, half expecting to hear his angry voice.

'Um, sorry, Pa,' she said.

'It's not the Prof. It's me, Zen. The crazy old coot wants me to cook a meal for you all on Sunday. I told him I couldn't do it, but he's insisting. What'll I do? I can only cook about four things, the ones you showed me. Sunday, it should be a roast. I never cooked a roast. I don't even know how big it should be or anything. And what about pudding? And how do you do roast potatoes?'

Her voice was rising.

'Calm down,' said Mary. 'It's bad for the babies. And don't worry, roasts are easy, it's just a matter of timing.'

'But...'

'I'll come over on Saturday and we'll get it all set up, and make some kind of pudding too.'

'Oh, would you? Can you really?'

'Of course. It'll be fun. And we won't tell them you had any help, just let them think you did it all.'

Zen giggled. 'Right. And you're sure I can do it?'

'My father thinks you can do anything you set your mind on, and I wouldn't dare question his judgement.'

'That's different. The work I do with him is in my mind. Intellectual.

Cooking's not like that, and he doesn't really know about that kind of thing. So, do *you* think I can do it?'

It was a novel kind of pleasure, to have her opinion given precedence over her father's.

'Yes, I'm quite sure you can,' she said warmly.

'Nice day,' said Alison.

'Yes, isn't it.' Mary thought that her answer had been a bit tepid, so she expanded. 'Lovely sunshine. And quite warm, too.'

'When you're out of the wind.'

'Yes, of course. But it is only March, after all.'

'Yes.'

They lapsed into silence. They sat in the back of the car, heading to Oxford. In the front John and David were talking golf as usual. Mary had wondered whether David wouldn't have preferred to sit in the back with Alison, so that they could hold hands and murmur to one another. He showed no signs of wanting to, and when she came to think of it she had never seen them behave like that anyway. They were more like an old married couple, she thought, than a newly engaged couple. In fact, they were depressingly like her and John. The prospect filled her with gloom. She sighed.

'You must be worried about your father,' said Alison sympathetically. Mary turned from looking out of the window. Alison's eyes were bright with – what? Sympathy, or curiosity?

'Worried? Well, a bit of course, but he's a great deal better. He's being quite good about taking his tablets these days, and the doctor seems to think there's not too much risk of another stroke, as long as he's sensible. Not that he is, of course, but still . . .'

'He's very clever, isn't he?' said Alison in tones of dubious reverence. 'But that wasn't quite what I meant. I was talking about that girl who's got her hooks into him.'

'I wouldn't have put it quite like that.'

'Oh, but surely . . . she sounds so peculiar.'

'Well, we're all a bit peculiar, aren't we? I mean, to somebody.'

'I suppose so.' Alison sounded affronted. She looked as though she thought that however odd the rest of the world might be, she herself could never under any circumstances be considered anything but normal. Mary suppressed another sigh, then initiated a banal conversation about Alison's work, which she managed to keep going until they arrived, mainly by asking rather inane questions that Alison seemed to enjoy answering. She would have made a good teacher, thought Mary. Her patience with the dim-witted was admirable.

The size and darkness of the hall seemed to daunt Alison somewhat, and Mary was pleased to see her edging closer to David. Professor Hill emerged from his study on a waft of peat smoke.

'Chimney needs sweeping,' he said. 'So, this is Alicia?'

'Alison,' corrected John. 'Good morning, Professor.'

The Professor accorded him a nod of greeting. John nudged David forward.

'Introduce Alison to your grandfather,' he instructed.

'Oh, er, yes. Of course.' David was flustered. As a child he had called the Professor 'Grandprof', but recently he had been made to feel that this was a little babyish. As a result he no longer knew what to call him, finding both 'Professor' and 'Grandfather' rather formal. Occasionally, to his chagrin, the influence of his schooldays reasserted itself and he found himself calling him 'sir'. Alison came to his rescue, stepping forward and holding out her hand.

'How do you do, Professor Hill? I'm Alison Sutton. I've heard so much about you.'

To Mary's relief her father shook the proffered hand – he had been known to ignore such gestures. Mary hoped that this meant he was intending to be agreeable.

'Yes, I expect you have,' was his disconcerting reply. 'I must hope to correct the balance today, must I not?'

Oh good, thought Mary. He's in one of his courtly moods. I wonder where Zen is? She glanced round surreptitiously. Beneath the tang of peat smoke she could smell the roasting pork, which was a good sign.

'A celebratory drink seems to be called for,' announced Professor Hill. 'I fear my study is untenantable until the smoke clears. We will repair to the drawing room.'

Mary raised her eyebrows at him. One eyelid drooped, and for a moment she was reminded of how he had been immediately after his stroke. Then she realised that he was winking.

The drawing room, that to Mary's knowledge had not been used for several years, had obviously been carefully spruced up. The sunshine streamed in on polished furniture and thoroughly vacuumed carpets. A vase of daffodils stood on the table between the pair of French windows, and a bowl of early primroses on the coffee table, and the fire (of logs, not peat) glowed and crackled cheerfully. Amid this genteel, if faded splendour sat Zen, like a Rackham goblin set in the middle of a Mabel Lucie Attwell picture.

Mary had entertained (and been ashamed of) a sneaking hope that Zen might have decided to tone down her appearance. Now she found she was rather pleased to see that, if anything, it was more striking than ever. A bright orange tee-shirt, its neck cut away (by hand, and by someone with a severe tremor by the look of it) so low that it scarcely covered her nipples, fought violently with a red skirt so short that it revealed the black suspenders that held up a pair of purple fishnet stockings. Her hair, as brightly coloured as ever and echoing, Mary noticed, the colours of her clothes, was brushed free of the little plaits, which had left it frizzed so that it stood out like a technicolour halo round her face that looked, in contrast, whiter than ever.

Zen stood up. She was wearing gold shoes with four-inch platform soles. Her red skirt, that rather resembled the little skirts Mary had worn to go ice skating in London during her childhood, was pushed out by the swell of her stomach so that it jutted forward like a lampshade. Mary's eyes met her father's bright blue ones that looked on with bland urbanity.

'Ah, there you are, Zen, my dear,' he said. 'Mary you know, of course, but allow me to introduce her husband, John,' he paused while John, holding his body as far away from her as feasible, stretched out an unwilling hand. 'And this is David, my grandson,' another pause, 'and Alice – I beg your pardon, Ali*son*, who is going to marry David at some unspecified time in the future.'

'That's great,' said Zen, shaking Alison's hand with enthusiasm and appearing not to notice that Alison was trying to pull it back. 'But why wait?'

'I don't believe in rushing into things,' said Alison primly. She glanced at her hand, as though checking for contamination, then allowed her eyes to veer sideways to Zen's all-too-protruding stomach. Mary felt a little niggle of rage somewhere round the base of her spine. 'We think it's important to do things properly, don't we, David? David!' she repeated more loudly, for David was standing transfixed, staring at Zen in such palpable astonishment that he appeared mesmerised. Mary was vividly reminded of a five-year-old David at the zoo, staring in terrified fascination at a brightly coloured snake. He started.

'What? Oh, yes, that's right. Do it properly. Um.' He looked, thought Mary sadly, rather foolish. Alison must have thought so too, because her lips tightened and she glared at David, summoning him peremptorily with a jerk of her head. Mary wondered whether this sharpness was something new. His stunned expression was replaced by a small frown.

There was a short, brittle pause while they all eyed one another.

'Didn't you say something about drinks, Pa?' asked Mary in desperation.

'Did I? Yes, of course I did. Champagne, I thought.' He went to the corner of the room, and all their eyes followed him. He busied himself with the bottle, taking a long time to untwist the wire. John shifted on his feet, longing to offer help but knowing from past experience that he would be rebuffed. At last the cork came free with a loud pop, and the wine hissed out. Deftly the Professor scooped a glass beneath the neck of the bottle and caught the first spurt, then poured the rest. He brought the glasses on a tray, jingling gently together as his hands shook slightly, and turned the tray in an alarming fashion to bring each glass near to its recipient. When they were all served he took his own glass and lifted it.

'I think I should mark the occasion by proposing a toast,' he said. 'So . . . to new beginnings.'

'New beginnings,' they all muttered, and sipped. Mary thought again how much she disliked champagne. There was another silence.

'Should you be drinking, in your, er, condition?' asked Alison accusingly. 'I've heard it can lead to problems. Lack of intelligence, that sort of thing . . .' There was, in her voice if not in her words, the clear implication that the babies were scarcely likely to be very bright anyway, born to such a mother. The little worm of rage stirred, and sent small electric *frissons* up Mary's spine, and David's frown deepened as he tried to catch Alison's eye. Zen smiled broadly, took another swig with every appearance of pleasure, then set down her empty glass. Her foot sneaked out to push the bottle of sparkling apple juice by the table further out of sight.

'I'll just go and check in the kitchen,' she said and moving lithely, in spite of her pregnancy and the platform soles, left the room.

'Well, *really*!' said Alison to no one in particular.

'Why don't we all sit down,' suggested Mary through gritted teeth. Alison promptly took her place on a sofa and looked up for David to join her. He leaned over her, murmuring in her ear. Mary, unashamedly eavesdropping, heard Alison say sharply, 'Don't be ridiculous, David. She's nothing but a tart.' David, to Alison's obvious rage and astonishment, turned abruptly away from her. In the end it was John who came to occupy the other seat on the sofa. The Professor took an armchair, Mary sat down in the matching sofa opposite Alison, and David, finally, wandered over to sit beside her. His grandfather, still behaving as though this were a perfectly normal party, asked him a question about his work, and Mary leaned back against the cushions and breathed slowly. She longed to rush to the kitchen and check that all was well, but they had agreed the day before that everything was to be left with Zen. Mary only hoped her protégée had not decided to spike up the joint with garlic and chilli, as she had half threatened to do.

John and Alison began a low-voiced conversation beneath the cover of the other voices. Mary had no difficulty in imagining what they would be saying. She tried to feel that glow of anger again to warm her, but even that had faded away into a dismal feeling of guilt; that if they had been children picking sides it would have been Zen's side and not her husband's she would have taken. Beside her, David was glowering at his glass.

Zen came back into the room. There was a little flush of pink beneath the white of her make-up.

'I think it's nearly ready,' she said.

'Oh, can I help you?' asked Alison. 'You must be rushed off your feet.' She glanced at the preposterous shoes, and John gave a sour little smile.

'Don't worry, Alison.' Mary was already standing up. 'You don't know this kitchen, it'll be better for me to go.' She was out of the door before Alison could protest, and pulled it firmly shut behind her.

'Does it look all right? I can't get the puddings out of the oven, they're catching on the top.'

'Don't worry, that just means they've risen beautifully,' said Mary calmly. It was one of her father's firmly held beliefs that Yorkshire pudding should be served with any roast, not just beef. They had settled on pork, since it was less likely to spoil by being overcooked, and Mary was relieved to see that the crackling was perfect, brown and crunchy and just the least bit scorched at the edges. 'I'll make the gravy, and you strain off the vegetables. Is the pudding there? We can put it in now the joint's in the warmer oven.'

Mary decided to do the carving, as she always did at home. Zen put the vegetable dishes on the table, then went to fetch the others.

'Eating in the dining room? We are grand today.' John's voice was as sour as his smile had been.

'Special occasion,' said the Professor. 'After all, we have a new member of the family.' Alison bridled smugly, but behind her back he was smiling at Zen. Mary, fortunately, was the only person who noticed.

The meal was delicious – Zen had adhered rigidly to the timetable she and Mary had worked out, and followed her every instruction to the letter. John refused the little stuffing balls because they had dried apricot in ('Funny idea, I always think, having fruit with meat') but everyone else enjoyed them, David even going so far as to remark on the crisp coating of sesame seeds. Alison darted him a meaningful glance, but he ignored it. She started to talk to the Professor.

'I gather you're still keeping up with your work,' she said, her polite tones barely masking the opinion that at his age it was scarcely worth the bother.

'I certainly am,' the Professor replied heartily. 'And do you manage to keep up with yours?'

Alison blinked, and decided to abandon this line.

'David calls you Grandprof, doesn't he? That's rather sweet.'

'Sweet. Hmf. Suitable for a small child.'

'So what shall I call you?' She tilted her head archly. 'Professor seems so formal.'

'Does it?' For once, he looked surprised. 'It's what everyone calls me. It's what I am.'

'But you must have a name,' she persisted. 'A. V. Hill, I've seen it on your books. What does the A. V. stand for?' Mary cringed, knowing what would come. Her father's eyebrows bristled, his eyes seemed to glow a brighter blue than ever.

'Archibald,' he said. 'Archibald Victor.'

Mary stifled a giggle. No one, as far as she could remember, had ever called her father Archibald. Or worse still, Archie. Even her mother, like Zen, had called him Prof. Maybe, far off in his childhood, his mother had called him Archibald, but no one since those distant days had ever used the much-disliked name. Alison, looking daunted, addressed herself to her plate.

'I gather my grandfather is teaching you,' David said to Zen, making the remark almost a question.

'That's right.' She chewed (with her mouth closed, Mary was relieved to see) and swallowed. 'He's been really kind. You're lucky to have a grandad like him.'

'Yes,' said David dubiously, not always having seen it quite in that light. 'But why do you want to learn history, in particular?'

'Oh, we don't just do history,' she replied blithely. 'We do everything. Writing, spelling, how to do things – it's not like school, everything cut up into separate things so you don't realise how they all connect. He tells me how to say things, and how to find things out – the other day he had me looking things up all morning in the library. He even told me how to hold my knife and fork, and how to eat!' She smiled, completely unselfconscious. John looked embarrassed. Table manners were something he felt very strongly about. He couldn't imagine how anyone could admit to needing to learn them.

David's brow wrinkled. He looked, Mary thought, just as he did when there was some discrepancy in the figures and he had to find the cause. 'Doesn't it bother you?' he asked. Zen looked puzzled. 'I mean, it's changing the way you are. Making you into something different.'

'Why should I mind that?' She laid a hand on her stomach. 'These little bas— – little beasts – are making me into something different, anyway. I've never been a mum before, have I? What's the difference?'

He shook his head. 'It is different. That sort of change is an external force.' He looked at her to see if she was following him, and she nodded. 'What, um, my grandfather is doing is imposing a different set of values on you.' He glanced rather nervously at the Professor, who leaned back in his chair and nodded, satisfied. 'It's a kind of criticism, isn't it? What if he started telling you, well, how to dress, for instance? You'd mind that, wouldn't you?'

Zen chewed thoughtfully.

'Depends,' she said in the end. She seemed to be picking up the Professor's telegraphic style, Mary thought. 'If I was–' ('Were,' corrected the Professor. 'Subjunctive.') '–were going to an interview, say. For a job in a posh shop.'

The Professor snorted. 'I'm not educating you just so you can sell expensive make-up to women with nothing better to do than buy it.'

'No, it's just a f'rinstance. If that was what I was – were – doing, I'd know I had to dress up a bit.' ('Down, surely,' murmured Alison.) 'I'd ask the Prof's advice, or Mary's. And I'd take it, too. I'd be mad not to.'

'Yes,' agreed David. 'But supposing he – the Professor – told you how to dress all the time, like he tells you how to speak. You wouldn't like that, would you?'

'No, 'course not. But I wouldn't take any notice of him.' David looked sceptical. He found it hard to imagine anyone not taking notice of his grandfather. ''S true. I'd tell him to kiss me where the monkeys go.'

Alison choked on her mouthful of pork, and had to be pounded on the back by John.

'What a bizarre phrase,' said the Professor. 'Bizarre, but telling. A combination, I suppose, of where the monkey put his nuts, and kiss me arse.' He smiled benignly round the table.

'It's what my nan always said,' Zen told him. 'She was a laugh, my nan. Still, that's not what we're talking about, is it? You still got problems?'

David, typically, was still worrying at the problem like a dog at a bone. He leaned forward earnestly.

'But isn't it, well, demeaning? The way you speak, the way you hold a knife and fork; those things aren't supposed to matter any more, are they?'

'Try telling that to someone when you go for a job. Of course they matter! They matter to you, don't they? Otherwise you'd be picking that bit of crackling up in your fingers, instead of trying to balance it on your fork!'

He looked down at his plate, startled. The piece of crackling, impervious to the tines of his fork, was balanced precariously on top of them.

'Pick it up, boy,' said Professor Hill testily. 'Remember *Cranford*!'

'Cranford?' repeated David. 'I don't think I know who Cranford is.'

'Not who. What! It's a book. Mrs Gaskell, nineteenth century. Wonderful bit where they go out to lunch with an old gentleman who still uses two-pronged forks, and they're given fresh young peas to eat. There they are, picking them up two by two, and they see the old chap shovelling them in on the blade of his knife. The old lady won't do it, but the young one does! "I saw, I imitated, I survived!" Wonderful stuff!'

Mary looked at Alison's shocked face, and felt a bubble of hilarity rise in her.

' "I eat my peas with honey," ' she murmured.

'I *beg* your pardon, dear?' John was looking at her as though she'd grown a second head but David, after a moment's puzzled reflection, grinned.

' "I've done it all my life," ' he said.

'Really, David!' said Alison, but he ignored her.

' "It makes the peas taste funny," ' continued Mary.

' "But it keeps them on the knife!" ' they finished in chorus. Mary smiled at David, suddenly seeing the dear little boy that he had been. 'You remember that one, then?'

'Of course I do! I used to think it was the funniest thing I'd ever heard!'

'It looks as though you still do,' said Alison sharply. 'I must say,' she said, turning to the Professor, 'it's very kind of you to do so much for, er, for Zen.' She spoke the name with distaste. 'I just hope it isn't too much for you. You should be careful, at your age and with your health. You don't want to overdo it.' She smiled at him as she spoke, all sweet concern. The implication that Zen had so much to learn that it was likely to wear him out was clear beneath the sugar-coated exterior.

'Overdo it.' He repeated the phrase slowly, his mouth pursing fastidiously as if the words were tainted. 'I am not a rib of beef. I will not be damaged by being "overdone". It is "underdoing", if you like, that is the curse of the old. Not enough to do, and too much time to do it in. Useless. I will not be useless.'

'Oh, I didn't mean . . .' bleated Alison. 'I only thought, since your stroke . . .' Her eyes moved helplessly to David and then, when she saw that his look was fixed on his plate, on to John.

'It's very nice of you to be concerned, dear,' he said to her kindly. 'Isn't it, Professor?'

The Professor opened his mouth to speak, encountered a furious glare from Zen and an entreating look from Mary, and closed it again.

'Of course it is, and she's quite right too,' said Zen. 'You always think you can do more than you can, Prof; you're as daft as a brush sometimes. But don't worry,' she smiled radiantly round the table. 'I'll take care of him.' There was a stunned silence. 'Anyone want seconds?' she asked. 'There's plenty, just help yourselves.'

Chapter 13

'How did the lunch go?' Rupert's voice was carefully neutral. Too neutral. Had her father been speaking to him? Mary scarcely cared. She took a scalding mouthful of cappuccino and licked the froth off her top lip. The cocoa that had been sprinkled on the froth was clean and bitter on the back of her tongue.

'Ghastly,' she said gloomily. 'They all behaved in a completely stereotypical way, if that's a word. Except David. Alison was so rude to Zen, and he's a very *chivalrous* boy, if that's not a silly thing to say. He was so annoyed with Alison that he talked much more to Zen than he might have done, and he found her very interesting.'

Rupert raised an eyebrow.

'*Interesting?* Or just interesting?'

'Oh, just interesting. I don't think he found her attractive, in the physical or the romantic sense. It was more as if she were some kind of exotic animal in the zoo – fascinating, but you wouldn't want to keep it as a pet. So they got on all right. But the rest of them!' She drew in a breath, tasting the vinegar tang of the pickled vegetables he was cutting. Rupert made a sound halfway between a grunt and a growl. It reminded her of a teddy bear she had once owned, that had emitted a similar sound when squeezed. It was a consoling noise, indicating interest, sympathy and amusement in equal proportions. Rupert the bear, she thought, with a private smile, and wondered how many times he must have been bored by that joke.

'Zen,' she continued, 'was in full, glorious technicolour, and then some. Her top – bright orange – was chopped away so low at the neck I thought her bosoms would fall out every time she leaned forward. Alison and John ganged up, went all precious and prissy. You know, I always thought that girl was so meek, without a thing to say for herself, but underneath that mimsy exterior she's got a sharp little way with her.

Of course she expected to be the Queen Bee, just engaged and all that, and Zen upstaged her, in spades. John, of course, is terrified that Zen will get some kind of hold over my father and that he'll go potty and leave everything to her – as if he would, or as if I'd care! – and he didn't know whether to be relieved by her outlandish get-up, or just appalled. I think appalled won. He thinks even henna is morally suspect and ought to be a prohibited substance, so you can imagine what he thought of her hair...' She took another pull at her coffee, sucking it in as though the fluid were life-giving. Rupert continued to slice, the economical rhythmic movement somehow soothing.

'As for my father, he was the worst of the lot. You know, he can be positively wicked sometimes! I'm quite sure he encouraged Zen to wear those clothes – four-inch platform soles, I ask you, for a girl six months pregnant! The thought of her going up and down stairs in them makes me feel quite sick! And encouraging Alison to make nasty, snide little remarks. Not that she needed encouragement, exactly. And I suppose he didn't precisely encourage, only I know very well he could easily have stopped her. But did he? No! He just sat there smiling inscrutably like a nasty, thin old Buddha.'

'But Zen wasn't upset, was she?'

'No, not a bit. I'm afraid she thought it was rather funny. They're both as bad as each other. Oh dear.' Mary gave a little hiccupping laugh that was only just not a sob.

'I wish I'd been there.'

'So do I. I was so grateful to you when Pa said you'd said no – did I tell you he wanted me to persuade you to change your mind? – but when it came to it I'd have been so thankful for just one normal human being. Am I really surrounded by freaks and weirdos, or does it just feel like that?'

'What's normal? All families are pretty weird, when you get close to them. And the "normal" ones,' his fingers sketched quote marks in the air, reminding Mary sharply of her father, 'are the weirdest of all.'

'Maybe.' Mary gave a reluctant laugh. 'I suppose it was rather funny, actually. You would have found it so, anyway.'

'Not necessarily,' he said mildly, scooping the chopped vegetables into a dish. 'Not if it was upsetting you.' A timer pinged and he bent to open an oven door. At once the air was filled with the rich brown smell of fruit and spices. Mary was distracted.

'What's that?'

'Simnel cake. I always make it for a few weeks of the year, from Mothering Sunday until a couple of weeks after Easter. It's very popular although it's so expensive – all the ground almonds in the marzipan cost a bomb – and it always sells well.'

'So why don't you make it all the year round?' Mary thought she knew the answer, and she did.

'Sentiment, I suppose. Die-hard traditionalism. It's a seasonal thing, like mince pies and Christmas puddings. I think people value them more if they're only available for a short time.'

I like this man, thought Mary. I really ought not to be here. It was surprising how often recently she had found herself shopping in Reading at a time when it would be convenient to drop in at the sandwich bar. It was also surprising to Mary how quickly she had fallen into the patterns of friendship with this man who, speaking honestly, she could not remember at all from earlier years. Should she be wary of him?

There was no element of flirtation in their dealings, no spark of sexual attraction that she was aware of. If anything, she found herself talking to Rupert more as she would to a close woman friend. How he felt about this was not clear, but he welcomed her always with a brotherly hug, and appeared pleased to see her and interested in what she had to say. That alone was a novelty to Mary. On the whole, she was accustomed to rate her attractions as a woman fairly low, and it seemed unlikely to her that Rupert would see her as anything other than a memory of his student past, or perhaps a fellow cooking enthusiast.

It was Tuesday morning, two days after the disastrous visit to Oxford. The atmosphere driving home in the car that afternoon had been crackling like static with unspoken words. This time, there had been no question at all of David sitting in the back of the car with Alison. She had sat tight-lipped while they ate the rhubarb crumble and almond ice cream that Zen brought out, picking at her portion and leaving most of it. David, still annoyed with her, made no attempt to mollify her, and John had kept up a desultory conversation with the Professor, which was difficult since they had almost no interests in common. Mary had ended up helping Zen with the washing up. They had left soon after, while Zen was still resting upstairs. David, with a defiant look at Alison, had asked the Professor to say goodbye for him. Alison and John, very pointedly, had not.

Mary had intended to give everyone tea and perhaps an early snack supper, but the younger couple wasted no time in leaving. After they had gone, John had turned on Mary.

'I just can't think what you're thinking of, if you're even thinking at all, encouraging that – that tarty little slut! A little gold-digger, if ever I saw one! She's bound to be on drugs – you've only got to look at her to see she's the type – and before you know where you are she'll be stealing things from the house to pay for them!'

'She told me she doesn't do drugs. I've never seen any sign of them in her behaviour, and she's certainly given up smoking completely.'

'Oh, you're so gullible you'd believe anything! What on earth do you know about drugs?'

Mary had to admit that she knew nothing, but, she thought rebelliously, nor did John. And she did know Zen. It was easier, however, to allow him to blow off steam for a while knowing that there was nothing he could actually do about it.

'John's very upset about Zen,' she said now, watching Rupert brush the top of the warm cake with melted apricot jam and then lay a rolled-out layer of marzipan skilfully over it. 'He thinks she's going to sell the family silver to buy drugs, and at the same time somehow persuade my father to make a will in her favour.'

'Yes, you said. Well, it does happen. I can't imagine Professor Hill doing anything like that, however senile he might get. Not that I can imagine him getting senile either, can you?'

'Maybe not senile, but I can certainly see him getting odd. Well, odder, really. Of course I don't think he'd do it, but he's such a tease, he's enjoying seeing John tie himself up in knots.'

'They don't get on?'

'Not really. John always admired my father's position, the fact that he's a professor. "My father-in-law, the Oxford professor" – you know. Basically they're chalk and cheese. It's a struggle for them to find anything to talk about. I suppose neutral co-existence just about sums it up.'

'And you're the buffer zone in the middle.' His voice was level, his eyes fixed on the marzipan he was rolling into balls to decorate the top of the cake.

'That's me. Just an old buffer.'

His face creased into a smile.

'Scarcely!' There was a small piece of marzipan left over. He cut it in half with scrupulous fairness, and passed her one piece. Mary, who

152

disliked marzipan, nibbled at it without enthusiasm, then brightened and ate the rest.

'Delicious! It's not like marzipan at all!'

'What you mean is, real marzipan is better than the bought stuff. No almond essence, that's the secret. Just a bit of lemon juice, to cut the sweetness.'

'Mum? It's me. David.'

'Yes, I thought it probably was.'

'Did you?'

'Well for one thing I recognise your voice, and for another thing you're the only person in the world who calls me Mum.'

There was a short pause. David was unused to this kind of levity from his mother. Perhaps I was a bit sarcastic, thought Mary guiltily.

'Anyway, it's lovely to hear from you, darling. How are you? And Alison? Is she better now?'

Alison, as might have been predicted, had gone down with a bad cold two days after the visit to Oxford. She had appeared to hold Zen responsible for this, although as far as Mary could see Zen was as free of germs as any human being could reasonably be. The cold had been heavy and chesty, and even two weeks later Alison could still produce a cough that sounded as if it came from a bronchial tramp.

'She's a bit better. She went to the doctor, and he's put her on antibiotics.'

'Yoghurt,' said Mary automatically.

'What? I thought you said yoghurt.'

'I did. She should eat it. Antibiotics kill off the beneficial flora in the stomach. Yoghurt replaces it.'

'Sounds revolting. Besides, she doesn't like yoghurt.' She wouldn't, thought Mary. 'She's feeling a lot better, anyway. We're having a night in London next weekend.'

'Oh, lovely. Staying with Graham?' Graham, Alison's brother, had a small, neat house in Camden where he lived a small, neat life that seemed to revolve mainly around the Rotary Club.

'No.' David sounded sheepish. 'As a matter of fact, we're going to a hotel. Thought we'd see a show, have a nice meal, that kind of thing. Just the two of us.'

'How romantic!' A reconciliation, Mary saw. Alison had finally forgiven David for the disastrous Sunday lunch.

'Well ... you know ... The thing is, Mum, that sort of thing costs a bit, and I don't want to have to eat into the money we've put by for a house. I suppose I could use some of the money we were saving for a holiday, but ...'

'Don't worry, darling. Let me pay for it.'

His shocked response was instant.

'No, no! That's not what I meant at all! I wouldn't ring you up to ask for money!'

'Wouldn't you?' Mary felt rather sad, almost hurt. 'But that's what parents are for.' Did Pa feel like this, that other day when he said about going to him for help? I hope not. He's not particularly sensitive, thank goodness. And I shouldn't be, either. I should be glad that David is so sensible and budgets so carefully. Saving for the house, saving for a holiday ... 'Of course you wouldn't, darling, you never do. But you do know I'd always be happy ... ?'

David's embarrassment was plain, even down the telephone.

'Of course, Mum. Thanks,' he said gruffly. 'But that wasn't it. The thing is, I'm going on a course in a few weeks. Five days, on money laundering.'

'Goodness. What fun. You'll be able to make a lot of money at that.'

'Not doing it, Mum!' David, already off-balance, was unsure how to take this. 'The course is in recognising it, so that we don't run any risk of being used, and then prosecuted.' Mary realised she had gone too far. Money, in the accountancy sense, was not something to be joked about.

'Yes, darling, of course. I was just being silly. Carry on.'

'Well, it's a five-day course and they're doing it in Oxford, so I thought, if I were to stay with Grandprof ...'

'You could save the cost of the hotel, and make up for the weekend in London. Good idea. Do you want me to speak to him?'

'No, it's not that. I can ask him myself, Mum. I'm not a child!'

'I know you're not. But why are you ringing me about it, then?'

'It's – it's not Grandprof. It's Zen. That girl.'

'Yes, I know who Zen is. But she won't mind. It's up to your grandfather who stays there, not her. Or is it ... oh dear, is it Alison? I suppose she doesn't like you to stay there while Zen's there?'

Mary tried hard (and successfully) to keep the disapproval out of her voice.

154

'No, she doesn't mind that. In fact, she thinks it's a good idea.' Does she indeed? thought Mary. I wonder why?

'Why?' she asked.

'She's decided the old chap is lonely, and that's why he's taken her in. She thinks that if I'm there, he'll see that family is better than outsiders, and he won't want her there any more.'

'And what do you think?'

'I think she's completely wrong,' he admitted. Mary felt a smile spreading across her face, and was glad they were on the telephone.

'So do I. Pa isn't lonely in that sense. It's not just someone around that he needs. If it were he could easily do something about it, have a live-in housekeeper or let some of the rooms to students. What he wants is someone he can teach. And to be honest, though I know he'll be delighted to have you to stay for as long as you like, you don't want to be taught by him, do you?'

Memories of childhood visits which had been more like high-powered lessons than family get-togethers gave added feeling to his answer.

'I certainly don't!'

'Right. So where's the problem?'

'It's Zen herself. Her . . . her condition. I called in the other day when I was going through Oxford and had half an hour to spare. She's so enormous. What if she goes into labour while I'm there? What do I do?'

There was real panic in his voice, and Mary managed to suppress her amusement.

'Well, darling, I'm not sure you'd have to do anything. For one thing, she's not really due until June – though of course with twins they usually come early. For another, having even one baby isn't exactly a quick process. I know there are people who have their babies in taxis on the way to the hospital, but it's pretty rare. If it should happen, the most you'd have to do would be to ring the hospital or the doctor, and even then you'd probably find Grandprof had beaten you to it. You know how he loves to be in charge.'

'I suppose so.' He sounded relieved. 'So I won't need to boil lots of water, or tell her how to breathe or anything?'

'I don't think so.' Mary's voice was warm with amusement and affection. This was so much the earnest little boy she remembered, anxious to do everything right. She had thought he had disappeared inside the self-confident young accountant. Had the change she had

155

perceived in Alison been apparent to him? Certainly there was more to her than the milk-and-water little creature that Mary had taken her for, but whether he had always been aware of these hidden depths (reefs?) in her, or whether she was only letting them show now that she had him, as it were, safely hooked, Mary could not guess. And while she hoped that his self-confidence was not dented, she could not help rejoicing a little in the slight vulnerability he was betraying. It made him more human.

'Thank goodness for that. I'll give Grandprof a ring, then. Is Dad there? I won't be able to manage golf on Saturday, of course, with going up to London.'

'No, he's out. Some kind of business get-together,' said Mary vaguely. 'He said he'd probably be late. I'll tell him for you, shall I?'

'Please. He seems to have a lot of these meetings these days. He didn't manage golf last Saturday, even, and you know how rarely he misses that.'

'Oh, but surely...' Mary stopped. She clearly remembered John going off the previous Saturday with his golf bag. Of course, he had not actually *said* he was playing with David, but she had certainly assumed so. Perhaps he had wanted to play elsewhere, with someone different, and had been wary of hurting David's feelings. Or could it be that these business events – and it was true, now she came to think of it, that he had been out in the evening much more often recently – were leading to a new job? He might well have decided to keep it a secret from her, until something was definitely settled. 'Silly me,' said Mary, 'I must have got the weekends muddled up. It's probably the first sign of senility. You'd better start looking for a Home for the Bewildered for me.'

David's laugh was genuine.

'Don't be silly, Mum! You're the sanest person I know, and the best balanced!'

'Am I?' Mary was astounded. 'You must know some very odd people.'

'No, really. You're as normal as – as bread and butter. I must go. Bye!'

Mary said goodbye absently. Bread and butter, she thought. How dull. Mother's Pride? No, probably something healthier, like wholemeal. Not a French stick, certainly, or the delicious Italian focaccia that Rupert used. She looked up at her reflection in the hall mirror. She seemed to have put on weight, particularly round the hips, or was it this skirt? A cottage loaf, I'm afraid, my dear, she said to herself. She cheered up. There were worse things in the world, she thought, than a nice home-made cottage loaf.

She went back to the kitchen. John had said he would be eating out this evening, so she had intended to have a nursery supper, a boiled egg. Now she decided she felt a bit funny about having bread and butter with the egg, and switched on the grill to make toast instead. She stood watching the slices of bread turn brown. Perhaps, she thought, I should book a course of sunbed treatments, get a bit of a tan before the summer? She closed her eyes for a moment, and with her back to the kitchen deliberately summoned up her fantasy.

'Hi!' Her lover lounged against the sink. 'How are you?'

It was the first time in ages that she had seen him, and Mary found herself feeling irrationally guilty.

'I'm sorry,' she said. 'I've been so busy . . .'

'I know, I know.' His voice was soothing as velvet. 'You don't have to worry about me. You know that.'

'Yes.'

'You're not convinced.'

'No. Yes. I don't know.' The problem was inherent in the situation. In the past Mary had dealt with it by ignoring it and thinking of other things. This time it seemed more difficult. A fantasy lover ought to be the ideal, and in many ways he was. Never out of temper, never moody; always interested, supportive, encouraging. This, in the past, had suited her very well. She had never envisaged there being a time when that very perfection might pall. The fact that she could ignore him for weeks, then summon him back when it suited her, without his ever resenting it, brought home to her that he was only a construct. Of course, if she wanted, he would behave differently. He could be hurt, resentful, even angry if – and that was the problem, *if* – she made the decision that he should be so.

'I can only be what you want me to be,' he said rather sadly.

'I know. And it always used to be enough. Why do I suddenly mind about it?'

'Because you've got someone else to talk to.'

The insight startled Mary, but of course it was correct. How could it be otherwise?

'Rupert? Yes, I suppose so. I have been talking to him quite a bit. But there are things I can't discuss with him . . .'

'Like John. You don't discuss him with me, either.'

'No, I know. But that's silly, isn't it?' Her previous scruples now seemed pointless, presumably because he was less real and, therefore, talking to him was no longer disloyal to John.

'It is rather. I wonder how he would see it?'

Mary laughed.

'He'd just send for the men in white coats to carry me off! You know John. He uses his imagination so rarely it's probably withered and dropped off.'

'I wouldn't say that. What about his game of golf last Saturday? Wasn't that imaginary?'

Mary dipped a finger of toast into her egg.

'I wonder.' She chewed thoughtfully. One advantage of talking to her lover was being able to talk with her mouth full, since of course all the conversation actually took place in her head. 'The trouble is, most Saturdays are so similar that it's difficult to remember t'other from which. But a Saturday when he *didn't* play, unless the weather were really impossible, surely that would stick in my mind? And last Saturday the weather was quite good, and I'm sure I remember him going off with his clubs.'

'He didn't say he was playing with David.'

'No, but ... come to think of it, he was quite late coming home, and he smelled different...'

'Aha.'

'Yes. Aha. He smelled of pubs – not that that's unusual, they often go for a drink after golf, though, mind you, they usually go to the members' bar at the club, and that smells different. Not so beery and cigarette smoky.'

'More g and t and cigar smoke?'

'Yes. But there was more to it than that. He smelled of perfume. Not much, just a bit. I didn't think anything of it. You know how sensitive my nose is, and in the past I've seen him peck someone's wife on the cheek, and smelled her perfume on him afterwards. But this was quite a strong one. Musky. It reminded me of someone ... I can't remember who.'

She glanced at him hopefully. He often remembered things for her, searched them out of her subconscious. This time he shook his head.

'Nothing, I'm afraid. Perhaps it's the perfume that's familiar rather than the person who wears it?'

'Perhaps. I know it's the sort of thing I wouldn't wear myself, and don't much like on other people.'

'Not like my aftershave.' Mary looked up from her egg, from which she was scraping the last mouthful of white. Her lover raised one eyebrow, and smiled slightly. Mary, to her annoyance, felt herself blushing.

'That's just coincidence! After all, you had that aftershave long before I ever met him!'

'Of course I did. And of course it is. But it's just one more thing to have in common, isn't it? Do you think that's why you felt at home with him so quickly? One of the reasons, anyway. After all, you don't remember him from before.'

'No. I feel bad about that. I wish I did. I have absolutely no image of him, how he looked, anything. I'd so like to know whether he's changed much. I mean, I can hardly ask whether he's put on a lot of weight recently, can I?'

'Difficult not to, with a job like that. It must be obligatory to taste everything.'

'And he's not fat,' said Mary defensively. 'Just well covered.' She considered having another slice of toast, with marmalade, but on the strength of her cottage loaf appearance decided reluctantly against it.

Mary was in bed when John came home. She had intended to stay awake, thinking it dismal for him to come home to a dark house and a snoring wife. She had tried to read, and fallen asleep with the book in her hand and the light on. When he took the book from her limp grasp she woke up with a start.

'Hello, John,' she said sleepily. 'Sorry, I meant to stay awake. Did you have a good evening?'

'You shouldn't have bothered, dear.' His usually pale face was rather pink, and he looked unaccountably put out. 'I didn't mean to disturb you. Go back to sleep.'

Mary glanced at the clock.

'Half past one! You must have had a good time. Where did you go?'

'Oh, nowhere special.' His vague reply was unusual. Generally, when there had been any kind of business outing he would return from it full of the details of where he had been, and the quality of the food and service.

'Do you want a hot drink? I left everything ready, I can do you one in no time.' John, unused to late nights, sometimes found them over-stimulating, and he considered a hot milk drink beneficial. Mary began to struggle out of bed. John backed off.

'No, no, it's all right. You stay there.' He almost pushed her back into the bed. 'I'll do it myself. You just go back to sleep.'

He hurried out of the room. Mary lay down again, but she was far from sleepy. When John had leaned forward to pull the covers back over her she had distinctly smelled perfume on him. It was the same she had smelled the previous Saturday. And now, quite suddenly, she found she remembered who wore it. Perhaps, during sleep, her unconscious mind had sorted through its filing system and come up with the answer. The only person, recently, who had smelled like that was Elaine Brantridge.

Her mind in a whirl, Mary closed her eyes. When John finally came back upstairs he went straight into the bathroom, and she heard the hiss of the shower. This more than anything else crystallised her suspicions. He never normally showered at night. But he knew, only too well, how sensitive her nose was.

Chapter 14

When Mary walked into Naseby's a few weeks later, she knew at once that something was wrong. There was no one on duty in the shop – not even one of 'the lads' – and although the shop door had given its usual loud double clang on opening and closing, no one came through. She saw, too, when she glanced round, that although the door was unlocked the sign on it read 'Open' on the side that faced her, which meant that it displayed a 'Closed' to the outside world. She glanced at her watch, wondering for a moment whether she had mistaken the time. The clocks had not changed again, had they? It was only three weeks since they had been put forward. Had the government, perhaps, introduced double summer time without her being aware of it? If nothing else, the confusion engendered might distract the country from the other disasters their policies had brought about.

It was an interesting thought, but unlikely. She might be quite capable of allowing such an event to pass her by unnoticed, but not John. John, who re-set his watch every morning by the time signal on the radio, and who became seriously disturbed if any clock in the house were more than a minute wrong. No, it was not that.

Mary found herself on tiptoe as she crossed the shop floor and lifted the counter hatch to go through. It moved without a sound, the hinges being well oiled and the hatch itself counter-weighted and balanced so that it lifted easily and went down again sweetly, with no more than a soft click as it closed. The click sounded loud this morning, however. The place was so quiet. Normally by now the radio would have been emitting a background blanket of sound: Radio 2 today, thought Mary after a moment's calculation.

Uncle liked Radio 2, and Dad preferred Radio 4 because he said, rather snobbishly, that it had more class. The battle over which was to be played had been fought with vicious determination. Everyone had

161

enjoyed it at first, but after a while, when it became apparent that ceasefires always ended in a renewed bout of hostilities, Mr Naseby had put his foot down and decreed alternate days. Occasionally, when they felt bored, one or other of the old gentlemen would initiate a random guerilla action and shift stations when he thought no one was looking, but by and large the system worked. Mary had marked up a calendar for them, taking into account half days and bank holidays, and this was referred to as the final arbitration in any dispute.

Mary put down her handbag and took off her coat. This is ridiculous, she thought. This isn't the *Marie Celeste*. There must be someone here, or the door wouldn't have been unlocked. I must go and find them. The shop shouldn't be left unattended like this. With a glance round the deserted showroom – everything in its place, the glass in the windows undamaged: not a break-in, then – she went reluctantly towards the closed door that led to the workshop. A sudden thought made her turn again and pick up her handbag. Madness to leave it in the empty shop, although of course the bell would give ample warning if anyone should come in. Besides, she felt safer with it in her hands. It was quite heavy, and it had a good strong leather strap. Should she find an escaped lunatic holding everyone at bay or, her imagination raced ahead, crouching over their bloodstained corpses, she could at least make shift to defend herself with it. Cheered by the ridiculous image she opened the door and went through.

The familiar smell met her. The smooth heavy overtones of oil were the mid-notes, pierced by the almost acid tang of newly cut or filed metal. They, the almost organic smells, were overlaid with a more artificial miasma of plastic that Mary, irrationally she knew, thought of as the smell of electricity. Through them all wove the base-notes of hot solder and, of course, cigarette smoke. Dad and Uncle rolled their own; thin, limp little cylinders that they assembled deftly, without looking. They burned sluggishly, adhering to the corners of their lips without apparently disturbing either their eyes or their ability to speak. The lads were not supposed to smoke in the shop or the workshop, and as a result tended to hang about in the passageway and smoke feverishly for a few minutes.

A low murmur of voices came from the workshop. Very much relieved, Mary pushed open the door (which was never usually shut) and went in. Four faces turned to look up at her. Four faces, not five. Uncle was not there.

'Mrs Marsh!' Mr Naseby was blundering to his feet, moving awkwardly as he never generally did. 'I'd forgotten ... what day it is, I mean ... I've been that upset. Gary! Put the kettle on again and make Mrs Marsh a cup of tea!'

'Don't worry,' said Mary. 'I'll make it.' Her eyes went instinctively to the shelf. One solitary pair of false teeth sat there, no longer grinning but seeming to grimace in a cry of pain. 'What's happened? Is Uncle ... ?'

'Heart attack,' said Mr Naseby gloomily. 'Last night.'

'Oh, no!' Mary sat limply on the stool that Mr Naseby, always courteous, pulled up for her. 'But he's never had any heart problems before, has he? Oh dear, I'm so very sorry.' Her eyes went to Dad. He sat hunched on his high stool, looking shrunken so that his clothes seemed too big, like a child in hand-me-downs. He looked suddenly old. Before, the seams and wrinkles of his face had looked more like the shrivelled skin of a prune, less an ageing than a transformation by sunshine and drying. Now the lines fell into the classic mask of old age, and the half-empty mug in his hand shook with a faint but ceaseless tremor. He was, Mary remembered, two years older than Uncle.

'Indigestion,' he mumbled. 'Always taking them indigestion tablets, he was. Told him to see a quack. Thought he'd got a stomach ulcer, didn't I? But he's such a stubborn old fool ... Now they say it's not indigestion at all, but his heart all along. I told him! I said, nobody but yourself to blame, I said. But he's always been the same, man and boy. I remember when he was no more than ten or eleven, and he would go and try out the ice on the pond near our house. I told him it wasn't strong enough, but would he listen? Not he. And who was it had to pull him out, and got frozen wet *and* a right bollocking from our mum into the bargain, for not taking better care of him!' He sniffed loudly.

One of the lads appeared at Mary's side with tea in the special cup and saucer Mr Naseby had insisted on providing for her. The rest of them had battered mugs. Mary smiled her gratitude, then returned her attention to Dad. He had put down his mug and was attempting to roll a cigarette. Little flakes of tobacco shook from the flimsy paper.

'You mustn't blame yourself,' said Mary gently. 'He wouldn't want you to do that.'

'Wouldn't he ever!' Dad looked up from his cigarette rolling and

163

fixed her with a look. 'That's just what he did do! "This is all your fault," he said. Lying there, stuck full of tubes and bits of wire and a nasty monitor screen going beep beep and a doctor that doesn't look like he's old enough to be out of nappies pushing me around and calling me Grandad . . .' His voice trembled and he hastily lifted the cigarette to his lips and stuck out the tip of his tongue to lick the gummed edge. Automatically his fingers moved to complete the rolling, but the paper had been the wrong way round and there was no glue on the part he had licked. The cigarette fell apart and with a grunt of annoyance he screwed it up in his fist and threw it away. Mary gazed at him.

'Stuck full of tubes . . . you mean, he's at the hospital?'

''Course he's at the hospital!' Never before had Dad spoken to her in that tetchy voice, but Mary scarcely noticed it.

'Oh, thank goodness! I thought you meant . . . I thought he had died!' Her eyes filled with tears of relief. She took a mouthful of the tea. It was tepid, and with part of her mind she thought with amusement that after all this time Gary still hadn't learned to get the kettle boiling properly before making tea.

'No thanks to him that he didn't,' said Dad grumpily.

'Now, Dad,' said Mr Naseby. 'Don't you go upsetting yourself.'

'Upset! I'm not upset!' shouted Dad. 'Not that anyone wouldn't be upset, finding that silly old fool lying there on the floor groaning and carrying on, and then having to deal with that young idiot on the telephone that kept arguing with me when I said we needed an ambulance!'

Mr Naseby and Mary looked at one another. The helpless pleading in his brown eyes made them look more spaniel-like than ever. Mary put down her cup. With anyone else she would have suggested that Dad go home and rest, but to send him back to the little house he shared with Uncle was unthinkable. The familiar surroundings of the workshop would soothe him more than his empty home, and the distraction of work would settle his mind more surely than rest. Mary finished her tea and put her cup down decisively.

'Well, that's a great relief. They'll have him up and about in no time, you'll see. By the time you go and see him this evening he'll be looking much better. Meanwhile, there's no one out in the shop, and the sign on the door still says closed.'

'Closed? At half past nine in the morning?' Dad was outraged. He sat up straighter and, miraculously, seemed to grow into his clothes again.

'What are you thinking of, Bill? That's no way to run a business. And what you two useless lumps are doing hanging around here is beyond me. What about that tumble drier you was stripping down yesterday? Don't tell me it's finished already. And there's those irons needing new flexes, and I don't know what else.'

Gary grinned at him. He and Mike seemed relieved to have Dad bullying them again.

Ten minutes later, Mary was at her desk. Normality, as far as possible, had returned. A quiet word with the lads had ensured that one or other of them would stay with Dad at all times.

Later, Mr Naseby came and perched in his usual place on her desk. He looked tired and anxious, and admitted that he had been worried about Dad and Uncle for some time.

'They won't let me put central heating into that little old house of theirs, that Dad bought when he and Mum were in their forties. It's cold, and a bit damp too. At least when they're here they're in the warm, but I worry about them working. Uncle's seventy-eight, you know, and Dad was eighty last birthday.'

'They're not! I had no idea! But they love coming to work. I think they'd die of having nothing to do if they had to stay at home.'

'Maybe. I don't know. The lease comes to an end on this place soon, and I'm in two minds what to do about it. I'm sixty myself, and I don't know that I want to commit myself to another howmany years.'

'No, I can see that. What about something smaller, perhaps further out of town so there's more parking? You could concentrate on the repairs – the retail side's more difficult now they're building these big out-of-town warehouses where everything's so cheap. Perhaps you could find a house to convert, have a flat upstairs for you, and one for Dad and Uncle downstairs. That way you'd have a bit of privacy, and you could still keep an eye on them.'

'It's a thought. Yes, it's certainly a thought.' He pondered, looking slightly more cheerful. 'And I hope you know, if we ever did anything like that, there'd always be a place for you.'

'Thank you, Bill. You don't mind if I call you Bill, do you? And do, please, call me Mary.'

He executed a bobbing little bow that was, for all its awkwardness, the very essence of courtesy.

'I should be honoured, Mary,' he said, his voice lowered reverently. 'But not in front of the lads. It wouldn't be suitable.'

Mary nodded seriously. Mr Naseby, looking far more cheerful, went back to the shop. Mary, out of interest, looked up the accounts for the last few years, and made a few pencilled notes on a piece of paper.

The following day, having given the house a cursory clean, Mary set off on the kind of expedition she had not made for years. In the past she had, without realising it, become well known in the local estate agents as the woman who spent hours looking in their windows but never came in and asked for details of anything. Then, her window shopping had been part of her fantasy life, but today it was rooted in reality. Both the rent and the rates of Naseby's were high, as she knew very well. It occurred to her that they could very well economise on both.

She had a very clear idea of what was needed. A house that could be divided up, with enough outbuildings to be used as workshops and a shop. There was no shortage of customer loyalty – many of the people who came in with items for repair had been coming for years, and not a few of them from some distance. As long as they knew where to go, they would come just as happily to a new place; more happily, if it had easier parking. The streets round the shop were notorious for being clogged with parked cars.

For the first time, Mary found herself going through the familiar doors. She found herself greeted as an old friend by older members of staff, and this embarrassed her when she discovered that they remembered her dreamy examinations of their window displays. They pressed leaflets on her, many describing houses which were completely unsuitable and too expensive, but she took them all away. On her next free day she drove round and looked at the outsides of the few promising ones, but most were disappointing. One, however, caught her imagination and she prowled round outside. Realising from its appearance that the whole place was empty, she ventured through the gate and into a yard where the original cobbles were invisible (though knobbly to the feet) beneath a healthy carpet of weeds.

Most of the outbuildings were unlocked, and she grew bolder as nobody challenged her. The house itself was firmly closed up, but she peered in through windows filthy with what looked like the grime of years. Inside it was dark and festooned with cobwebs, though the air, when she boldly pushed open the letter box and put her nose to it, smelled dry and relatively fresh. At last, regretfully, she climbed back into her car. She meant – she really meant – to go home and hang out the washing she had left churning in the washing machine. Instead she found herself driving into Reading and parking in the now familiar car park.

It was nearly midday. Mary had visited the sandwich bar quite often recently, though usually she tried to time her visits with the quiet patches of the day. This time the sandwich bar was full, every inch of the wall counter taken up by people eating and drinking, and a queue stretching out of the door and along the window. Quickly, Mary ran her eyes round the throng, and was faintly relieved to see that John was not among them.

Once or twice she had met him while he was buying his lunch, and although he had never gone so far as to pretend he hadn't seen her, she had been left with the distinct impression that he resented seeing her there, intruding into his daytime existence. Mary had been saddened by this, but for once had made the decision to please herself rather than him. She had long been aware that she should make the effort to meet more people, to make friends. The trouble was, she had always found it difficult to know where to start. The classic advice – join a club, go to evening classes – filled her with alarm, and her good intentions had invariably evaporated. Now that she had found a place so congenial to her, and a person she could talk to, she would not allow anything to prevent her from visiting.

Mary joined the back of the queue, unwilling to break the ingrained British tradition of standing in a line, until Rupert caught sight of her when he glanced up from serving.

'Mary!' he bellowed. 'Come on in!' The queue, as one, turned to look at her and Mary blushed hotly. They made way for her perfectly cheerfully, however; a crowd of office workers for the most part, young go-getters as busy eyeing up one another as reading the choice of fillings on the blackboard. Mary, wishing heartily that she were small and willowy, wriggled her way through them, apologising at every step. A door in the wall, almost invisible behind the large blackboard that was re-written every morning, opened a crack and she squeezed through it.

'Thanks,' she said breathlessly, her face still glowing.

'One advantage of being big,' he said, his hands flying as he assembled sandwiches. 'Me, that is. You get to see over people's heads.'

'I'm not exactly tiny, either. Compared to all those slim little girls.'

167

He waved a hand, dismissing them.

'Skinny. Nothing to them. Don't eat properly, most of them – except when they come here, of course! Coffee?'

'Please, but I'll get it. I know how to work the machine.'

As she filled her mug she heard requests for tea and coffee from customers being served. The two boys were working flat out stuffing slabs of focaccia from the dishes of prepared fillings, so she set down her mug after a sip, washed her hands, and helped out. After a few moments they settled into a rhythm, the others seeing to the food while Mary set up the drinks and took the money. The time flew by, and when she finally glanced up and saw that the queue had dwindled to a trickle she realised, to her amazement, that it was after two. She made herself a sandwich oozing with filling (spicy chicken and chickpeas, with cucumber and yoghurt), and sat on a stool in the tiny kitchen. Rupert came and joined her.

'Thanks for your help,' he said, squashing his piece of bread between large hands so that he could get it into his mouth. 'I shall have to see about taking on a part-timer to help out with lunches. Most of those people have only got an hour; they don't want to spend it standing in a queue.'

'You know,' said Mary thoughtfully, 'they probably all work fairly nearby. There are quite a few large companies with offices in this area, and quite a lot of them were buying for other people, to take back to the office. You could organise some kind of delivery service locally. Have a printed menu list that they could tick off for the following day, take them round in the late morning before the rush gets going. They do it in London, why not here?'

'It's an idea.' He looked thoughtful, then interested. 'Yes, it really is an idea! I'll look into it. We'd need packaging, of course.'

'Something that looks nice. I've always loved the idea of those Japanese lunchboxes, in layers, but I suppose that would be terribly expensive.'

'Something to work up to, perhaps. Or a two-tier system, perhaps? Executive lunchboxes? And call it something witty-witty like Upper Crust. But it's definitely a thought. It was great fun setting this up, but now it's settled and running I feel ready to expand a bit. Empire building, you know. The Caesar of the Sandwich Bars, that kind of thing.' They chewed companionably. Mary told him about Uncle and then, rather shyly, admitted what she had been doing that morning.

'It's terribly interfering of me. I don't know what's got into me, I'm not usually like this. And now telling you how to run this place, too! I deserve that you should kick me out.'

'Hardly, when you've just saved our lives in the lunchtime rush. You've made me realise we really need to move on; it was so much easier with just one extra person. And I don't have to follow your suggestions, any more than your Bill does. Or should I say Mr Naseby?'

Mary laughed.

'Oh, dear Bill. He is such a gentleman, and so old-fashioned!'

'He's probably madly in love with you, poor chap.'

'Don't be ridiculous!' Mary was embarrassed. 'It's not like that at all. I'm not the sort of person people fall madly in love with.'

Rupert smiled gently, saying nothing. Mary hurried to change the subject.

'I was in Oxford the other day – by the way, Pa loved the peanut sauce. Thank you for going over there again.'

'Nothing else to do on a Sunday,' he said cheerfully, robbing the words of self-pity. 'Besides, I enjoy it. He's wonderful company, the Professor, and he and Zen together are getting to be like a pair of cross-talk comedians. I could listen to them for hours.'

'She *has* come on, hasn't she? I must admit, when Pa first took her in I was worried. It seemed – oh, I don't know – as if he were taking her over, experimenting on her as if she were a guinea pig. But she can hold her own, can't she? He says she's reading everything she can lay her hands on, no matter what the subject, and making the most extra-ordinary connections of ideas. And she's writing, too, now. Her spelling's a bit bizarre and the grammar's still a bit wobbly, but she has the most amazing grasp of how to use words . . . It's as if they were toys, and she were playing with them, experimenting to see what they can do. She showed me a few pages, and I was stunned. It was so – so real, so immediate. It sort of sparkled in your mind. That sounds ridiculous, but I don't know how to express it. And that's just it, because she *does*. Every word is precisely chosen. She told me she'd re-written one sentence fifteen times.'

'One of these days,' said Rupert soberly, 'we'll be dining out on the fact that we knew her when she was just beginning, before she won the Booker and got famous.'

'We might, at that. And she's so excited by it! She's drunk with words, I think. Do you know what the first thing she said to me was, the other day? She said, "I've just found a phrase I *really* like. Raymond Carver. It was 'shoals of remarkable fish'. Isn't that great? He could have spent a whole sentence describing those fish, their colour, their shape, how unusual they are, but no. 'Remarkable fish' says it all, doesn't it?" Now I wouldn't even have noticed that, but when you think about it, she's right, isn't she? It is just the right word.'

'Mm. Remarkable Fish.' He tasted the words, then grinned. 'It would do for a recipe. Or a restaurant. Now there's an idea!'

'Oh, you!' Mary had to laugh. 'You've got no soul.'

'Me? I'm all soul. Dover, of course, not lemon.' Mary giggled helplessly. She thought she had not felt so light-hearted for years. Or was it ever? I must be going into my second childhood, she thought. Well, why not? It seems rather fun. Remarkable Fish. Oh dear.

By half past three the place was busy again, but since most of the customers wanted cakes rather than sandwiches the pressure was less, and Mary thought it was time she took herself out of the way. She was rather dismayed to find how reluctant she was to leave, and how still more reluctant she was to return to her empty house. On impulse she drove to Oxford.

She found Zen and her father in the kitchen. The table was littered with books, and Zen was chopping onions while the Professor read to her.

'Don't let me interrupt,' she said unnecessarily, since neither showed any sign of stopping. Zen smiled, sniffed, blinked away onion tears and reached for a head of garlic. Professor Hill continued to read – Milton, Mary vaguely recognised, his voice filling the room. Mary filled the kettle and made tea. Her father finished his reading, and allowed a moment of silence while the echoes of his voice died away, then closed the book carefully and reached for his cup.

'Hello Pa, Zen. What's cooking – *Samson Agonistes* stew?'

'*Comus* curry,' said Zen with composure, sniffing again and beginning to peel a piece of ginger. 'Well, I've learned something important, anyway.'

'Oh?' Professor Hill looked smug.

'Yes. To chop the onions last, not first. Bloody things are making my mascara run.'

Mary glanced slightly anxiously at her father, but he grinned.

'Neglecting her studies,' he growled. 'Fussing in the kitchen.'

'I thought you wanted Zen to learn to cook?'

'That was plan B, if I kick the bucket.'

'Really, Pa!' Mary was worried about Zen's feelings now, but she only laughed.

'Take no notice of him, Mary. He's just grumpy because it's David's favourite. He wanted chicken chasseur.'

'Of course, David started his course this week. I'd forgotten. How's it going?'

'The course sounds suitably tedious.' Professor Hill dismissed it with a wave of his hand. 'Fortunately, he doesn't go on about it. In fact.' He paused, as if wondering whether to continue. 'In fact the boy's quite good company. For an accountant.'

'And that,' said Zen, competently slicing the ginger into slivers, 'is his idea of a compliment.'

'I should say it is!' Mary, knowing her father, was impressed. 'My dear Zen, that's the equivalent of an illuminated scroll with gold leaf and a wax seal!'

'I don't know what's caused it, and I can't believe it's due to that dismal little Alison, but he's definitely improved.'

'Has he?' asked Mary, rather wistfully. It was a long time since her father had praised David. 'Not that he wasn't pretty special already,' she added firmly. Professor Hill dismissed such maternal partiality with a grunt.

'He's been teaching me maths,' said Zen cheerfully. 'Really patient, he's been. Makes it interesting, like a puzzle, you know?'

Mary felt such a glow of pleasure that her eyes filled with moisture. 'That's wonderful, Zen. I'm so pleased.'

'Not that we're doing anything special, mind. Nothing complicated, just going back over the basics, really. Said the Prof was making me unbalanced, all arty-farty. Well, that's not what he said, but it's what he meant.'

'Sensible,' put in Professor Hill unexpectedly. 'Practical lad. Going to teach her a bit of basic book-keeping, that kind of thing. Deadly, but useful. Thought of getting him to teach me, too, but it's a bit of a new trick for this old dog. Besides, to change the metaphor, why keep a dog and bark yourself?' He raised and lowered his eyebrows, and put up his hand in the familiar gesture of pushing his fingers through his hair.

'He's really polite to me, too,' said Zen, sounding almost puzzled. 'Thought he was kidding me at first. That Alison's on to a good thing, I reckon. I mean, he don't – doesn't – come on to me.' Seeing Mary's puzzled expression, she elaborated. 'No funny stuff. Doesn't try to get his hand into my knickers.'

'Oh, good,' said Mary weakly.

'Yes, he's a real gentleman. Opens the door for me, that kind of thing.'

'I thought that kind of thing was considered sexist nowadays? Patronising?'

Zen stared at her.

'Come off it! It's lovely! Makes me feel really special.'

'You don't need to have a door opened for you to tell you that,' grumbled Professor Hill.

'Don't worry,' said Zen kindly. 'I don't expect you to do it. Now, I must get this curry started, or it'll never be done for supper. Long, slow simmering to bring out the flavour of the spices, that's what the book says.'

Mary was reminded that the meat she intended to cook for John's and her supper was still in the freezer. Reluctantly, for she would have loved to stay and see David in this new incarnation, she left.

Chapter 15

The harsh ring of the telephone, waking her out of a deep sleep, brought Mary to shaking, heart-pounding life. She waited for a second – John generally answered night-time calls, seeing it as part of his duty as man of the house – but it continued to ring. The room was pitch black. Mary disliked the livid glow of street lights, and had lined the thick curtains with black so that not a glimmer came in. Clumsy with haste and anxiety she fumbled for the telephone. It slipped from her sweaty hand and clattered back into the cradle, cutting it off. Cursing, she listened to the hum of the dialling tone.

'Blast it,' she muttered. 'John! John?'

There was no answer. John had been out for the evening. Out for the evening *again*, her mind pointed out. Mary had gone to bed after she could no longer keep awake over a book or the television, and after dozing off once had switched off the light, feeling defiant. Now her hand went to the switch of the bedside lamp, finding it by instinct. It dazzled her for a moment and she squinted across at the other side of the bed. It was empty, the pillows and duvet smooth and undented.

Mary glanced at the bedside clock – twenty to three. Had there been an accident? Her eyes dropped to the telephone receiver in her hand. Perhaps that had been John, trying to call her. Quickly she replaced it and sat staring at it. After a few moments it rang again, and she snatched it up.

'Hello? John? Hello?'

'Mum!' David's voice, sharp with anxiety, cut through hers.

'David! What's the matter? Is it Pa, or Zen?'

'Both.' The word fell like a stone into her mind.

'Oh God. Is he dead?'

'No!' His voice was horrified. 'Sorry, Mum, I'm doing this all wrong.

It's just all happened so suddenly, I don't—' She heard him draw in a long breath. 'Zen's gone into labour. Went into labour. She said she had a bit of back ache in the evening, but I never thought – you didn't *tell* me about that – anyway, she was calling out, but I didn't hear her. You know me, the original log. Anyway, Grandprof did, went up to see what was wrong, went down to telephone the hospital and slipped on the stairs.' He paused for breath, or for dramatic effect.

'Go on, for heaven's sake,' said Mary crossly.

'Sorry. He's not hurt. Not much hurt, nothing broken or anything. But he's very shaken up, and I don't like to leave him on his own.'

'I should think not! He might have another stroke! But why do you need to leave him on his own? Where are you going?'

'To the hospital.' He lowered his voice to a breathy whisper. 'Zen's in a complete panic. She's terrified out of her wits, poor kid. She's convinced it's far too early, that the babies will die, all that sort of thing. The doctor's tried to reassure her, but he told me privately that the babies are a bit small, and that if the contractions can't be stopped it might be a bit touch and go. Trouble is, the poor kid waited until the pain got really bad before trying to wake us, so things are fairly advanced. She keeps hanging on to my hand and begging me to go with her, and Grandprof thinks I should. In fact, he insists. What the *hell* he thinks I'm going to do . . . Anyway, can you come? The ambulance'll be here any minute, they said . . .'

'Of course.' Mary was already out of bed, pulling off her nightie one-handed and reaching for her clothes. 'Tell Pa I'll be there in a moment – or perhaps not, it'll only fret him. I've got a key, I'll just turn up. Shouldn't take long at this time of night.'

'For God's sake drive carefully. It won't help to have you in hospital as well. Or . . . couldn't Dad drive you?'

'Dad's away for the night,' said Mary swiftly.

'Away? That's not like him. Is – hang on, I can hear something. Think it's the ambulance. I must go.'

'Yes. Give my love to Zen, tell her not to worry, everything'll be fine, *convince* her of it. Good luck, love.'

He was already gone. Mary scrambled into the rest of her clothes – she had managed knickers, socks and track-suit trousers one-handed – dragged a brush through her hair, and gave her teeth a hasty scrub which made her feel instantly more awake and able to cope.

It was a fine night. At last, in late April, the weather seemed to be settling into warmer, more spring-like patterns. The air smelled alive and fresh, and Mary kept the car window open to enjoy it, turning the heater to full to counteract the chill. The roads were empty and driving was almost a pleasure. Mary found herself humming and stopped, rather shocked by her callousness. She was fully awake now: more awake, in a strange way, than she felt herself to be in the daytime. Her senses were more receptive than usual, all her nerve endings alert and sensitive.

Dim lights shone through the windows of the house. She stepped into its familiar chill.

'Pa?' she called softly, in case he was asleep. 'Pa?'

'Who's there? Who's that? I can see you, you know.'

The querulous voice came from the study. Mary went to the door and pushed it open.

'It's all right, Pa, it's me.'

He looked up at her from his usual chair. In his pyjamas, his hair tousled, he looked small, and old. Someone, David presumably, had brought a rug and tucked it round him, and the fire glowed dimly, sending out little warmth.

'What are you doing here?' he said crossly.

'I was just passing, thought I'd call in.'

'Don't get clever with *me*, my girl! I suppose David called you. Time he learned to stand on his own feet instead of running back to his mother every five minutes.'

'Really, Pa!' Mary was stung into defence of her son. 'Of course he rang me! Not for him, but for you! You don't seriously expect him to go swanning off and leave you alone, do you?'

'And why not? I'm perfectly all right on my own. I'm not a baby!'

Sitting in his chair, the rug tucked neatly round him, he did in fact look not unlike a large, bony baby. Mary felt her irritation vanish. She went over and bent to kiss him on his bristly cheek.

'Of course you're not. You're a cantankerous, ungrateful old devil and I don't know why I bother with you. Shall I make us some coffee, or something? I suppose a milk drink might be better at this time of night.'

'Coffee. You know I abominate milk drinks.' He was mollified but trying to hide it, flattered rather than otherwise by her words. 'I've no intention of going back to sleep now, and I don't suppose you have, either.'

'No, I've never felt more awake in my life. Shall we have something to eat? For some reason I'm ravenous.'

He grinned.

'Bacon and egg would be good. And fried bread. And I believe there are some mushrooms in the fridge.'

'If anyone had told me I'd fancy a fry-up at four in the morning, I'd never have believed them. In the kitchen, or shall I bring it through here?'

He stirred, then leaned back in his chair with a grimace.

'In here.' He sounded, if anything, ashamed.

'All right,' said Mary cheerfully. 'I'll just make up the fire a bit, shall I? We might as well make ourselves cosy.'

'What a dreadful word. Cosy. Next you'll be putting something fluffy round my shoulders, and offering me a drinkie. Not like that, you fool! Surely you know how to lay a peat fire, at your age?'

Mary, who had done it on purpose to cheer him up, meekly replaced the slabs of peat to his satisfaction, then went out to the kitchen.

By the time he had eaten his plateful, the Professor looked far less shaky, the bones of his face less prominent and skull-like. Mary took away their trays, made a fresh pot of coffee, and settled with a sigh back into her chair. From outside came the first isolated chirpings of what would soon be a frantic dawn chorus.

'What happened, then? David didn't have time to tell me much. I gather you heard Zen calling?'

'Not calling. Moaning. Silly little fool, didn't want to disturb anyone.' His anger was a measure of his anxiety. 'Seems it had been going on for hours, but she thought if she lay quiet it would go away. Said she thought it was some kind of practice contractions with a stupid name, like pickles. That's what comes of going to these classes, fills their heads with useless information. By the time she realised it wasn't going to stop she was frightened to get out of bed or do anything. As I said, she was worried about disturbing us so she thought she'd wait until it got light. Luckily I got up to go the bathroom.' He glared at her, daring her with his eyes to ask after the state of his prostate. 'Heard her groaning, went up to see what was going on. Terrified she was, poor kid. Convinced it's too early. Told her it was no such thing, plenty of babies born at seven and a half months with no problem at all. Six weeks early, she is. Told her I knew for certain.' He shook his head. 'Lied, of course. Not something I know anything much about, in spite of the books.' He looked at her anxiously, unable to ask outright for reassurance.

'It should be all right. I hope. Twins are always smaller, of course, but the Radcliffe is very good; they'll have special incubators and so on. She couldn't be in a better place.'

Knowing him as she did, she could see the infinitesimal easing of the skin round eyes and mouth that meant relief. Mary felt touched. As far as she could remember, her father had never before needed her reassurance. Even when he had had his stroke, he had needed her physical care but neither her mental nor her emotional support. His own fierce resolve, and his deeply held belief that his will was strong enough to conquer any bodily weakness, were sufficient.

'Lucky you heard her, anyway.'

He grunted. 'Would have been, if I hadn't slipped.' He thumped at his leg with a frustrated fist. 'This bloody leg of mine. Most of the time it's all right, but every so often it goes weak on me. I was hurrying, of course. Didn't bother to put the lights on – know the way round my own house after all these years, don't need to see. Leg gave out on me, grabbed at the banister and missed it. Lucky I was only one step up, and I didn't fall hard. Nothing broken, just the odd bruise. Gave me a fright, though.'

It was an extraordinary admission. Mary was careful not to react too much.

'Yes, that sort of thing does, especially in the dark. It makes you feel silly, too, doesn't it? Like when you trip over a paving stone, and look round to see if anyone's noticed.'

He grunted agreement. 'So I lay there a moment, to see whether anything was going to happen. Moved my arms and legs, that kind of thing.' He spoke calmly, but Mary felt her heart contract, imagining him lying in the dark, feeling for broken bones, waiting for the warning signs that presaged the onset of a stroke.

'You should have one of those mobile phones,' she said suddenly. 'That way you can keep it by you, telephone from anywhere. I can't think why we didn't think of it sooner.'

'Modern rubbish,' he said automatically. 'Don't interrupt.'

'Sorry, Pa.'

'Then all the lights came on, and that boy of yours appeared. He'd heard me fall; well, I believe I did give a bit of a shout when my leg gave way. Silly fool would keep fussing round me when I kept telling him to

177

phone for am ambulance for Zen. Got through to him in the end. Got him to help me through here – didn't want Zen to see me lying there, give her a fright . . . That's all, really.'

'What about a doctor? Didn't he call the doctor, to check you were all right?'

'Wanted to, but I wouldn't let him. Knew I was OK. One of the ambulance men did a quick MOT, said I was roadworthy. Why doesn't that damned boy ring? He must know we're waiting to hear what's happening.'

'Presumably because there's no news. I'm sure he'll let us know as soon as anything happens. These things take time. But there's nothing to stop me telephoning the hospital.'

'No. You've done enough for a bit. You're right, he'll call if there's any news. He may be a bit of a dull stick, but that's a good boy you've got there.'

His voice was gruff. Mary was stunned into silence. They sat peacefully together. The room rang, now, with birdsong, and already the grey light of a new day was making the electric lights look sickly. Mary went to the window and opened it. The air was cool and damp, heavy with the sweet balsam scent of the poplars that grew beyond the end of the garden. It was a smell which, more than any other, carried Mary back to her childhood when each season seemed to stretch beyond the horizons of time.

'Remarkable fish,' she murmured.

'What? What fish?'

'Remarkable. It's Zen's perfect phrase, at the moment. Never mind.'

'Mmn. Clever girl, isn't she.' It was not a question.

'Very. I had my doubts, of course I did, but now I've got to know her, I can see it. She's got – oh, I don't know. Something I've never had, but I can recognise it when I see it.'

'Something I've never had either. True originality, I suppose. And a first-class brain. Well, I've got that, but the other . . . that's a remarkable fish, if you like.'

Mary shivered, and closed the window.

'I think,' she said, out of the blue, 'that John is being unfaithful.'

There was a short pause, and Mary wondered if her father had heard her. Then he stirred in his chair.

'Has he ever been anything else?'

Mary was nettled.

'Of course he has! He's been a very good husband. Steady, reliable, a good provider ... and I'm sure there's never been any other woman. Until now, that is.'

'Faithful is more than not going to bed with his secretary. Faithful is ... having faith in someone. Believing in them.'

'What am I, then? A figment of his imagination?'

'No. But you're someone he's never bothered to get to know. You're not a real person to him, just a convenience.'

'Perhaps that's all I am. All I'm capable of.' Mary could not help thinking that her father, also, could have been accused of similar behaviour.

'"Ever so 'umble, Master Copperfield"?' It was practically a sneer.

'Do you think of me as a person?' she snapped back.

'Probably not. But then I don't with anybody. Why do you think your mother left me? I'm not interested in people, only minds. Intellects. Ideas.'

'Would you have liked me to be like Zen?'

He considered.

'Not really.' He smiled grimly. 'I'd have been jealous of you,' he admitted, with a devastating honesty that it was impossible not to respect. 'I like you as you are. You're a good woman, Mary.'

She felt her eyes wash over with tears that stung like acid. She shook her head, her throat too hard and aching for speech.

'Yes, you are. And you deserve better than John. Whether or not he's being unfaithful to you.'

'You've left it rather late to say so,' said Mary mildly. 'I've been married to him for nearly twenty-five years. Why didn't you object at the beginning? Or did you not see him like that then?'

'I wasn't much drawn to him. But he seemed to be what you wanted, and I never believed in interfering in your private life. You were a sensible child. I always assumed you knew what you were doing.'

'Does anyone? At any age?'

'I always do.'

'Well, I don't. And I don't know what John's doing, either. I just suspect he's having an affair. It sounds so sordid.'

'You don't sound particularly upset.'

'Oh dear, that's the trouble. I'm not, really. It's dreadful; I'm sure I should mind far more than I do. I don't even feel angry, or insulted, or any of the things you're supposed to feel. If anything, I just feel sorry for him. And ...'

'And?'

'And *amused*.'

'*Amused?*'

Mary laughed.

'Now I've shocked you! Yes, amused. You see, I think he's spending his time with that woman who stabbed him. Elaine Brantridge.'

'Ha! Oh, ha ha ha!' Mary thought that she had never heard him laugh so uninhibitedly.

'The way to a man's heart ...' she said in a stifled voice.

'Cupid's dart – modern version, a kitchen knife. Oh, ha ha ha! Perhaps he's not such a dead loss after all!'

Mary giggled. It was true that a new element had entered into her feelings for John. Where before there had been a muddle of gratitude, resentment, the fondness of old habit and a kind of exasperated pity, there was now a new warmth. Was it, perhaps, that for almost the first time in his life he was behaving like a fallible human being? Certainly his position, for someone who had been unable to admit to being out of work, was a very difficult one.

'Do you have any proof? Or is this just feminine intuition?'

'Feminine intuition. I expect I'm just imagining the whole thing.'

'Not necessarily. But something must have made you think it's this Elaine person.'

'Only that it's all started so suddenly. And – I smelled her perfume on him. At least, the perfume she was wearing that night. It's very strong. Heavy.' Her nose wrinkled at the memory. He nodded.

'I'd trust your sense of smell. So, what do you want to do about it?'

'I don't know,' said Mary helplessly. 'What should I do?'

'You're asking me? I'm not exactly a shining example of marital success, am I? How do you feel about it? Apart from amused, that is.'

'I don't know that, either. None of the things I ought to feel, anyway. I don't really mind very much, though I'm sure I should. Is that dreadful? The only thing that really worries me is how it can be sorted out. All that fuss ...' She sighed. The curious intimacy engendered by lack of sleep, by anxiety, and by the silent emptiness of the dawn world where they two seemed to be the only people alive in a slumbering universe, made it suddenly possible to ask the kind of question she had never been able to frame before. 'How did you feel? When Mom went off?'

'Relieved,' he said.

'Is that all?' She was not altogether surprised, but it seemed rather stark.

'Oh, sad, I suppose. Anxious about you. Annoyed with myself for having been foolish enough to marry her in the first place. How much do you remember of her?'

'How she looked. Her accent. The food she cooked.'

He nodded. 'The best things about her. The accent excluded, perhaps, though that had a certain exotic charm to me, at one time.' He shook his head. 'Poor girl. We neither of us got what we expected. I don't know what she saw in me. Some romantic idea of Old England, moated granges and so on. And I saw a pretty face and a good figure, and a kind of superficial sparkle and gloss, the knack of being articulate on many subjects that a good American education gives, and, God help me, I took it for brilliance. By the time she had found out I was only a fuddy-duddy don, and I that she was a shallow socialite, it was too late. I'm sorry. That sounds harsh. But she did care about you. She may not have been the greatest mother in the world, but she tried hard.'

'She went off and left me. I don't call that trying very hard.' The old hurt still ached. He looked surprised.

'But she tried to take you. Didn't you know?'

Mary shook her head.

'She came back to get you. You were at school. She gave up rather too easily, so I telephoned the school and told them not to allow you out of the building under any circumstances. They thought I was mad, but I insisted that your teacher keep you within sight for several days, and I came to fetch you myself. She tried turning up at the school twice, but she soon realised it wasn't going to work. That chap of hers wasn't going to hang around for a kid, and they left. She wrote to me several times, begging me to let you go out there, but I refused. Surely ... I suppose I kept it from you. I didn't want to upset you. And I suppose I was afraid ... Children cling more to their mothers. I thought you might want to go with her ... Perhaps ...' The words came out slowly, as if forced. 'Perhaps I wasn't very fair, to you or to her. But it didn't seem like the right sort of life for a child. For you.'

Mary came and crouched by his chair. She put her hands over his, feeling the brittle hardness of his bones beneath the thin old skin.

'I thought it was a nuisance to you, that she left me behind.'

He looked horrified.

'Did you? I must have been a worse father than I realised. You were always such a self-contained little thing. I'm sorry, Mary.'

It would not be true to say that he had never apologised to Mary before. A man of scrupulous honesty, he had from her early childhood been prepared to accept that he was not always fair, although seldom that he was not right. Nevertheless, Mary had never known him sound so humble. She wasn't very sure that she liked it. She clasped his hands more firmly, and shook them gently.

'No need for that. I don't think I was a particularly good mother for David – certainly not the kind of mother he needed – but I did my best, and so did you. No one's perfect, and other platitudes. Anyway, it was all so long ago. "And besides..."' She stopped, not sure if the quotation should continue.

'"...the wench is dead"?' She should have known he would pick it up. 'Tasteless, but apt.' His hands turned beneath hers, and returned her clasp for a moment before withdrawing. He began to unwrap the enveloping rug. Mary helped him.

'Have to go for a pee. Too much coffee.' Mary was rather relieved. Too much emotion was probably not good for either of them, and the moment did not need to be prolonged. She took the coffee tray back to the kitchen, and washed up. The hot water was pleasant on her hands, and she felt suddenly sleepy. She stood at the sink, swilling the cloth gently round in the water, half dreaming and at peace. Then the telephone rang, shattering her mood. Not waiting to dry her hands, she rushed to the hall and almost collided with her father, emerging from the cloakroom. She beat him by a short head.

'Hello?' Her voice was breathless.

'Mary!' John's voice came from the receiver so loudly that it rang in her head. 'Where the hell are you?'

'Well, I'm here, of course,' she said crossly.

'Yes, but where have you *been*? No, you've been there, I know that, what I mean is ... why? You might have left me a note.'

He sounded aggrieved.

'You weren't there,' Mary pointed out quietly. 'And you didn't think to let me know where you were, did you? David phoned me, and you weren't there, so I just left.'

'David phoned you? Why? That dreadful girl, I suppose.'

'As a matter of fact, I'm here because of Pa. He had a bit of a fall, but he's all right. And Zen has gone to hospital. To have the babies. And we're waiting for a telephone call, so I'm afraid you'll have to get off the line.'

'But Mary—'

'I'm sorry, John,' she said firmly. 'You're welcome to come over here, if you want. But I really have to go now.'

She put the telephone down. Faintly, as the receiver left her ear, she heard his voice – 'Mary!' – then she replaced it firmly. Almost at once, it rang again.

'Really, John,' she began to say crossly.

'Mum! It's me! A boy and a girl, mum! She's had a boy and a girl! About half an hour ago. They did a Caesarean. Zen's all right, they're still tidying her up. That's what they call it. The babies are so tiny...' His voice faded. He was obviously deeply moved. 'So tiny. But they're all right. Breathing, and everything. They're in incubators, they've taken them up to some special unit. I promised Zen I'd go and check on them for her, but I said I must call you and Grandprof first. Is he all right?'

'He's fine.' Mary broke in on the flow of words. 'A boy and a girl,' she said to her waiting father, 'very tiny and in incubators, but all right. Zen had a Caesarean, but she's all right too.' Her father nodded.

'I'll stay here for a bit longer,' David continued. 'It's all been so extraordinary ... I'll have to get back, though, and have a wash and a shave. I can't very well miss the course, it's almost the last day and I don't know that they'd understand. I suppose I could say my grandfather was ill...'

'Certainly not,' said Mary briskly. 'Zen will want to sleep, and the babies won't run away. Ask whether we can come and visit later, will you, and what time? I'll get some breakfast ready for you.'

'Thanks, Mum. I'm starving. See you soon, then. Oh, by the way...' He sounded suddenly rather shy. 'Zen says she's going to call the boy David.'

'How lovely!'

'It should have been after Grandprof, really, but Archibald...'

'Quite. There are limits.'

'Yes, even if you do call yourself Zen. It's not her real name, did you know? Her real name's Rosie. Rosie O'Hara.'

'Pretty. Well, give her our love, and the babies too. See you soon.'

This time, when the telephone rang again, she knew it must be John again. He was not at all interested in Zen's twins, and was inclined to think it an insult that one of them should be named after any member of his family.

'It's outrageous! What will people think?'

'Who knows?' Mary felt suddenly light-hearted. 'Who cares?'

'Now that's typical of your attitude, Mary. Of course it matters. You don't want people to say that David's the father, do you?'

'Not really, though since it certainly isn't true I can't see what difference it makes. Anyway, if you are coming over here, would you bring me some clothes? And my wash things? I'm afraid I rushed out without anything useful, and it looks as though I'll need to stay for a few days.'

'I'm afraid that won't be possible,' he answered stiffly. 'I'm afraid I shan't be coming over. You may choose to encourage David to associate with this girl, but I certainly shall not. Nor do I think it anything but deplorable that your father should have her actually living in his house with him, with nobody else there.'

'For one thing she's not here, she's in hospital. And for another, David's here, and so am I.'

'That's even worse. I do not choose to be a party to it. I shall be staying with friends. I will let you know when I intend to return.'

Chapter 16

Mary put down the telephone and stood looking at it thoughtfully, rather as though she thought it might explode. Behind her, Professor Hill cleared his throat, and she jumped.

'I think I'll go and have a bath,' was all he said, however. Mary was grateful for this unusual tact. She was quite sure that her father, whose hearing was still excellent, would have been able to make out most of what John had shouted, and had guessed the rest from Mary's replies. She was not sure how she felt, apart from guiltily relieved that John would not be coming over to make trouble in person, and preferred not to discuss it with anyone just yet. The important thing, after all, was Zen and the babies. She would concentrate on that for the time being, and let everything else happen as it came along.

'Good idea,' she said cheerfully. 'I'll do the same.' Another legacy of her long-ago mother was a copious supply of hot water. 'David will be back soon, wanting some breakfast. I'd better get a move on. Do you want any help?'

He was moving slowly up the stairs.

'Certainly not,' he snapped back. 'I can still manage to keep myself clean.'

'I know you can, but you've had a long night and quite a lot of excitement. At least don't lock the bathroom door, Pa, please.'

He grunted. Mary braced herself.

'Perhaps I'll have a shower instead of a bath.'

Mary was so astounded by this sudden display of good sense that she said nothing, which was probably the best thing she could have done. By the time she had pulled herself together he had gone. She remembered that she must hurry, and ran up to the room she still thought of as hers.

Luckily she had a basic collection of clothes, underwear and wash things left here from the time when her father had been recovering from his stroke. She collected them while she waited for her father to finish his shower; her bathroom was nearer the hot water tank than his, and if she were to turn her shower on his was liable to go suddenly cold.

When the sound of water in the pipes died away she showered quickly, dressed in clean clothes and brushed her teeth and her hair, swiftly plaiting and twisting it up with fingers that moved automatically, without any need to look at what she was doing. Her face in the mirror looked tired and there were bags under her eyes. She told herself that the lighting in this bathroom had always been unflattering, which was true enough, and that in any case there was no one she needed to impress. Her only make-up was what she had in her handbag – powder and a lipstick; but she foraged through the bathroom cupboard and found an old mascara, rather dried up, which encouraged her. She went back down to the kitchen feeling surprisingly cheerful and optimistic.

David arrived almost immediately after. His clothes, usually so carefully chosen to be appropriate to the occasion, indicated his perturbation of mind. The suit trousers and jacket that he must have been wearing for the course were teamed with an old rugby shirt which he kept for relaxing in during the evening. His hair was tousled, his eyes red-rimmed but bright with excitement. He kissed her with more exuberance than his usual dutiful peck.

'Hi, Mum. Is breakfast ready? I'm starving!'

'It'll be about ten minutes. Why don't you shower and shave? Pa will be down in a minute, and he'll want to hear all about it. At least, I suppose he will. I certainly do. Did you see the babies again? Are they all right?'

'Yes, and they're fine. Well, they haven't got all those drips and things that some of them have got, just tubes down their noses for feeding, so I reckon that's a good sign, don't you?' He yawned widely, his jaw cracking. 'God, I'm tired. Don't know how I'm going to get through the course today.' He leaned across the table, picking at the loaf she had set out. Mary turned him round and pushed him towards the door.

The bacon was grilling, the pan heating for the eggs, when the doorbell rang. Nobody else was downstairs. Mary cursed and pulled the frying pan off the heat. Could it be John? she wondered as she crossed the hall. Surely not. He never went back on his decisions. And yet who else would be turning up here at – she looked at her watch – ten past seven in the morning? It must be John, then. Her heart sank at the prospect of his disapproval.

She opened the front door reluctantly, peering round it rather than pulling it hospitably wide. Because she was expecting John her eyes were already lifted to someone tall. The height was right, but the build . . . against the early morning light, he looked huge. What could John be wearing to make him look so bulky?

'Mary! Won't you let me in?'

The voice, warm and amused, pulled her eyes to his face which she had been subconsciously avoiding. Not John at all.

'Rupert!' She pulled the door wide. 'I thought you were John!'

His eyebrows lifted, but he said nothing. Coming into the hall he enveloped her in a hug and kissed her firmly on the cheek. It was very comfortable, and Mary allowed herself to lean, for a moment, against his friendly bulk. At the sound of rapid footsteps on the stairs she pulled herself free, feeling flustered.

'Oh, David! This is, um, Rupert. Rupert Greenwood. One of Grandprof's old students. This is my son, David.'

They shook hands, David warily, Rupert without any of the embarrassment Mary was feeling.

'Something smells good,' he said.

'Goodness, the bacon!' Mary flew back into the kitchen. 'It won't be a moment. I've just got to fry the eggs. The coffee's ready, help yourselves, and there's toast in the warmer. Are you hungry, Rupert?'

'Naturally. I always am,' he answered simply. Mary put more bacon to grill and filled a plate for David, who began to eat hungrily. The Professor came in, greeted Rupert imperturbably, and joined them at the table.

'Seen them again, have you?'

David nodded, his mouth full. He swallowed, looked regretfully at the next mouthful already poised on his fork, and laid it down reluctantly.

'Yes. Tiny little pink scraps, hideous really, but amazing! They let me hold them for a moment, before they put them into the incubators. Terrifying. I thought they'd break if I touched them. But the boy looked at me . . . he really did. Such a look . . .' His own eyes took on a faraway expression, he waved his hands in the air, unable to express what he meant.

187

'I know. Infinite wisdom,' said Rupert. 'You think they can see right through into your soul, and they don't think much of it.'

'Yes, that's it.' David nodded.

'Can't focus their eyes, at that age,' said the Professor gruffly. 'Couldn't even see you. Why would they let you hold them, anyway? Nothing to do with you.'

'Pa! You're jealous! Zen's had her babies,' Mary explained belatedly to Rupert.

'Yes, I rather gathered. And you were there? Lucky chap!'

David grinned through the forkful of food he had gone back to.

'Jealous! I'm never jealous,' spluttered the Professor. 'Don't like babies, anyway. Noisy. Smelly. Troublesome.'

'So you won't want to go and see them later on today, then?' Mary caught Rupert's eye, and he winked at her.

'I didn't say that, did I? Of course I'll go and see Zen, and make polite noises about the brats. You know me. The soul of tact.' The other three exploded into laughter. 'What are you laughing at? Bunch of lunatics,' he muttered, which made them laugh still more. David looked at his watch.

'One more slice of toast, and I must go.' He crunched his way hurriedly through it, and stood up with the last corner still in his hand. 'See you later,' he said in a muffled voice. They heard him taking the stairs two at a time. Professor Hill finished his coffee and stood up.

'I shall have a sleep,' he said. 'Wake me up at eleven o'clock, Mary.' He nodded to Rupert.

Left alone with Rupert, Mary felt suddenly awkward.

'More toast? And coffee?'

'Yes please, to both.' He held out his cup. 'Very good marmalade. Yours?' She nodded. 'I thought so. Most people don't bother to cut it so carefully.' He leaned back in his chair, seeming to have all the time in the world.

'The sandwich bar!' said Mary suddenly. 'You should have been there hours ago! You told me you were usually there by seven at the latest!'

'Left it to the others,' he said airily. 'Be good for them, a bit of a challenge. See if they can do it.'

'They'll be rushed off their feet. You don't want to upset your customers.'

188

'No, they're all pretty faithful. I said to tell them it was a crisis. People love a crisis. Dunkirk spirit, and all that.'

'What crisis?' Mary thought about it. 'You couldn't have known about Zen before you got here. And, come to that, why are you here? Not that it's not good to see you...'

He stirred his coffee, though Mary knew he never had sugar in it. His gaze was fixed on the swirling liquid as if he could read the future – or the past – in its muddy depths.

'I had a phone call. From John.'

'From John? So you did know about Zen. But why would John ring to tell you that? And so early in the morning?'

Still he did not look at her.

'It wasn't to tell me about Zen. He rang earlier. About half past five or so. He said he'd just got in, and that you weren't there.'

He lifted the cup to his face and drank slowly. That coffee must be cold, Mary thought. I poured it out ages ago.

'So why did he ring you?' she asked. As she spoke she felt the colour flame up her body. It seemed to start somewhere round her navel and spread outwards: she thought she could have charted its movement, like watching the steady rise of mercury in a thermometer. When it reached her neck she knew that it would show, and automatically put her hands up to shield it. Then it was in her face. Goodness, she thought. Is this a hot flush? That's what it feels like – a lavatory in reverse with the liquid swirling up instead of down.

With difficulty she took her hands from her face and laid them carefully on the table, palms down. She looked at them. Large, capable hands, the nails filed short and unpolished, the skin always slightly rough because she disliked rubber gloves. Unadorned, no rings except the plain gold band of her wedding ring. Straightforward hands. Hands that since her marriage had never – except in her fantasies – touched intimately any man but her husband or her son.

'He thought I was with you.' The words came out flatly: as flat as her hands on the table. She almost thought she could see them lying there, plain words in a black, unadorned typeface. He thought I was with you. Her fingers twitched and she knew that she was typing them; a habit started in her student days, of picking up a word and a phrase and typing it in her head. If I make a mistake, she thought, I'll have to retype it three times. But there was no mistake. The words were too easy.

'Yes.' Yes, she typed. Yes full stop space space space.

189

'How did he get your number? Oh! Oh, of course!' Mary shook her head. 'It's my fault. I scribbled your name and number on the notepad by the phone. I meant to ring you about the office lunches, and I looked up your home number in the book, then didn't get round to doing it. He must have looked to see if I'd left him a note, and seen it. I'm very sorry.' The apology came out stiffly. He looked up at her, his face unreadable.

'So am I.' S o space a m space shift i full stop typed her fingers. He put down his cup and stretched his hand across the table, laying it across hers. It was big enough almost to cover them.

'You're twitching,' he said. 'It's all right.'

'I'm typing,' she said.

'You're what?'

'Typing. Typing what we're saying. It's a kind of habit. A nervous habit. I'm sorry.'

His fingers gripped, shook her hands.

'You don't have to keep apologising. I don't mind if you play arpeggios with your toes, if that's what you want to do.'

'I don't think I could,' she said seriously, considering it. 'They're not long enough. Chromatic scales . . .'

'Mary!'

For the first time she lifted up her eyes and looked at him properly.

'It's all right,' she said. 'I'm not upset. I'm embarrassed, of course. Was he very rude to you? Did he shout?'

He shook his head.

'Not at all. He was really very polite. I'm so sorry to disturb you, but do you know where my wife is – that sort of thing. Extraordinary, if he had really thought you were with me at five in the morning. I mean, he didn't sound jealous or anything. Just rather put out to find you weren't there. I said no. I don't know if he believed me, but he apologised for waking me up. I suggested you might be here, and he agreed, and we said goodbye in a very civilised way. I don't think I've ever had quite such a bizarre conversation. Is he . . . is he under a lot of stress?'

'Having a nervous breakdown, do you mean? I don't know. I don't think so.' Mary hesitated, but under the circumstances it seemed a bit late for discretion. 'I think he's having an affair. In fact, I'm fairly sure he was spending the night with her. He hadn't come home, you see, when David rang me in the night. I rushed off without thinking to leave a note, because Pa had fallen on the stairs and I didn't want him to be on his own while David went to the hospital with Zen.' He nodded his comprehension. 'I think, perhaps, that's why he suspected me. You're the only man, apart from Bill Naseby, that I see at all often, and of course he knows I've been visiting the sandwich bar. And because he's being unfaithful, he thinks I must be as well.'

'Wants to think,' he corrected her. 'It makes it more legitimate for him, if he can persuade himself that you're doing it too. He must know, deep down, that you're not the type. Unfortunately.'

The last word was spoken quietly. Mary ignored it.

'I still can't believe he rang you. He must have been in agonies of embarrassment when he found I wasn't there. You'd think he'd be relieved, but he seems so angry with me,' she said, not complaining, but as one stating a curious fact.

'Of course he is. There's nothing worse than being in the wrong, and knowing it. When you feel guilty, the person you most resent is the one you're guilty about. If you know what I mean.'

'I suppose I've never felt that guilty.'

'Lucky girl!' He smiled at her. 'What an innocent life you must have led.'

'I don't know.' She struggled to find the words. 'I'm beginning to think I've never really had a life at all.'

'Get a life!' he grinned. Mary looked at him, startled. 'It's what the kids say about someone they think is, oh, a bit wet. Not that you're wet. And you don't seem like the sort of person who hasn't got a life.'

'Perhaps. But all the interesting bits have been in my head.'

'Aren't everyone's?'

'Not exclusively. I mean, I have these fantasies . . .' She felt herself blush again, suddenly aware that the word usually carried a strong sexual connotation. 'About houses, I mean. And a kitchen – I've got a kitchen in my head that feels more like home than anywhere I've ever actually been in. And I have a cat. And . . . a friend. Well, more than a friend, I suppose.' She blushed once more.

He thought it unutterably sad, but smiled encouragingly. 'We all have our dreams. Some of them can be realised, most of them not. There's no harm in it.'

'Isn't there? Not even if the dreams are more important than the reality?'

'Only if you confuse the two. You don't do that, surely?'

'No.' She shook her head, sadly. 'Sometimes I'd like to. I'm aware of the possibility. But then it's men in white coats time, isn't it?' She began to gather up the breakfast dishes and stack them in the dishwasher. He helped her, rinsing the plates and slotting the knives and forks neatly into the basket with the automatic movements of one who did this all day, every day. Mary could not help thinking of John, who had clearly defined parameters regarding men's and women's work. He would dutifully spend an hour mending the dishwasher, but he never filled or emptied it. It was extraordinary, she thought, how comfortable she felt with Rupert. Even the awkwardness over John's telephone call had passed quickly. Was he somehow familiar to her, because he had once been her father's student and was therefore part of her earlier life, however little remembered? Or was it merely that they seemed to like so many of the same things, and to think alike so often?

Trying to step back and be objective, she examined her feelings for him. Interest, liking, and friendship, of course. Attraction? In a physical sense she had to admit that the answer was yes, although she was always careful not to think or speculate about that. It never occurred to her to think of herself as sexually interesting or available, and Rupert was so physically demonstrative that the hug or the kiss on the cheek with which he frequently greeted her seemed perfectly normal.

Thinking about it, she realised that her relationship with Rupert was, in many ways, similar to her relationship with her imaginary lover. He was someone she could talk to, someone who understood what she said, who laughed at the same things. In that respect he was more like a close woman friend, and she had often thought that it was partly because she had her lover to talk to that she had not made more effort to find the kind of close supportive bond many women had with their female friends. Such closeness was something she had never, sadly, been able to reach with John.

'Good Lord, what day is it?' she asked suddenly. The thought of John had recalled her to the exigencies of everyday life.

'Friday. Why?'

She checked her watch.

'Half past nine! I'm supposed to be at work!' She looked wildly round the kitchen, as though she expected it to transform itself into her cubbyhole at Naseby's. 'I must go!'

'Hang on!' He caught at her arm as she went towards the door. 'Can't they manage without you for one day? Your father needs you more than they do, not to mention Zen. Can't you give them a ring?'

'What? Oh yes. Yes, of course.' She put up a hand to rub her forehead. 'I don't know what's the matter with me. I'm usually much more sensible than this.'

'You're tired, and you've had a lot on your mind.'

'You can say that again!' She went to the telephone. Bill Naseby was so relieved to hear that she was all right – she had never been late like this before – that he told her at once to take as much time off as she needed.

'Oh, I'm sure I'll be back on Monday,' she said. 'My father was only a bit shaken, not really hurt. And there's nothing urgent. I sent off the end-of-year stuff to the accountant last week. If you're sure . . .'

'Of course I am. Not that we won't miss you, of course. But you take as long as you need. We're managing. Uncle's back. I don't let him do too much by way of work, but he's chirpy as a cricket to be here again, fighting with Dad.'

'Oh, that is good! That he's back, I mean. Give him my love!'

'I'll do that. And I'm sure he'd ask me to give you his kind regards.'

Mary rang off, thinking how very much more civilised Bill Naseby was than most men.

Back in the kitchen, she found herself telling Rupert about the house she had visited.

'It really would have been quite suitable,' she said enthusiastically, 'only it's probably too big and too expensive.'

'What was it like?'

'Quite old – traditional stone built. A farm, really, but they'd sold off all the land separately and there were too many outbuildings and bits and pieces for it to be sold as a normal home. The actual farmhouse wasn't very big, either, only two bedrooms, and although there was another little two-bedroomed cottage it wasn't next to it. You couldn't make them into one, or anything. It was the outbuildings, really. A lovely old barn, timber-framed. The sort that farmers hate, because it's too small for their machinery and too good just to demolish. A dairy next to it – the slate shelves are still there – and on the end by the barn a big stone trough with water bubbling out of it.'

'Out of it? Something wrong with the plumbing, you mean?'

'I don't think so. It wasn't that kind of trough. It was low on the

193

ground, sunk into it a bit. I think it was a spring. They probably used it to cool the churns of milk.'

'Sounds pretty.'

'Yes, it was. But very dilapidated. Not really suitable for Naseby's. Silly, really. And the thing I liked best about it – apart from the trough – was the garden, though I didn't actually see it. It's walled, and the gate was locked. But on the details it said it was quite big, nearly an acre, and full of fruit trees, and they're protected or something. I didn't really understand that bit. But I thought it sounded nice. Not very practical, I suppose. The barn's too big, and the house is too small.'

He looked thoughtful. 'Where did you say this place was?'

'About ten miles outside Oxford. Why?'

'Why don't we go and see it this afternoon?'

'Go and see it? You mean, properly? With the agent?'

'Why not? It's not very far. We could take your father, if you like. It's a beautiful day. We could have tea somewhere.'

'Checking out the opposition?'

'Nothing like a bit of industrial espionage. I'll go back to Reading now, and get the lunchtime rush out of the way, then come back by about four. What do you think?'

'Well . . . I should be . . .'

'There are always I-should-bes. Look on this day as a kind of present. You would have been working, so none of the other things would have been done anyway. Come on, it'll be fun. I'd enjoy it: I haven't had a day off that wasn't a Sunday or a bank holiday since I set up the sandwich bar, almost. If you say no, I'll have to stay and work.'

'Blackmail is an ugly word, Mr Greenwood.'

'But effective, madam. With a certain kind of person.'

'The weak, easily led ones?'

'The kind-hearted ones. Go on, Mary. Say yes.'

'All right. Yes. But it's a waste of time. It's not at all suitable for Naseby's.'

'Bother Naseby's. It sounds intriguing. Half past four. Promise?'

'I promise,' said Mary weakly. He surged out of the kitchen, leaving the room feeling suddenly echoingly empty. The thought of spending some of the afternoon with him made her feel, for a moment, as elated as a young girl going on a date. She gave herself a mental shake. Go to the shops, she told herself. Get something for lunch. Get presents for the babies. Get something for Zen, and pick her some flowers from the garden. Pack her up clean nighties, and her wash things – not very likely that David would have thought of all that, under the circumstances. Feeling suddenly full of vigour, she wrote a note to her father and went into Oxford.

Chapter 17

'Zen, they're beautiful. Really beautiful.'
  'If you like pink frogs.'
'Love them.' Mary leaned over to peer through the plastic top of the incubator. It was true that in their aquarium-like cribs, their little limbs splayed out, the twins did look like something from a wildlife programme. Mary heard the hushed David Attenborough tones. One of the babies – David, she thought – twitched, its minute fingers clenching for a moment into a parody of a winner's air punch. Zen, from her chair between the two incubators, put her hand in and stroked him gently. The wrinkled little eyelids opened for a moment, and Mary found herself more than half expecting the revealed eyes to be milky and unseeing. Instead a glance like a laser scanned the room, fixing, she thought, on her own face for a moment before moving on to find Zen's. They rested there for a second or two, as though assessing her, then the eyelids came down again.
  'Goodness,' said Mary shakily. 'David said they had X-ray eyes, but I didn't realise ... Are they both like that?'
  'Yeah. They don't do it very often, but when they do open their eyes I could swear they know exactly what they're seeing. Be a handful, they will.'
  'What are you calling the little girl?'
  'Molly. After my mum.'
  'Molly – I like that. Quite unusual nowadays, a bit old-fashioned, but nice. Is she pleased? Have you spoken to her?'
  'Yeah. She's coming down to see us tomorrow.' She glanced at Mary. 'Molly ... it's short for Mary. Well, not short for, but ...'
  'I know. Thank you, Zen, I feel very honoured. And I know David is too.'

'Poor old David!' Zen laughed. 'He was terrified! But he stuck it out, didn't faint or anything. It was good of him. I know he doesn't think much of me. But he likes the babies.'

'Of course he does. And I don't agree that he doesn't think much of you. He's just never met anyone quite like you before, and he's having all his preconceptions turned on their heads. It's very good for him. It should have happened years ago. I've obviously failed him as a mother.'

It was meant as a joke, but Zen's face was serious.

'That's how it's going to be from now on, isn't it? I never realised before.'

'What, people judging you by your appearance?' Zen shook her head. Her rainbow hair, which Mary was so used to that she no longer noticed it, had been trimmed a few days earlier and now lay in a neat cap over her head, the colour freshly applied and glowing.

'No, not that. I mean, being responsible. Being a good mother. I used to think it just came naturally, that when the baby was born you knew how to do it, like you know how to breathe when you're born, even though you've been swimming around in water for nine months. But those books I read ... I thought it was just feeding and changing and cuddling, and being a bit strict with them when they got older so they didn't go out mugging old ladies and ram-raiding ... Now I wonder whether I'm going to spend the rest of my life looking at everything I do and say, and wondering whether I couldn't have done it better...' Her lips, carefully painted with purple lipstick, suddenly trembled like a child's, and her grey eyes were awash with tears.

'Oh, my dear...' Mary bent over Zen's chair and hugged her rather tentatively. Usually such gestures were inhibited by her size, which made her feel clumsy and awkward, but Zen's skinny body was so childlike in its smallness that it seemed quite natural to gather her into her arms. Zen drooped her head into Mary's shoulder and sobbed. Mary rocked her, and made soothing noises, and after a while the sobs died away to hiccups and snuffles. Mary reached into her pocket for a handkerchief.

'I'll get make-up on it. There's lipstick on your blouse. It'll mark. Ooooh!' Zen wailed, ceasing at once when the babies stirred. 'Sorry,' Zen whispered. 'I'm sorry. It's just...'

'The baby blues,' said Mary matter-of-factly. 'Perfectly normal, if a bit early. But you had an exhausting night, and you probably shouldn't be here now, should you?'

'Not really.' Zen managed a wobbly smile. 'They said I could stay for a few minutes, but the porter's forgotten me. They won't let me walk more than a few steps, so I had to come in this 'orrible chair, like some kind of cripple. I feel better now.' She sounded surprised.

'Of course you do. There's nothing like a nice cry, and why shouldn't you? I don't blame you. It's just a pity it's not your mother here, instead of me.'

'Mum would just tell me to pull meself together,' said Zen with a faint grin, blowing her nose vigorously. 'Crying over spilt milk, she'd call this. She don't seem to worry about things, Mum, just gets on with them.'

'I bet she does really, only she's too busy to let on. So will you be, when these little darlings are out of here. You mustn't worry too much about what you read in the books. They'll give you a lot of advice, and most of it's good, but in the end you must trust your instincts and do what seems right to you. There's no such thing as a perfect mother. All you can do is do the best under the circumstances you find yourself in, and remember that people are born, as well as made. Whatever you do, they'll be themselves, just as you are you in spite of whatever your mother, or your teachers, or my father, may try to do to change you.'

'I wish I'd never read them now,' said Zen crossly. 'My mum never had no books. Any books.' Her self-correction was completely automatic.

Mary nodded. 'The more you know, the more you know you don't know,' she said. 'That's the price you pay, I'm afraid. It's part of what my father's work with you has done, one of the things I was worried about. You will be a different person because of him. You already are a different person. I just hope you won't regret it all.'

'Regret it?' Zen was astonished. 'Why would I regret it? It's the best thing that ever happened to me, meeting him. I could have gone all through my life not knowing, like some kind of zombie. I may worry more about some things, but at least I know they're there to worry about. And the babies . . .' Her eyes rested on each tiny form. 'I'll make sure they get their chance, too. If they're clever, then they'll learn, or I'll want to know why!'

'Good.' Mary hesitated. 'My father – he may not be able to teach you for as long as he'd like to, but . . .'

'I know,' Zen broke in. 'That fall! I was so frightened. He's all right, isn't he? He seemed OK when you brought him in earlier.'

'Yes, he's fine. Just a few bruises. But if he were to have another stroke...'

'Yeah. Poor old duck.' She looked shyly at Mary. 'I'd look after him, you know. I helped Mum with my nan, after she broke her hip. I don't mind anything, incontinence pads and all that, if it'll help. Nurses cost a fortune, and he'd hate it in a home, wouldn't he? All those old wrecks, watching game shows on the telly.'

Mary patted her hand.

'I know you would, my dear. And I wouldn't say no, either, though I suspect you'd be too busy with the twins to be able to do much. But if the worst came to the worst, you know I'll try to make sure you're all right, don't you? I mean, you won't find yourself thrown out on the streets or anything.'

Zen frowned.

'I don't need charity. I can look after myself, and the kids.'

'I know you can. It's nothing to do with charity. But we've agreed that things have changed for you, that you're a different person since you met my father. He looks on you – don't be cross – as his creation, almost. He feels responsible for you, in the same way that you feel responsible for the babies. I told him at the beginning that it wouldn't be fair of him to drop dead and leave you in the lurch, so he said...' she paused, dubiously, 'he said he'd leave you to me. As a kind of legacy. Not that he needed to,' she added hastily. 'I mean, I'd have been there anyway. But you see...'

'A legacy.' Mary held her breath. Zen gave a hoot of laughter. 'Isn't that just like the old bugger? Oh, sorry.'

Mary laughed too, with relief.

'Don't apologise. He is an old bugger. And although I will do anything I can to help you, I have to tell you now that my husband would strenuously resist any attempt to give you a home with us, although there's plenty of room now David's moved out. But I'm sure we could find somewhere.' She stirred. 'Listen to us, behaving as though Pa were at death's door. He'll probably see us both out, surprise us all. It's seeing these little scraps, I suppose.' She nodded at the babies. 'Somehow, just having them there makes you more aware of the future.'

'Yeah.' Zen's eyes suddenly looked heavy, her face pale now that much of her make-up had been wept off.

'Come on,' said Mary. 'I'm going to wheel you back to your ward. You need to rest while you've got the chance.'

Obediently, Zen put her hand into the cribs to caress each sleeping child.

'Thanks, Mary,' was all she said, but Mary knew that it was for more than the ride in the wheelchair.

'No sweat,' she said in a fake Australian accent. 'She'll be right, Sheila.'

'And cobblers to you too, cobber,' Zen returned with a flash of her old self. 'Where's that bed? You can plant me in it like one of your daisies.'

'Daisies are weeds,' said Mary primly, pushing her out into the corridor. 'You don't plant them, you dig them up.'

'Oh well. Same difference.'

'I don't know why we're doing this,' said Mary crossly. 'It's quite ridiculous.'

Rupert glanced at her. She sat hunched slightly forward in her seat, tense, the seatbelt pulling taut and a perceptible gap between her back and the car seat. He eased his foot off the accelerator and pushed his own large shoulders into the cushioned backrest. The car, an ancient Mercedes, was beginning to show signs of rust at the edges, but the seats were still comfortable.

'Relax,' he said equably. 'It's a beautiful day. We're driving out into the country. Sit back and enjoy it.'

'I can't.'

'Can't relax, or can't enjoy it?'

'Both. It just seems ... wrong.' As soon as she had said it she felt embarrassed by the implications, but his face was placid as he negotiated the narrow lane.

'Protestant work ethic,' he murmured. 'If you enjoy it, it must be bad for you. On that basis, cooking and eating good food is downright immoral.'

Mary laughed. Some of the tension oozed from her body, and she allowed herself to lean back in the seat.

'That's better. You looked as though you were about to draw in a sharp breath and clutch at the door handle, like my old auntie used to do, and I rather pride myself on my driving.'

Mary looked down at her hands, and saw how they were gripped together. She prised her fingers apart, and drew in a deep breath.

'You're right. I am allowed to go out and do what I want, from time to time. After all, John's away with friends, Zen's safe in hospital and Pa's having a quiet afternoon, with his housekeeper there to keep an eye on him. Nobody needs me to do anything. Even Mr Naseby. And it is partly on his behalf that I'm going to this place, though I don't really think it's at all suitable for him. Still, it might be.'

'You don't have to justify it,' he said, changing gear smoothly. 'If you must, why not say it's for me? Here I am, overworked, stressed, in desperate need of a bit of country air to keep me sane . . .' He shook his head ponderously. Mary laughed.

'Poor old you. I can't really see that going to look at a crumbling old place which some pushy young high pressure negotiator will try to bully us into buying is the answer to anyone's incipient nervous breakdown, but don't forget this was all your idea.'

'Yes, it was. No pushy salesman, however. Didn't I tell you? I've got the keys.'

'Got the keys? To the house? How did you manage that?'

'It's me honest face, guv. No, as a matter of fact, that pushy young salesman was at school with my elder son. He used to spend half his time at our house. I just offered to share some of the wilder exploits of his youth with his colleagues – like the time he fell off the roof and nearly drowned, stuck head first in the water butt, or the time he got his willy caught in his zip and we had to take him to Casualty – and he caved in at once. The place has been on the market for more than a year, anyway, and empty for longer than that.'

'What's wrong with it? I thought it seemed too good to be true, that it hadn't been snapped up. I thought places like that were still selling well, in spite of the recession.'

'You'd think so. The trouble is, the house and the cottage are so small in relation to the number of outbuildings, and there's no land for horseyculture. That alone might have been all right, but it seems there is some kind of restriction on the garden.'

'On the garden? The one with the trees in?'

'That's the one. The trees are protected, or something. It's written into the deeds. He didn't have much time to explain it to me, but it makes it impossible to extend the house or do anything else with the garden, and it puts people off. So there it is.'

'Oh.' Mary felt rather daunted. 'Still, I suppose Mr Naseby might not mind about that. He doesn't want a big house, and as far as I know he's never been very keen on gardening. And surely all this must have brought the price down?'

'Not on paper, but I think the owners would be glad to have an offer. It belonged to an old lady who died, and it's her children who are selling. They both live miles away – Scotland and so on – and they just want to be shot of it. That's what Jason told me, privately, of course. Anyway, they've had two or three people who seemed interested, but they all faded out when they realised the local farmers weren't likely to let them have any land for ponies, and that they would be stuck with a two-bedroomed house and all those trees.'

'What a funny thing to do. I mean, I like trees, whatever they are, but to fill the garden with them and make them sacrosanct – she must have been a bit weird.'

'One sandwich short of a picnic, and obsessive with it. Fell out with her family, fell out with the neighbours, wouldn't have a telephone and refused to use electricity, though it's all laid on. And mains water. Said it was full of chemicals, and insisted on drinking from the spring.'

'The spring! That stone trough, you mean?'

'Presumably. Hang on, I think we're nearly there. Does this look familiar?'

'I think so, but I was coming from the other direction. Yes, there it is, on the right! I know I went past it, because there's no for sale board up.'

'They're worried about squatters. Yes, this is it. Goodness, what a fine crop of weeds.'

He pulled up in the gateway, and Mary got out to open the gate. Wooden, with a heavy metal sprung latch, it sagged on its hinges once released and she had to lift it to get it further than a few inches open. Rupert drove slowly into the middle of the courtyard and stopped. Mary stayed where she was, looking despondently around. Somehow the place looked more run-down than she had remembered it, the empty buildings crumbly with rotten wood, the cobbles matted with weeds. In the little house an old curtain, faded an indeterminate grey and ragged at the edges, hung at the window like a stage cobweb, just visible through the grime. It all looked hopeless and desolate. Mary felt ashamed of it, as if it had been an elderly relative discovered partially clothed and without her teeth in.

Rupert climbed out of the car and stood stretching and looking round him.

'I'm sorry,' said Mary, picking her way over the cobbles. 'It's a bit of a wasted journey, I'm afraid.' Under no circumstances could she see the Nasebys, father, uncle and son town-dwellers to a man, settling into this weed-smothered collection of agricultural buildings.

'Wasted? Not a bit of it. It's fascinating. Come on, what shall we look at first? The house, or the barn?'

'The house, I suppose. Goodness, is that the key?' Mary eyed the huge iron key with awe.

'Wonderful, isn't it? With that on your keyring you'd never lose it in the bottom of your handbag. In fact it would probably double as a handy tyre lever.' He fitted it into the heavy door where it turned silently, though the door itself had swollen into the frame and needed all Rupert's not inconsiderable strength and weight to force it open.

Inside, it was less depressing than Mary had feared. The old lady's relatives had obviously done a clean sweep, for the house was bare. Mary had dreaded that there would be shabby old furniture and pathetic little relics of her life, the small everyday objects of no value that could so poignantly call up a vanished past. Instead the floor, solidly boarded beneath a gentle sifting of dust, rang to their footsteps, the sound bouncing off plain, cream-painted walls.

The front door opened directly into a good sized room, the full depth of the house, with windows front and back and a deep chimney recess which housed an old-fashioned solid fuel stove.

'It's called "kitchen stroke living room" in the detail,' said Rupert, consulting the paper in his hand. 'Because of the stove, I suppose. There's no sink, though. Oh, a scullery off it. Which door, do you suppose?'

There were two in the left-hand wall. Mary opened the first.

'Not this, anyway. This is a dark little passage and stairs upstairs, and a door to the other room. What do they call that?'

' "Sitting room". I'd call it the parlour, wouldn't you? It's just crying out for a really uncomfortable horsehair sofa, all slippery and prickly, and lots of little tables with bobble-fringed cloths and hundreds of ornaments. Smells all right, though, doesn't it? No damp, or rot.'

'No. It seems quite sound, at least. Come on, let's find the scullery before we look upstairs.'

With more enthusiasm Mary led the way back to the other room, and opened the further door.

'Phew,' she said, recoiling. 'Now that *does* smell damp.'

Rupert went past her through the doorway.

'Old plumbing, I think, though,' he said, bending to peer at the pipework beneath a deep rectangular sink. 'And this wooden draining board has been left under the drips, and rotted a bit. Easy enough to fix.'

'There's a back door, too. Have you got a key for it? Oh, no, it's just bolted.' Mary wrestled with the bolts. 'Stable door, that's nice. Good heavens! The garden! Well, orchard, really. And walled, too. Blast this door, I can't open the bottom half.'

'Let me have a go.' With a protesting screech the stable door opened, and they stepped out.

The garden was almost an acre, but, as Mary said, it ought really to be called an orchard, for there were no beds at all except a narrow one along the back wall of the house, that was tangled with the woody stems of untrimmed herbs. Sage, rosemary and thyme Mary recognised easily, and the green rosettes of mint that were thrusting their way through everywhere; something feathery she vaguely thought might be sweet cicely, and tall dead stems of something that surely could not be hogweed? She pinched a sprouting leaf.

'I do believe this is angelica,' she said, but Rupert was halfway down the garden. Mary followed him.

A narrow stone path ran round its perimeter, about four feet in from the high brick wall that enclosed the whole area and created a microclimate that warmed the air to summer. Blossom and young leaves starred the branches of trees that had been fan-trained against the walls.

'Peaches,' breathed Rupert. 'Apricots. Pears. Plums. Needing pruning, but still . . .'

The grass in the enclosed plot was knee-high, more like June than late April. Seedheads and drooping leaves showed where daffodils and narcissi had flowered thickly round the trunks of the dozen or so trees set there. Of these, half were apple trees in full blossom. Mary went over to stand among them, her eyes closed and head raised to breathe in the sweetness. She heard Rupert's feet swishing through the grass, and opened her eyes.

'What about those ones?' She nodded to the remaining trees, that showed no blossom and only a faint hint of green where leaves were breaking from the buds. In contrast to the other trees, that were overgrown and bristly with sprouting twigs, these were neat and shapely, their crowns smoothly rounded as though trimmed. 'I don't recognise them, and there's no blossom.'

Rupert pulled a twig towards him, and examined the leaves.

'I wouldn't swear to it,' he said reverently, releasing the twig gently, 'but I think I know. They're what gave this place its name.'

'Its name? What is its name?' He held out the piece of paper to her. Mary looked at it. 'Mulberry Court,' she read. 'You mean, they're mulberries? How extraordinary. And so many of them. They look quite young, too. She must have planted them in the last few years.'

'Twenty years, probably. They're very slow growing, don't even fruit for ten years. That's why hardly anyone plants them. That, and the mess. The fruit drops, and it stains dreadfully. Delicious, though...' He sank into a culinary reverie. Mary leaned against an apple tree, watching a bee work its way through the blossom, and wished she had brought a picnic tea with her. The sound of cars passing in the lane might have been in another world. She was unaware that Rupert had roused from his dream and was watching her. His face was very still and intent as he looked at her, remembering the way she had rested against him that morning, fitting into his arms as if she belonged there. Which, he thought fiercely, she did. If only he could make her see it.

He shook his head, smiling in wry self-mockery. They had come to see the buildings, and he was no longer a romantic teenager. While it was true that he welcomed the chance to spend time alone with Mary, he had to admit that his primary concern had been with his own plans and the long-term aim that the brief description of the place had brought to the forefront of his mind.

'Come on, let's look at the rest.' Reluctantly, Mary dragged herself away from the tree and followed him. The scullery seemed darker and damper than before, and she was glad to emerge into the freshness of the cobbled courtyard.

The house was at the far left-hand corner of a three-sided block of buildings, with a row of looseboxes separating it from the still smaller cottage that fronted the little lane. On the other side of the house, and forming the bottom side of the courtyard, was the dairy, which they examined briefly, then the deep stone trough where the water, its surface dimpled by the upward pressure of the spring that supplied it, flowed out into a stone-lined gully that entered the barn through an arched opening.

The barn occupied the whole of the third side of the rectangle, and Mary was surprised by how long Rupert spent in it. He examined the timbering closely, climbed up to look at the roof, and scraped away patches of mouldering straw to look at the floor. Mary, sneezing at the dust, retreated to the open doorway and stood in the sunshine, thinking sadly of the walled garden. There was no doubt that this would never do for Mr Naseby, even if he could have afforded it . . .

'It's perfect!' Rupert was standing beside her. His face blazed with excitement. 'You clever, clever girl, it's absolutely and utterly and completely perfect. I could kiss you. In fact, I will.'

As once before, his arms went round her, but this time not just in a friendly hug. Mary felt herself lifted from her feet – a novel experience that made her suddenly feel quite small and vulnerable – and swung round in a circle, before he kissed her soundly on the mouth. His lips were warm and surprisingly soft. It was an altogether enjoyable experience, and Mary abandoned herself to the pleasure with no feelings of guilt. Swept off my feet, she told herself happily. So she was not Mary, heavy, lumpy Mary at all. This was a new Mary, light and fragile as the apple blossom.

'That was nice,' said Rupert. 'I've wanted to do that for a long time. About twenty-five years, actually.'

'Twenty-five years! But that's before I married John!'

'Exactly. And it's a long time to make up for.' He kissed her again, and this time there was no mistaking his passionate intentions. Mary, responding with enthusiasm, knew she ought to be shocked. In fact the only thing that shocked her was that she wasn't. This, she knew, was where she should call a halt, be sensible, pull away from him. Instead she kissed him back, rejoicing in the sureness of his hands as they held and caressed her. She thought she had never felt so alive, so real. Her fantasy world and lover could not have had less relevance. She allowed herself to be lowered onto a heap of old straw without even noticing how prickly it was. For ever afterwards, the dank mildewy smell that rose from their impromptu bed was to be, to them both, one of the most erotic fragrances in the world.

Afterwards, he shifted carefully so that his body was beside and curled round hers. Mary, her eyes half closed, nuzzled her head into his neck. His shirt was spread on the straw under their heads, and through the musty reek of their bedding she could smell the freshness of his aftershave, stronger than usual today. He generally wore very little, because of working in the kitchen, and she sniffed his skin appreciatively.

'Mmm.' she said. 'Lovely.'

'Not too heavy for you? I didn't squash you?'

'Not that I was aware of.' She wriggled closer to him. 'We fit together well, don't we?'

'Very well.' He ran his hand down her flank, and she felt her skin quiver with pleasure. 'I didn't plan this. You do know that, don't you?'

'Yes. Though it would have been quite flattering.'

'Fishing for compliments?' His fingers counted their way up her vertebrae. 'You must have noticed that I fancied you rotten. I hoped it would happen, but I didn't expect it to.'

'You didn't realise I was so promiscuous?'

He slapped her, quite stingingly, on the bottom.

'That's not what I meant at all, and you know it. I just don't want you to hate me, later.'

'I'm more likely to hate myself. But I don't think I will,' she said thoughtfully, as his arms tightened around her. She pulled away a little bit, so that she could look him in the face. 'And it's nothing to do with John telephoning you, either. I'm not using you to get back at him. In fact, I never gave him a thought. Poor old John.' She spoke as she felt, with kindly regret, and let him pull her close again. His hands moved, purposefully. 'Again? Already?'

'Making the most of my opportunities,' he murmured. 'A lot of catching up to do.'

Later, shaking out their clothes and dressing, they both began to cough.

'The dust...' said Mary. 'I'm so thirsty. Do you think the spring is drinkable?'

'I don't know. The old lady drank it, but she'd probably built up a resistance ... There's the tap in the scullery.'

Mary pulled a face. 'I think I'd prefer the spring. After all, it's flowing through all the time. If we take it where it actually bubbles up...'

Together they cupped their hands in it and drank, each watching the other.

'Well, if there's anything, we've both got it. That'll be fun to explain away to everyone.'

'It's lovely,' said Mary, drinking again. 'I'm sure it's all right. That's the trouble with you food-sellers, you're permanently hung up on Health and Safety.'

'So would you be, if you'd ever been inspected by them. Worse than taking a driving test.' He stood up, and looked round the courtyard. 'They're going to love this,' he said.

'They're not going to see it, are they? Surely,' Mary wrinkled her brow, 'you don't have to tell them that you drank this water, do you? I mean, it's not likely to have legionnaire's disease, or hepatitis, is it?'

He looked at her blankly, then laughed.

'That wasn't what I meant at all! Don't you remember, in the barn, when I said it was perfect?'

'Of course I do. I thought you meant, perfect for, um, us.'

'Oh, dear! I'm afraid that at that moment even lust was incidental. No, I meant perfect for a restaurant.' Mary gaped at him. 'It's just the sort of place I've had at the back of my mind. The sandwich bar is all very well. I've enjoyed it, and it's doing well, but it doesn't need me any more, and it's not enough. I want to do proper cooking. The full works. Look...' He swung her round, pointing. 'The restaurant itself in the barn. Plenty of space, lovely old timbers – clean it up, lay a proper floor. Kitchens in the dairy – enclose that bit behind the trough and make it a connecting corridor. Seats out here in the summer, even some tables maybe. Live in the house. Staff in the cottage. Storerooms in the looseboxes.'

'You must use the spring. Cool the wine bottles in it or something. People love that kind of thing. Or trout – what about live trout? It's big enough.'

'Yes – and the mulberries! Don't forget the mulberries! Mulberry sorbet. Mulberry ice cream. Mulberry fool. They freeze beautifully, such a strong flavour.'

'Mulberry liqueur,' broke in Mary, equally carried away. 'For aperitifs, with white wine or champagne. Like kir, but with mulberry instead of cassis. A kind of – of signature dish. Or drink. Oh, Rupert, I think it could really work! I know it could!'

'Yes,' he said more soberly. 'I think so too.'

Mary wondered whether it was only the restaurant he was thinking of.

Chapter 18

'Still here, Mum?'

'More or less.'

'Oh, good,' said David vaguely, looking at his mother in some concern. It was not the kind of answer she usually gave. 'What's for supper?' That, he obviously thought, was the kind of question that would return her to normal.

'Nothing.'

'Nothing? But I'm starving!' He sounded like an outraged little boy. It was Friday evening, the end of his course except for a lunch the following day, and he had been up for most of the night with Zen at the hospital. Then his face changed. Mary could read his thoughts clearly as they popped up in his brain: women – funny moods – difficult age – must make allowances. What would he say, she wondered, if she were to tell him that she was suffering from post-coital depression? The thought of his embarrassment and horror sent a shiver through her, and induced a wild desire to laugh. David eyed her. 'I expect you're tired. I'll go and get fish and chips, shall I?'

Mary felt her eyes grow hot with tears. She stood up briskly.

'Sorry, darling. I am a bit tired, but it's nothing much. I can find something in the freezer. Grandprof doesn't like fish and chips.'

'Being difficult, is he?'

'Not particularly. He's spent most of the day in bed.'

'He can't come to much harm there, I suppose.' He thought. 'One of your working days today, wasn't it?'

'Yes, but I didn't go. When I rang this morning they said to take as much time as I liked. I didn't mean to, but then I thought, why not? No one's indispensable.' Particularly not me, she thought. Except when it's supper time, and even then there's always fish and chips. She went to the freezer and took out a container of basic pasta sauce. David

211

fidgeted round the kitchen. Mary found herself wanting to snap at him, which wasn't like her.

'Why don't you go up and change, then go and have a chat to Pa until the meal's ready. It won't be very long.'

'Yes. Right.' He left the room with visible relief. Mary ran water into the bowl to wash the salad. She felt the tension prickle across her shoulders, and moved them in an attempt to relieve it. She felt full of crackling energy, like a thundercloud before a storm, but could think of no way of dissipating it. Her hands moved mechanically as she prepared the meal, but her mind was miles away. Not, surprisingly, at Mulberry Court which seemed farther away and harder to believe in than heaven, but back at the house which she supposed she should call 'home', the house she shared with John.

Or did she? Sharing, surely, implied an equal interest in something? Financially, half the house was legally hers. But emotionally? She cared for it, because she saw that as part of her job, but she certainly didn't really care about it. People who had been burgled, she knew, frequently felt as though they themselves had been violated, knowing that a stranger had been in their home. It was true that she would very much dislike the idea of a burglar rifling through her clothes, or going through her cupboards and drawers, but she knew she would not find it upsetting in any way other than the practical.

All she could think, at the moment, was how very reluctant she was to go back there. Staying here in her childhood home was a peculiar experience. It was at once so familiar and so strange that she found it difficult at times to remember that she was a middle-aged married woman. Some of the things she had hoped she had grown out of – the fear of other people and the world, the deep-seated feelings of inadequacy – seemed to hang around in the dark corners of the house ready to swoop down on her the moment she relaxed her guard. At the same time, conversely, elements of the security of home were here, comfortable and consoling as a warm woollen blanket and a night light.

Would the events of the afternoon have happened if she had not set out from this house? Could her sudden and complete abandonment, as she could not help seeing it, of all the values and principles she had believed herself to hold be put down to an emotional return to the freedoms of adolescence? The worst thing, in her own eyes, was that even now she felt no kind of guilt about what had happened. It was true that she suspected John of behaving equally dishonestly, but in the past she would never have seen that as a reason to free her from the constraints of what she felt to be right. She could honestly say that there was no element of tit-for-tat, no wish for revenge or even any feeling of redressing a balance. It had seemed so simple and right that notions of values and principles were utterly irrelevant. Even now, facing her son, the only guilt she had felt was that she felt none.

As for the future, it was no less vague than it had always been. It was a long time since Mary had bothered to look ahead of the immediate present. Before, it had been empty in a dull way. Now the emptiness was shot through with anxiety and uncertainty. She was unable to imagine repeating what had happened with Rupert. That had been an event out of time, something that had more in common with her fantasy world than with reality. The thing about it that she minded most was that it was difficult to imagine continuing the easy friendship they had fallen into. It was not until now, when it looked as though she would no longer be able to do it, that she realised how much she would miss visiting the sandwich bar. It was a depressing thought.

The weekend passed slowly. David finished his course and left. Mary kept herself as busy as possible, to avoid the necessity for thought or, worse still, conversation with her father who after years of seeming scarcely aware of her existence was suddenly exhibiting an alarming penetration into her mind. She cooked and cleaned, visited Zen and the babies, who continued to make good progress, and toured the second-hand shops for nursery equipment. Zen, thinking she still had several weeks to go and perhaps feeling superstitious about buying too much, had pitifully little. Mary cleaned out the room next to Zen's, and was delighted to find some cheap fabric in the covered market that would replace the sombre old curtains.

On Sunday she went home to fetch her sewing machine, some clothes, and to rifle through the loft for David's old pram. As she turned into the drive her heart pounded, but as she had hoped John's car was not there, the garage was empty and the house, when she let herself in, had the dead, closed-up atmosphere of an unlived-in home. Mary gathered up the dead flowers from hall, sitting room and dining room and took them down to the compost heap. She saw that John, although he had neither dusted nor vacuumed indoors, had cut the grass and tied up the dead daffodil leaves into tight knots, a form of vegetable torture she particularly disliked. John, she knew, would have preferred to forego the pleasures of spring bulbs in order to avoid the aftermath of drooping foliage.

Dismally, but with a compulsion to duty, she picked fresh leaves and a few flowers, arranging them swiftly in the accustomed containers and setting them in the usual places. To run the vacuum and a duster round the tidy rooms took no more than half an hour. Sorting through the things in the loft took longer because everything was neatly wrapped and packed away, but luckily John's sense of order was such that having found one thing – the pram – everything else left from David's baby days was neatly ranged next to it. Getting them all down, even though there were sloping telescopic stairs rather than a mere ladder from the hatch, was an exhausting affair, and by the time she had packed them, and the sewing machine, into the car Mary felt grubby and tired. She longed for a cup of tea, but some atavistic feeling made her reluctant to eat or drink in that house, so she climbed wearily up the stairs to her bedroom for her clothes.

The mirror door on the fitted wardrobe confronted her with her unflattering reflection. Knowing that she would be going up into the loft she had dressed sensibly in old trousers and a baggy pullover that was covered with bobbles and snags, and hung unbecomingly from her broad shoulders, making her look fat and shapeless. Her face was pale and smudged with dirt, her hair slipping down and covered with wispy bits of escaped hair. Mary found herself imagining how Elaine Brantridge might have looked under the same circumstances. Elaine, she thought sourly, would have had more sense than to go up into the loft in the first place. She would have fluttered her eyelashes and persuaded someone else – male – to go, and remained immaculate downstairs, ready with admiring remarks.

Mary went into the bathroom. With the tips of her fingers she turned on the taps, then washed her hands and face, dipping her head down to the water and rubbing her skin with wet hands. She looked at the towels, neatly folded on the heated rail. The one on the right was 'hers', but somehow she felt reluctant to touch it. In the end, feeling foolish, she pulled double handfuls of paper from the roll by the lavatory and dabbed her face and hands dry. It disintegrated in her wet hands and stuck unpleasantly to her face. She had to pick little bits off which adhered in turn to her fingers, so she had to flick them into the lavatory bowl.

Feeling only slightly cleaner she fetched a holdall and dropped in deodorant, talc, her make-up bag, her washbag, then went back to the bedroom and collected clothes at random, shoving them into the bag until it was full. After a moment's thought she picked up three pairs of shoes and dropped them into a plastic carrier. She was unable to stop feeling like a burglar. Her senses were alert, stretched to any slight sound or change in atmosphere that might signal the arrival of someone else. Of John, of course, for who else would be coming to the house?

Her packing done she went downstairs with relief. Longing to leave, she went to the notepad by the telephone and wrote a message to John, saying simply that her father was shaken but all right, and that she would stay a day or two more in Oxford. She signed it, after some thought, 'love, Mary', because that was what she always did and she felt unable to change it. However she did not, as she usually did, put an extra line across the hanging tail of the y to make it into an x, a kiss. It was a subtlety that she felt sure John would not notice.

As she put the pen back into its holder by the pad, the doorbell rang. Mary froze. She had heard no car on the drive, something she had been listening for in case John should return. Scarcely breathing, she heard the faint shuffle of feet as the person on the doorstep moved, and she thought with relief that the visitor was going. Then the bell rang again, a long ring. The person must know she was there, or be eager to speak to her. Reluctantly she went to the door and looked through the spyhole to see one of her neighbours. The woman – Wendy, she recalled after a moment's thought – who lived in the next house but one. As she hesitated, Wendy turned her face so that she seemed to be looking back at Mary through the lens of the spyhole, and lifted her hand to the bell again.

Before she could ring it, Mary opened the door.

'Hello, Wendy,' she said, tepidly polite. 'Is something wrong?'

'That's what I was going to ask you.' Wendy did not move, but Mary could not bring herself to keep her standing on the step and moved backwards, opening the door wider. 'I don't want to bother you, but when I saw your car in the drive I thought I'd just check. You've not been around much, and nor has John.' She saw the look on Mary's face, and laughed. 'I sound like a real nosy neighbour, don't I? Please don't think I spend my time peering round the net curtains and noting every-body's comings and goings! It's just that I walk the dog three times a day, and you get used to everybody's routines. Sort of Neighbourhood Watch, if you like.'

Her laugh was infectious, and Mary found herself smiling back.

'I know what you mean. As a matter of fact, my father had a bit of a fall . . .'

Wendy nodded. 'I thought it must be something like that. I knew he'd had a stroke a while back, so I was afraid . . . I'm so sorry, is he all right?'

'Yes, thank goodness. He hasn't had another stroke, but I'm keeping an eye on him.'

It was the longest conversation Mary had ever had with Wendy. Slender and dark, her face carefully and vividly made up, her clothes elegant and eyecatching, she had always made Mary feel awkward and frumpy, and now she was more than ever conscious of her grubby and untidy appearance. Indeed, Wendy was looking into her face and Mary wondered whether she had left a smudge of dust on it.

'You look tired. Why don't you come back with me and have a cup of tea? Unless you've got to rush back?'

'That's very kind of you,' Mary said, thinking guiltily that she had misjudged the other woman. 'If you're sure?'

Wendy smiled, and Mary was surprised to see a look of sadness in her face.

'As a matter of fact, I'd love it.' She lifted her chin a fraction. 'You probably don't know, but I'm on my own at the moment. Jeremy's left me.'

'Oh, Wendy! I had no idea! I'm so sorry.' All thoughts of her unkempt appearance vanished. Mary glanced round the hall, and picked up her bags. 'Let me just dump these in the car and lock the house. Um, can I move my car into your drive?'

Wendy looked at her intelligently.

'Put it in my garage, if you like,' she said. 'There's plenty of room.'

Mary felt her eyes crinkle with the beginnings of a conspiratorial smile.

'That would be perfect,' she said.

Later, driving back to Oxford, Mary thought how extraordinary it was that you could suddenly see someone with completely new eyes. Sitting in Wendy's sparkling new conservatory, she had felt a moment of uncertainty, but this had vanished when Wendy poured the tea and Mary saw that her hand was shaking so that the saucers were awash. She put down the teapot with a crash.

'I'm sorry,' she said. 'I just don't seem to be able to pull myself together. You're the first person I've spoken to since he went, apart from my cleaning lady, and I couldn't discuss it with her. I didn't mean to bother you with it either, and I really was concerned that your father was ill, but . . . I always thought you had such a nice face,' she finished inconsequentially. The flesh round her mouth seemed to shrivel as she controlled its tremble. 'I feel such a *failure*,' she said. 'It's not even that he's got another woman. I could *fight* that. But he just says he needs space. Space!' Her eyes filled with tears.

Mary sympathised and comforted, and told Wendy about John. They abandoned the tea and drank a bottle of wine, after which Mary found herself telling Wendy about Rupert too.

'He sounds lovely,' said Wendy wistfully. 'I think you should *definitely* go for him.'

'Well . . .' Mary shook her head. 'I just don't know what I feel. In fact, I can't really believe it was me at all. It's as if I'd read it in a book, or dreamed it or something.'

'Have you spoken to him since?'

'No. He'd have been busy on Saturday, of course, and I left pretty early this morning . . .'

'Avoiding him?' Mary nodded, smiling ruefully.

'Yes, I suppose I was. I can't help thinking he might be regretting it. It was the place he was really excited about, and I just happened to be . . . there.'

'Don't be daft! You were there because he wanted you to be there. He could just as easily have gone on his own. Don't worry about what he's thinking, what matters is what you think. Do you like him? As a friend, I mean?'

'Yes.' The answer came without hesitation, before Mary had time to think. 'Yes, I do,' she said more slowly. 'He makes me laugh.'

'And if you went back there tomorrow . . . would you do it again?'

'Yes.' Again Mary did not need to stop and think. 'I would,' she added, with fervour. They both laughed.

'There you are, then.' Wendy leaned back in her chair, with the look of one with all the answers.

'But . . . John . . . and everything . . .'

'Give it time. It sounds to me as though it'll sort itself out. Wait till your mind is more settled, till you've got your own feelings sorted out, and then – go with the flow! God!' she added, 'Why is it so much easier to organise other people's lives than one's own?'

By the time Mary left, she felt not only happier in herself but with the added warmth of having discovered a friend. As she drove out of the close she felt a wave of warmth wash over her, benign and comforting. She noticed for the first time that the sun was shining, and even the slow-moving Sunday morning traffic on the Oxford road did not shadow the feeling of release that sent her, cheerful as a child let out of school, back to the city.

Her father too seemed unusually good-humoured when she reached the house. He made no complaint when Mary assembled the pram and parked it in the hall, even going so far as to inspect it with some interest.

'They should fit into that for quite a while. What a monster! Where did you get it?'

'You gave it to me,' answered Mary rather shortly. She felt tired, and the wine she had drunk with Wendy made her feel rather heavy.

'Did I? No wonder it's a good one.' He patted it with genuine pride, impervious to her mood. 'What are we having for lunch?'

Mary sighed, and glanced at her watch. Quarter to one already.

'There's some soup. I thought we'd have that, and bread and cheese. I'll do a proper meal tonight, but I wanted to get these things this morning, and there wasn't time to cook as well. Why? Are you hungry?'

'Not especially. But that chap rang, and I asked him to lunch. Forgot you were out.'

'Which chap?' Mary's heart sank.

'Your friend. Took you out for a drive the other day. Greenwood.'

'Rupert?' Mary's hands flew to her hair. She remembered all too clearly how she had looked in the bedroom mirror. 'Today? Now? Really, Pa . . .'

'No need for all that fuss,' he said testily. 'Told him we weren't having a proper meal. Said an improper one would suit him just as well. Young fool.'

'But, Pa, I wish I'd known. When did he ring?'

'This morning, just before you left. Didn't see any point in stopping you, flapping around like a headless hen as you were. Come to think of it, he did seem a bit worried, said was I sure you wouldn't mind. So of course I said it was fine, you'd be pleased to see him.'

'Yes. Of course.' No time, thought Mary. No time for a shower and a change, and to brush out her hair and put it up again. Powder and lipstick, at least? Blast Pa, blast and damn him, how could he do this to me? And Rupert too, turning up out of the blue. Well, it's too bad. He can see me just as I am. That should do the trick.

Her mind did not specify what trick was to be done. Feeling decidedly put out, she went to the kitchen to taste the soup. She might look like a witch, but at least what came out of her cauldron would be as good as she could manage.

The doorbell rang as she was stirring the soup to keep it from boiling. Her hands twitched, but resolutely she kept them down, away from her hair and face. She heard her father's step, still slightly halting, cross the hall to the front door, and their voices as they moved into the study. She laid the table, setting out bread and butter, cheese and fruit, then went back to the soup. The kitchen door opened and Rupert came in.

'Smells good. Lemon grass?' It was a characteristic greeting. He crossed the room with his big stride and put an arm round her as familiarly as a brother, bending to kiss her cheek and to sniff the steam from the saucepan.

'And lime leaves. It's a kind of Thai tom yam, but with a bit of coconut in as well.'

'Delicious.' As if absent-mindedly he kissed her again before releasing her. Mary kept her back turned to him, her head lowered as if concentrating fiercely on the stirring. There was a slight creak which Mary, knowing every sound in this kitchen, diagnosed as him sitting on the corner of the kitchen table.

'Your father didn't tell you I was coming, did he?'

'No,' she answered shortly.

'I'm sorry. Do you want me to go away?' His tone was even and relaxed. Mary knew that if she were to say yes, he would go at once, quietly and without resentment.

'No.'

'That's all right, then,' he said comfortably. He did not offer to help, for which she was grateful. It was good to have something to do, even if it was only unnecessary stirring. 'I've been looking into your idea,' he continued. 'You know, I think it would really work.'

Mary found herself unable to remember having had an idea. Any idea, ever.

'What idea?' She knew she still sounded gruff, but was unable to do anything about it.

'About the lunches. Delivering them to the offices. I did a quick opinion poll during the week. Asked all the people who came in. They seemed enthusiastic. Said it would be great, particularly during the winter. I sat down and worked out a basic menu and price list; and I've been in touch with a couple of firms that do catering supplies, for packaging.'

Mary was impressed, and interested enough to lose some of her self-consciousness.

'Already? That was quick.'

'I want to get it up and running now before I get too involved in anything else.'

'Who's going to do the deliveries?'

'Me, of course. For the first few days anyway. I want to get the feel of it, see whether it's going to take off. You can only do that by being there yourself, talking to people, getting their reactions, finding out what they want. I wondered . . .' He paused. 'Would you be able to help out for a few hours, Tuesdays and Thursdays? I'd pay you, of course,' he added hurriedly. 'I wouldn't expect you to do it for nothing. And if you're too busy, I'd quite understand. You've got the other job already, and the house, and the Professor . . .'

'I'd love to,' Mary broke in calmly, soothed by his obvious uncertainty.

'Are you sure? I don't want to – to take advantage of you. Of your good nature,' he added hastily.

Too late, however. Mary's eyes flew to his face, and her sense of humour got the better of her.

'Oh, zurr,' she said, in Mummerset. ''Ee wouldn't be meaning to take advantage of a poor maid, would 'ee? Oi be a good girl, Oi be.'

He frowned.

'You forward wench! How dare you speak to me like that? Don't you know that I have rights of socage and poundage and turbary, not to mention *droit de seigneur* and the right to gather rosebuds on the second Thursday of every month without an R in it?'

They smiled at one another.

'I love you, you know,' he said, conversationally.

'Do you?' Mary thought, belatedly, that it sounded as though she was asking for flowery speeches, when all she really meant was 'How extraordinary'.

'Yes.'

'Oh.' She felt that he deserved rather more than that in response, but was unable to find any words, since she had no idea how she actually felt. I don't know, she wanted to say, about love. I thought I was 'in love' with Maxim, all those years ago, and perhaps I was, but it's all so long ago and I can't even remember properly what he looked like. I thought I 'loved' John. Doesn't staying married for twenty-four years mean that we 'love' each other? Or is it just habit, and inertia? I love David, I know that for sure. But I don't always *like* him, and sometimes he irritates me beyond bearing. And Pa the same. Maybe there's something missing in me, and I'm incapable of love. But I like Rupert, and he makes me laugh, and the sex was great. Would he settle for that, I wonder?

'I don't know...' she said feebly.

'I know. It's all right. I just wanted you to know, that's all.' He seemed quite unperturbed by her tepid response, and Mary felt reassured.

'Oh. Well, thank you.'

'So, you'll do Tuesdays and Thursdays?' He returned to the matter in hand, as though there had been no digression. Mary relaxed still further.

'Yes, I'd love to. Not this week, of course, but I could start the week after, if everything's all right here.'

'Good. Is the soup ready? I'll go and call your father.'

The following week passed quickly. By Tuesday Zen was home, but spending most of the day in the hospital where the babies were making good progress, needing only to reach a better weight before being allowed home. She and the Professor still spent several hours together each day, reading and talking. Mary felt herself to be slightly extraneous, but for once this failed to bother her. She filled the freezer until it was practically bulging at the seams, and in her spare time went for long rambles round Oxford. The endless flow of tourists was so familiar that she was less aware of them than she might have been of a herd of cows on a country walk, merely picking her way round them when they were pointing their cameras, or when they came to a sudden halt in the middle of the pavement. She felt peaceful, becalmed in a tranquil sea. Like the Ancient Mariner after his conversion she was benignly disposed to all creation, and would have blessed even the tourists, those happy living things.

She did not see Rupert, although he telephoned twice and they chatted without constraint, mostly about the lunchbox deliveries. On Thursday, also, John telephoned, and rather stiffly asked how she was.

'Oh, fine,' she said vaguely. 'How about you?'

'I'm all right. And the Professor?' Rather pointedly, he refrained from asking after Zen or the babies.

'He's very well. He doesn't really need me here any more.'

'So you'll be coming home?'

Mary paused. Drifting along as she had been, she had closed her mind to the future.

'Do you want me to?' she asked, to give herself time.

'Of course.' Was that uncertainty in his voice?

I don't have to go, thought Mary. I could stay here, help Zen with the babies, work for Rupert . . . Oddly, knowing that she had a choice made it easier to decide. She would go back, because she owed it to herself and to the years she had spent with John to do things properly. Maybe the new Mary she increasingly felt herself to be might even be able to talk to John, to find some way of reaching an understanding.

'I'll probably come back tomorrow, or Saturday.'

'Which?'

'Saturday, then. Are you playing golf?'

'Yes.' Mary was aware, without being sure how she knew, that he was back at the house, and alone. She thought that she really should go back on Friday, but hardened her heart. Surely he could manage for one more day?

Back at her house, Mary flung all the windows wide and whirled through the rooms, cleaning at least the bits that showed. With fresh flowers on the carefully laid table, clean sheets and towels in bedroom and bathroom, a bottle of good claret uncorked and a rib of beef sizzling in the oven, the house was as welcoming as she knew how to make it. Mary even put on one of her good summer dresses – a bit chilly for early May, but it was a fine evening – and sprayed on one of her favourite Penhaligon floral perfumes. The hyacinth smell, sweet and sharp, reminded her vividly of her fantasy kitchen, but she pushed the thought away and went downstairs.

At the sound of John's key in the door she went, rather nervously, into the hall.

'Hello, John.'

He stood framed in the doorway, his tall figure stooping rather more than she remembered.

'Hello, dear.' He came in, and bent over to kiss her. His moustache was bristly against her cheek. It was all so familiar that Mary wondered if she had ever been away, whether it had all been a dream or, worse, a figment of her imagination. Another fantasy.

Chapter 19

'Mary! It's Wendy. How are you doing?'

Mary was glad she had answered the telephone upstairs. It was evening, and John had settled himself firmly in front of the television after supper, to watch a two-hour documentary. Mary had come up to fetch her book, and now she kicked off her shoes and lay down on the bed, only too happy to spend some time gossiping. Since her return she had had little opportunity to see Wendy, since she now worked every weekday and had to fit the housework, which formerly had occupied so much of her time, into the edges and corners of life.

'I'm fine,' she said, not altogether truthfully. 'More to the point, how are *you* doing?'

'He wants to come back,' said Wendy hollowly.

'Oh. And how do you feel?'

Wendy, it seemed, wasn't sure.

'I've had long enough to get used to being on my own. I've joined a bridge club, and started going to aerobics classes. He seems to think we can just take up where we left off, as if nothing has happened.'

'I know,' sighed Mary.

'Is that how John is?'

'That's *exactly* how John is. There are all the classic signs – coming home late, evenings out "on business" that he won't talk about, telephone calls that are always wrong numbers if I answer them – but when I try to talk about it he just clams up. Walks out of the room, out of the house even. And it's not as if I were making scenes. I mean, I don't even *mind* that much.'

'That's probably what he doesn't like.'

'You mean he'd rather I was screaming accusations and throwing the china at him? Oh!'

225

'Thought of something?'

'It just reminded me. You could be right, at that. I have known John to respond to violence . . .'

'Better get a few old plates together. You don't want to break any good ones.'

'No,' said Mary. 'It may be what he wants, but I'm not going to do it. I've spent all my married life, more or less, doing things the way I thought he wanted them done. This time I'm going to do things my way.'

'And that is?'

Mary laughed.

'Good point. I'm not altogether sure! All I know is, we can't go back to the way things were. I can't believe he doesn't know it, but he just won't admit that things have changed. Poor John, I think he finds it all terribly frightening. That's why I came back, and why I'm still here. I just feel I must help him to make the transition, if I can. The trouble is, I'm not sure that my being here is much help.'

'What about Rupert?'

'He's rushed off his feet setting up this new delivery service. We see one another in the sandwich bar, of course, and it's all fine . . .'

'But? He hasn't made any more . . . advances? No canoodling by the cooker, or frisking by the freezer?'

Mary laughed.

'Hardly! For one thing there's no room, and for another there's always other people around. Besides, I more or less told him I wasn't sure.'

'Mary, you didn't! Why?'

'Because I wasn't sure,' said Mary reasonably.

'So there's no progress at all.' Wendy sounded disappointed.

'Not much, sorry. We all seem to be marking time.'

'Something will happen,' said Wendy with certainty. 'You'll see. You can't just drift on like this. What you need is a crisis!'

'Do I?' Mary was dubious. 'Perhaps you're right. But I'm afraid I'm not the one to provide it.'

'You can't spend the rest of your days waiting for things to happen to you. You have to take charge of your life.'

'You've been reading too many magazines. I am taking charge of it, in my own way. Anyway, you were the one who told me to give myself time. You can't have it both ways!'

'Why not? We must get together soon. Are you still working every day?'

'Yes, but not for much longer. My old job with Naseby's is coming to an end. They're moving to somewhere smaller, which was my idea so I've more or less talked myself out of a job. I don't really mind, though I'll miss them. I want to have more time to go to Oxford.'

'And to the sandwich bar?'

'Well...' Mary laughed. 'Perhaps. But I do want to have more time with Zen and the twins. She's got a bit of help – did I tell you? Pa's housekeeper's daughter. She's fifteen, and wants to train to be a nanny. She's thrilled to bits to have the twins to practise on, and of course in the school holidays she's got the time.'

The twins, now two months old and growing at an alarming rate, were developing distinct and fascinating characters, and Mary found them absorbingly interesting. They seemed to change with every week that passed, and Mary found that they already welcomed her with beguiling, gummy smiles and seemed to take it for granted that she would entertain them. Mary found herself making mobiles to hang over their cribs, and reviving her somewhat creaky piano playing, abandoned in mid-adolescence. She almost longed for them to be weaned, and was already mentally devising little dishes to puree that would teach them to enjoy the new world of taste and smell.

Returning one Saturday from just such an afternoon of playing with the babies, Mary was startled to find that John had already returned from his afternoon of golf with David. She had made an effort to get back early, since the week before she had been particularly late, having been beguiled by a sunny day into taking Zen and the twins for a picnic by the river. She had returned to find John, tight-lipped, grilling the chops she had left for their dinner. He had turned the grill up too high and the chops were spluttering, coating every nearby surface with spangles of grease and filling the kitchen with smoke. The jacket potatoes intended to accompany them had been microwaved too long and had collapsed into themselves, shrivelled like leaky balloons, and the broccoli was boiled almost to mush. As she walked into the kitchen the fat in the grill ignited, and John gave a howl of anguish.

'Oh, John, you shouldn't have bothered...'

'Someone had to *bother*,' he said crossly. 'I was hungry.'

'Why didn't you have a snack? Some biscuits, or a piece of cake? There's a fresh one in the tin.'

His face lengthened disapprovingly.

'You know I don't believe in snacking. Ruins the digestion. Besides, I'd had a drink at the club. You don't want to go back to sweet stuff after a drink.'

In the end, of course, Mary had had to begin preparing the meal again, and as a result they had eaten late and John had suffered with indigestion all night. Mary, who had never had indigestion in her life, refrained from pointing out that if he had left everything to her she could have had the meal ready in less than fifteen minutes. It was hard to be patient, knowing that he had started cooking not because he wanted to help her, but merely to force home a point and to make her feel guilty. He resented every moment she spent with the twins; they were something never spoken of, but once he found a small fluffy duck in the back of her car and dropped it in the dustbin with as much distaste as if it had been a dirty tissue.

Mary checked her watch. Half past five – much earlier than her usual time and at least an hour before John normally came home. His back, perhaps? Oh, please not. She let herself in quietly through the garage door to the lobby. From the kitchen she could hear the low murmur of voices from the sitting room. John, and David. That, too, was unusual. Since the weekend when David and Alison had been to London they had been spending even more time together, and she was sure they had been intending to go to a party that evening. With some trepidation she opened the sitting-room door and went in.

They were both sitting there looking gloomy. John flicked a glance at her, but said nothing, though she noticed with relief that he wasn't sitting in that peculiarly still, careful way that meant his back was hurting. David turned his head towards her without looking at her.

'Hi, Mum,' he said.

'Hello, darling. You're both back early. Is something wrong?'

David hunched his shoulders.

'The engagement's off,' he mumbled. Mary knew that later on she would be glad of it, but for the moment all she could see was her son's misery.

'Off? Your engagement with Alison? Oh, darling, I'm so sorry. Why?'

He shrugged, not looking at her. Mary's eyes turned to John, questioning. To her surprise she was met with a glare of fury.

'You might well ask why! This is all down to that wretched girl your father's infatuated with! I said at the beginning that it would be a disaster, and I was right, but would you listen? Oh, no. No, you had to go encouraging her, didn't you? Treating her as though she belonged in the family, fussing over her, *giving* her things! And now look what's happened! David's life ruined, his future in jeopardy for all we know. And whose fault is it, I'd like to know?'

'Well, I don't really see how it can be Zen's. David's scarcely seen her for weeks.'

'Poor little Alison never liked her. She always said that girl put funny ideas into David's head, and she was right. Little tramp!'

'David hasn't ... Zen wouldn't ...'

'Of course I haven't,' David broke in angrily. 'It's nothing like that. Zen's a friend, that's all. It's not her fault.'

'So whose fault is it, then? You can't blame poor little Alison!' Mary wished that John wouldn't keep calling Alison that.

'Mine, I suppose,' said Mary without heat. Her hope had been to startle him into silence, but he scarcely paused for breath.

'Yes! Yes, yours! At least you have the decency to admit it, now it's too late! Much good that'll do David, or poor little Alison!' Small triangles of spittle were collecting, white at the corners of his mouth. His bony face looked suddenly pointed and feral, Mary half expected to see his teeth sharp and pointy beneath the smudge of moustache. David stood up abruptly and left the room, brushing past Mary as if she did not exist. She heard the slam of the front door closing behind him, and held her breath. There was no sound of a car door or of his engine starting, though, and she was relieved until she remembered that his car had not been here, only John's.

'Where's he gone?' she asked wildly, rushing to the front door. 'He hasn't got his car! David? David?' She ran out into the drive and along it to the road of the close. David's figure, walking so fast he was almost running, was already some way away. Mary would have gone running after him, but John came up behind her and grabbed her arm.

'For heaven's sake!' It was a whispered shout. 'Don't make such an exhibition of yourself, dashing about and screeching! What will the neighbours think?'

'*Sod* the neighbours,' she said fiercely. 'What does it *matter* what they think! That's our *son*, and he's unhappy! Let me go!'

He began to pull her back to the house. Although he was so skinny he had a wiry strength that Mary could not resist. His bony fingers were digging painfully into the muscle of her upper arm, but he had a fixed grimace of a smile on his face, determined to show the neighbours that everything was quite normal. Mary was tempted to scream at him, to vomit up some of the violence that was boiling in her and let it out as obscenities. To drive John further down his angry road would do David no good, however. She took a deep breath and stopped resisting. He kept his hand on her, though, until they were inside the house again. Then he let her go at once and stalked back into the sitting room, where he poured himself a drink. Mary sat down, and waited until he had drunk half of it with unusual speed; generally he drank in parsimonious sips, making it last.

'Tell me what's happened,' she said calmly.

'I already did.'

'Yes, but not really. Only the basic fact. Is David very unhappy? He won't . . . he's just gone to walk it off, hasn't he? Or has he gone for his car? Where is it?'

'At the club.' Reluctantly, he answered her questions in reverse order. 'We had a drink or two. Didn't feel like going on with the game, under the circumstances. I thought he'd had a bit too much, that he'd better not drive. Didn't want him to risk losing his licence *as well*. Thought he'd better stay the night here, and I'd drive him back to fetch his car in the morning. He won't have gone to fetch it, it's too far. Besides, I've got his keys.' He jingled them in his pocket with an air of angry triumph as though he had scored a point. 'He'll be back, when he's tired. He's not unhappy. Just angry.'

'Poor David.' Mary smoothed her hands down her skirt, absently picking off a piece of torn sticky tape that had come, she knew, from a disposable nappy. 'He's angry now, but he'll be unhappy later.'

'Bloody psychological claptrap. Your son's a fool.'

My son, thought Mary. My fault. Oh well, why not?

'If you want me to carry the can, you'll have to introduce me to the worms in it first,' she said.

'That's just like you, making it all into a joke. Don't you *care* that he's made such a mess of things?'

'Of course I care, very much. But I don't know that he has made a mess of things, do I? If things haven't worked out with Alison, well, better they should find out now than after they married. There are plenty more fish in the sea. As they say.' And Alison, she thought, was a bit fish-like. Cold blooded.

'They do. I don't.'

Mary sighed. It seemed as though she was never going to learn what had happened, or not from John at least. She stood up.

'Where are you going?'

'To the kitchen. We've still got to eat, after all. And if David comes back he might be hungry.' Without waiting for an answer she walked out of the room. As she had hoped, he followed her, wanting to tell her what had happened but under his own terms and at the time of his choosing.

Mary settled to scraping new potatoes at the sink so that she could keep her eyes and hands occupied, which might encourage him to talk. He paced up and down, unable to settle, and speaking more to himself than to her.

'It's such a *mess*,' he fumed. 'That trip to London. If only they hadn't done that trip to London.' Wisely Mary said nothing. 'Not that they could be *sure* that that was when it happened, he said, but it seemed likely. Romantic weekend, just the two of them, a drink too many ... easy enough to forget the precautions.'

The knife slipped in Mary's hand, and she cut her thumb.

'Ouch!' she said, turning on the tap and rinsing the cut, which was bleeding freely. 'Don't tell me Alison's pregnant!' It seemed so wildly improbable. Hard enough to imagine Alison, that meek cold fish, having sex with anyone. Harder still to imagine her pregnant, giving birth, suckling a baby at those small pointed breasts. Her mind darted off to the possibilities – wedding as soon as possible; living together and having the baby – but no, of course, the engagement was ended, they were no longer a couple. Certainly not an embryonic family. With sudden clarity she knew what had happened.

'She's had an abortion.'

John winced at such plain speaking.

'A termination, they call it. Perfectly sensible, under the circumstances.'

'I suppose so.' Mary felt a pang of regret, surprisingly fierce, for the baby that was not to be. She felt ambivalent about abortions: disliking the idea of ending a life, at however early a stage, she also had strong views that every baby should be wanted and, if possible, planned for. She was positive in her support for the idea that a woman had the right to the choice of whether or not to have a baby, and yet ... 'Poor little thing.'

'You can't call it a baby, not at that stage. Just a blob,' he corrected fastidiously. Mary, who had studied pictures in the colour supplements, disagreed but could see no point in saying so.

'So what was the problem? Surely David doesn't want to start a family yet, does he?'

'Of course he doesn't. Not really. I can't understand what all the fuss is about. As far as I can make out, he didn't exactly mind that she'd done it, but that she didn't discuss it with him first. After all, it's her body.' He brought out this last phrase with self-conscious political correctness. Mary could have laughed, if she hadn't minded so much.

'There must be more to it than that?'

'That's all he told me. Then he went all silent, you know how he is. Sulky. Wouldn't tell me anything.'

Oh yes, thought Mary, I know how he is. And how you are, too. You went for him, didn't you? Before he'd had a chance to explain himself, so he clammed up. And you're right, it is my fault in a way, because David was there when Zen's babies were born, and it's all too recent in his mind. When she told him what she'd done, he would have seen those babies, so tiny and scarcely formed. And it was his baby. They say the fathers feel bereaved, sometimes, but no one takes account of that. Poor David, poor love. And what can I say? Because I'm pleased, really. Oh, not pleased about the way it's happened, but pleased the engagement is broken off.

'You never liked her, did you?' John's words mirrored her thoughts with startling accuracy.

'Not much,' she admitted. His lips tightened. Alison, Mary thought, had been exactly the daughter-in-law he wanted. She was, perhaps, the kind of girl he should have married. Had he thought Mary was like that, and been disappointed? Had Mary been like that? On the outside, maybe, but not really, not inside.

They ate their meal in silence, then sat mute in front of the television. Mary's ears were strained for the sound of David returning. At half past ten John went upstairs. Mary followed him, but when she got into bed she felt so wide awake that, having lain listening to John's light snoring breath for half an hour, she crept out of bed again and went downstairs. She made a pot of tea and sat at the kitchen table in the semi-darkness of a summer night to drink it, tucking her bare feet up on the rung of the chair away from the chill of the floor.

She was halfway through her first cup when she heard David's key in the door. She put the cup down carefully, holding her breath. He came slowly through the hall, stopping for a moment by the sitting room before appearing in the kitchen doorway. He stood still, and Mary wondered if he could see that she was there, whether his eyes were still dazzled by the street lights. She said nothing, reluctant to intrude on his privacy.

'Is there any tea left in that pot, Mum?' His voice was pitched low, but it was calm and controlled. Mary felt the prickle of tension leaving her body.

'Yes, I've only just made it.' He felt his way forward, and she realised that he could scarcely see anything yet. She fetched another cup, and filled it. He picked it up and drank thirstily.

'How did you know there was tea?'

'Smelled it.' Mary nodded. She should have guessed: David had inherited her sensitive nose. 'That's how I knew it was you. That, and your face cream.'

'Elementary, my dear Watson.'

They drank in companionable silence.

'Sorry about that. Going off like that, I mean. I just couldn't bear ... Dad's really upset, isn't he?'

'He'll get over it. He liked Alison very much, and he thinks you've made a mistake, but he'll come round. He wants the best for you, really, he just always thinks that his way is the best.'

'Yes. They got on well, didn't they? I used to tease her, say she was only marrying me to be with him. Poor old Dad.'

'Mmm. And poor old you?'

'Not really.' He sounded surprised. 'I believe I've known for a long time that it wouldn't work, but I couldn't bring myself to confront it or do anything about it.' He leaned forward to refill his cup. 'Did Dad tell you?'

'Yes. I'm sorry.'

'I really minded.' His voice ached with pain. 'Ridiculous, isn't it? But I kept seeing ...' His voice went husky.

'I know. So did I, a bit. Your child. My grandchild. But there will be others. Planned for, and wanted.'

'That's just it. I could have accepted it – I wouldn't have liked it, but I can see perfectly well that it would really make things unbelievably complicated to have had a baby now – if only she'd discussed it with me first. But she just went ahead and did it, and even seemed surprised that I might have wanted to be involved! It was as if she'd had a wisdom tooth out, only marginally easier. I suppose I'd have got over that, we'd have patched things up again, only she said she wasn't going to risk it happening again.'

'Not going to risk it? You mean...?'

He gave a small laugh.

'No, not that! Celibacy has no place in Alison's life! No, she wanted one of us to be sterilised. She was quite happy for it to be her, in fact she preferred it, but the doctor was reluctant because she's so young, and besides it's slightly more complicated for a woman. So she suggested that I should have it done.'

Like father, like son, thought Mary with slight hysteria. Is sterility hereditary?

'Ridiculous!' she exclaimed. 'How dare she!'

'Yes, I was a bit taken aback too. In fact I couldn't believe it. I thought she was joking. But when I found she was serious...' He shook his head. 'I've never really thought about having children. I mean, at my age... But I always assumed that I would, when the time was right. It was stupid of me not to have discussed it with her, but it all seemed so far in the future. I mean, we weren't even going to get married for a year or two. If she'd said, when we first got engaged, that she didn't want to have children, I don't believe it would have worried me all that much. I know I'm not ready for that, and there's no reason she should be either. But when she said she'd got rid of it – that's what she said – and that she'd prefer not to have any at all, it was... frightening. A kind of denial of life. I felt as though she were a complete stranger, and I couldn't believe I'd ever really thought I loved her enough to marry her. Does that make sense?'

'Oh, yes.' For the first time, Mary dared to go round the table and put her arms round him. He leaned against her without awkwardness. She felt a little heave in his breath and tightened her arms, but when he spoke he was laughing.

'Dad's afraid I'm going to go off with Zen and become a New Age accountant, isn't he?'

Mary laughed too.

'He's a bit paranoid about Zen. I'm afraid she embodies everything about the yoof of today that he most fears and dislikes. He'll blame her for anything that goes wrong in the family, just because she's there.'

'I do like her; she's made me think about things in a way I never did before. As a matter of fact, I did once...' He looked embarrassed.

'Make a pass at her? I'm not altogether surprised,' said Mary calmly. 'You stayed there all that time, and you're both young. Maybe deep down you already knew that Alison wasn't right for you.'

'Maybe. We used to sit up late and talk, in the kitchen. One night I'd had rather too much wine, and I just suggested, jokingly, that we might ... I'm a bit ashamed of it, actually. But Zen didn't mind. She wasn't angry, or shocked, or anything. She said what you did.' He sounded surprised.

'Mother knows best,' murmured Mary, to lighten the atmosphere. David laughed.

'Yes, both you mothers! She said she knew I didn't really mean it, and that we were too good as friends to spoil things between us. I was stubborn, because of the drink, and said I did mean it and it wouldn't spoil things, and she said I should think very carefully about my feelings for Alison. I didn't altogether like it at the time, but she was right of course. Zen's not the girl for me, any more than Alison is.'

'Plenty of time.'

'Yes.'

Mary thought that when the time came, the girl for David might well prove to be a kind of compromise between Alison and Zen, with the good points of both. She wondered whether to say so, but decided against it.

'Dad'll come round,' she said again. 'He just needs to get used to the idea. He doesn't like things changing.'

'Poor old Dad.'

It sounded, in Mary's ears, almost like an epitaph.

Chapter 20

By the middle of August Mary was running the sandwich bar almost on her own. Naseby's had closed down for a month while the business was transferred to its new premises, and Rupert was spending more and more time out on his own. Mary presumed that he was going ahead with his ideas for Mulberry Court, but on the rare occasions when they saw one another it was in a crowd of busy people in the sandwich bar, and because he did not mention it, neither did Mary. He was friendly but withdrawn, and Mary could not tell whether it was simply that he was preoccupied with his plans, or for some other reason. It occurred to her that he might be regretting his involvement with her.

'He's changed his mind,' she said gloomily to Wendy. 'I expect he wishes I wasn't working for him any more.'

'Don't be daft,' said Wendy. 'It's more likely he's thinking the same about you. After all, you're the one who's moved back in with your husband.'

'Yes, but that doesn't mean anything,' said Mary unreasonably.

'Well, he doesn't know that, does he?'

'I never get it right, do I?'

'You will. It's a pity you never see him on his own.'

'Yes. He calls and sees my father sometimes, in the evening.'

'Does your father know what's what?'

'According to him, he knows everything. Unfortunately, he's usually right.'

'There you are, then. He'll put Rupert straight in no time.'

Mary thought it unlikely.

The lunch deliveries were going very well – word had spread; and it was not unusual for them to be asked to supply an up-market 'directors' lunch', for which Mary ordered more elaborate boxes with inner containers, reminiscent of the Japanese boxes she had originally envisaged.

At the end of the school term she had engaged two sixth-form students on a part-time basis: a girl and a boy to help in the kitchen. She also took on a sixteen-year-old school leaver, a large, cheerful youth with a pronounced stammer, to do the deliveries. He made nothing of carrying the stacked-up boxes, his long arms encompassing them carefully, and in spite – or perhaps because – of his speech impediment he became very popular with his clients. They treated him as something between a pet and a protégé, and since he seemed perfectly happy to amuse them with his attempts to recite tongue-twisters and was at the same time both reliable and conscientious, Mary hoped that he would stay for as long as possible.

David, judging that his father would get over his annoyance better if he did not have the cause of it under his nose for a while, had accepted an offer from his firm to spend a few months in Hong Kong where they had a subsidiary office. This, although not particularly well paid since the living expenses were high, was seen as something of a pat on the back, and John had been delighted, even going so far as to wonder whether they might not manage a week or two out there themselves. He and Mary were living in a state of careful neutrality: John said nothing at all about Mary's frequent absences to the sandwich bar, and to Oxford, and Mary for her part never questioned the late evenings when he came back smelling of perfume, or the occasional nights and weekends away. It was, if not satisfactory, at least bearable as a *modus vivendi*. Mary saw it as a temporary phase, but when she tried to suggest this to John he reacted with such anxiety that Mary had been alarmed.

'You're not going to leave me, surely? Not that, Mary!'

'I just thought that maybe the time had come to look at our lives together, and to the future. It's not a question of either of us leaving the other. It's just a progression, a change.'

'I don't want anything to change!' It was a cry from the heart, and Mary saw that for John it represented the ultimate catastrophe.

'Things have to change,' she said gently. 'That's how life is. David has grown up, your parents have died, Pa had his stroke – those were all changes, and we coped with them.' She did not mention his job, but it was implicit in her words.

'That's what I mean! We've had so many things to get used

238

to. But those were things that happened to us, we couldn't do anything about them. Surely we don't want to bring about any more
changes?'

His voice was truculent, but he was pleading with her. Mary
remembered how, all those years ago, she had committed herself to
caring for him. That mad promise, with no thought of the con-
sequences, still bound her, mind and heart. The fact that she had made
it to no one but herself made it all the more impossible to break it. She
could only hope that John would come to realise that things could not
go on as they were.

It felt, against all odds, rather numbingly permanent. Mary could
imagine this situation continuing through the months and years, with
herself becoming more of a zombie with every passing day. She read a
report in a newspaper about a new kind of artificial heart that pumped
the blood round the recipient's body in one continuous flow, without
the surges of an actual beat, and was appalled by the thought. She
found it unimaginable that anyone could properly exist without that
background rhythm of life, and took to putting a hand up to her neck to
feel her own pulse in case it had somehow stopped without her being
aware of it.

Zen and her father, on the other hand, seemed so vibrant with life
that it was as though their pulses were permanently racing. Zen had her
eighteenth birthday, and they celebrated with a small party to which
Zen's mother came. Mary was interested to meet her, and found her to
be a sensible, down-to-earth woman with a great deal of Irish charm
and wit, though without her daughter's needle-sharp intellect. Mrs
O'Hara, for her part, was relieved to find someone relatively normal to
talk to. She appeared to regard the Professor, and those of his
colleagues he had invited along, with a mixture of respect and kindly
contempt, as if they had been small children who had somehow learned
to do remarkable tricks but were still liable to make puddles on the floor
or eat too much ice cream and be sick.

Zen was working hard, and Professor Hill confided in Mary that he
hoped to put Zen forward to take the Oxford entrance exam in
November.

'This November? Don't you think that's a bit soon? And shouldn't
she take some A levels first?'

'A levels!' His hands swatted them away like troublesome flies. 'No
point in jumping through those hoops. That's the whole point of the

entrance exams, after all. They're looking for people who can think –
who are rare – not people who can pass A levels, who are two a penny.'

'But she's only just eighteen. She can afford another year, surely.'

'But I can't.' He said it calmly, but Mary heard the undertone of
frustration. She eyed him warily, knowing how much he resented any
kind of sympathy.

'You'll live for years yet, if you give yourself a chance,' she said.

'Give myself a chance? What's that supposed to mean?'

'It means doing what the doctor tells you. It means being sensible. It
means not driving yourself too hard. If you give Zen another year, you
might give yourself one too.'

'Or I might not.' He grinned. 'I'm not going to "go gentle into that
good night". I'm more one of your "rage, rage" sort.'

'You don't say. And does Zen think she'll be ready?'

'*Zen*,' he said with heavy sarcasm, 'has faith in me. *Zen* believes that if
I say she can do it, she can.'

'Well, *Zen*'s only known you for about seven months, not forty-eight
years. But how is she going to feel if you kill yourself trying to rush her
into college?' Mary thought this was rather a crafty hit, but she had
reckoned without her father.

'She'd work all the harder, to make it worthwhile.' He sat there,
looking smug. 'Besides, it's not just me. I've recruited a few helpers.
Drafted them in, as you might say.'

'You haven't been pestering the Fellows, have you, Pa?'

'Certainly not! I never pester. But these young ones have more time
on their hands than they know what to do with. All those vacations.
And most of them don't take on half as many students as I used to, or do
as many lectures.'

'Oh, I'm sure they're all very grateful to you for livening up their
lives.' The trouble was, thought Mary, that they probably were. People
in love with their subjects liked nothing more than to talk about them,
and without the constraints of set courses the extra-curricular teaching
of one bright girl would seem more pleasure than annoyance.

Mary went early to the sandwich bar one morning a few weeks later.
She had had an idea for something new that she wanted to try out,
based on a Turkish pizza made with a very thin layer of dough, with the
sides folded inwards over the filling. She found that the filling tended to
ooze out of the ends, and she had learned very early on that the one

thing people in offices did not want was food that dripped down their clothes or on to their desks. She wanted to try pinching the dough together, as if making a pastie.

She had made three fillings – spicy vegetable, chicken with ginger and mushrooms, and chilli beef – and was re-kneading the dough she had left to rise when she heard footsteps in the shop. About to call out, she realised that she knew those long, decisive strides. Much to her annoyance, she felt her heart give one tremendous thump. She breathed in, expanding her chest to contain the explosion, and swallowed. Really, she thought, one's body never did play fair. You could always rely on it to produce a spot when you were going to something smart, have a period and blow up like a balloon just before a holiday in the sun or, as now, react to feelings that she was not, as yet, ready to acknowledge. To punish it, she made her hands continue kneading, using more force than usual in the movement to still the slight tremors in her fingers.

'Smells good,' Rupert said, as he had done in her father's kitchen. 'What are you making?'

Mary explained her idea, and he nodded.

'Great! They should go like – well, like hot cakes! I knew you'd be better at this than me.'

'Oh, no!' Mary was horrified. 'I'm just going on with what you started. I could never have set it all up like this. I wouldn't know where to begin.'

'I had some help,' he admitted. 'A friend of my son's did a course in hotel management, concentrating on the restaurant and the kitchen side. He's working as a chef, now. Well, sous-chef.' For some reason he looked embarrassed. He turned away and began to wipe down the kitchen surfaces, quite unnecessarily since they had all been scrubbed the previous day, at the end of the afternoon. Mary, made more relaxed by his discomfort, began to divide her dough up into pieces ready for rolling.

'Are you busy this afternoon?' he asked, so casually that the air rang with tension.

'Um,' said Mary. 'Yes, I am. Well, there's here, for one thing, all the afternoon teas and things, and I really ought to . . .' She stopped, unable to think what she ought to be doing. Ironing, of course. There was always that. And the garden . . . 'But I'm sure they could manage without me.' She stopped, aghast at the sound of her own calm voice.

She had not said it, surely? It had not been her tongue that had uttered those unambiguous words.

'Good. I've got something to show you.' They both jumped as there was a thud from the door – Jason, one of the original employees, by the sound of it, loaded with salad stuff and bread, and pushing the door open with the corner of the boxes. 'I'll pick you up at three,' Rupert said hurriedly, filling the kettle and switching it on. Cappuccino machine or no cappuccino machine, Jason liked to start his shift with a mug of strong sweet tea with plenty of milk in it. He came in, peering at them over the pile of trays and boxes he carried. Rupert was always telling him not to move so many in one go, but although the stack frequently wobbled perilously, he had never dropped anything yet.

'Morning,' he said cheerfully. 'What're you up to, then?' Mary felt a guilty look spread over her face, but Jason nodded at the lumps of dough, standing like an improbable growth of puffballs on the board. Once again she explained her idea, and he nodded judiciously.

'Reckon you could do smaller ones, with a sweet filling?' he suggested. 'Apple, say, or mincemeat? Or chocolate and nut?' Jason was supremely uninterested in any form of savoury food, but existed almost entirely on a diet of sweets and cakes. In spite of this he was neither fat nor unhealthy-looking, a fact which Mary put down to the nourishing qualities of their home-made cakes. She had not as yet plucked up enough courage to ask about the state of his teeth.

'It might work,' she said dubiously. 'The dough would have to be a bit thicker, though, and richer. More like brioche. It's worth a try, if these ones go all right.'

'Trust him,' said Rupert. 'The English are a nation of sweet-eaters, and when it comes to sweet food he knows whereof he speaks. I must go, I've got a meeting. I'll see you later.'

'Never here these days, is he?' remarked Jason cheerfully. 'Reckon he's two-timing us?' He began to unpack and sort the produce he had brought in. 'Another sandwich place, I mean?' he added, glancing at Mary's averted face.

'Oh, surely not! He wouldn't risk harming our business, this place means too much to him. And where else is there he might start somewhere? Oxford? I doubt if there's room for another, the place is full of them already, and some of them are almost as good as this.' Jason grinned at this blatantly biased assessment.

'Well, he's up to something, Mrs M.,' he said. 'I know the type. This place is fine, but it's not enough for him any more. He's too big for it – and I don't mean his size. The deliveries were a good idea, kept him buzzing around, but now that's up and running he's all set to break out again. You'll see. My dad's the same, only with him it's women, not business. Six marriages and five divorces he's been through, and every time he gets that look about him; you get to recognise it. He's got it now, and if I were his lawyer I'd be rubbing my hands with glee. Made a mint out of him over the years, they have.'

Mary abandoned her rolling pin and turned to look at him.

'Six marriages? *Six?*'

He nodded, unperturbed. 'Shocking, ennit? Henry the Eighth got nothing on him, except he don't cut their heads off, of course. Got it down to a fine art, he has. Somehow he manages to persuade them that splitting up's all their own idea, and he seems so hurt they feel sorry for him, and it stops them turning nasty. Quite good friends with them, he is. You should see the house on his birthday, bursting with all his exes.'

'Don't you mind? And your mother?'

'I minded all right when I was a kid. But you get used to anything in time, don't you? I reckon he just can't help it. And he's been a good dad, really. I'm the only boy; I've got three half-sisters, one older and two younger. And Mum's all right. She married again and went to live in New Zealand. She still sends him a card on his birthday, though.'

Mary turned back to her dough, silent in the face of this insouciant tolerance.

With the arrival of Jamie and Helen the morning work got going. Since space in the kitchen was limited they had evolved a rigid pattern of movements, formal as an old country dance. For the most part their conversations were confined to the business in hand as they worked their way through the lunchbox orders and assembled sandwich fillings, salads and cakes. At the back of Mary's mind as she worked was the thought of the afternoon.

It seemed very clear to her that she was about to reach a crossroads. The tension in Rupert's manner told her that today was going to be the turning point. If he regretted what had been between them, then she must accept it and find her own path into the future, perhaps by moving back to Oxford and looking for another job. If not . . . she scarcely dared to contemplate that. The weeks of uncertainty had shown her at least that she was far from indifferent to Rupert. When he was near her she was physically conscious of him, feeling his presence as if he gave off tangible rays of heat or cold. The thought that he might not want her made her realise, at last, how much she needed him in her life. She would fight for him; if necessary she would throw herself at him.

She felt a shiver of desire at the thought, followed almost at once by a shiver of anxiety. It might not happen, she told herself, but if it did . . . Halfway through the morning she slipped out of the shop and went down to Marks & Spencers. She had dressed that morning in her usual working clothes, a cotton skirt and a short-sleeved blouse that were comfortable in the kitchen and looked fresh and neat when she was serving behind the counter. It had, however, been several days since she had loaded the washing machine, and the underclothes she had found that morning were old, the elastic inclined to sag and the nylon a dingy greyish colour because of a navy face flannel that had somehow been buried in a white wash.

As she queued to pay for the knickers and bra she had chosen Mary found herself avoiding the eyes of the other people in her line, and when she handed them to the cashier she was blushing as if everyone must know why she was buying them. They were, perhaps, slightly more lacy and flimsy than what she would normally have bought, but Mary felt as guilty as if she were buying red satin with black lace. She took her change and the green carrier bag with a glowing, averted face, and stuffed everything into her handbag as if they had the word 'adulterer' embossed on them in neon letters.

The lavatory at the sandwich bar was tiny, and the thought of trying to undress and dress unobtrusively, with her elbows banging against the wooden partition walls, made her go hot with embarrassment again. She went into the nearest department store, picked up a garment at random and changed in the changing cubicle. Thank goodness, she thought, they had abandoned the communal changing area. Somehow the new underwear made her feel that it was less, rather than more, likely that any kind of romantic interlude with Rupert would happen. She half wished she hadn't bothered, but decided it was better to have done it, just in case.

The lunchtime rush was busy enough to stop her thinking about anything but keeping pace with the demand. Her pizza pasties sold well, she was pleased to see, and she determined to sit down and work out costings as soon as possible, bearing in mind that they were labour intensive to make. Once the crowds wanting sandwiches, drinks and cakes thinned out, however, she glanced at her watch and saw that she had only about half an hour before Rupert fetched her. Nervously she checked her appearance in the small, spotted mirror. Her hair was still neat – one advantage of the plaited, pinned-up style was that it stayed tidy – but her nose was shiny. She blotted it with a piece of toilet roll, then dabbed on some powder. Her lipstick had worn off – she had been chewing nervously at her lips – and she renewed it carefully, checking her teeth to make sure it had not got on to them.

When Rupert's car pulled up outside she was ready and watching out for him. Jason had gone off duty, and Jamie and Helen were busy with clearing up, listing the lunchbox orders for the following day, and replacing the cakes eaten at lunch with fresh ones for the afternoon tea trade. They made no remark when Mary mumbled a goodbye and slipped out of the door. She got carefully into the car, feeling as though her new underwear must be shining luminously through her clothes. The car was pulling away from the kerb almost before she had shut her door. Mary did up her seatbelt.

'How did they go?'

Mary felt confused.

'What? I mean, how did what go?'

'The pizza things. The ones you were making this morning.'

Mary relaxed. How typical of him, she thought.

'Oh, those. Yes, they went well. I thought I'd do the costings tonight.' They discussed the sandwich bar for a while and Mary was able to relax a little, though part of her attention was always on the roads they were taking. It did not take her very long to be sure that they were going to Mulberry Court, which was what she had expected anyway. For the last few miles they both fell silent, and Mary felt the tension mounting between them.

As they turned into the gates, Mary could not at first think what it was that was different. Then she saw that the cobbled courtyard, which had been green before, was now clean and weeded. He stopped the car just inside the gateway, and forgetting everything else she climbed out. The cobbles looked so clean they might have been scrubbed: they were lumpy beneath her feet as she walked over them.

The barn doors were wide open, and the inside had been swept clean. She felt a small pang, seeing that the pile of straw was gone. Coming out again, she caught a glitter of reflected sunshine and followed it to the water trough. It, too, had been cleaned and scrubbed inside and out. The crystal water bubbled up through a layer of pebbles that seemed to have been polished, their colours were so rich and clear against the golden stone of the trough. A bottle of champagne stood in the water, and on a trestle table nearby were two sparkling champagne flutes and, next to them, a covered glass jug that glowed a deep garnet red. At the other end of the table were several large pieces of paper, their curling ends held down with more stones.

Mary looked at them. The plans and drawing leaped off the paper at her, as immediate as if she were seeing the actual building. She saw the barn transformed: tall, thin windows discreetly inserted between the timbering; a flooring of terracotta tiles that the artist had colour-washed softly faded with age; concealed lighting indicated by splashes of pale gold; plants and flowers and, above all, the tables. Restaurant tables, larger and smaller, arranged so that each had an illusion of privacy and space and yet none of the area was wasted. Tables set with linen, silver, glass, candles . . . all shown with economy, a line here, a dot of colour there, and yet real, ready, waiting for the customers.

She riffled through the other sheets of paper. Kitchens, beneath which the old dairy was still visible. A storeroom. Looseboxes converted into living accommodation, with a query, Staff? written beneath them. The cottage. Plans, fine-drawn and detailed. Nothing for the house. Mary looked up from the drawings and towards the house. She had not noticed before that there was scaffolding up one side, and that part of the roof was under tarpaulin. How could she have missed that?

Rupert had walked from the car, halting a few feet from her as if keeping carefully out of reach. His hands were pushed deep into the pockets of his trousers, not so much hidden as restrained.

'It doesn't need much doing to it. Not architecturally, that is. Rewiring, roofing, new bathroom, that kind of thing. Kitchen . . . He said he could re-design it, but I thought . . .' His eyes were fixed on her face. 'I hoped you might prefer to do that yourself.'

Now it had come there was no surprise, no uncertainty.

'Yes,' said Mary. 'Yes, I would.'

'As simple as that?'

'As simple as that.' Mary thought that later, perhaps, she would feel elation, anxiety or guilt. Now she was filled with a tremendous calm, a kind of inner peace that she could not recall ever experiencing before. It won't last, she told herself. It will be like those rare moments when you realise you're happy, when the very realisation and the feeling that you must grab it and hold on to it make the happiness slide away. But you remember them, and I will remember this. What ever happens, I will always remember this.

Rupert took his hands from his pockets and walked nearer. With great care he uncovered the jug and poured a little of the dark liquid into the bottom of the glasses, then he fetched the bottle of champagne from the water trough. He untwisted the wire with practised fingers and eased the cork out. It came not with a firework explosion but with a neat, satisfying pop. He poured slowly and neatly, then lifted the pink-tinged glasses and brought one to Mary. She took it, feeling the coolness of the wine through the glass against her fingers. Seriously, without speaking, they touched their glasses together, more of a kiss than a clink.

Mary took a sip. The prickle of bubbles, which she found unpleasant when the wine was icy cold, seemed gentler in the water-cooled liquid, and the rich sweet flavour of mulberry filled her mouth, before the acidity of the wine cut satisfyingly through it. She took another sip and held it lingeringly in her mouth, savouring the combination and swallowing with reluctance.

'It's wonderful,' she said. 'Better even than I'd hoped.'

'It's not a proper liqueur,' he said, lifting the jug and examining it critically against the light. 'There wasn't time to make any yet, though I've got some started. It's good, though, isn't it? And unusual.'

'Unique, practically.'

'Yes. Unique.' His eyes were fixed on her, and quite suddenly all her uncertainty vanished. 'That's what I think this place can be, too. It will take time, and a lot of hard work, but . . .'

She answered the unspoken question. 'We've got time. And I've never been afraid of hard work.'

He took the glass out of her hand and set them both down so that he could kiss her. Mary thought how good it was to be in his arms again. He kept one arm round her as he refilled their glasses. They touched them together, and drank again.

'You are quite sure?'

'Yes. Perfectly sure.' Mary thought she had never in all her life been so sure of anything. 'But I don't know how to do it. I can't just . . . up sticks and leave, after all these years.'

'Is it going to be difficult? Acrimonious?'

'Not exactly acrimonious, but very difficult, I'm afraid. I can't just leave John. He doesn't love me, in fact in some ways I think he despises me, but he needs me. For all the wrong reasons, I'm afraid, but it's my own fault. In a way I've protected him too much, and now he can't manage without my protection. I believe – I'm *sure* – he's ready to change, to come out of the pupa he's spun around himself. But it has to come from him. I can't make him do it. If I'm right, and I hope I am, then there's someone else who can drag him out of that shell, but it's going to be . . . awkward. It may take a while.'

'Then I'll wait. But not patiently.' He looked at her over the rim of his glass and she knew that in a while, without any unseemly haste, they would go into the house or, since the day was warm, perhaps into the privacy of the walled garden, and make love. It would be an unspoken affirmation of their future, and she would feel no guilt. Afterwards, she thought, she would tell him about the new underwear, and they would laugh together. My lucky knickers, she thought, that's what these are going to be. I'll probably wear them for the wedding, if we get married. And for the opening.

'Penny for them?' Rupert was studying her face, trying to follow the various expressions moving across it. Mary burst into laughter.

'I couldn't possibly tell you! At least, I will, but not just now!'

Chapter 21

It was after seven o'clock before Mary got back to Reading. There was a tiny yard behind the sandwich bar where she parked her car, and Rupert drove her into it. He got out when she did, and came round the car to kiss her. Eventually, reluctantly, Mary went to unlock her car, but it was not until she had actually got into it that she saw the sheet of paper tucked under her windscreen wiper. She climbed out of the car again, pulled it free, and stood looking at it. Rupert, his attention attracted by her stillness, came over and she handed him the note.

'Zen rang,' he read. 'Your father is ill. Please contact at once. So sorry.' It was signed by Helen.

'I must go there now. Straight away. He must have had another stroke.'

'Yes, of course.' His hands were on hers, preventing her from opening the car door. 'But let's telephone first, so we know where to go. He might be at the hospital. Come on.'

The idea seemed to bounce off her mind, so that at first she resisted his pull towards the building. Then she accepted what he had said, and was running with him, ahead of him, fumbling with her key until he took it from her hand and unlocked the door.

'Oh, Mary!' Zen's voice was full of relief, and the babies were wailing in the background. 'I didn't know where to find you, I've been ringing everywhere. Mary, I'm so sorry, the Prof's had a stroke. He's not dead,' she added hastily. 'They've taken him off in an ambulance, he's at the Radcliffe again. I couldn't go with him, because of the babies, and he was unconscious. But I've been ringing them, and he's stable. They say he's comfortable, bloody idiots.'

'They always say that,' said Mary numbly, 'unless you're actually screaming in agony. I expect they said he's as well as can be expected?'

249

'Yes!' Zen gave a high laugh. 'Sorry. Mary, I'm sorry. We were reading together, and he – he—'

'It's all right. It would have happened anyway. At least you were there, to get help. I'll go straight to the hospital. Don't worry. Are you on your own?'

'Yes, I sent Theresa home. She said she'd come back if she was needed, and her mum too. They've been great.'

'Good. I'll ring you from the hospital.'

Mary turned to find that Rupert had picked up her car keys and put them in his pocket. Now he was at the refrigerator, swiftly pulling out containers.

'What are you doing?'

'Making you some sandwiches. It's a long time since lunch, and you could be hanging around the hospital half the night.'

Mary felt her throat close at the thought of food, but she knew he was right. She sat down, keeping out of his way as he assembled one of the lunchboxes and filled it.

'There. That should keep us going. Come on.'

They were outside, locking up his car and opening the passenger door of hers almost before she could catch her breath. He held the door wide, not getting in.

'What are you doing?' It seemed to be all she could say.

'You don't think I'm going to let you drive to Oxford in this state, on top of that champagne, do you? I'll take you, and stay with you. Unless you'd rather I didn't?'

'But your car...'

'It'll be all right here. You'll need to have yours there. I can get a train back, pick mine up later. In you get.' Limp with relief, Mary got into the car. At the hospital, once they had established that her father was stable and resting, Rupert tactfully took himself off.

'You know where I am,' he said, scribbling a number on a piece of paper. 'This is for my mobile phone. I'd have given it to you before but I've only just got it. Promise me,' his eyes looked fiercely into hers, 'that you'll call me if you need me. Any time. *Any* time. All right?'

'Yes. Thank you.' His hand clasped her shoulder warmly, then he was gone. Mary sat beside her father's bed watching him as he slept, and it was not until late that night that she realised she hadn't told John. Guiltily she went to the pay phone, scrabbling in her purse for coins.

The ringing sound went unanswered, however, and in the end she gave up. I'll catch him in the morning, she thought.

The following morning she tried again, with the same result. Counting hours on her fingers she telephoned Hong Kong, and spoke to David, touched when he offered to come straight back.

'I don't think you need to,' she said. 'They've assured me he's not dying or anything, and in fact he doesn't seem too bad this morning, only he can't talk much. He hates people seeing him like this – you know how he is.'

'But what about you, Mum? Are you all right?'

Mary felt her throat tighten. She coughed.

'Yes, I'm fine,' she said, forcing her face into a smile so that her voice would sound positive. 'Don't worry about me. The only thing is, I can't get hold of your father. He was out yesterday evening when I rang, and I missed him this morning. He'll guess where I am, but I know he won't ring to find out because he's got this silly thing about Zen. He may ring you.'

If David was surprised at having to mediate between his parents via Hong Kong, he did not betray it.

'Don't worry, today's his day to ring me anyway. I'll put him in the picture. Um, what do you want him to do? Come, or stay away?'

'Oh, David, I don't know. Whatever he wants, I suppose.'

In the end, John visited the hospital only once. He was ill at ease, speaking to his father-in-law in unnaturally slow, loud tones which Mary knew would infuriate her father. He seemed reluctant to be alone with Mary, and left with the air of one making his escape. Mary, peering out of the window of her father's room, saw his foreshortened figure hurrying across the car park to a red sports car. He got into the passenger side.

'Smile?' said the Professor, with difficulty. He still noticed more than he should, thought Mary, primming her lips and banishing the smile he had queried.

'Oh, I was just watching John leave.' His blue eyes twinkled at her. 'No, I'm not glad to see the back of him.' She said no more, and he accepted her reticence. Perhaps, she thought, she should be grateful to her father if his continuing presence in hospital was driving John into Elaine Brantridge's arms.

'I want to take him home.'

The doctor was younger than Mary, which should have given her an advantage but didn't, because he clearly felt that middle-aged women who were not even patients, but only relatives of patients, came so low in the scheme of things that they were practically non-existent.

'Out of the question.'

He was already turning away. Mary moved to get in front of him again.

'Of course it isn't. You've just said yourself that you couldn't do any more for him. So he doesn't need to stay here.'

'Nothing for him medically. We haven't got any magic pills to make him better.' He spoke as to a pestering child, and Mary hated him. 'But he needs constant nursing. Day and night. Physiotherapy. Perhaps speech therapy, if he recovers enough. Can you give him all that? Any of it?'

'I don't see why not. He's not poor, and he's got excellent health insurance cover. I can hire nurses.'

'If you can find any. I'm afraid the days when you simply paid for a nurse to live in went out with Agatha Christie. Will you let me pass, please? I have other patients, you know.'

'If I can find nurses, and a physiotherapist and all the rest of it—'

'And a special bed,' he broke in.

'And a special bed, is there any reason why he shouldn't be at home?'

'And if he has another stroke?'

'If he has another stroke he'll die anyway. And I think he'd prefer that to being stuck in here.'

'How do you know? He can't talk.'

'I know,' said Mary fiercely, 'because he's my father, and I love him.'

Having been facing up to her aggressively, this ultimate in four letter words had the doctor backing nervously away. Mary was amazed, as much with what she had said as the effect of it. Surely it couldn't be true? The ties that bound her to her father were, she had always considered, of duty and of habit, rather than affection.

'I can't stop you, of course . . .'

'Good. Then kindly don't do so. I will make the arrangements and notify the hospital. Will he be sent home in an ambulance, or must I arrange for that also?'

'That,' he said grandly, 'is the kind of detail you can arrange with Sister. Now, if you will kindly excuse me . . .'

Mary watched him walk away. Even from the back you could see the self-satisfaction all over him. His shiny brown shoes were planted firmly and crisply down, the toes pointing slightly outwards. His bottom was round and protruding, exaggerated by his confident stance that curved his spine forward and his shoulders back. A bumptious bottom, she thought. Bumptious bum . . . bumptious bum . . . the clack of his footsteps on the polished hospital flooring receded, and with them the phrase.

Mary went back to her father's room. He was awake, his one good eye fixed on the door while the other, drooping, parodied a conniving wink.

'I'm taking you home,' she said firmly. He made a sound between a grunt and a gurgle. Mary had been assured that it was only his speech that was affected by a mixture of damage to the speech centre and paralysis to one side of his face. His mind still works, a helpful nurse had told her, and Mary had been appalled, seeing him trapped in the small space of his skull, unable to escape with words. She came towards the bed and sat down in the chair. Her body knew that chair, was intimately acquainted with the too-soft padding of the seat, the hardness of the frame, and the place where the fabric had worn thin. She had sat in that chair, on and off, for days, ever since she had arrived at the hospital and found her father in this bed.

Now the tubes and drips were gone, his bodily functions were returning, and on his good side at least the strength was coming back so that an optimistic physiotherapist had said he would soon be well enough for a wheelchair. He fed himself, slowly and fastidiously, his distaste for the hospital food apparent but forcing down the necessary nutriments with grim determination. Everything was coming back except for the speech, which seemed not to improve although the attempts he made to communicate were painfully strenuous. Now Mary believed she heard pleasure in the sound he made.

'The doctor wasn't very pleased,' she told her father. 'I don't really see why, when he'd just told me there was nothing further he could do for you. They're always going on about a shortage of hospital beds, I'd have thought they'd have been pleased to have another one empty.' The bright blue eye looked sardonically at her. 'It's power, isn't it?' said Mary dreamily. 'The decisions are supposed to come from him. Have you noticed his bottom?' The blue iris flickered sideways. 'The way he stands, sticking it out, so pleased with himself. Bumptious bum, I call him.'

The door opened, and the doctor came in. Mary rose to her feet in a flurry, embarrassed that he might have heard her. He ignored her, however, and spoke to her father, raising his voice slightly.

'Your daughter seems to think you want to go home, Mr Hill.'

He made a sound in which three syllables could clearly be heard.

'Is that a yes or a no, Mr Hill? What about, let's see, one sound for yes, two for no? Mr Hill?'

The three syllables were repeated, with more emphasis.

'Professor,' said Mary. 'Not Mr Hill. Professor Hill. Like calling you mister, not doctor, if you work your way up to being a surgeon.'

He gave her a look of deep dislike.

'Professor Hill, then,' he said with exaggerated patience. 'Do you want to go home? Will you feel safe there? It may not be easy to get nursing help.'

'Uh.' They waited.

'Is that yes, Professor Hill?'

'Uh!' The effort of the noise lifted him in the bed. Mary put her hand on his shoulder.

'It's your decision, of course,' said the doctor stiffly. 'I can't stop you.'

'Uh uh.'

'No, you can't,' Mary interpreted, unnecessarily. 'Thank you for your concern. I can assure you that I will take every possible care of my father.'

The doctor stood for a moment. He was slightly turned away from them, and against the window the shape of his body was clearly outlined. Mary, her hand still on her father's shoulder, felt a tremor shake his body. Alarmed, she bent down to look at him. His good eye was fixed on the other man; specifically, on the rounded silhouette of his buttocks. He held his stare, then transferred his look to Mary's face. The blue eye was as vivid as ever. Mary giggled. The doctor sniffed, and walked out of the room. Mary sat weakly down in her chair and laughed until her eyes ran and her stomach ached.

It was two days before it was possible to bring Professor Hill home. Mary managed to get a bed like the hospital ones, with adjustable height and ends that moved. She had it put in the study, judging it to be the room he felt happiest in, and after spending several hours on the telephone managed to find a nurse who would be there from first thing in the morning until lunchtime, and then return in the evening to help with settling him for the night. A sophisticated type of baby alarm was fitted between the study and Mary's bedroom, and the social services arranged for the loan of a commode and a rather sophisticated wheelchair, which the Professor seemed quite pleased with and which Zen treated as a motorised toy, whizzing round the ground floor of the house with shrieks of delight.

A new routine evolved. Mary went in the mornings to the sandwich bar, returning in the middle of the day and bringing their lunch home with her. She spent her afternoons with her father, and sometimes with the babies also, when Zen was out studying with one of her other co-opted tutors.

'I shouldn't be doing all this,' she said. 'I should stay here and help look after him.'

'I can just imagine what he'd have to say about that,' said Mary. 'Well, think about it, anyway. You know how proud he is of you, and that he's counting on your taking the entrance exam this autumn. The best thing you can do for him is to study as hard as the babies will let you.'

'I'll work my balls off for him – metaphorically,' said Zen. Mary looked at her. With the resilience of the young her figure had long since returned to its natural slimness, but the high protein diet with its emphasis on fresh produce had done away with her skinniness, while breast feeding the twins, which she was still, amazingly, managing to do, meant that her breasts rounded in a way that drew wolf whistles when she walked through Oxford. Mary no longer noticed the outrageous clothes or the brilliantly colourful hair, they were just a part of Zen, an expression perhaps of her unusual mind. Mary felt extraordinarily close to her, as if she had known her for years. Closer to her, in fact, than she had ever felt to John.

Her mind shied away from the thought of her husband. He had telephoned once or twice, but had not offered to visit again. The only time Mary called him, to tell him that her father was going home, the call had been answered by someone who did not speak. Mary contemplated talking into that silence, leaving a message for John, but in the end she simply replaced the receiver.

Unwilling to try again, she telephoned David in Hong Kong.

'I'm coming home soon,' he said. 'How is he?'

'Pretty bad,' she admitted. 'He still has a lot of trouble talking. I can usually understand him, and so can Zen, but he has to stick to simple words and he absolutely hates it. The wheelchair, too, although it does give him a bit more freedom. He's just so frustrated all the time, and though we all do what we can it doesn't help much, because he so dislikes losing his independence.'

'It's a pity, really . . .'

'That he survived? Yes, I know, and yet how can I want it otherwise? By the way, Dad doesn't know Pa is home. I couldn't get hold of him to tell him.'

'OK, I'll pass it on. Um . . . how would you feel about a Chinese daughter-in-law?'

His voice held a note in it that Mary had never heard before. She felt a smile spreading over her face.

'What if I say, over my dead body?' She knew he would hear the smile.

'Then lie down and die. But only temporarily, because I want you to meet her. And she wants to meet you.'

'Oh darling, how lovely. What's her name?'

'Lin. Well, Say-Lin, really. She works in the office out here – as a matter of fact, she's my boss. She's . . . well, she's special. I've only known her for a few weeks, but it's as if I've known her all my life. You know?'

'I know. Darling David, I'm very happy for you. Can I tell people, or is it a secret?'

'Well, we haven't spoken to her parents yet, but I don't think they'll be very surprised. They might have preferred her to marry someone of her own race, but I think it'll be all right. They're moving to Canada anyway, because of 'ninety-seven. They seem to like me all right. The only thing is . . . Pa.'

'Oh dear. Yes. I don't know what he'll say. But she – Lin – is obviously clever, and successful.'

'Her parents are quite well off. Rich, actually.'

'Yes, that might help. At least she couldn't be as bad as Zen, in his eyes. I'm sure it'll be all right.'

'Poor old Dad.'

'Yes.'

Mary went back downstairs, feeling almost light-headed with pleasure. She went into the study, meaning to tell the Professor about David, but one sight of the room drove all thoughts of anything else away. Her father was lying on the floor, his wheelchair tipped over, surrounded by numbers of books. Above him, wide gaps in the shelves gaped like missing teeth. He was growling crossly to himself, struggling to pull himself up with his good arm.

'Pa!' She ran to help him. For almost the first time in her life, for the past week she had been thankful for her size, which made it possible for her to move her father's bony body. Now she hauled him up, realised too late that she should have righted the wheelchair first, then half carried him to his old seat by the desk. He dropped into it, the air coming with a whoosh from his lungs as she lost her grip and he fell the last few inches. 'Sorry, Pa,' she panted. He shook his head, gasping a little. Mary propped herself against the desk, struggling for breath that had been driven out by a combination of shock and exertion.

'What happened?' she asked at last. 'Were you trying to reach a book? Surely you could have waited a few minutes, until I came back?'

An extraordinary look came over the mobile half of his face, a mixture of irritation and cunning. His eyes slid away from her.

'Doesn't matter,' he said with difficulty. 'Nothing.'

Mary waited for a moment, then pulled herself away from the desk. The wheelchair was heavy, and it was an effort to lift it back on to its wheels. When she had managed it, and moved it out of the way, she set to work to replace the books. Since they were all arranged alphabetically this was a time-consuming job. At length she replaced the last one and turned. Professor Hill was watching her, and the misery and despair in his face caught at her heart.

She came and crouched at his feet, looking up at him. He turned his head away, lifting his good hand and swiping clumsily at his cheek where a tear trickled sluggishly down.

'Oh, Pa. Won't you let me help you?'

He turned his face back towards her. During his illness, Mary had become adept not only at understanding his garbled speech, but at reading his expression. Sometimes, though he did not speak, she could hear his voice clearly in her head, rather as she had previously heard her fantasy lover. At times she found herself answering this inner voice out loud, and they sometimes conducted quite long conversations in this fashion. Now his look spoke to her clearly.

'You can't help me. It's something I have to do myself.'

'Something private?'

He nodded.

Mary followed his eyes back to where they rested longingly on the bookshelves.

'You were trying to reach something? A book?' It had to be. There was nothing there but books. She went back across the room, looking at the books she had replaced. Not one of them, obviously, but near them? She turned back to him, saw the hunger in his face.

'Let me find it. I won't look.' Perhaps, she thought, there was a diary he wanted to destroy, or papers, or photographs? What ever it was he had a right to his privacy, which he had always protected so fiercely. Certainly she did not wish to be discovering any revelations when, eventually, she had to clear this room.

He watched her, considering. She lifted her hand, ran it along a shelf, glanced back at him. His eyes lifted, and she raised her hand to the shelf above. Authors, she noted, beginning with E. One by one she fingered her way along the books, her eyes constantly checking his face. If it had not been for that she would have missed it, an insignificant book, neither larger nor smaller than those on either side of it, its brown cloth cover blending with the others. Unlike them, however, it had no author name, only *Enquire Within* in faded gold letters.

'*Enquire Within*? Isn't that one of those "How to get ink stains off the housemaid's knee" type of books?' As she joked she pulled at the book. The shelf was tightly packed, and the book resisted. She slipped her hand over the top and got the tips of her fingers just behind it. A swift jerk brought it loose, but it was lighter than she had expected and once it was free it came tumbling down. She caught at it with her other hand, and heard a distinct rattling sound from inside it as she grabbed it. The sound distracted her and she missed. The book fell to the floor, not with the hollow thud of a true book but with the lighter bounce of something hollow. Of a box.

Across the room they confronted one another.

'Don't look,' said his eyes. 'Just give it to me, and don't look.'

Mary did not move.

'I can't,' she said.

'You promised...' His voice in her head was bitter.

'I know I promised. But this is different. Isn't it?'

His face acknowledged the truth of it. But—

'Open it, then.' He spoke the words, as clearly as he could. Slowly Mary bent, reaching for the object on the rug. Her fingers approached it reluctantly, as if it might give her an electric shock.

When she picked it up, it still looked like a book, only it weighed too little in her hand. She examined it. The cloth binding was real, slightly scuffed along the spine like a much-borrowed library book. The edges of the pages were a faded blue. Mary ran her fingers across them and they felt as they should, only they did not part. Only the front cover moved, lifting with a little sucking hiss to reveal the well-sealed little compartment within. There was nothing in it but a small plastic bottle. A chemist's bottle, with perhaps a dozen pills in it. It had no label, and the cap was an ordinary old-fashioned metal screwtop, not a child-proof plastic one.

The pills were plain and white. They looked innocuous, like aspirins. With difficulty she raised her eyes to his face. She didn't know what to say. He held her gaze.

'So,' she said at length, 'I have to decide, do I? Whether to give them to you, or not?'

His physical voice said 'Sorry.' In her mind he spoke. 'I wanted to protect you from this. It wasn't my wish to make you face this kind of choice. It's mine. My life. My choice. My death.'

'If I hand them to you, I'll be killing you,' she said bleakly.

'Not at all. The means of death is all around us every day. A car. A sharp knife. A rope. A river. Only, those options are no longer open to me. I am reduced to ... this.'

'Where did you get them from?'

His eyes glazed over.

'Long time,' he said aloud. 'Your mother...'

'My *mother* gave them to you?'

He gave a gesture of irritation; the Professor with a slow student.

''Course not. Doctor. After. Sleeping. Warned me – not more than two.'

Mary looked down at the bottle again. It was true, she thought, that in those days such things were handed out more freely. In those innocent days, strong sleeping pills for someone under stress were given easily, particularly if the patient and the doctor knew one another well. Their family doctor in those days, who had seen her through all her childhood ailments and had administered those first, almost revolutionary injections against polio, had been a family friend. And, she thought, he's been dead for ten years, without ever giving another thought to these pills. Pills which my father has hoarded all these years.

'All these years,' she said wonderingly. 'You've kept them all these years. Will they still work?'

A flash of humour warmed the blue of his eye.

'Don't know.' He invited her to share the joke, but she could not. 'Comforting,' he said, struggling with the syllables.

Mary thought of the things in which she had taken comfort, through all the years of her life. Little things – food, and hot water bottles, and favourite books. The thought of David. Her phantom lover, and her phantom kitchen. And now, Rupert.

'I'm going to leave John,' she said inconsequentially. 'Rupert's found a place in the country. We're going to run it together, as a restaurant.'

He nodded.

'Busy,' he said aloud. 'You'll be busy,' said his voice in her head. 'You don't need all the extra work of looking after me. Get on and live your life, and let me have my death.'

'We won't get many customers if word gets round I poisoned my father,' she pointed out. He made the grunting wheeze that was, these days, his laugh.

'Won't know. Old man. Stroke. Could. Go. Any. Time.' The single words shot from his mouth like slow bullets.

'Then why not wait, and let nature take its course? Why must you be so – so impatient all the time? Must everything *always* be done on your terms?'

'Yes!' His voice was loud and certain. 'Selfish,' he added. Mary looked at him, not sure whether this was an accusation or self-indictment. 'Me,' he clarified. He gestured to the wheelchair, the commode, to his own useless body, and finally to his books, row upon row of them. 'Done your best,' he said earnestly, 'but . . .' 'But it's not a life,' he continued in her head. 'Not like this. Uncomfortable, undignified, pointless. Let me go.'

Mary looked at him. She saw that he, who seldom asked and never begged, was pleading with her. She saw, quite clearly, that denying him would be like refusing water to a man in a desert. Quickly, giving herself no more time to think, she crossed the room and put the little bottle in his hand.

His fingers closed over it greedily. They rubbed at the bottle, caressing it, almost . . . polishing it? Mary looked up from those busy fingers into his face, and gave a sob of laughter.

'Oh, Pa! Fingerprints?'

260

He met her look with one of happy amusement, as candid as his earlier expression had been cunning. Mary felt her throat go hard and painful; her eyes burned with scalding tears.

'Must you, Pa? What about Zen? Won't you wait until she's taken her exams? It's not so long.'

He shook his head.

'Too long. Can't wait...'

She thought of David, who would be sad not to have been here but whom she could not summon. Of Zen, who would weep, and throw herself still harder into her work, in his memory.

'When...?' The hardest question she had ever had to ask.

'Not yet. Soon. One night.' He shook the little bottle, rattling the pills. 'Forget these. Think ... another stroke. But peaceful. Asleep.' His blurred voice was warm with relief, and she knew she could not deny him.

'No goodbyes, then?'

He rested his head against the back of the chair.

'No goodbyes. Just ... goodnight.'

Chapter 22

It was, against all odds, a happy evening. The presence of Zen, high as a kite on a mixture of intellectual excitement and maternal pride, brought both Mary and Professor Hill back from the tenebrous realms where their spirits had been wandering. Theresa, the housekeeper's daughter, had two weeks before secretly taken Molly and David to a department store where the local newspaper, in conjunction with a portrait photographer, was running a Beautiful Baby competition. Now four months old, the twins had made up much of their early lack of size, but they were still quite tiny, so that the only clothes that really fitted them were made for the newborn. Theresa, thinking this rather shameful (as if she, at fifteen, had to wear clothes made for a ten-year-old), had found some oddments of fabric and made them what she considered more appropriate garments: tiny dungarees in red trimmed with green for David, and a bib-topped pinafore in green trimmed with red for Molly.

Both the babies in the last two months had produced heads of fine curling hair. Mary, who had secretly been hoping for a clue about Zen's natural hair colour, had laughed at herself, because while David's hair was almost black, Molly's was bright golden red. Their faces, however, were very similar, and both had Zen's grey eyes, fringed with dark lashes. Apart, they were pretty babies, but together they were startling and it was not surprising that the photograph of the pair of them, propped together like a set of book-ends and regarding the camera with wide-eyed interest, won the competition. Theresa had taken the babies down to the newspaper offices that afternoon, just to check, and had been given an advance copy of the newspaper as well as the photograph, framed, which she had brought back in triumph to give to Zen.

Zen returned from her afternoon session studying English literature, her mind overflowing with a rich diet of Shakespeare and Marlowe.

Momentarily stunned by the sight of her children's faces looking up at her from the pages of the newspaper – in colour too; the paper was really splashing out – she had then shrieked with excitement. She was, Mary realised, still very young and in many ways unsophisticated. To have one's picture in a paper, even a local paper, was to her the kind of fame she had never thought to achieve. Mary thought that although in the future it might well be that Zen herself would appear in publications more prestigious than this, nothing would ever again bring such pure pride and delight.

She opened a bottle of champagne and, since the evening was fine, wheeled the Professor out on to the lawn in the back garden. The babies, bathed by Theresa and fed, lay on a rug on the grass near his feet and they toasted them ceremoniously, though Theresa turned up her nose at the sour taste of the champagne. Professor Hill flatly refused to drink wine out of the plastic beaker with a spout that was what he could manage most easily, and Mary put it in a glass, hoping that the grass would cushion it from breaking if he dropped it, but not caring very much so long as there was no broken glass left on the lawn. He drank with enjoyment, savouring the wine, and if some of it went down his front, what did it matter? They toasted the twins again and, when Mary belatedly remembered her news, drank again to David and Lin.

In almost holiday mood, Mary found steaks in the freezer and Zen lit the barbecue, which she had improvised earlier in the summer from an old biscuit tin and a metal grid. The smell of burning charcoal, sour and delicious, floated on the still evening air, and Mary collected twigs from the overgrown herbs to lay on the coals. Her father, who could not chew the steak and hated having his food mashed up for him, had buttered crab. A varnish of melted butter coated his chin, and the hospital nurses would have been appalled by the richness of the dish, but Mary had found that since his stroke he particularly relished intensely flavoured food. The mixture of brown and white crabmeat (carefully picked over by Mary in case of stray pieces of shell), flavoured with nutmeg and brightened with lemon rind and juice before being drenched in melted butter and cooked slowly in a bain-marie, was easy to eat with one hand and exactly suited him. Mary and Zen sat on the grass by the babies and ate their steaks with their fingers, tucked into crusty rolls so that they resembled, Zen said, very aristocratic burgers. They had some of Rupert's chilli sauce with them, which gave Mary a carefully hidden frisson of pleasure.

They sat on long into the twilight. Mary had left the radio in the kitchen on, as she often did, tuned in to Radio Three. A programme of Mozart and Haydn drifted out to them: Mary recognised the flute and harp concerto which was one of her favourites. The air was cooler. Reluctant to go indoors, Mary and Zen picked up a baby each. Mary felt the warm, sleepy little body relax against hers, was aware of the fractional addition of heaviness as the child fell into sleep. The dying barbecue gave off wisps of vapour, enough to keep the midges away, and the sound of the music seemed to blend with the scents from grass and flowers, lapping at Mary in well-being and peace. When, in the summer darkness, they found their way indoors they said their goodnights quietly, without strain, and Mary at least fell into deep, untroubled sleep and woke clear-headed.

She had no fear of what she would find when she went to her father's study first thing in the morning. She had told Zen when he first came out of hospital not to go in there unless he called for her, and certainly with two babies needing attention her early mornings were busy times. Mary thought that if she were to find the Professor cold in his bed that morning it would be not unfitting, but in fact he was awake, his good eye glinting blue like a sunlit iceberg as he greeted her.

'Still here, then?' It seemed possible to make a kind of joke of it, even.

'Still here,' he agreed tranquilly. 'Not for long, but for now, anyway,' said his imagined voice. 'What doing today?'

'I'm going back to fetch my things.' The idea appeared in her head at that moment, with as much certainty as if she had been thinking it over for hours. 'It's time I sorted things out.'

'And John?'

'Have to sort him out, too, I suppose.'

She had expected the house to feel chilly and dead. Certainly its windows stared blankly at her as she drove up to the garage, rejecting her presence. The garden looked immaculate. John had obviously cut the grass. He had also, she saw, cut back the flowering shrubs and pruned the roses drastically. He would have preferred not to have roses, regarding them as untidy in winter and a nuisance in the summer, with their tendency to greenfly and black spot, and the necessity to cut off dead heads. The garden looked alien. Even the front door seemed awkward, the key stiff in the lock so that for a moment she thought she would not be able to turn it.

As soon as she stepped into the hall, she knew that something had changed. She had expected the air to smell closed up; she had expected wilting flowers and a thin layer of dust on everything. She smelled, instead, the aggressive aroma of spray polish – the heavily scented kind that she never used – and a whiff of disinfectant that was stronger than anything at the hospital. The flowers on the hall table had been cleared away, and in their place was a stiff little arrangement of silk leaves and flowers, delicately and improbably coloured in various shades of pink and mauve. It was as if she had walked into someone else's house. Mary actually looked down at the key in her hand and then out of the hall window. Yes, she was in the right place.

'Hello?' she called out. Her voice sounded thin and frightened. She tried again. 'Hello?' This time she sounded aggressive. In other circumstances she might have giggled. There was no answer, no movement of the sickly air or sound of a footstep. The house was empty.

Mary went into the kitchen. It was tidy, sparkling with cleanliness. Even the windows looked cleaner than usual, though that might have been her imagination. The knives on the wall rack were out of order, though, and when she opened the cupboards there were subtle changes in their arrangement that told her someone else had been cooking in her kitchen. John? It seemed unlikely. Left to his own devices he would either live on bread and cheese or eat in pubs (or sandwich bars, said her mind, with a hoot of hysterical laughter). Crossly, she opened the window wide and re-arranged the knives. Then, thinking again, she replaced them. This was no longer her kitchen.

Mary went upstairs. In the doorway of her bedroom she paused, sniffing the air. Here at least nothing seemed different. She should be pleased, she knew. At least John had not slept with Her in this room. But it's my kitchen I really mind about, she thought. Not this room, not even this double bed that we shared. She went to the spare bedroom. The double bed there was neatly made, there were no intrusive objects on bedside tables or the dressing table. But the smell! That heavy, musky perfume! It filled the room like a miasma.

Returning to her old bedroom, where the vitiated air seemed pure and fresh by comparison, she took out a suitcase and packed it with clothes and underwear, then fetched a plastic bag and filled it with shoes. She felt frantic with the necessity for speed, unable to bear the thought of staying a moment longer than she must. It was almost as if she were a burglar, intruding in someone else's home. In her haste she did not notice the sound of the car in the drive until the slam of two car doors brought her to quivering stillness. Her first instinct was to hide. Would they know she was here? Out of habit she had put her car into the empty garage, but her actions had been so much of habit that she could not remember whether she had pulled the door closed, as she usually did. She stood frozen, listening. Voices speaking indistinguishable words – no attempt at concealment – and then a key in the front door.

'. . . Can't have double locked,' said John's voice, with less anger than he would normally display at such a breach of security.

'The kitchen window's wide open!' Unmistakably the voice of Elaine Brantridge, shrill with anxiety. 'Have we been burgled?'

Mary heard John's footsteps on the parquet floor of the hall as he crossed to check the sitting room, then the dining room. She wished desperately that she had not come, or that she had telephoned first. Somehow it had never occurred to her that Elaine might be living here. She had imagined speaking to John, calmly and reasonably, but Elaine's presence made all that seem unreal.

'Nothing's been touched.' In his voice was a tone of indulgent reassurance such as she had never heard from him. He was more inclined to be irritated by displays of female weakness. Mary glanced around her, seeking some means of escape but knowing there was none, short of leaping from a window. Hiding, then? The little fourth bedroom, that was never used for guests now that David no longer lived at home and had declined into a storage room, would be safe, but she might be stuck there for hours, even for the rest of the day. The idea was ridiculous, and her foolish panic ebbed. She had told her father, after all, that she was going to sort things out with John. At the time it had been scarcely more than words, but when would she ever have a better opportunity? All the same, she wished they had not caught her upstairs, rifling through her things.

She moved, took a tentative step towards the door. Then, remembering her suitcase, she retreated towards it. A loose floorboard creaked beneath her weight. If only I weren't so heavy, she thought desperately.

'There's someone upstairs!' Elaine said, between outrage and fear. 'Be careful, John!'

Mary, knowing she was trapped, grabbed at her suitcase. She was not clear in her mind whether she meant to hide it or hang on to it as some form of protection. It hung forgotten from her hand as John pushed the door wide. He stood back from the opening, turned sideways as if anticipating a violent rush by a masked intruder in a striped sweater. He looked – odd. Mary wondered if she was simply seeing him differently, more clearly, but then she realised what it was. The carefully trained slick of hair had vanished from the top of his head. Or rather, what had vanished was the shiny scalp beneath it. A toupee, she thought wildly. He's got a toupee. What on earth do I say? Do I mention it? As a matter of fact it does look better, but then anything would look better than that long lock of hair. She was so distracted by it that it was not for several moments that she realised that there were more crucial things to talk about than John's hairpiece.

When he saw Mary his hand flew instantly to his head, patting it as if making sure everything was in the right place. Then, self-consciously, he snatched his hand down again, pulled his body straight and frowned.

'Mary! What are you doing here?' He sounded more affronted than guilty. A number of answers ran through Mary's head: 'I live here, this is my home', for instance. She rejected that immediately as being, in some way, untrue. A more sarcastic 'I might say the same to you' did not come easily to one of her temperament. In the end she said, weakly, 'I've just come to fetch a few things.'

'Who is it? Shall I call the police?' Elaine had stayed prudently downstairs, and it was true that with her diminutive size and build she would not be much use against the average burglar. Unless, of course, she had a handy kitchen knife . . .

'It's all right, Mrs Brantridge. It's Mary.'

At least, thought Mary, he didn't say 'only Mary', though he might just as well have done. And 'Mrs Brantridge'! How typical of John! There was a thoughtful silence from downstairs.

'Isn't this one of your working days?' He managed to sound accusing, as though he had caught her out cheating. He also put metaphorical parentheses round the word 'working', as though what she did at Naseby's or the sandwich bar did not really qualify for the term. If I had done something suitable, like flower arranging for weddings, he would have been proud of me, she thought sadly.

'I'm having a few days off. And I'm not working at Naseby's at the moment, they're moving. They want me to carry on doing a few days a month, though.'

'No doubt.' Mary wondered if she were being hypersensitive, whether she had imagined the overtones in the simple rejoinder. She took a tentative step forward, and for a moment it looked as though he would not give way but would barricade her in the bedroom. Then he stepped back and allowed her to precede him down the stairs.

The suitcase was heavy and awkward, catching at her legs, and as she had not managed to zip it up properly there were ends of garments, very obviously not folded but shoved anyhow into the case, bulging out of the opening. In the hall Elaine Brantridge stood, her body expressing watchful stillness. She was immaculately dressed, Mary saw, her hair recently done and her make-up carefully and skilfully applied to her pussy-cat face. Maquillage, thought Mary regretfully. By the time she was halfway down to the hall Mary could smell the familiar perfume.

'Mrs Marsh! What a nice surprise! I hope your father is better? Mr Marsh told me he had been unwell, when we ran into one another in the library.'

Under other circumstances, Mary could have been impressed. The tone was just right, that of a chance acquaintance who had come back for a cup of coffee. The polite enquiry, and the casual explanation of her presence that managed not to fall into the trap of being too detailed – it was beautifully done. Mary did not believe a word of it, but felt unable to challenge her. Next to Elaine's trim, petite appearance she felt herself to be lumbering, both physically and mentally.

'He's all right,' she said vaguely.

'Oh, good. Well, I won't stop now. I expect you two have things to talk about.'

'Oh, no!' Mary was surprised at the strength of her own denial. 'I mean, yes, of course we do have things to talk about, but I think you should stay, don't you? I mean, you're one of the things, surely.'

'Mary—' John's voice behind her was a protest, though whether against the thought of discussing things or against the description of Elaine as a thing Mary could not have said. Elaine's watchful look intensified.

'Perhaps you're right,' she said. Her eyes travelled past Mary. 'It's all right, John,' she said briskly. 'You know it's got to be discussed some time. Perhaps this is sooner than we intended, but that might be all to the good. Shall we all sit down?' She led the way, not into the sitting room but to the dining-room table. Mary followed her meekly, reminded of her suitcase only when it banged into the doorframe and rebounded into her legs. Sheepishly she went back to the hall and put it down near the front door. Ready for a quick getaway, she thought.

When she returned to the dining room John was sitting in his accustomed place at the foot of the table, with Elaine on his left. Mary wondered whether he had tactfully waved her away from the chair on his right, which was where she herself usually sat when they were alone. She sat down. It's like a board meeting, she thought. We should have blotters and notepads, and glasses with a carafe of water.

The light in the dining room was better than it had been upstairs. Mary discreetly studied John's appearance. She had to admit that the toupee was an improvement. He looked younger, and perhaps a little less gaunt. Or was that the effect of Elaine's cooking? In any case, the hairpiece was obviously well made and had probably been very expensive. Its colour was subtly matched to John's own, and some strands of grey were carefully set in it, avoiding the all-over-youthful look that was often such a give-away. Poor John, thought Mary. I'd never have thought of that in a million years, but it *is* an improvement, and he's obviously much happier.

There was a long pause. Mary felt that the situation was not of her making and had passed beyond her control, and waited for Elaine to say something. Elaine, however, looked expectantly at John, her head tilted to one side like a bird's. He kept his eyes fixed on the table and said nothing.

'John,' said Elaine with gentle authority. He hunched his shoulders a little, and slumped in his chair so that he appeared to have shrunk. Elaine gave a half-exasperated shake of her head. 'It's very difficult for him,' she confided in Mary. 'He's so sensitive. And of course we neither of us want to hurt you.'

'Thank you,' said Mary. She felt an insane desire to giggle. It was rather like taking part in a play, only she had no idea of her lines. She had hoped for a confrontation with John, for the chance to make him see, somehow, that they could not continue as they were. Not just because of Rupert, but because she, Mary, had changed too much. Somehow she had never envisioned anything like this.

'I don't think we should talk about it now,' said John. 'Mary's father's ill . . .'

'Don't be silly, John.' Elaine spoke crisply. 'The fact is, Mrs Marsh, that John and I are . . . in love.' Her eyes dropped coyly to her lap.

She sounded smug, triumphant. Almost as though, Mary thought, she expects me to congratulate her. What am I supposed to say? Come to that, what am I supposed to feel? This all seems so unreal. Perhaps I'm in shock. Yes, that's it. The body's way of protecting the mind from reality. She looked at John, this new John who still looked as though he would rather be anywhere but in this room.

'That's right,' he said lugubriously.

There was another pause.

'Of course I realise that this must come as a great shock to you,' said Elaine tenderly, having apparently understood that she would have to carry the burden of talking herself. 'And I hope you will believe me when I say again that we neither of us want to hurt you. Not in any way.' She leaned forward earnestly. 'We really care about you. We want to be . . . to be *there* for you.'

Where? wondered Mary. Here, presumably. What a ghastly thought.

'Thank you,' she said neutrally. 'But I'm sure it won't be necessary.'

'We're all *civilised* people,' Elaine continued, as if Mary hadn't spoken. 'Adults. I'm sure this can all be arranged . . . tastefully.' Mary looked at the basket of silk flowers that now sat primly in the middle of the table, its subtle chemical colours reflected in the mirror-gloss of silicon wax spray. Tastefully. Oh yuk. She looked at John.

'Elaine's right,' she said. 'We do have to talk about this. It's time to get things out in the open, to move on. What exactly do you want? A separation? A divorce?' He winced like an old maid at a Victorian tea party. 'Come on, John,' she said gently. 'You must have thought about it. Discussed it.'

The eyes he raised to her were haunted, full of helpless appeal. She realised with a pang that this was the only thing she had ever truly found lovable in him; this usually well-hidden core of helplessness, the basic lack of self-confidence that manifested itself in finicking attention to detail, in rigid adherence to a self-imposed pattern that reminded her strongly of a rat in a maze.

What did he want from her? Other men, she thought, would look for the easy way out. Wanting things to be easy and comfortable, they would be glad to have a wife who was prepared to let go easily, who would accept the fiction that they had drifted apart, and would be prepared to come to terms with a new kind of extended family that included the new partners of each. That, presumably, was what Elaine meant by 'civilised'. Other men, happy in a new love, might even be glad that the woman they were leaving also had someone else, freeing

271

them from the guilt of infidelity. But John? Whatever Elaine might want, he was not like that. John would never, in future, suggest that they all have Christmas together, or share a party to celebrate any future engagement that David might enter into. David's wedding photographs, whomever he married, would not feature father and step-father chatting amicably together.

It seemed to Mary, in that moment of intuition that was no more than a few seconds, but which seemed to her to last an eternity, that while she might have had a fantasy lover and a fantasy kitchen, it was John who was out of touch with reality. She, at least, was aware that her fantasy was a creation. While she might have escaped into it as a sanctuary, it had been no more than a stratagem for spiritual survival, less harmful than alcohol or tranquillisers, though equally addictive if not kept under control.

John, on the other hand, lived in a world that was almost entirely a construct. A world where he had been unable to admit even to his wife that he had lost his job. A world that could not accept the unexpected, like Zen. A world that Mary, in all their years together, had never been able entirely to enter but which Elaine, inexplicably, was part of. And now he wanted something from her, she who had always tried to be the wife he had wanted but had failed. Now, if ever, was her chance to put that right.

What he wanted, she saw, was that she should *mind*. Not that she should accept their parting gracefully, but that she should be hurt and upset by it. It was as if he had to prove to himself, or perhaps to Elaine, that what they had had, their marriage, had been of value. A small, mean part of her wanted to punish him, to withhold this last gift and have a revenge for all the things she had missed. With a few dismissive words she could force him to confront the reality of their marriage, but she could not do it. She would not go to Rupert smirched with that sin, for so she felt it would be; the damage, if not the destruction, of another's soul.

At the same time, she could not pretend. No longer was she prepared to be something she was not, to keep John happy. She saw very clearly that her future relationship with Rupert could not be built on dishonesty.

'John,' she said. 'Dear John. I always wanted you to be happy.' Elaine opened her mouth to interrupt, but Mary gave her a glance so unexpectedly fierce that she subsided. John eased himself up in his chair, pulling himself a little bit taller. 'We did well, John, don't you think? Twenty-four years is a good marriage, by anyone's standards. And there's David.' John lifted his head, looking at her. 'I think we did well with David, don't you? We can both be proud of him.' John nodded. 'It's sad when something comes to an end. Someone once said that the end of every relationship is like a kind of little death. So . . . I am bereaved.' Elaine would have spoken, but this time it was John who lifted his hand and stopped her. 'I wish it could have been otherwise,' said Mary truthfully. John reached out and took her hand. Looking at him, Mary thought that he loved her more at this moment than perhaps he had ever done, and the sadness of that made her eyes fill with tears. And so he was satisfied, because he would not, could not know that the tears were for him.

Chapter 23

Mary sat in the study of her father's house in Oxford. There was a mug of tea in her hand, and from time to time she sipped at it without noticing that it was almost cold. A second mug, with a skin already forming over its cool surface, stood near her on the desk. The room was very quiet, though in the garden a few birds sang to welcome the day. The curtains were pulled back, and the pearly light of early morning lay gently on the room.

Mary had woken very early that day, with an inexplicable feeling of joy. It was true that for the last few weeks everything had seemed to go well for her. Work at Mulberry Court was progressing well, and already they were working on colour schemes, looking at china and cutlery and glass. Money was tight, but with Rupert's saved capital and the money Mary would get from her share of the house, they would manage with only a small loan from the bank. John had offered to buy out Mary's half of the house. He had been rather unflatteringly surprised to hear that Mary and Rupert intended to go into partnership. At first he had assumed that this was merely a business venture, but when Mary had gently told him that she and Rupert intended to get married he had been struck silent.

'I don't know why you're so surprised,' Mary said, not unkindly. 'After all, you did once assume that I was spending the night with Rupert.'

He had the grace to look ashamed.

'I was overwrought,' he blustered. 'Not myself at all. Besides, you weren't with him. So how was I supposed to know?'

How indeed? thought Mary.

'Well, I hope you wish us happiness.' She spoke with a kind of pleasant firmness that he had not experienced in her before.

'Of course I do,' he said, in the tones of one who holds out little hope.

'You'll have the cooking in common, at least,' he said dubiously. 'You'll have to watch your weight.'

'Yes, I will,' said Mary meekly.

'You're laughing at me!'

'Well, yes, I am a bit,' admitted Mary. 'Never mind, John. At least it won't be you who's lumbered with a barrage balloon for a wife. And think how much money we'll save if Rupert and I do the reception for David's wedding!' David was due back in England in two weeks, and he was bringing Lin with him. Her parents were busy with preparations for their move to Canada, and it seemed sensible to have the wedding in England.

John's face dropped.

'That's another thing,' he grumbled. 'This Chinese girl. I don't know what to say to my friends about that.'

'Well, you can't keep it a secret. What does Elaine say?'

'She says I must be careful not to sound like a racist.' He sounded bewildered.

'Well, she's quite right,' said Mary briskly. Goodness, she thought, we're actually having a proper conversation. Well done, Elaine. Perhaps we'll have that wedding photo with all the step-parents after all.

Mary tactfully asked him how he would manage for money if he bought out her share of the house.

'You'll never believe it,' Mary told Rupert later. 'That husband of hers – the one who didn't commit suicide – died after all, in an accident. Rather dreadful, really; he'd had too much to drink and drove his car into a river, so he actually drowned after all. The payments on all his life insurance had been kept up, and although the insurance company are screaming fit to bust, it looks as though they'll have to pay.'

'Poor devil. Are they sure it wasn't just a successful suicide this time?'

'Yes, more or less, because he'd booked quite an expensive holiday for the following week, and paid for it as well. It seems he'd had some money put by, in his girlfriend's name. She'll get to keep that, presumably. Anyway, it means that John can pay me my share fairly soon, even though the divorce won't go through for a while yet.'

'Are you really sure you want to sink it all into this venture? It's not very safe. You ought to have something put by.'

'For a rainy day? No, I prefer it this way. If the worst comes to the worst, we can always come and live at Pa's, or something.' No need, between them, to spell it out. Professor Hill would not be needing his house much longer, and then Mary would inherit enough to shelter her for several rainy days, and Zen too.

Zen was working like one possessed, and it began to be more and more of an accepted thing that she would take the entrance exam in November. Naseby's was now open in its new incarnation, Dad and Uncle wrangling happily in their new flat. Bill Naseby had admitted, sadly, that he didn't need Mary there more than an hour or two a week, just to keep the books under control, and even those were largely being taken over by the sensible girl he had recently employed. He had brightened considerably, however, when Mary had told him that she was sure they would need his expertise to help with various mechanical difficulties connected with the restaurant, and particularly with the second-hand machinery they had bought, very cheaply at auction, for the kitchen.

Waking that morning to a feeling of pleasurable anticipation, Mary had looked at her clock and, realising how early it was, had turned over and tried to go back to sleep. After ten minutes she had realised it was impossible, and got out of bed. A glance out of the window had revealed the beginnings of a beautiful day, so she had put on her dressing gown – the air was chilly – and gone downstairs to make a cup of tea.

In the hall she had hesitated outside the study door. Very often, she knew, her father was awake at this time of day, and might welcome a cup of tea as well. The door was not quite closed, but she could hear nothing. Very gently she pushed the door wider, and put her head in the room.

Some quality in the silence told her, at once, what had happened. She walked without haste across to the bed that had been moved in there, set between the desk and the window so that he could see out into the garden. He slept, always, with the curtains open, and there was enough light to see his face. He had slept – arranged himself? – on his side, his head propped on the pillows so that his jaw did not sag open. His eyes were closed, but not completely, so that a little rim of white showed, fine as a new moon, between the lids. Mary touched one of his hands where it lay relaxed on the blankets and folded-down sheet. It was cool, but not yet cold. She did not need to feel for a pulse or check that still chest for breathing. He was dead.

Very gently she let go of his hand, and went out to the kitchen. In a kind of trance she boiled the kettle and made tea, waited for it to infuse and then carefully poured two mugs, remembering to use the strainer and to give him the top of the milk, which he liked. Then she went back to the study and sat in the chair by his bed. His mug of tea she left on the desk. She took his hand in her free one, and sat holding it quietly, forgetting to drink her tea until it was tepid and then sipping at it.

His hand already seemed colder than it had been a few minutes before, or perhaps it was the contrast with the warm mugs. It was limp, slightly unpleasantly so, but the bones within the skin were reassuringly hard and solid. Mary let her eyes roam round his bed. She looked for the little bottle the pills had been in, but there was no sign of it. Not under the pillow, or under the bed, or in the pockets of the dressing gown laid neatly over the back of the chair she was sitting in. The only thing that caught her eye was an envelope, tucked as a bookmark into the book on the bedside table. She picked up the book, knowing the well-worn paperback as a familiar friend.

This, his bedtime reading, was for once neither history nor philosophy, but *The Good Soldier Schweik*. It was a book that he loved and re-read constantly. It always made him laugh.

'So, you died laughing did you, Pa, you old devil?' She looked at the envelope. It was a used one, addressed to Professor Hill and postmarked some weeks earlier. She looked in it. Empty. Feeling rather foolish she ran her finger along the bottom fold but it came out clean. Not even, when she touched it to her tongue, the tiniest hint of whatever medicinal bitterness might have been left behind. The envelope had been carelessly opened and was creased with several folds. She put it carefully back into the same page of the book.

'Last laugh's on you, Pa,' she said. 'I'll never know, will I, whether you did it or not? Though I bet you did. You never had any patience, did you?' She put the book back exactly where she had found it, next to the crumpled tissue and the half drunk glass of water. That meant nothing, of course. He always had a glass of water by his bed, and always drank from it in the night.

The light was getting stronger. Soon the babies would wake Zen, and she would come downstairs. Mary would have to tell her, to comfort her and endure being comforted. There would be all the official things to do – the doctor, the undertaker. People to telephone, arrangements to be made. Meanwhile she could cherish this time of quiet, hold her own private vigil for her father. She was intensely thankful for it, and for the fact that David had come back from Hong Kong just a week earlier, had seen his grandfather, and would be there for the funeral. She was pleased, too, that her father had met Lin. He had flirted with her outrageously, and David had sat watching them, smiling. Had her father waited for that, she wondered? Another thing she would never know.

She took his hand again, that she had let go to examine the book. It was definitely colder now, but she did not allow that to distress her. She had the feeling that the gradual cooling was a kind of departure, that some small part of him still remained with her, but was slipping away like a boat slipping its moorings and drifting from the shore. No ticker tape, she thought. No bands and cheering crowds. Not even a Viking funeral, the burning ship a floating pyre. It seemed strange that she had no impulse to weep. Was it because she was in a state of shock? She felt quite ordinary, perfectly calm. There had been times in the past when she had thought that she disliked him, even hated him. Recently they had grown closer; but was it enough? Her eyes had filled with tears for John, but had she none for her father?

She closed her eyes for a moment, hiding from the thought. When she opened them again, a shadowy figure sat at the foot of the bed. He turned his head, and she recognised her lover.

'What are you doing here?'

'You needed me.' His voice in her head was so familiar, although she now realised that she had not summoned him for months, not since Rupert became her real lover.

'I didn't . . . think of you.' Before, she would have said 'summon', but now that word made him seem frightening, as if he were a ghost, a familiar spirit, a genie.

'But I'm here.' It was unanswerable. The early morning light lit the auburn of his hair, and she even thought she could smell a drift of his aftershave – Rupert's aftershave, she thought with a pang – through the study smell of peat fires and old books.

'My father is dead.' It seemed necessary to make some kind of explanation.

'Yes. I'm sorry.'

'Are you?'

'Of course. He was a good man. He used what he had.'

It seemed a strange thing to say. Long ago memories of scripture lessons came back to her.

'You mean – like the parable of the talents?'

He smiled. 'A bit like that, yes.'

Mary looked at him. He looked quite real, although of course she knew that beneath his body the end of the bed was smooth, neither dipping nor wrinkling beneath his weight. She felt quite extraordinarily shy of him, as though he were no longer the creation of her own lonely heart but something external, that she scarcely knew.

'Are you an angel?' she asked, feeling foolish. He threw back his head, and laughed his old laugh.

'An angel! No. And not a devil, either. I'm just me.'

'I don't know who that is any more,' she said, rather sadly.

'We none of us know ourselves as well as we think we do. Or other people, either.'

'I didn't know him.' She nodded to her father's still form.

'If we don't know ourselves, how can we ever know anyone else? You knew some aspects of him. More than most people. And recently you'd got to know him better, hadn't you? Since his first stroke. And since Zen came to live here.'

'Zen. Yes. It's strange, she was a kind of catalyst between us. A bridge. But all those years...'

'It's hard for children to know their parents. All those memories of childhood. All the bitterness of seeing someone as a kind of god, and then learning that they're only fallible human beings after all. All the problems of responsibility, of resentment, all the balance of give and take. It blurs things.'

'I didn't even like him, some of the time. A lot of the time.'

'There's no law says you have to like your family. If anything, it's probably harder to like them than anyone else, because you're stuck with them.'

'Not with John I'm not!' She found she could laugh.

'Well, he's not family exactly, is he? Except that he's David's father. More of a distant relative, I'd say, wouldn't you?'

Mary smiled, acknowledging the rightness of this. She looked down at the hand she held.

'I'm not sure that I even loved him.' There, she had said it. That was the thing that came like a glass wall between her and the rest of the world.

280

'Of course you did.' His voice was very gentle.

'How do you know?' She was desperate for his answer. If he said so, it had to be true, didn't it? After all, he knew her, knew everything that was in her mind better than she did. But then, she thought despairingly, would he not tell her what she wanted to hear, because he knew that she wanted to hear it? She shook her head, as if to quiet the scampering thoughts. 'I just don't know any more. What's real, and what isn't. I thought John was like that, living in a world of make-believe, but I'm just as bad, aren't I?'

'You loved him,' he said with absolute certainty. 'I know it, and so do you. And so did he. Because of what you did.'

'Because I gave him the pills? But they were to kill him! Suppose it wasn't love, but hate?'

He shook his head.

'No. The only reason you could give them to him was because you loved him. If you hadn't felt as you did, you would never have been able to put them in his hand. You know that's true.'

Mary thought about it. The panic in her thoughts subsided.

'You're right,' she said. 'If I hadn't loved him, I couldn't have done it.'

She pulled in a deep breath, on and on until she was filled with clean air. Very distantly, two floors above, she heard the high murmur of baby voices. The twins were awake.

He had heard them too.

'Time for me to go, I think.' He stood up.

'Will I ever see you again?'

'Who knows? Maybe one day, if you need me.'

'Will you be ... with him?' She glanced at her father.

'Of course. We're both a part of you.'

'Take care of him.'

He smiled lovingly at her.

'We'll take care of each other.' He faded as he spoke, and was gone.

'Goodbye,' she whispered. 'Goodbye.' The room felt empty, as if some residue of her father's spirit had vanished too, and his hand was cold. She laid it gently down on the bed.

What have I become, she wondered? I am not the woman I was. Have I changed, or was I always like this? An adulterer. Perhaps, even, a murderer. Evil things in themselves, and yet I don't feel any evil in me. I feel ... alive! Yes, how extraordinary. After all these years, I feel properly alive. I shall be me, not just John's wife, or Pa's daughter, or David's mother. Me.

She sat on in the quiet room, waiting for the sound of Zen's footsteps on the stairs. Waiting for the start of another day.